Clare Connelly was raised i[] among a family of avid reade[] of her childhood up a tree, M[] hand. Clare is married to her own real-life hero, and they live in a bungalow near the sea with their two children. She is frequently found staring into space—a surefire sign that she's in the world of her characters. She has a penchant for French food and ice-cold champagne, and Mills & Boon novels continue to be her favourite ever books. Writing for Modern is a long-held dream. Clare can be contacted via clareconnelly.com or at her Facebook page.

Emmy Grayson wrote her first book at the age of seven, about a spooky ghost. Her passion for romance novels began a few years later, with the discovery of a worn copy of Kathleen E. Woodiwiss's *A Rose in Winter* buried on her mother's bookshelf. She lives in the US Midwest countryside with her husband—who's also her ex-husband!—their baby boy, and enough animals to start their own zoo.

TRAPPED BY DESIRE

CLARE CONNELLY

EMMY GRAYSON

MILLS & BOON

First published in Great Britain 2024
by Mills & Boon, an imprint of HarperCollins*Publishers* Ltd,
1 London Bridge Street, London, SE1 9GF

www.harpercollins.co.uk

HarperCollins*Publishers*, Macken House, 39/40 Mayor Street Upper,
Dublin 1, D01 C9W8, Ireland

Trapped by Desire © 2024 Harlequin Enterprises ULC

His Runaway Royal © 2024 Clare Connelly

Stranded and Seduced © 2024 Emmy Grayson

ISBN: 978-0-263-32015-2

07/24

This book contains FSC™ certified paper
and other controlled sources to ensure responsible forest management.

For more information visit www.harpercollins.co.uk/green.

Printed and Bound in the UK using 100% Renewable Electricity
at CPI Group (UK) Ltd, Croydon, CR0 4YY

HIS RUNAWAY ROYAL

CLARE CONNELLY

MILLS & BOON

PROLOGUE

FINALLY ENSCONCED IN the seclusion of Benedetto di Vassi's exclusive suite in the heart of the opulent, private members' Diamond Club, Benedetto turned to his friend and spoke, his accented voice gravelled courtesy of the lateness of the hour.

'What is it?'

Crown Prince Anton strode to the windows that framed a postcard view of the London street. 'I need a favour.'

'So I gather,' Benedetto responded, voice droll, but inside he acknowledged that whatever Anton asked of him, he would agree to, for the simple reason that Anton had stood by him through everything that had happened—had been at his side in the worst days of grief, had supported him when Benedetto would have given up entirely.

There was *nothing* he wouldn't do for the man.

'It's Amelia.'

Benedetto knew all about the spoiled younger sister of the Catarno royal family—the Runaway Royal, as she'd been dubbed in the media, because she'd simply woken up one day and decided to abdicate all of her royal duties—and responsibilities to her family—and disappear.

'Go on.'

Anton paused as the door opened and one of the club stewards entered with a silver tray atop which sat a pair of whisky glasses. Both men waited silently for them to be placed on a nearby table.

Though the staff at the club signed strict confidentiality agreements, neither Anton nor Benedetto saw discretion as optional.

'I need her to come home.'

Benedetto moved to the whisky, lifted both glasses, carried one to his friend.

'The wedding is in two weeks. Already the media is in a frenzy about whether or not she'll be attending—it's all they can focus on.' Frustration was obvious in Anton's features. 'This day is supposed to be joyous. Vanessa deserves that much, doesn't she?' he asked, his eyes lightening as he spoke of his fiancée.

'Yes, she deserves that,' Benedetto agreed, finding it impossible to keep the censure from his tone when he thought of the spoiled princess Amelia. What a brat she was, not only to have run away in the first place, but also to have stayed away even as the wedding of her oldest brother, and the heir to the throne, approached.

'Frankly, I just need Amelia to come home, wear a pretty dress, stand beside us and smile.'

'Yes,' Benedetto said, because of course that made sense. Otherwise the media would go on about her absence and it would overshadow everything else. 'And she's said no?'

Anton nodded. 'She said it's best if she stays away. I know the media has given her a hard time in the past—she always copped it worse than Rowan and me—but this is really too much.'

Benedetto didn't reply. He wasn't inclined to cut Amelia any slack. After all, the media was capable of saying or writing whatever they wanted but, at the end of the day, it was just words.

Words only had the power to wound if you ceded that to them; she should have known better. Besides, the glare of the newspapers was nothing compared to the grief of losing a child—until you'd felt that loss and desolation, you didn't understand true suffering.

Everything in Benedetto's life was benchmarked against that pain he'd known and continued to know each and every day of his life.

Until his dying day, he would think of Sasha with an emptiness inside that simply wouldn't quit. It was an emptiness he relished, though. What right did he have to enjoy his life in any way when he hadn't been able to save his beautiful, sweet daughter?

'We've generally taken a policy of allowing Amelia to be Amelia. Let her sort out whatever's going on in her head and come home when she's ready. Of course—' he laughed without humour '—we thought it would be a matter of weeks. Maybe months. But she's now two years into this self-imposed exile with no sign of returning. It's gone too far.' He took a drink of his whisky, winced as the flavour hit the back of his throat. 'My parents are suffering far more than they let on. They miss her. We all do.'

Benedetto kept his own thoughts private from his friend. He'd never met Amelia—most of his time with Anton had been spent abroad, here in London or over in the States, and when he had gone to the small, yet exceptionally wealthy, country of Catarno, he had only met the King and Queen and Anton's brother once. He had, however, heard enough about Amelia, read enough about her, known enough women like her over the years, to have formed a pretty good idea of what she was like.

Nonetheless, she was Anton's sister and he understood the way families and loyalty worked.

'How can I help?'

Anton's relief was visible. 'Would you go to her, Ben? You're the only one I could ever trust with this. I need you to do whatever it takes to bring her home.' He took a step closer to his friend, eyes closed a moment. 'Please.'

The last word was unnecessary—most of the request had been. Benedetto had decided to help from the moment Anton had asked. Determination glinted in the depths of Benedetto's obsidian eyes. 'I'll have her there for the wedding—I promise.'

CHAPTER ONE

BEFORE BOARDING THE yacht Amelia stared east across the sparkling ocean, as she did each and every day—looking towards home. It was a long way away, separated from her by land, sea, miles and too vast an array of problems for Amelia to ever imagine traversing, but that didn't mean she didn't miss it, didn't yearn to be back with all her heart. She could never go home, though—she couldn't risk it.

She narrowed her eyes a little, imagining what her parents were doing, her brothers, imagining the palace she'd grown up in and always loved, with the light sloping in through the fourteenth-century windows. She visualised the gardens at this time of year. Amelia always thought they were prettiest in summer when the fragrance of blossom was heavy in the air, and the roses were abundant.

She imagined walking amongst them, running her hands over the petals, picking one, lifting it to her nose. But when she inhaled from her vantage point, all she caught was the heady tang of sea water and citrus.

This was home now. On the outskirts of Valencia, where she had been able to reinvent herself, to emerge from her pain and shock-induced chrysalis as someone new. Someone independent. Most importantly, someone *not* royal. She might desperately want to go back to the palace and her family but that didn't mean she hadn't also fallen in love with her life here. It was quiet and dull, by most people's standards, but Amelia was not the average twenty-four-year-old. She'd been to more than enough parties, balls and overseas holidays to last a lifetime. Now she was very happy to simply exist.

Perhaps she hadn't emerged from her chrysalis after all? These could well be indications of still being in a state of retreat, of desperately needing to heal from her shock and heartbreak, from the deep sense of betrayal that had made her withdraw from the world.

A seagull flew overhead, dipping low towards the ocean, scouring with great talent and experience, minimal effort expended in a wide-span glide until the perfect moment, when the bird dived straight down, half disappearing into the ocean and emerging victoriously only seconds later with a small fish in its beak. A natural predator. The fish swimming just beneath the surface hadn't stood a chance when the bird had decided to strike. Poor defenceless fish!

Amelia grimaced wistfully, pulled on the strap of her backpack and began to move again, away from the pretty wildness of the beach towards the pristine, perfectly maintained marina, where almost all of the boats were pleasure crafts—though she was gratified to see a handful of working fishing boats still amongst them.

But, more and more, this had become a place of wealth and luxury, and the marina reflected that. Amongst the impressive yachts, one in particular stood out. A sixth sense alerted her that it would be the boat she was looking for without even needing to read the name, but as she approached, the words *Il Galassia* caught her eye.

Bingo, she thought.

Her experience in real-estate photography was relatively limited, though she'd received positive feedback from her clients and enjoyed the work. She'd been hired through her agency to capture high-end apartments and homes prior to sale, and she'd thrived at that task. A yacht, though, was something new, different from the standard homes she'd been photographing.

She'd always loved the water. As a girl, she'd summered aboard the royal yacht, and handsome naval officers had served as crew, teaching Amelia all about the operations with good humour and answering her millions of questions without even a hint of impatience.

She stilled exactly where she was, noting the way the afternoon sun caught the glistening white of the mega yacht, and her fingers twitched. Without another moment's hesitation, she removed her backpack and lifted out the camera, bringing it to her face and looking through the lens as she shifted it slightly, until the sunbeams seemed almost to cut through the bow, and then she adjusted the focus, took a deep breath and clicked.

For Amelia, photography was an almost spiritual act. It always had been. Capturing a moment, a memory, seemed kind of magical. But ever since leaving behind everyone she knew and loved, all the places that had until a few years ago defined her, Amelia hadn't understood quite how important her photos would be, for they were reminders of what she'd walked away from, what she'd cared enough about saving to sacrifice from her life.

She held the camera out so she could see the image, and flashed a quick smile of satisfaction, with no concept of the man behind one of the many tinted windows of the yacht, looking out at her with a disapproving scowl on his face.

To Benedetto di Vassi, Princess Amelia looked exactly as he'd thought she would: very beautiful, almost hauntingly so, with her slender, willowy figure and long, waving blonde hair pulled into a loose braid that fell with the appearance of carelessness over one shoulder. Her skin was a deep tan, a colour that spoke of much time spent sunbathing for the sake of vanity, and her dress was floaty, like something from the seventies—falling to her ankles, revealing brown leather sandals. It was as though she'd just stepped off a photoshoot—she was the last word in beach chic. The only concession to her profession was the backpack she wore, from which she'd just removed a camera.

Lips tightening into a line on his handsome face, Benedetto pushed away from the window, rubbing a hand over his chin.

He'd agreed to help Anton and he didn't regret it, but he wasn't a total Neanderthal. The idea of kidnapping a woman wasn't something he relished. Nor was he thrilled about involving his staff in the whole business, so he'd carefully selected only his two most trusted team members: Cassidy and Christopher. Between them, they'd pilot the yacht, take care of the housekeeping duties, cooking, cleaning, anything that was needed. But it didn't matter how comfortable he made the princess for this voyage.

At the end of the day, he was taking her liberty.

He was taking her back home.

And given that she'd spent the last couple of years assiduously disappearing into obscurity, it was natural to presume she wouldn't be thrilled.

His loyalty was not to Amelia, though. It was Anton he owed everything to, Anton he had promised to help. No matter what.

'Cassidy, you said?'

'Yeah.' The woman's accent was Australian. She had hair that was only a slightly darker brown than her skin, and her eyes were mesmerisingly beautiful. She grinned, revealing perfect white teeth. 'Ben's waiting for you.'

Amelia raised a brow, feasting on the details of the yacht.

Her agent hadn't specified how many pictures would be needed, so, as with any listing, Amelia figured she'd take an abundance and work it out later. There was certainly no shortage of stunning angles. The yacht looked to be almost brand new—she wondered what could have happened to require its sale.

'Is Ben the sales agent?' Amelia asked, falling into step beside the other woman.

'Nah, he's the owner.'

'Oh.' Amelia frowned. Her agent hadn't mentioned that the owner would be on board. Usually, the residences she photographed were empty, giving Amelia the run of the place, and she preferred it that way. She'd been drawn to real-estate photography particularly because it was a solitary task, with little interaction required with anyone besides her agent. A friend of a friend, he always respected her boundaries, never pushed her about her other life.

'Well, I'll try to stay out of his way.'

'That won't be necessary,' a man said. His voice was deep and rough, and as he spoke a summer breeze rustled past them, so Amelia's hair brushed her cheek and she felt as though his voice had somehow transformed into a caress, the lightest of touches. She shivered, turned without meaning to, bracing herself, though she couldn't have said why she felt that was necessary.

Electricity flooded the very air around them, the summer breeze morphing into a fierce storm in which Amelia was caught.

She hadn't expected to meet anyone on board the yacht except perhaps the crew, and she certainly hadn't expected to meet anyone like this.

Casting about, she tried to rationalise her reaction, to understand what it was about the man that was so immediately unsettling, so threatening. Physically, he was obviously very strong, with broad shoulders and a toned abdomen hinted at by the white business shirt he wore, making her mouth weirdly dry. He wore chinos, a caramel-brown colour, with a dark brown belt, but his feet were bare—an odd discrepancy with the rest of his formal outfit. Amelia tried to swallow but a lump had formed that made it difficult.

Jerking her attention back to his face, she catalogued everything she saw there with what she told herself was a photographer's interest: the symmetry of his features, strong, harsh, angular yet somehow incredibly compelling, as though he had secrets to tell, and she was suddenly desperate to hear them. His jaw was square, belying an inner strength that was further conveyed by the harsh set of his lips. But it was his eyes that threatened to turn her knees to jelly. They were almost jet-black, and *fierce*. It was the only word she could think of. They radiated an intense anger, an emotion that made no sense, and yet she was sure he was looking at her as though...

But then he blinked, and his eyes softened, just enough to make her doubt her first, silly interpretations.

How long did they stand there, neither speaking? What was he thinking about her? Had he been looking at her the way she had him? Amelia had been so caught up in her own inspection she hadn't noticed, but surely one of them needed to say something. The electricity in the air arced and sizzled. Amelia felt parched and over-warm.

'This is the photographer,' Cassidy interjected in her cheery Australian voice. 'Millie, right?'

Grateful to have someone else there to cut through the strange vortex of tension, Amelia cast her glance sideways.

Hearing the diminutive version of her name, that she'd used since leaving home, was slightly mollifying. 'Yes, right. Millie.'

'This is Ben, and this beautiful thing is his.' Cassidy ran her hand over the railing of the boat, then turned back to Ben. 'I was just going to give Millie a tour.'

Ben shook his head. 'I'll do it.'

Amelia's insides clenched. She wasn't sure if she was happy with that pronouncement, or filled with dread, but her whole body seemed to react to his statement in an alarming way. Heat flooded her veins, and her fingers shook, so she clasped them together in front of herself.

Cassidy left quickly, with one last look in Amelia's direction—an expression of apology. Had she seen the anger on Ben's face too? Was he a grumpy person, habitually, and was Cassidy regretting the necessity of leaving them alone together?

Amelia's mouth pulled to the side, her eyes shifting quickly to the gangplank, wondering how bad it would be for her career if she were to quickly abscond.

Strictly speaking, she didn't need the money.

She had a trust fund that had come through her mother's family, nothing to do with the royal lineage. She had accessed it only since leaving the palace, to buy a small apartment, and any of the necessities absolutely required. But the thrill of earning her own money had caught Amelia by surprise. The pay was hardly extravagant, and yet it was all hers, accrued through her hard work and skill, and she'd become addicted to that.

There was no way she could turn her back on this commission, even when there was something about the owner of the boat that set her nerves on edge.

'Let me show you the entertaining spaces first.'

Amelia's instincts went into overdrive, but she ignored them with effort.

'Lead the way.' She spoke, finally, realising that, apart from confirming her name, she had yet to offer any intelligible words. Her voice sounded prim to her own ears, formal, driven back to the comfort and familiarity of the persona she'd adopted when forced to attend state events. She attempted to soften the words with a smile, but even that felt tight. She looked away instead, giving up.

Impressing him wasn't part of her job description. She was there to take photos, nothing more.

And yet, as he led the way to a wide set of doors, she was aware of him on a soul-deep level. Every step he took, even his inhalations, seemed almost as though they were her own. The hairs on the back of her neck were standing, and her stomach felt as if it were rolling around in a washing machine.

'This is one of the lounge areas,' he said, apparently unaware of the tension eddies assaulting Amelia from the inside out. She did her best to focus on the tour instead, regarding the space with a trained eye. Perhaps if she'd been less exposed to wealth and luxury, she might have been overawed by the sheer opulence of this room, but Amelia had known such extravagance all her life and so barely gave it a second thought. She shifted her backpack from a shoulder to her hand, unzipping it and removing her camera with an easy grace, too focused on her job to notice how he was looking at her, the way his eyes lingered on her bare shoulder with its faint pink line from the backpack.

When she turned to face him, his gaze had returned to her face, his eyes narrowed analytically, as though he was waiting for her to speak, so she nodded. 'It's very nice.'

Nice was a bland way to describe the beauty of the room, which was large and expansive, furnished in cream leather, pale Scandinavian-style minimalist decor, with timber floor-boards leading the eye towards the enormous wall of windows offering a breathtaking view of the water from this side, and the marina on the other.

It was stunning, and yet, somehow, she wasn't sure it felt like what she imagined this man would choose. She barely knew him, but her first impression had been of someone quite wild and untamed, someone virile and overtly masculine. So what? she thought, hiding a smile by tilting her head. Had she expected black leather and animal prints?

'You are amused?'

Damn it. She grimaced inwardly, composed her features, then turned to him with an expression of wide-eyed innocence. 'Not at all. Shall I start here?' She lifted her camera, to remind them both of her reason for being in his private space.

'Let me show you the rest of the boat first, then you can decide.'

'Okay.' She shrugged, her mouth drying as his eyes dropped from her face to one of her shoulders, lingering there just long enough for her skin to respond by lifting in goosebumps. Shockingly to Amelia, in addition to that visible response, she experienced the unfamiliar sensation of her nipples tingling almost painfully, hardening against the soft cotton of her dress—she wore no bra. Life in Valencia was warm and free. Besides, Amelia hadn't been endowed with the kind of figure that required restraint. How often she'd looked at her curvier friends and wished, more than anything, that she'd been the recipient of well-rounded breasts. Alas, it was not her lot in life to set the world on fire with spectacular cleavage. 'You're such a clothes horse, you lucky thing,' her mother had remarked on multiple occasions, probably trying to make Amelia feel good about her naturally slender frame.

Now she wished for the protective armour of a bra, or ten

of the things, as her whole body seemed to come alive as though being licked by flames, white-hot and destructive.

She turned away from him, breath snagging in her throat so her voice emerged breathy and light. 'Where to next?'

'Well, not that way,' he drawled, sardonic amusement in his tone. 'Unless you are planning a swim.'

Her eyes focused beyond the wall of glass on a pool, spectacularly aquamarine, with the appearance of disappearing out into the ocean. Now *that* she was impressed by.

'It does look inviting,' she murmured truthfully, as heat threatened to send her pulse haywire.

'Another time, perhaps,' he responded, so she immediately snapped herself out of it.

Another time?

No. Amelia shut the thought down instantly. There would be no other time.

For as determined as she was to escape her past, she knew that meant limiting her exposure in the present. She missed her friends, and there were times when she was unspeakably lonely, but this was the life she'd chosen for herself. It was the way it had to be. She could never risk getting close to anyone again. Not after what had happened. How could she ever trust anyone again, after her boyfriend had betrayed her, had blackmailed her with revealing Amelia's most personal secret?

Although, it wasn't really *her* secret.

She was the by-product of it, the evidence, but it was her mother who'd cheated, and fallen pregnant to someone other than the King. Her mother who'd conceived Amelia outside the marital bed, who'd lied to all and sundry about Amelia's parentage. It was her mother who'd foisted Amelia upon the royal family, who'd raised her to believe her father a man who was no such thing, who'd raised Amelia to see her brothers as that, rather than half-brothers, who would likely disown her if they knew the truth.

It was for the Queen, her mother's sake, that she'd run away.

And also King Timothy, the man who'd raised her, for if he learned the truth it would surely destroy him.

Tears threatened to spark in Amelia's eyes and she blinked rapidly to forestall them. Of all the times to let her life story seep into her present, this was not it. She dragged practised defences around herself like a wall of steel.

'Have you organised with the realtor to send someone for the floor plan?' Her voice wobbled a little. She cleared her throat, dug her nails into her palm and tried again. 'Then again, the yacht looks very new, so perhaps you have one from construction?'

'I do,' he confirmed, with no mention of the emotion in her voice. She was glad. Much like when you fell over and the worst thing a bystander could do was ask if you were okay, she didn't want him to check on her, as she feared she might weaken and confess that she wasn't. Why now? Why this man?

She blinked quickly, assumed a businesslike expression. 'Lead the way, Mr...?' She let the question hang in the air between them.

He was quiet, thoughtful. Too thoughtful for such a simple query, but, a moment later, answered. 'Di Vassi. Benedetto di Vassi.'

'Di Vassi,' she murmured, wondering why the name was familiar to her. It was an unusual surname and yet she was sure she'd heard it before. 'Have we met?'

'No,' he said with easy confidence, and so she believed him, yet the slight warning bell dinging in the back of her mind didn't ease up, even as he led her into yet another opulent living space, this time with a large dining table and bar. The next room showed a grand piano and several leather sofas. Finally, there was a room that was both a library and office, a timber desk in the middle of the room, a floor-to-ceiling window revealing more stunning views of the ocean, and a wall that was lined with books. As a bibliophile from way back, Amelia itched to move closer to the shelves and scan the spines, but there'd be time for that later, once he'd finished the tour and she was exploring on her own.

They stepped into a corridor. Several doors were shut on the other side.

'Bedrooms,' he said. 'Shall we?'

But her body revolted at the idea. She was terrified of the very notion of being in a bedroom with this man when her pulse was going crazy and her insides were a melting pot of awareness.

'Later,' she managed to say.

'Fine. Come downstairs, then.'

Was she imagining the hesitation in his voice? The hint of emotion?

Her feet wouldn't shift. She remained where she was, planted in the middle of the hallway, so when he stepped forward to lead her to the wide staircase, Amelia still didn't move, and their bodies were brought within a couple of inches of each other. She caught a hint of his fragrance—masculine, pine and pepper, spicy and seductive—and she closed her eyes as a wave of desire, unmistakable and powerful, washed over her. Her lips parted as she tried to process these feelings, to understand why they should be besieging her here, now, of all places.

'I—perhaps I should finish looking around on my own,' she suggested haltingly, self-preservation driving the suggestion because, inwardly, what she wanted most of all was more time with this man, whom she found unspeakably compelling.

'For what reason?' he asked, and stepped forward once more, so their bodies were now almost touching.

She let out a soft groan, because she felt as though she were fighting a losing battle. When had she last been kissed? Touched? Looked at with longing?

That was easy to answer. She'd broken up with Daniel a week before leaving Catarno. It had been the beginning of the worst week of her life, and ever since, she'd avoided men like the plague. But even before their break-up, it hadn't been a passionate relationship. They'd fallen in love slowly and safely, which had only made his betrayal worse. He'd been her friend first, and then he'd used her for financial gain.

This was all overpowering, and, to Amelia's surprise, she found she *liked* the way it felt to be overcome by attraction, even when it was simultaneously terrifying.

What would happen if she gave into temptation? If she lifted up onto the tips of her toes—even though she was quite tall, he was taller still, by several inches—and kissed him? Would he be shocked? Or was he as attracted to her as she was to him?

Somewhere, far away from Amelia and the fantasy world she'd begun to inhabit, she was aware of a soft rumbling sound, a feeling that made her legs vibrate a little beneath her. Or was that yet another indication of her attraction to this man?

His eyes flared, as if she'd spoken the thought aloud, and then he lifted a hand, large and capable, fingers dark with short nails, and took hold of her face. Not gently, not even sensually. This was a touch of possession and curiosity, as though he had every right, and she was reminded of how he'd looked at her on the deck, the anger in his eyes, and she wondered if that same emotion was driving his touch now.

But then he expelled a long, slow breath, warm against her temples, and his gaze narrowed as if he was confused. 'Your eyes are so different.'

She blinked, not understanding. 'From what?'

Something must have happened to cause the water beneath them to roll—perhaps another large boat departing the marina—because she lost her balance a little, and it took Benedetto's hand reaching out to steady her. It was quickly done, a clinical touch at first, but then with another, faster, rougher breath, he shifted the hand from her arm to her hip, then around her back, pressing her forward with the same easy command as he'd touched her face seconds earlier.

'I— Ben—' she said, frowning, because she had no idea what to say. Her first instinct had been to protest his overfamiliarity, because it was completely inappropriate.

But that was the response of Princess Amelia Moretti, who always had to be conscious of her reputation, and how she was perceived by the public. There was no such requirement here. But still, how could she trust him not to betray her if she gave into this? How could she ever trust anyone? The saving grace was that he didn't know who she was. To him, she was just a photographer, not a princess with a small fortune at her fingertips.

His hand at her back moved lower, to the dip above her bottom, and his fingers were splayed wide, moving slowly, hypnotically, seductively, so she struggled to make sense of anything.

'What do you want?' he asked, rough, deep.

Amelia was totally swept away, and yet there was a small part of her brain capable of rational thought and in it she marvelled at this sudden strange turn of events. She'd never been the kind of woman to go for strong-man types, yet here she was, desperate to strip naked and make love to a man who was really more beast than anything else.

'I—shouldn't—'

His smile was mocking. God, he was insufferable. 'You shouldn't?' he prompted, and now when he stepped forward, he pulled her with him, or rather shifted her, so her back pressed against the wall of the corridor, and his body formed an equally hard frame, one hand pressed to the wall beside her head, the other still on her face. His knee, somehow, had come between her legs, and she thanked heaven for that because without the support she wasn't sure she could stand upright. And yet, she found herself dying to press lower against him, to rub her sex against his skin, and her cheeks flushed a deep pink at the very X-rated direction of her thoughts.

'We shouldn't,' she said, but then her hand lifted, bunched in his shirt, her eyes hooked to his, begging, willing him to kiss her. Full lips parted on a sigh, a hope, and then, when he didn't move, she leaned forward a little, inviting him more obviously.

'You say we shouldn't with your mouth…' his eyes fell to that part of her body '…and yet your body is suggesting you want something else entirely.'

He was right. She was sending mixed messages. But that wasn't Amelia's fault. Her brain was completely scrambled.

'Saying we shouldn't doesn't mean I don't want to,' she said honestly, a moment later, the confession whispered. 'Does that make sense?'

'You have no idea how much sense,' he admitted darkly, eyes flashing to hers as he moved forward, and her heart skipped a beat as she waited to be kissed. But he didn't take her mouth. Instead, it was Amelia who pushed up, heat in her veins, desperation firing through her as she fused her mouth to his and felt as though a thousand lightning bolts were striking through her soul.

She hadn't known what to expect…but it wasn't this. Her whole body rejoiced at the contact, her mouth exploring his with passionate hunger and need, her hands roaming his body possessively, from his arms to his shoulders to his nape, tangling in the hair there, so her breasts were crushed to his chest. He made a noise low in his throat and Amelia felt as though she might almost lose consciousness. It was a kiss that managed to throw everything from her mind, all thought and knowledge dissipated in the face of such an onslaught of white-hot passion, and Amelia could not have cared less.

CHAPTER TWO

THIS HAD *NOT* been a part of the plan. Not exactly. He'd known he would need to distract her, as the boat left the marina, and he hadn't worked out how. Their clear mutual attraction had caught him off guard. Capitalising on it was an easy solution, but it was more than that. He *wanted* to kiss her. He *wanted* all of her, and he was totally blindsided by that.

Hell, this was his best friend's younger sister. A woman he despised, a spoilt, selfish brat he'd been begged to bring home with her tail between her legs. At no point had he considered seducing her, or being seduced by her, so what the hell was happening?

Just because something shouldn't happen it doesn't mean you don't want it to.

Damn straight.

But Benedetto was no inexperienced teenager. He was a man well into his thirties, who'd lived a full life in all aspects, and had plenty of relationships to have learned from. He didn't need to slake his libido with Princess Amelia. There were dozens of women he could call on for that, if and when he decided he was in the mood. So what the hell was he doing? There were other ways to distract her; he didn't need to do this—and yet he couldn't stop.

She moaned again, this time louder, and rolled her hips, her body imploring him to do something more than just taste her, and before he realised what he was doing, his hands moved roughly, impatient now for what he'd wanted the moment she'd strolled onto the boat, a picture of casual summer beauty. He'd seen enough photographs of Amelia, and it had never occurred to him to be attracted to her. She was in every way off limits to him.

But he'd never actually met her.

And despite the experience that should have inured him to this kind of attraction, it had also taught him to respect the laws of chemistry. Sometimes, you just couldn't fight it.

Besides, the Crown Prince had told Benedetto to bring Amelia home, whatever it took. Okay, Anton wouldn't have had this in mind, but Benedetto wasn't going to fail his friend.

Acknowledging, in the back of his mind, that he was simply making excuses to justify his weakness, he nonetheless allowed himself to succumb to temptation, figuring he'd sort out the consequences later. After.

'Are you sure we don't know each other?' she asked, huskily, momentarily piercing his fog of desire.

'We've never met,' he responded, though it didn't quite answer her question. She'd clearly recognised his name— undoubtedly her brother had mentioned him at some point over the years. But theirs was not a personal connection. Or at least, it hadn't been.

'Okay.' She tilted her head back, giving him better access to her throat, and he took it without hesitation. Now it was Benedetto's turn to groan as he brushed his stubble over her skin, so soft it was like velvet, feeling her purr.

Her dress was simple—elasticised across the torso in a style a woman would probably know the name of—with no straps, so it was the easiest thing in the world for him to tug at the side and lower it. She gasped as he revealed one of her perfect, neat breasts, the darkened areola taut and firm, so he was drawn like a moth to a flame to pull the nipple into his mouth and suck on it, harder perhaps than he'd intended, so she bucked against his leg in surprise, her whole body jerking with the strength of her physical response.

'Do you want me to stop?' he asked, dark anger in his voice—an anger that was directed at himself, for having insufficient willpower.

She shook her head quickly, but her eyes were huge, a look of awakening in them that had him briefly questioning her experience with men. 'You're not a virgin, are you?' After all, he had to draw the line somewhere, and he had no interest in being Anton's sister's first sexual experience.

She shook her head again and relief surged through him.

'But I'm— I haven't—' She grimaced. 'Never mind.'

He did as she requested, thrusting aside whatever she'd been about to say and instead giving himself full access to her body, pulling the dress down on the other side so he could lose himself in her breasts, her nipples, exploring them hungrily with his mouth and then his hands, enjoying the way her pupils dilated when he squeezed her nipples as he rolled them, the way she bit down on her lip as he palmed her breasts, her hands desperately running over her body when he pulled away, as though she were on fire and needed extinguishing.

It was all getting away from him.

He should stop this. The boat had to be out of the marina by now. She was his ward for the next week, the time it would take to sail to Catarno. He had to take control of the situation. Didn't he?

'Please,' she whimpered, the fire raging out of control. He understood; he felt it too.

'Please what?'

'What do you mean?'

'What do you want from me, Amelia?' he demanded, eyes

latched to hers, so he saw something shift in them, a frown tugging on her lips.

'I want—what did you call me?'

His heart thumped against his chest as he belatedly re-alised his mistake. He'd used her christened name, rather than what she went by now.

Pride stopped him from lying. His arousal was straining hard against his trousers, his whole body was taut with need, and yet he stood straight, dropped his hands to his sides and regarded her as though nothing had happened between them whatsoever. Even when desire was threatening to turn him to mush, making him want to forget everyone and every-thing but her, he held onto sanity just long enough to know he couldn't lie to her. Not when asked a direct question.

'It is your name, *si*?'

She flinched, confusion and betrayal writ large across her face. 'We *have* met,' she said, lifting her fingers to her lips. 'You know who I am.'

She was so shocked she didn't even think to draw her dress back up, so Benedetto had the vantage point of her feminine form, mottled pink by his stubble and the desper-ate need of his touch.

'No,' he said, crossing his arms over his chest simply to stop himself from reaching for her. She looked so hurt, so crestfallen, it was impossible not to feel sorry for her.

Benedetto had to remind himself of everything he knew about Amelia: her spoiled, overindulged ways, the only daughter of parents who doted on her, the fact she'd cast her family aside and disappeared into the ether, hurtfully ignor-ing almost all their attempts at contact. He hated women like her, who had no loyalty nor respect for other people. 'And yes,' he finished, interested in her reaction.

Her eyes swept shut, her lips parted, and her features were

so defeated, her expression so haunted, it was impossible not to experience an overarching sense of compunction for his place in all of it.

'Why? How did you find me?'

'You are not so well hidden away, Princess,' he responded.

He'd never been into role play but apparently when it was a real-life princess that was a different matter. Out of nowhere, he had an image of her in a palace, and he her concubine, existing purely to service her needs, and felt a thrill of something that surprised him. Benedetto had never needed a woman for longer than it suited him. He'd never really been wired to seek relationships, but after those awful days of grief and loss, he'd known he wouldn't again risk that kind of pain—nor emotional connection. He didn't deserve it.

'So what was all this?' She gestured to the boat and then, belatedly realising she was half naked, she pulled up her dress, shielding herself from his view so he wanted to cry out in objection, to reach forward and remove the dress altogether. 'Why am I here?' she demanded, and then her eyes widened as she looked around, lifted a hand to her lips. 'Oh, my God. The boat's moving, isn't it? Why is the boat moving?'

'Because we're leaving port,' he responded simply. He was angry with her for what she'd put her family through, so he'd thought he'd enjoy this moment, but the truth was Benedetto felt as though he was speaking words that were at odds with how he should be acting. He'd committed to this path though; he had to follow through. Besides, he'd run the plan briefly via Anton, who'd said only that she had to be brought home.

'We can deal with her anger when she's back in Catarno.'

And so here Benedetto was, a tool of the palace. This wasn't his fight, and it wasn't his business. He was simply doing as he'd been asked by the one person he could never say no to.

'You're kidnapping me,' she said quietly, shaking like a leaf. 'Oh, my God.'

'No.'

But it was obvious she didn't believe him. 'You're kidnapping me,' she said again. 'At least have the decency to be honest about it.' She was clearly terrified and yet she still had such strength and dignity.

'I am not kidnapping you,' he said, then frowned. Because wasn't that exactly what he was doing? 'At least, not for any nefarious reason. You can relax, Princess.'

'Oh, gee, can I?'

'All I am doing is taking you home.'

It was as if he'd said he planned to kill her. She paled before his eyes, her skin losing any hint of a tan, even her lips draining of colour, so he reached forward on instinct alone, because it was clear what was about to happen. Sure enough, she collapsed the second his arms connected with her body, her frame going limp, and a thousand memories jolted through him.

Memories of Sasha slammed into him hard, so his own skin paled, his heart raced, his palms felt sweaty as remembered trauma flooded his body. And yet, just as he had then, he pushed past those feelings to act as was necessary, scooping Amelia up against his chest and carrying her, watching her face—but this wasn't a seizure, not as Sash used to experience. This was different. Amelia had fainted from shock. He didn't need to worry that she was going to swallow her tongue, that she was going to die because he wasn't paying attention.

Nonetheless, the memories of his daughter in that last year were an indelible part of his being, haunting him mercilessly.

He laid Amelia down on the cream sofa, staring at her with an overwhelming sense of regret, guilt, anger and frustration, pressing a hand against her forehead, then moving it to her arm. So warm, so vital.

She wasn't dying.

He slowed his breathing, focused on the moment, on becoming himself again, on getting rid of the anxiety that was plaguing him, so that when Amelia blinked her eyes open, she'd see no vestige of emotional ache on his features—it was a pain he never intended to show anyone but Anton, who'd been there through the worst of it with him.

Amelia felt as though she were coming to the surface of the water from a long, long way down, the depth of the ocean almost overwhelming, so she struggled to breathe, to think, to see. Her eyes opened and everything swirled in front of her, nothing making sense. Where was she? And who was that?

She scrambled to a seated position, then wished she hadn't when her head began to spin again.

Benedetto stood watchful but unmoving, arms crossed, eyes on her as if held by some invisible force.

'I'm not going home,' she said quickly, the last few moments clarifying in her mind, his words reverberating inside her brain. 'And you cannot make me.'

His lips curled derisively. 'Want to bet?'

'You can't be serious?'

He lifted one shoulder, one beautiful, broad, strong shoulder, so Amelia's mind scattered in a direction she most definitely wouldn't allow it to go.

'Anton is getting married. Your presence is required.'

'I think you mean requested,' she replied with the appearance of calm, when her insides were jangling all over the place. 'And I've already told my family that I cannot make it.'

'You misunderstand. Your attendance is not optional.'

She ground her teeth together, wondering why her body was trembling with something other than anger and fear. Why did she find his awful bossiness…sexy? It was more of that horrid caveman behaviour, which Amelia found abhorrent. Didn't she?

'I'm sorry, since when did you become the boss of me?' she responded with saccharine sweetness, moving to stand.

But he was quicker, closing the space between them and pressing a hand to her shoulder. 'Stay there. I don't particularly want you to pass out again.'

'Thanks for the concern,' she muttered sarcastically. 'But I'll be fine.'

'Maybe, maybe not. Stay where you are.'

It wasn't just that she was angry, she was spoiling for a fight. He'd stirred up a frenetic energy inside Amelia and all she wanted was to expel it *somehow*. If that was by fighting with him, then so be it.

So she stood up, and pushed at his chest, a thrill of pleasure running through her at how good it felt to take out her annoyance on the man who'd caused it. 'Stop telling me what to do.'

'It's for your own good.'

'Oh, yeah, right, and you're what, a doctor?' she prompted sceptically. 'Some kind of fainting expert?'

His lips clenched. 'Fine, have it your way,' he said, a strange quality to his voice. 'But don't expect me to catch you next time.'

'I didn't expect you to catch me this time,' she responded firmly.

'That doesn't sound like "thank you".'

'You seriously expect me to thank you? I fainted out of shock, a shock caused by your pronouncement that you're attempting to kidnap me against my wishes and return me home, also very much against my wishes. Tell me, what exactly should I be grateful to you for?'

'Kidnapping is, I think, always against a person's wishes,' he said, concentrating on the semantics of her accusation, earning an eye roll from Amelia.

'By all means, correct my sentence structure,' she snapped. 'But that doesn't change the fact you've broken about a million laws. You do realise I'm under the protection of the Catarno royal guard?'

'Are you?' he replied. 'Where are they?'

She floundered. Damn it, that was an easy lie to catch her in. 'I mean, in theory,' she responded testily. 'I have no need for them here, but what you're doing is a serious crime in Catarno. You'd be stupid to take me there and not expect consequences for this.'

'Fine, I'll drop you off just outside the waters of your country,' he said with something like amusement, which only served to strengthen her anger.

'You will do no such thing.' She drew herself up to her full height, no idea that she looked like a modern-day Boudicca with her hair wild around her shoulders and a quiet, dignified strength emanating from her.

'No?'

She shook her head. 'You will have your crew turn this boat around and put it back into dock. I will leave, and never see you again.'

His laugh was a short, sharp sound, filled with the same anger she'd detected in him at their first meeting. 'No.'

'No?' Her nostrils flared. 'What do you mean "no"?'

'Your brother asked me to bring you home, and that's what I'm doing.' She blanched once more, and, despite what he'd said minutes ago, he moved swiftly, as if anticipating the worst, but stopped short of touching her.

'This is absolutely *not* simple,' she said, hands on hips, staring across at him. 'Did it occur to you that I left Catarno for a reason?'

'I presume you had reasons you thought were valid at the time. Perhaps you didn't realise how hard it would be on your family. Or perhaps you just didn't care about them. Maybe you're only capable of caring about yourself and your own happiness,' he added, eyes lancing hers with an accusation that made the bottom fall out of her world.

Was that really what he thought of her?

And had he formed that opinion based on what Anton had disclosed? Was that how Anton viewed her? Nausea flooded Amelia's body, so she spun away to conceal the way her throat moved and her mouth tightened.

'It's none of your business,' she said unevenly, after a long, pained pause. 'I left. I'm a free person, capable of making my own decisions. None of that is your concern.'

'No,' he agreed quickly, so she was gratified. 'And yet, you're hurting someone I owe a huge debt of gratitude to, someone who wants—needs—you to return to Catarno, for one week only.'

'You really think I can go home for a week, attend the wedding, then disappear into my life again? Do you have any idea how impossible that will be? Escaping once was a god-damned miracle, there's no way I'll be able to do it again.'

'Escaping?' He homed in on her use of the word. 'What exactly did you need to escape? A life of idle luxury? Of low expectations and a schedule that was one hundred per cent geared to pleasure-seeking?'

Amelia gasped, shocked by the level of her anger, and by the hand that lifted and struck his cheek, by how good it felt to slap him, to release that tension, shocked by the way his flesh changed colour, darkening red in the shape of her palm, and at the way her stomach knotted—and not from tension so much as something infinitely darker and more dangerous. Shocked and delighted at how he gripped her wrist the moment after she'd connected with his skin, the way his fingers curled around her, held her hand in the air, so much stronger than she was, so easily able to command her body with his.

'Did that feel good?' he asked, eyes like lasers, cutting through her.

'Yes.' She didn't bother to lie. 'It felt bloody great, actually,' she admitted, even when she knew she should feel ashamed. She'd never condoned violence, and it didn't matter that she was his physical inferior, much slighter and weaker, it was still violence. It was still wrong.

His eyes flared, and heat arced between them, so despite her hatred for him, her fear at the thought of going home, that same heady throb of need was tormenting her, making it almost impossible to remember where she was, with whom, and why she had to fight this.

'Do you want to hit me again?' His thumb stroked the flesh of her inner wrist.

She shook her head, confused.

'Don't you?'

'I don't know what I want.'

His eyes flared at the unintentionally provocative comment. 'You're angry with me.'

'Do you blame me?'

His lip contorted into something like a half-smile, but it was rich with sardonic mockery.

'What I don't understand,' she continued, 'is why *you're* angry with *me*?' Her pulse quickened, her body so close to his, the hand on her wrist too benign to explain the impact his proximity was having.

'What makes you say that I am angry?'

'I can tell.'

'Are you a mind-reader?'

'Don't do that,' she murmured.

'Do what?'

'Gaslight me. I know what I feel from you, and it's anger.'

'Yes,' he admitted, though she saw surprise in his features, and something like grudging respect. 'Fine, I am angry with you too.'

'Why?'

'Because of what you have put your family through. Because of how careless and selfish you have been.'

There it was again! A twitch in her fingers, an ache to slap him. Instead, she jerked at her hand, attempting to pull it free, but he held on and so her action had the unintended consequence of bringing her whole body forward, ramming it into his.

She closed her eyes on a husky, terrified groan of surrender.

His nostrils flared. 'They love you, and you have turned your back on them, no matter the consequences.'

'You don't know what you're talking about.'

'Don't I? Unlike you, I have been around to witness the consequences.'

She shook her head, wanting to argue with him, wanting to tell him that they weren't even her family anyway, that if they knew the truth, they wouldn't want her...but how could she begin to explain? Besides, it was a secret she could never tell another soul, for her mother and father's sake. She had to bear this burden herself—she'd learned her lesson after Daniel.

'You think you know my family, but you don't know me, and I have no intention of explaining my innermost thoughts to you. You don't get to know what I'm feeling. That's for me, and me alone. But I will tell you this: if I go home, it will complicate everything. It will potentially overshadow Anton's wedding and ruin my parents' lives. I'm not joking,' she responded, when his lips curled once more into that hateful, derisive half-smile.

'Anton has mentioned your flair for drama,' he said simply, and then she wanted to slap him more than ever. Again she jerked at her wrist, but when he didn't release it, she lifted her foot instead and stamped down on his, satisfied because he was barefoot and she still wore her sandals. She saw his immediate pain response, a tightening in his face, but otherwise he didn't react, and shame at her base instinct quickly followed the satisfaction of having landed another strike against him.

'Screw you,' she said angrily, her breath coming in ragged spurts now as she glared up at him, something else entirely overtaking her. Her gaze dropped to his mouth, and silently she willed him to kiss her.

'You are going home, Amelia. There is no sense arguing about it now.'

'You are insufferable!' she shouted, shocked by her anger, by her lack of decorum, imagining what her tutors would say if they could see her now, wild and overpowered by rage.

'Be that as it may, you shall have to learn to suffer me, for the next week at least.'

'I will swim to shore if you do not turn this boat around.'

He laughed. He actually laughed!

Amelia couldn't take it any more. She lifted her small fists and pummelled his chest, tears of frustration and impotence sparkling on her lashes. 'I hate you!' she said. 'How dare you do this to me? How dare you?'

'This conversation is futile,' he said. 'The next time this boat stops, it will be in a Catarno port. I suggest you take the next week to make your peace with that, and start working out how you can make amends to your long-suffering family.'

Her nostrils flared at his haughty, judgemental tone.

'In the meantime, your bedroom is through there. As you clearly can't stand being around me,' he said, with indolent mockery layered over the words, 'I suggest you go and make use of it.'

Amelia ground her teeth. He was the most arrogant, infuriating man she'd ever met. 'This is a mistake.'

He lifted one shoulder, careless now. 'Dinner is served at eight. Please feel free to join me. If you think you are capable of behaving with a level of basic civility, that is.'

'You get what you deserve,' she muttered, spinning on her heel and leaving the room, thinking she'd never been so glad to walk out on someone in her life.

CHAPTER THREE

THERE WERE SOME things Benedetto found almost too painful to think about, some memories he kept permanently shelved because they still had the power to tear him down, even now, years after his entire life had been torn asunder.

When he thought of Sasha, he preferred to focus on what their life had been before her diagnosis. Before he'd learned that her fainting and exhaustion and poor eyesight had been caused by an inoperable brain tumour. Before he'd had to come face to face with his greatest fear as a single parent and acknowledge that he would lose her.

His best memories of Sasha were of her as a baby, her sweet, chubby, competent frame dragging across the floor at only five months of age, before she crawled a month later. She'd been walking by eight months, babbling and smiling almost constantly. There'd never been a happier child, he was sure of it.

He remembered her first day at nursery school, how she'd marched in without a backwards glance, confidently making friends and teaching the other children her favourite games, before waving him off with a grin that spread from ear to ear. He remembered how great she'd been at everything she tried—a natural reader, athletic, kind, considerate.

She had been his daughter and so he'd loved her, but it

had been impossible *not* to love Sasha. Everyone had felt it. She had been magical.

At her funeral, the priest had said that she'd glowed so brightly, even if just for a short time, and Benedetto had been struck by the truth of that. Perhaps people were born with a certain amount of light to shine, and Sasha had shone all hers out early.

Afterwards, when she was gone, and he'd had to accept that, no matter how much money he'd spent on chasing down state-of-the-art treatments, his failure had equated to her death, he'd been in a state that defied explanation. There were no words to describe his grief. He had been bereft, almost deranged with his sadness.

He'd sought solace in liquor, in women, in dropping out of his life altogether. The fortune he'd been steadily building since seventeen, when he'd founded his first company, had gradually floundered owing to his total inattention.

And Benedetto hadn't cared.

If it hadn't been for Anton stepping in and appointing an interim CEO, it would have all been lost. But Anton had known.

Somehow, he'd understood that the clouds would eventually clear, that Benedetto would come up for air and look for the hallmarks of his life, for some semblance of what had been before, and that there had to be *something* for him to return to. Perhaps Anton had known that the challenge of rebuilding his business would be the one thing to draw Benedetto out of his grief. And so Anton had overseen operations as much as his role as heir to the throne of Catarno had allowed, had made sure that Benedetto would have something to return to one day, even when his personal wealth had been decimated.

Anton hadn't just been there for Benedetto, he'd shown

him every step of the way that he would *always* be there for him.

Benedetto owed him an enormous debt of gratitude, and repaying it was immensely important. While kidnapping Amelia, and whatever the hell had happened between them, didn't sit well with him, he knew it didn't really matter. Not as much as helping Anton.

Anton had grown up with the weight of the world on his shoulders, his royal legacy meaning he'd had to be the best at everything, had been scrutinised mercilessly lest he put a foot wrong. It was Amelia who'd had the freedom to enjoy her royal lifestyle without the responsibilities. It was high time she faced up to them, Anton was right.

The first thing Amelia did when she got to her room was drop down onto the bed and scream into one of the pillows, a scream of abject anger and frustration, of a thousand million emotions that were setting her nerves jangling and making her want to dive off the side of the boat.

The second was to move to a window to ascertain the sense of that plan. If she were to jump ship, could she actually swim to shore?

A quick scan of the view from her windows showed her that they'd moved fast—Valencia was just a speck in the distance now. Even for a confident swimmer like her, that would be pushing it.

Or was it that she didn't truly want to escape?

As if to prove to herself that wasn't the case, she went to reach for her camera backpack, to grab her phone, only to remember it had been left in the corridor, presumably when she'd fainted.

With a racing heart—not from fear but from the adrenaline and possibility of running into Benedetto again—she moved quickly, striding across the room, ignoring the pulsing heat between her legs, the yearning that remained unabated in her body, and dragged open the door. She looked left and right, saw no one, so stepped out, looking for her bag.

It was nowhere.

Damn it.

Might it be in the other room? Where he'd taken her when she fainted? She looked down the corridor, decided to chance it, and jogged to that door, pulled it open. A quick inspection showed the room to be empty. But her bag was also missing.

The only conclusion she could draw was that Benedetto had taken it, and, with it, her only way of contacting—

But who would she have called anyway?

Her family? Who'd clearly ordered this kidnapping? They might sympathise with her plight but inwardly they'd be rejoicing at her imminent return, even if it was against her will. And who else was there? The friends she'd unceremoniously dumped when she'd left the country because she wasn't sure if she could trust them either? After Daniel, she hadn't known where to turn. And who could blame her?

Suddenly, Amelia felt so unspeakably alone, so awfully ganged up on, that she ran just as quickly back through the boat, to the solitude of her room. She closed the door and slumped against it, falling to the floor in a heap and dropping her head to her knees, a silent tear trickling down her cheek as she acknowledged the helplessness of her situation.

Going home would be a disaster. She knew it would be.

She knew her family would want to know why she'd left. They'd asked her over and over in email and text, even in the voicemails they'd left when she'd first disappeared. But Amelia hadn't answered. She hadn't been able to.

The discovery of her illegitimacy was still too raw, too

painful to discuss, too dangerous to everyone she loved most.
Even to her family's position?

That was one of the thoughts that had tortured her most.
The civil war was all but a distant memory now, something
that had happened three generations back, and yet, for Amelia, the thought of her family being deposed and thrown out
by the people had always struck her as particularly horrify-
ing. She'd known even as a young girl she'd do everything
she could to avoid that fate.

Unfortunately for Amelia, no matter how well behaved
she was, she seemed to find herself getting into some sort
of scrape or another. A scandal in high school to do with her
friendship group taking drugs—never Amelia, but far be it
from her to tell other people how to live their lives—or a
cheating scandal at college. Amelia hadn't cheated, but the
mud had stuck, and rumours continued to swirl. Even in her
own family, she was sure there were suspicions about her
grades. The media had loved to print stories about her, so
many of them made up, some of them so wild they actually
made Amelia laugh, but at the heart of it all was a deep and
growing sense of not belonging. Of being different.

And then she'd learned why she'd always felt that way.
The root of her sense of displacement.

She *didn't* belong.

She wasn't royal.

The blood of which her family was so proud didn't even
flow through her veins.

And in her being she held the power to destroy her parents' marriage, her family's happiness.

Worst of all was the knowledge that the one person she'd
turned to when she'd learned the truth, whom she had believed she loved, and had loved her back, had used her secret to blackmail Amelia for financial gain. She'd confided

in Daniel because she'd needed to speak to someone about it, and he'd betrayed her. That he still held this piece of information about Amelia, and could use it at any point to damage her and her family, was what had kept her in hiding for two full years.

How could she go back?

How could she risk it?

Fear made her skin crawl.

She stood and began to pace the suite she'd been dumped into, distractedly investigating it simply to assess her situation for the next week. A bathroom, palatial in size and appointment, with a window right on the edge of the boat showcasing yet another spectacular view of the still ever-diminishing Spanish mainland, framed by timber, and placed perfectly behind a claw-foot bath. There was a large shower, a double sink, and when she idly opened one of the drawers she saw that it had been stocked with high-end products—moisturisers, cleansers, even a set of nail polishes, and make-up.

The next drawer housed hair products—a brush, hairdryer, straightener, leave-in conditioner. A quick inspection of the shower confirmed that she'd also been supplied with shampoo, conditioner, toner. A very thoughtful kidnapping indeed, she admitted, but without a hint of a smile, because there was no atonement for what he'd done to her. No atonement for what he *hadn't* done to her either.

Leaving the bathroom, she pressed on the next door along, gasping to discover a full wardrobe of clothes just her size. Her hands ran over the brightly coloured designer outfits—dresses, skirts, bathers, shirts, jackets, everything she could want for a year, not just a week. There were shoes too—sandals and sneakers, as if she might be going to do more than pace a hole in the floorboards of her bedroom!

The final door revealed an office of sorts. It was very

small, designed to be tucked out of the way, with a narrow desk pressed to the wall, and cables for a laptop, screen, charger, anything she might need to use while here. But Amelia had brought only her camera and phone, for the simple reason that she hadn't intended to be staying long.

With a sigh, she turned back to the bed and lay down, determined to stare up at the ceiling in the kind of grumpy state a teenager would be proud of, and she spent the next several hours mulling over her predicament and trying to fathom exactly how she could escape this situation.

Because there was no way she could go back to Catarno, and definitely not for Anton's wedding... She simply couldn't risk anything happening that might ruin his happiness. Staying away might have seemed heartless but Amelia had long since decided it was one of the ways in which she was being cruel to be kind.

So how could she get her grumpy captor to understand that?

By eight o'clock, Amelia was famished. She'd been in her room a long time, with no food, no drink, and no desire to go out in search of either. Pride had made her stick to that point. But as he'd 'invited' her to join him for dinner—or rather demanded—she supposed it wouldn't hurt to accede.

She had to work out how to get through to him, after all.

He'd said they had a week together, from which she could only presume he intended for them to travel to Catarno by boat, and that the journey would last that duration. Okay, she could go along with that. A week would definitely afford an opportunity to make him see that she wasn't the person he believed her to be.

Without admitting the truth behind her estrangement, she might be able to convince him of the necessity of her staying away. After all, if he was Anton's best friend, then surely he had a reasonable side.

And pigs might fly, she thought to herself, all hopes of Benedetto being, deep down, a benevolent, kind-hearted billionaire evaporating when she stepped onto the deck to find him glaring out at the ocean as though it had personally committed some great wrong against him.

He was so entrenched in his thoughts that he didn't hear her arrive at first, so she had a moment to study him, and in that moment all of the new-found determination to simply, logically reason her way out of this situation disappeared.

There was nothing reasonable about this man.

Nothing measured or calm.

He was pure animal, pure instinct.

And didn't that just turn her insides to jelly?

She had always regarded herself as a feminist, so it was damned hard to make her peace with this side of her nature. Besides, that would be a job for later. For now, she had to focus on concealing how she felt, what he inspired in her.

First step? Dinner.

Finally becoming aware of her presence, he tilted his head, even that simple movement imbued with arrogant disdain, so she was aware of her hackles rising, her irritation growing back to the levels it had been earlier. And not just her irritation. Her insides churned and her skin suddenly felt clammy and warm.

She reached up and pulled her hair over one shoulder, seeking the relief of a light ocean breeze against her nape. Instead, her temperature spiked when his eyes fell from her face to her breasts as though they were his and his alone.

And she was back to feeling parched, and totally flummoxed.

'You said dinner would be at eight?' she reminded him

crisply, doing her best to tamp down the feelings assaulting her.

But his knowing smile showed that he saw right through her. 'Would you like a drink?'

Amelia moved to the edge of the boat, wrapped her hands around the cool metal balustrade for strength. 'I'll have what you're having.'

'I doubt it.'

'Oh?'

'Whisky?'

Her eyes narrowed. 'Why not?'

He considered her a moment, shrugged as if he had not a care in the world, then disappeared inside. She watched him go, trying not to notice how pleasingly masculine his waist was, how well his trousers moulded his bottom, how tall and athletic he was. She quickly turned back to the water, seeking in it a reprieve, a blast of sanity and calm when everything else was threatening to overwhelm her. But the ocean was at her favourite state—bathed in dusk light, with the moon rising through the orange and pink sky, the waves gentle and undulating, rhythmic and talkative, so there was an inherent romance to the water that was definitely no help to her present mindset.

He returned with a whisky, handed it to her, and, despite the fact she rarely touched strong liquor, she forced herself to lift it to her lips. It practically burned, yet it also reminded her of her brothers, with whom she'd shared this drink often over the years, and her heart panged with missing them, so she threw back the entire measure to disguise her reaction.

The Scotch acted like a balm on her overwrought nerves and she expelled a long, slow breath before returning the glass to him. Her smile was over-sweet. 'Thank you very much.'

'No problems, Princess,' and she felt things tip beneath her.

It had been a long time since anyone had called her that. Two years, in fact.

'Don't,' she whispered, digging her nails into her palm.

'Why not? You're going home. Isn't it time to get used to your title again? Or would you prefer Your Highness?'

She shook her head in consternation. 'Neither, please.'

'So I shall simply call you Amelia while you are on board?'

'I prefer Millie now,' she corrected.

'Millie is not a princess's name.'

'Maybe not, but it's my name.'

'Are you so angry with your parents that you would even want to disavow your connection to the royal family?'

Her face drained of colour. 'I'd prefer not to discuss it.'

'That's a shame, as we have nothing but time ahead of us.'

'A week,' she said, thinking of how much she had to achieve in six or seven days. Could she change his mind in that time? Could she convince him to let her go? It wasn't long, and yet, with the two of them, it might turn out to be an eternity. Already she felt her nerves stretching well past breaking point.

'Tell me how you know my brother,' she invited, surprised that her voice could emerge so calm when her insides were fluttering.

'We met a long time ago.' His answer was short, his gaze direct, yet he was holding so much back, she couldn't help but laugh.

'That's funny?'

'No, but how assiduously you're trying not to answer my question is.'

It was clear that Benedetto was not a man used to being called out. He glowered for a moment before something like a smile flickered on his face, like lightning way out on the horizon, so quick and breathtakingly bright that you could almost swear you'd imagined it.

'We met through a mutual friend when I was in my twenties. Younger even than you,' he drawled, as if to remind them both of the age gap between them.

She narrowed her eyes. 'Which was how many years ago?'

'Twelve.' He moved closer, lifting a hand to her face on the pretence—and it was most definitely a pretence—of tucking hair behind her ear, to contain it in defiance of the light sea breeze. 'I am thirty-six, Princess.'

Her stomach rolled with the power of these conflicting emotions. Desire warred with frustration, and fear. She wasn't a princess, she wanted to scream, even when she knew she could never proclaim that to another soul.

'Older than Anton,' she murmured.

His eyes flashed with hers. 'And too old for you.'

'And yet you're touching me.'

'Haven't we already covered that?' he responded, but dropped his hand, so she could have kicked herself for even bringing it up. She glanced away, buying time to assume an expression of calm.

'How come I haven't met you?' she pushed, but he didn't answer immediately, instead gesturing to the table across the deck from them. Amelia eyed it, her stomach giving a little growl as she remembered that she'd been starving moments earlier.

'Happenstance,' he said non-committally. 'I've been to Catarno a couple of times. I've met your parents, your brother. You weren't at home.'

She considered that. 'Uni, perhaps.'

'Or with friends.'

She heard the veiled criticism and bristled. She'd gone to a few high-profile parties in her first year at university and from that moment on she'd been dubbed the Playgirl Princess. On the one hand, she'd been pleased to see that the treatment often meted out to young, single male royals was being dispensed to her—because gender shouldn't determine such things. On the other, it had been spectacularly unfair. In reality, Amelia had worked hard at her studies and had been a member of the track and polo teams, competing at a high level for both. If she'd missed seeing Benedetto, it had probably been because she'd had a meet.

There was no point explaining that to him though. It was all too apparent he'd made up his mind about her. It pained Amelia to imagine how Anton must speak and think of her, for Benedetto to have formed such a particular dislike.

'Why are you so loyal to him?'

He held out a seat for her, their eyes sparking as she moved towards it. She sat, ignoring the way his hands brushed her shoulders as if by accident, and the way her body responded immediately. How was it that a single touch could unsettle her so completely?

'You don't think he deserves it?'

'I didn't say that.'

Benedetto took the seat opposite, his long legs brushing hers beneath the table. Another accident? Her hand shook as she reached for her water glass, glad to take a sip to dilute the whisky flavour in her mouth.

'I'm just curious,' she continued after a moment in which he didn't speak, 'as to why you'd owe him such an allegiance that you'd consider committing a criminal offence.'

'I've done more than consider it,' Benedetto pointed out. 'And I'm more curious as to why you'd be intent on seducing someone who's kidnapped you. You kissed me before you knew, so you can't blame Stockholm syndrome.'

She actually laughed, it was so absurd, but it was a laugh

that bordered on the maniacal, hysterical and unhinged, so she dropped her face into her hands and held it a moment.

'I don't know,' was the simple, honest answer. 'It just felt... I just wanted to.'

A frown jerked at his lips.

'You kept pointing out that you have more experience than me, so presumably you've felt that before. I don't like you. I mean, I really, really actively *dis*like you, and yet there's something about you that...'

'Yes?' He growled.

'Makes me want to tear your clothes off.' She blinked away from him, both embarrassed and proud of her frankness.

'And you haven't felt that before.'

She wanted to lie. She certainly didn't want to give him the ego-boost of admitting he was the only man who'd ever had that effect on her, but to what end? His ego was already full to the brim, a little extra wouldn't make a fundamental difference to his behaviour. 'No.'

He arched a brow, silently imploring her to continue, but Amelia was reticent to discuss Daniel.

'You've dated men?' Benedetto pushed.

Amelia bit into her lip. 'Yes.'

'And?'

'And what?'

'You didn't feel a desire for them?'

Amelia hesitated. 'I've dated men, but only one seriously, and it was...' she searched for the right words, her cheeks flushing pink '...slow to warm up.'

Benedetto's eyes met Amelia's and held in a way that caused her whole body to simmer.

Amelia reached for her water, and was sipping it gratefully, when Cassidy strolled towards them. 'Sorry, guys, I burned the first set of prawns and had to make more. But they look delicious. Hope you enjoy.'

The Australian woman was a veritable breath of fresh air after the intensity of Amelia's conversation with Benedetto—not the conversation itself, but the way she felt when they were alone, as if there were an oppressive weight bearing down on her, making it hard to breathe and think and do anything but crave him.

Cassidy placed their meals down—a serving of enormous prawns in a sticky sweet sauce with a large salad. It was exactly the kind of thing Amelia might have ordered in a restaurant, had it been on the menu, and as her gaze drifted from their dinner to the view, the dusky sky quite breathtaking from the colours that burst through it, she thought how perfect and sublime this all would be under very different circumstances. If she'd met Benedetto in a bar, or on the street, instead of like this.

'So if I'd met you some other way, if we weren't connected through Antón, would you have stopped us from… you know…?'

He reached for his cutlery, slicing through one of his prawns. 'I don't deal in hypotheticals.'

'Sure you do. Every time you consider your options for any decision you're planning to make, you consider the hypothetical outcomes. That is just your way of saying you don't want to talk about this.'

A smile was her reward, his appreciation for her quick retort obvious. 'Fine. Let's imagine then that we met randomly, and somehow ended up in a private space, with the chemistry we share.' He kicked back in his seat, his legs brushing hers again, but this time, they stayed where they were, forming a trap around her own legs, so every time she shifted, even a little, she felt him, the static charge of electricity energising her. 'It's likely we would have shared a one-night stand.'

'Only one night?' she prompted, then could have kicked herself. Was she really offended by his reply to a hypothetical scenario that could never be?

He lifted his shoulders. 'Perhaps a few nights.'

'And then what?'

'We'd part ways.'

'That easily, huh?'

'Why not?'

'I just—it seems like a very limiting way to live your life.'

'That's what I like about it.'

She frowned. 'I don't understand.'

'I have no plans to get married, and absolutely no plans to have children. It shifts the parameters of what my relationships are about.' His eyes scanned hers. 'But I am not a subject we need to discuss.'

Her stomach tightened with frustration, but she let it go for now. There was no sense pushing him. Amelia needed time to regroup and form a new strategy, to reconcile what she'd learned about him tonight and how best to use it to her advantage. Lost in thought, she shifted beneath the table, their legs brushed and it was as though an invisible rubber band that had been tightening around them finally snapped.

He jerked his gaze back to her face, his eyes boring into hers, an invisible war being fought, but Amelia couldn't have said who was winning or who was losing, she knew only that she felt as though she were fighting for her survival. Her breath was held, her body stiff, her senses all finely honed on the man opposite.

'You need to understand, Anton is my closest friend,' Benedetto ground out, pushing back his chair, leaving the battlefield altogether. 'Someone who stood by me when no one else would.' He stared at her. 'And you are his sister.'

Anger fizzed inside Amelia. 'I am also my own person. Me.' She stood, jabbing her fingers towards her chest, to indicate the centre of her being. 'I am not just an adjunct to Anton. I'm not a princess. I'm just Millie Moretti and I wish you'd—'

'Don't say it.' He held up a hand, eyes warning her.

'I wish you'd remember who I am,' she finished defiantly. 'Not act as if my only defining characteristic is being related to Anton. But what did you think I was going to say?' she demanded, moving around the table, towards him, until they were toe to toe. 'Did you think I was going to say I wish you'd make love to me?' She threw the gauntlet down between them. 'And if so, why are you so threatened by that?'

'You know why. It can't happen.'

'I don't even know if I want it to happen,' she lied, hating how much she *did* want him. 'But I find it strange that a man with your experience can't be a little more sanguine about the whole affair.'

He responded with a harsh bark of laughter. 'I have kidnapped you and yet you persist in throwing yourself at me. Why?'

If he'd intended to hurt her, then he couldn't have chosen his words more wisely. After Daniel, she'd lost her confidence completely. She'd thought they were in love, but he'd been using her, and it had made her feel dispensable and worthless. She'd sworn she'd never let another man have that kind of power over her again, and yet here she was, not twelve hours after meeting Benedetto, and clearly he already had the ability to wound her.

She shuddered and took a step back, staring at him and

trying to make sense of everything, but most of all wanting to escape, to get away from him and his intently watchful gaze.

'You're right.' She shivered despite the fact it was a warm night. 'I must be mad.' There was no other explanation for this. It simply didn't make sense. 'Excuse me.'

She turned on her heel and left. But before she'd reached the door to the corridor, his voice arrested her. 'Wait.'

She stopped walking but didn't turn around. 'What for, Benedetto?'

'I meant what I said before.'

She sucked in a breath.

'If you weren't his sister, and we'd met, as you proposed, in some other way, you would already be naked in my bed. This is not one-sided, Princess.'

She gasped, spinning to find him standing right behind her, so close they were almost touching. 'I don't know what to say to that.'

He held a finger up to her lips, to silence her anyway, but it was an incendiary touch. Sparks ignited.

'Don't say anything. There's no point. It's never going to happen between us so whatever we might be tempted to, it's a far better idea if we just…ignore each other from now on. *Va bene?*'

CHAPTER FOUR

IGNORE HER? YEAH, RIGHT. Given the lack of other occupations, Princess Amelia Moretti had taken to sunbathing on the deck in one of the swimming costumes Cassidy had bought for her, which—Cassidy being a free spirit who'd grown up surfing—was barely sufficient to cover Amelia's body.

His dreams had been filled with Amelia, with imaginings of her, naked and sensual, straddling him so her long hair formed curtains around her face, and yet now that he stared at her in a way that was making it impossible to keep his distance, he realised how much more desirable her body was in the real world, how much more beautiful and graceful, than he'd been able to conjure in his dreams.

So ignoring her wasn't going to work, but nor could he act on his feelings.

Which basically put him in a form of hell for the next six days.

There was one way he could stay true to what he knew to be the right thing.

Eyes on Amelia, he removed his phone from a pocket and loaded up a text to Anton.

I have her. She'll be home within the week.

He sent the message but didn't experience an accompanying sense of relief. If anything, knowing that Anton was aware of the predicament felt strangely oppressive. It also felt like a direct betrayal of Amelia. To whom he owed nothing! And yet he found he couldn't completely disregard her obvious misgivings about returning home.

From Benedetto's perspective, the royal family of Catarno was surprisingly normal and loving, all things considered. He'd never had an example of that, of a real family. He'd been an only child and his father, while not physically abusive, had drunk too much and had a short fuse, meaning it hadn't taken much for him to lose his temper and explode at whomever happened to be nearby—Benedetto, or Benedetto's mother. As children in volatile situations often did, Benedetto had become adept from a young age at appearing to ignore the outbursts, to compartmentalise his fear and panic responses. When his father had died of a heart attack, and Benedetto was only fourteen, he'd been relieved.

Despite the fact the death had plunged Benedetto and his mother from living hand to mouth to abject poverty, the silence and lack of living on tenterhooks had been an immense relief, for both of them. They'd been happy, but only eighteen months later, his mother had been talking on the phone and stepped out from the kerb right into a bus. She'd died instantly. Her, he did mourn.

So his experience with family was limited. Meeting Anton's brother and parents had blown him away—to see the easy love and connection, the way they were all so respectful of one another.

And Amelia had simply turned her back on that, as though it held no value whatsoever. It was a callous, childish, hurtful thing to have done, and yet he wasn't sure Amelia was any of those things.

True, he barely knew her, but his childhood had made him an excellent judge of character. He also didn't have the sort of pride that would prevent him from admitting when he'd made a mistake, and at least on this score he had, potentially, been wrong about Amelia.

And so what? he asked himself angrily. What did it matter to him? Beyond the wedding, he wouldn't need to see her again. She'd be free to live her life.

And what would that look like?

Would she stay in Catarno? Would the wedding be the start of a new phase in her relationship with her parents and siblings? Or would she escape again as soon as she possibly could? Return to Valencia, or somewhere else, now that her cover had been blown?

She turned at that moment, tilting her face. He wasn't sure if he'd moved, or done something else to draw her attention, but her eyes flicked sidewards and landed directly on his— catching him staring at her, pondering. He didn't look away. He held his ground, arms by his sides, every part of him focused on her.

She tilted her face away again, looking out to sea, her expression mutinous.

'It's a far better idea if we just...ignore each other from now on.'

He'd said it. It was his idea, and it was the right idea, so why did he find his legs carrying him across the deck towards her against his own better judgement?

His shadow cast across her chest, long and dark, but it was a warm enough day not to make a hint of difference to Amelia's enjoyment. If anything, his proximity fired something new to life inside her, so she stretched languidly, shifting one leg over the other, crossing them at the ankles, and positioning an arm behind her head, a study in relaxation.

'Are you wearing lotion?'

She was so angry with him, and yet the hitch in his voice pulled at that anger, undoing it a little, making her vulnerable to an awareness of him she was doing her best to fight.

'Is this your idea of ignoring me?'

'I can hardly hand you over to your family with bright red sunburn.'

She bristled at that. 'I'm not an object,' she reminded him coldly. 'No one is handing me to anyone else.'

'I'll take that as a no.'

She ground her teeth together. 'It's none of your business. I'm not your business, regardless of what you and my brother might have discussed.'

'We have not discussed you often, *cara*.'

The term of endearment surprised her, but it surprised him more, going by the look on his face. He seemed to wish to swallow the word right back up again.

'And yet you appear to know a lot about me. Or think that you do.'

'I know what I've perceived, through your absence. Through how that absence has affected your family.'

She could easily believe her family was suffering, but it was nothing compared to the hell they'd be living through if she'd stayed, and they'd learned what kind of mess Amelia had exposed them to.

'I had no interest in hurting them,' she said truthfully. 'And I can't see why any of that matters to you. Friendship with Anton aside, this is a private matter.'

'He asked me to retrieve you, and so I did.'

She jerked to standing, eyes flashing with his, and it was only when she met his gaze that she began to suspect he might have been deliberately goading her. 'Retrieve me?' she repeated with incredulity. 'Seriously? Like a lost pet, or a missing suitcase or something?'

His smile irritated her even as she was captivated by the way it transformed his features.

'Don't laugh at me.'

'I'm not.' He lifted a hand in surrender. 'You're funny, that's all.'

'I'm not meaning to be.'

He lifted his shoulders. 'You still are.'

She expelled a long, calming breath. 'Did you come out here just to ask me about sunscreen?' she asked, determined to shut down their conversation. Maybe he'd been right the night before? Maybe they needed to either ignore each other or at least pretend to, if every one of their conversations led to an argument.

'Yes,' he said, without moving.

'Well, then, you've done your duty. You can go.' She gestured across the deck for him to leave.

He arched a brow.

'You're the one who suggested we ignore each other.'

'Easier said than done,' he drawled.

'God, Benedetto, you're impossible.'

'So I've been told.'

'I'm serious. You're like a whole bundle of mixed messages. Why don't you just decide what you want and let me know?' And with that, she settled back onto the sun lounger and pulled her glasses over her eyes, feigning sleep.

But not for long.

Not five minutes later a splashing sound alerted her to the fact she wasn't alone, and a quick shift of her head showed Benedetto in the pool across the deck. He was swimming through the water, powerful and confident, and although the pool wasn't Olympic length, he had enough space to complete a lap and turn under water, swimming back the other way, where he paused against the coping, his powerful, tanned arms mesmerising, covered in water and delightfully tempting.

She blinked away.

Only, he was right there, half naked, tanned, wet, relaxed, and even when she knew the smartest thing to do was disappear off the deck and away from temptation, she found herself lasting barely ten minutes before she stood and paced to the edge of the pool, an unimpressed scowl on her face.

'Yes?' he asked at the water's edge, standing with legs braced wide apart, blinking up at her through eyes that were rimmed with dark, wet lashes, hair slicked back showing a high brow.

She glared at him. 'Don't you have work to do or something?'

'I've been working,' he replied with a shrug. 'Late last night, and from early this morning. Does it bother you for me to have a break?'

That wasn't what she'd meant. 'It's none of my business,' she muttered, holding up her hands in surrender. 'It just seems like you're going out of your way to aggravate me.'

'By swimming?'

She raised her brows. 'By swimming when I'm right here.' She gestured to the deck.

'There are two of us,' he pointed out. 'You could go somewhere else if my presence bothers you that much. It's a big ship.'

The water was so tempting, and suddenly all Amelia wanted was to dip into it, just for a moment, to cool off. She'd been lying in the sun for hours and she was quite warm all over. But there was no way she'd show even a hint of her thoughts to Benedetto. There'd be time later to swim—for now, she needed to escape.

'Great idea. Thanks for the suggestion,' she said with mocking obedience in her tone. She followed it up by doing an overly exaggerated salute. 'See you later.'

She felt his eyes on her the whole way across the deck.

Inside, she fixed herself a sandwich and took it to her room to eat, brooding as she stared out at the ocean. Once finished, she decided she couldn't pass the rest of her time sulking and staring into space, and there were limited alternatives on board. And so she made her way back to the library, intending to grab a book. But when she strode in, without knocking, it was to find Benedetto there, hair still wet, body mercifully covered now in a T-shirt and fresh, dry shorts.

'Oh!' She startled, and he looked just as surprised. 'I didn't realise you were in here.'

He regarded her for several seconds without moving. 'Well, I am.'

'I see that now.'

'What can I do for you?'

'I came to get a book.' She gestured to the shelves.

'A book?'

'To read,' she babbled, then clamped her lips together. Caught off guard, she was on the back foot, not sounding as assertive or confident as she wanted. 'As I have literally nothing else to do, I presume you won't mind?'

'I don't mind at all,' he said, waving a hand to the wall of titles. 'Take whatever you want.'

'Oh, thank you so much,' she replied, heavy with angry sarcasm. 'What a considerate kidnapper you are. Is there somewhere online I can leave a five-star rating?'

Another smile, which he was quick to smother, but Amelia saw it and her stomach did a strange flopping motion.

'There's a cinema downstairs, you know.'

She glanced over her shoulder. 'A cinema?'

'And a gym. A spa. I was going to show you yesterday, but then you asked me to kiss you...'

'I seem to remember *you* kissing *me*,' she said, though in fact, while his body had come close to hers, it was Amelia who'd sought his lips. She coloured to the roots of her hair.

'We'll have to agree to disagree.'

'You are seriously the worst.'

His eyes bored into hers. 'Do you want to finish the tour?'

'I can probably work it out for myself,' she said after a beat.

'Afraid to be alone with me?'

She ground her teeth together. 'Of course not. Just trying to follow your instructions.'

'Okay.' He didn't move, and her stomach dropped to her toes, the emotion easily identifiable as disappointment. 'Suit yourself.'

Amelia's lips parted but she left the room before she could say something really stupid and beg him to show her.

Unfortunately, when Amelia made her way to the end of the corridor and down the wide stairs, it was to discover a door at the bottom wouldn't open. Had he known?

With a noise of frustration, she turned on her heel, strode back into his office without knocking, hands on hips. 'It's locked.'

Head bent over some documents, Benedetto took a moment before looking at her. She hadn't really given his desk any proper attention, but now she saw it was incredibly ordered, as though he could only function when everything was in its place. There was a laptop, a pile of papers, a leather-bound diary, and, from where she stood, the back of a photo frame. Curiosity had her wanting to move forward to see what kind of picture a man like Benedetto would keep on his desk, but Amelia would die before she'd show that much interest in his life.

'I'll open it, then,' he said simply, standing.

'Why is it locked? We're on a boat.'

'It's a security feature—the door's self-locking. It doubles as a safe room. There's an alternative bridge down there, a backup command system. In case the boat's ever breached.'

She blinked at him, the thought unsettling. 'Is that likely?'

'I'm a very wealthy man. It's not unlikely.'

She shivered.

'You've lived with security precautions all your life. You can't be surprised by that?'

'I just...you're a private citizen.'

'Yes, with a lot of money, which motivates some people to do very bad things. Hence the security features.'

'What else?' she asked curiously, falling into step beside him.

'Planning your escape or your rescue? I should tell you, neither's likely.'

She blinked up at him. 'Do I need to be rescued?'

'I haven't decided yet,' he said, but without humour. 'Maybe I'm the one who should send out an SOS?'

'Oh?'

'I'm starting to think you're trouble with a capital T.'

'You can always let me off at the nearest port.'

'And call the Catarno guard to come collect you? That's not a bad idea.'

She stopped walking, staring at him. 'Benedetto, listen to me—' She inhaled sharply, searching for words. But how could she get through to him? He seemed so determined, without even a hint of doubt about his plan to return her to the family she'd left for their own good.

'I know you're doing this out of loyalty to Anton. I know

you think you're doing the right thing, but you're really not. Nothing good can come from making me go back.'

He stopped walking, stared at her for a long time, silence crackling between them.

'Did someone there hurt you, *cara*?'

She flinched. Not because his term of endearment was unwelcome, but because it was entirely too welcome, too comforting. It made her want to cry to think even for a moment that this man might be on her side. He wasn't. Of course he wasn't. He was operating on Anton's behalf, and while she loved her brother, in this matter their wishes were diametrically opposed. But what if Benedetto saw Amelia's perspective? What if he actually went in to bat for her? She couldn't fathom what it would be like to have a defender such as Benedetto.

'Amelia?' he demanded, his expression pinched, as though genuinely worried about what might have happened to her.

She swallowed hard, blinking away. Yes, someone had hurt her. Daniel had destroyed her childish faith in love, he'd taken her trust and trampled it. And worse, he still knew a secret that had the power to destroy Amelia's family. Fear rose in her throat, making it hard to breathe. What a mess it all was.

'I can't go home.' The words were bleak. 'If you have any decency in your heart, any whatsoever, you'll take me at my word and let me go.'

He looked momentarily surprised and then anguished. 'Why does it bother me,' he mused a moment later, 'for you to say I have no decency?'

Her emotions lurched all over the place. 'I don't know.' A whisper. Tears were threatening. She looked away, determined not to show such weakness.

'Do you know why I decided to take you to Catarno by boat?'

She lifted her shoulders. 'Because it was a sure-fire way of getting me out of Valencia?'

'True, but I have a helicopter on board. I could fly you there tomorrow and be done with this.'

Fear made her heart hurt.

'I thought this would be best for you. To have time to get used to the idea, to work through whatever issues you have with your family, to make your peace with the necessity of seeing them again and being at your brother's wedding. Of being able to put your best foot forward and show your family that you've changed.'

But Amelia hadn't changed. She was still an illegitimate love child, a secret, a shame. And a target for blackmail because she'd opened her big mouth to the wrong person.

'Am I supposed to thank you?' she whispered, anguished.

'No.' He moved closer, putting a hand on her arm solicitously, staring into her eyes with obvious concern. 'Tell me why you ran away.'

'I can't.' Her voice caught. 'I really can't. But believe me when I tell you it was the best thing for everyone. I can't go home, Benedetto. I can't.'

CHAPTER FIVE

DESPITE HER REPUTATION, Amelia was not prone to dramatic fits but as she said, 'I can't' over and over again, she felt herself growing hysterical, frustrated, terrified of the prospect of being home and having to keep this enormous secret, terrified of what Daniel might do or ask if she returned, terrified that Anton's wedding would be ruined because of her.

Amelia could hardly breathe.

Benedetto grabbed her other arm, shaking her a little, so she looked up at him, eyes huge.

'Hey,' he said firmly. 'Stop. Stop.'

She was trembling, she realised, and weak. Without his touch, she wasn't sure she could stay standing.

'Tell me what's going on. Is it just that you're afraid of their reaction? Because I can tell you this: they love you.' His voice was gravelled. 'They want you back, more than anything.'

She shook her head, stomach in knots. 'You don't understand. I can't. I can't.'

And then, perhaps because he saw no other way to silence her, he claimed her mouth with his own, kissing her hard and fast and desperately, absorbing her panic, her anguish, placating her without words or promises to listen and be her champion, but somehow still reassuring her.

Everything inside Amelia shifted. Her hands lifted to his shirt, bunched into it as if holding on for dear life, as if she couldn't possibly survive without him, as if this kiss and he were her lifelines.

It was all so confusing, so wrong, so right. She whimpered into his mouth, lifted one leg, wrapping her heel behind his knee, then higher, aching to be closer to him, so much closer than this. His kiss grew more urgent, more intense, harder, his tongue lashing hers, his mouth pressing her head back against the wall, until he lifted her, carrying Amelia with her legs wrapped around his waist the rest of the way down the stairs to the door that was locked.

He cursed into her mouth, reached over her shoulder and fumbled the buttons on a keypad; the door swung open. Amelia barely noticed. She was utterly captivated by this moment, by him, by what they were sharing, by how her body was reacting and, most importantly, by the way his kiss was wiping everything else from her mind, so she no longer felt as though she were losing to a rising tide of panic, but surfing along a current of desire that was engulfing her in the best possible way.

Through the door, he strode purposefully to a wide arch and stepped through it. She was conscious of only the surface-level details—a sofa, huge, wide, long, beige in colour, which he laid her down on, barely breaking their kiss for even a moment, his hands pushing at the summery dress she'd pulled on over her bathers while she ate lunch, revealing her near-naked body. She had no self-consciousness around nudity, but this was different. Benedetto stripping her bathers was a whole new level and in the back of her mind she knew she should stop this, slow things down, that they both had reasons for not acting on their attraction, but to hell with it. That kind of rational thought felt just outside Amelia's grip.

She was terrified about going home but when Benedetto

touched her, nothing else mattered. Didn't she deserve this? Just a little?

'This is crazy.' He seemed to echo her thoughts.

'I know.'

He pushed up onto his elbow, staring down at her, eyes conflicted, lips tense. 'Amelia—'

'Don't stop,' she pleaded, dropping her hands to his sides and pushing up his shirt, revealing his torso, which she lifted up a little to kiss. He groaned, and the power she had over him was a heady, glorious feeling.

'This is complicated.'

'No, it's simple,' she murmured, arching her back. 'I still don't like you, you know. This is just sex, desire, chemistry, whatever. It doesn't mean anything. That's what we both want, isn't it?'

He looked at her as though she'd spoken in a foreign language. 'Your brother—'

'I'm pretty sure neither of us wants to think about Anton right now. But in case you're worried I'm going to tell him about this, don't be. It's not my style to kiss and tell.'

'Nor mine.'

'Then?' she asked, shifting her hips and, this time, removing his shirt fully, throwing it across the room without looking away from Benedetto.

'We'll both regret this.'

She lifted her shoulders. 'Do you want to stop?'

'What do you think?'

She smiled, her heart lifting. 'I think this is out of our control and that's okay.'

He shook his head. 'That's not generally my philosophy.'

And yet, despite that, they were kissing again, lips melded, hands running over each other, naked bodies writhing, moving so one moment she was on top of him and the next him on her until they rolled off the sofa and onto the floor, both laughing at the unexpectedness of that before they kissed once more, and the passion building between them made laughing or speaking entirely impossible.

Benedetto stepped out of his trousers swiftly, removing a slim leather wallet from his pocket and from that wallet a familiar foil square, which Amelia was delighted to see, as she'd been so swept up in the moment she'd almost forgotten contraception.

He stripped naked and sheathed himself and Amelia's mouth grew dry at the sight of his enormous arousal, the size of him alone quite frightening as she imagined taking him inside her. But then he was back on the floor with her, his weight on top of her body, his mouth seeking hers before he moved to her breasts, kissing her as he had the day before, rolling her nipple in his mouth, tasting, tormenting, his hands at her hips shifting lower, between her legs, separating her there, teasing the entry to her sex, promising so much that she was moaning his name over and over, crying out with nonsensical sounds driven by white-hot need and passion. Finally his tip was there, and she was no longer afraid but euphoric and desperate, so she lifted her hips and pulled him in, crying out with relief as he breached her most intimate space and possessed her in a way she'd never known possible.

Hers was a guttural cry of relief, his of restraint, as he thrust as gently as he could deeper, deeper, until finally his entire length was buried in Amelia and she grew still, eyes wide, staring at him. He ran a hand over her face.

'Okay?'

His concern touched something deep in her chest. She could only nod.

He kissed her then, his tongue moving in time with each shift of his hips, each powerful thrust, the hairs on his chest rough against her over-sensitised nipples, her whole body on fire, pleasure a violent storm now, rather than just a rising current. She felt as though she were being rocked in a thousand directions; as if her body were entirely unfamiliar to her. Every part of her, every nerve ending, every fibre, was exploding, jangling, radiating a whole new frequency. She scraped her nails down his back, crying out as her body began to quiver and tremble as if she were tipping over the edge of a chasm with no ground in sight, only stars and heaven and beautiful sky. She was flying through the stars, the heavens, all celestial, perfect radiant life encapsulated in her as she dug her heels into the base of his spine and held him deep, held him still, as her muscles tensed and spasmed, her body exploding in a powerful, all-consuming release that left Amelia utterly breathless.

She lay, eyes closed, the waves still rolling over her, the tide still lapping at her sides, and then he was moving again, gently at first, letting her get used to the feeling as her insides were still squeezing with release, and then he began to move faster, his mouth seeking first one breast, then the other, his hands roaming her body freely, moving between her legs, stroking her there as he thrust inside her so the pleasures were almost impossible to bear. And she felt the madness returning, threatening to devour her, she felt pleasure filling each pore of her body and threatening to explode it and then she was on the brink of losing herself once more just as he did, so their euphoria was mutual, shared, a total joining of passion and pleasure, of release and relief.

He weaved their fingers together, holding her hands above her as he stilled, and she felt his release, she felt her own body spasm and cried out because it was all so perfect, so desperately, hauntingly right.

'I—don't know what to say,' she murmured after a long

time, when their breathing had returned to normal but neither had moved.

'Do we need to say anything?' he asked, and then he did shift, pulling away from her, rolling to his side, propping up on one elbow to study her.

'I guess not,' she agreed, brows knitted together. Her mind though was swirling with thoughts, awakenings, needs, reassurances. Namely, she wanted to know that this wasn't going to be the only time they experienced that. 'I like you more when you make me feel like that,' she said softly, and he laughed, a sound that filled her body with another kind of pleasure.

She smiled, closed her eyes, turned her head and then blinked languidly, scanning the room for the first time. And gasping. She'd been vaguely aware of an enormous piece of wall-size art when they'd entered but had been too caught up in Benedetto to give it another moment's thought. But now she realised it wasn't artwork so much as windows beneath the water giving the most stunning view of the ocean, which was teeming with brightly coloured fish. She scrambled to sit despite the cataclysmic shift that had just taken place inside herself, and saw that the floor also had a large strip of glass, revealing yet another vista. She reached for his arm and gripped it, simply because she almost couldn't believe what she was witnessing.

'It's so beautiful, Benedetto. It's just incredible.'

He was quiet. She spun to face him, smiling, lost in her appreciation for this room, so didn't see the way he was watching her.

'I've never seen anything like it.'

'It's a nice feature,' he agreed belatedly.

'The stone benchtops in the bathrooms are a nice feature,' she contradicted. 'This is mesmerising.'

She pulled her knees to her chest, rested her chin on them. 'I could stay in here for hours, watching the fish swim by. Or us swim by them, whichever it is.'

'Both.'

'Right.' She smiled again, her eyes trained on the water.

'When we stop, it's better. They become curious and swim right up to the boat.'

'Oh, I'd like to see that.'

'I'll arrange it.'

She resisted the urge to ask him to stop them for ever.

For ever wasn't right anyway, but there would be worse places—and worse people—to hide out with for the rest of her days.

'Do you feel better?'

She blinked, something fraying on the edges of her mind before jolting into her fully, reminding her of their conversation Before.

She turned to face him as he reached for a blanket off the edge of the sofa and passed it to her. She took it gratefully, wrapping it around her shoulders, but it wasn't her body that felt exposed so much as her innermost thoughts and worries.

'I feel pleasantly distracted,' she said honestly. 'Can we just keep doing that? Then I won't have time to worry about home.'

'Why are you worried?' He asked the question gently, perhaps concerned that she might devolve into yet another panic attack. Amelia was surprised by how tempted she was to be honest with him. But she'd confided in Daniel, and he'd taken that information and threatened to use it against her. Amelia had learned she had to keep her secrets close to her chest.

'I've been away a long time,' she said eventually, haltingly. 'But nothing's changed. This is going to be a disaster.'

Silence fell between them, heavy and thoughtful. 'You

know, I never had a family like yours,' he said, so slowly she felt as though the words were being dragged from him against his will. 'My dad was a mean drunk who seemed to hate me and my mother. He had a raging temper and would lose it often. She was browbeaten by him, and never argued back. After a while, I didn't either.'

'Were you afraid of him?' she asked, leaning back a little, against Benedetto's chest, craving that closeness, but also wanting to comfort him by being near.

'He was not violent,' Benedetto said. 'At least, not physically, but his outbursts certainly had those characteristics. They seemed to erupt from him totally without his control, a temper that was fierce, unjust, unpredictable, and inconsistent. I felt at times that I was living on eggshells, not afraid for myself so much as my mother, who would wither a little whenever he shouted, belittling her with his cruel, awful insults. He would call her dumb, lazy, ugly, a waste of skin. His names for me were worse. Often he told me he wished I'd never been born, that I ruined his life just by existing.'

Amelia sucked in an outraged breath. 'That's a horrible thing to say.'

'Yes.'

'Did your mother leave him?'

'No. She would still be with him today, I'm sure, if he hadn't done us all a favour and died.'

She flinched a little at his words, but she understood them.

'I was so glad, *cara*. I hated the man. He made our lives a misery and yet we were stuck with him. Many times, I contemplated running away, but I was worried for my mother. In the back of my mind there was always a risk he might become physically violent towards her, and at least by being there, I could protect her.'

'Of course you felt that way. What an unfair burden for a young man to carry.'

'When he died, there were mountains of debts in his name. The estate was a mess. I have never known anything quite like the pain of that poverty, and the joy of our freedom. It didn't matter that we often didn't have enough to eat, or spent weeks at a time sleeping in cars. We were free of him.'

'Are you really, though?' Amelia asked, genuinely curious, pressing a hand to his chest. 'I've often wondered about the wounds left by a childhood like that. The insults spoken by someone who's supposed to love you and instead treats you as though you're worthless. Is there a part of you that still carries those wounds, Benedetto?'

'I'm not stupid enough to deny that,' he said with a lift of his shoulders. 'We are all shaped by experiences, and for the first fourteen years of my life, I lived with a man who told me every day that I was worthless. But if he shaped me,' Benedetto added, fixing her with a steady, cold gaze, 'it was probably for the better. Every day I knew that I would never become like him. I would never allow my temper to get the better of me. I would control my emotions, not the other way around. I would be better than alcohol, gambling, addiction, cruelty. I would prove him wrong. And I did.'

'Yes, you did.'

'When I first met your family, I could not believe how loving everyone was. Your parents seem to enjoy each other's company. They listen to one another's opinions. They are the definition of a team. Your brothers are friends. It's all so amiable and…nice. So warm. I cannot imagine what it must have been like, growing up in that environment.'

She stiffened, the mention of her family something she didn't welcome, bringing their conversation to a place she refused to go.

'To you, from the outside, I'm sure it did seem like that.'

'Does that mean I've missed something? Is it your family you are afraid of?'

'I can't talk about it.'

'Why not?'

'Because I can't.' She pulled up to standing, frustrated, aware of him watching her as she paced to the window. 'My family are fine. Loving, as you say. Almost to a fault. Whatever issues I have with them, and, like anyone, things they do annoy me sometimes and I'm sure that's mutual, I still love them. I don't want to hurt them. But I can't...' Her voice faded off into nothing as she ground her teeth. 'It doesn't matter.' She turned to face him. 'Nothing I say will change your mind, will it?'

He looked at her long and hard, spectacularly naked, strong, handsome, desirable, so close to being perfect that she realised, belatedly, that was exactly the case: Benedetto was a mirage. Stranded with him, she saw only what she wanted to see, but, ultimately, he was going to hurt her, just as Daniel had. She had to accept that.

'I'm sorry. I gave Anton my word.' He rose then, coming to stand in front of her, pressing a finger beneath her chin and lifting it. 'But I also think it is the right thing for you.'

Her smile was laced with sorrow. 'That's just something you're telling yourself to assuage your guilt.'

'They love you. Whatever you're running from, they want to help you. Let them.'

She closed her eyes, the first step in blanking him from her mind, body, and heart. When they'd made love, she'd had some kind of hope that she could get through to him, that maybe he'd come to see things from her perspective, but now she realised: he never would. Sleeping with him was the best she'd ever felt but it was also a mistake, one she couldn't repeat no matter how much she wanted to.

'I'm not an idiot, Benedetto. When I ran away from home, I did so knowing how it would hurt them, knowing what it would mean for all of us. I did it anyway. I weighed up all my options and chose the one that was right—not just for me, but for them too. In fact, it was agony for me, but it had to be done. I did them the courtesy of keeping my reasoning to myself, but that doesn't invalidate it. You're infantilising me and treating me with a complete lack of respect by making me go home.' She pressed a hand to his chest, pushed it lightly, then stepped backwards. 'I'm sorry, I can't say anything to ease your conscience. You're doing the wrong thing, and you should feel bad about it.'

She was beautiful and softly spoken, the total opposite to how his father had been, and yet her words, so gently delivered, cut him to the quick more than almost anything had in his life. She'd called him out on what he was doing, echoing his own deepest-held misgivings, which he'd pushed aside purely out of loyalty to his friend, but hearing her charges, after what had just happened, put him in a position he couldn't defend.

'I do.'

Her eyes widened, her lips parted. 'But it's not too late. We're only a couple of days out of Valencia. Surely you could fly me back? Take me anywhere,' she pleaded. 'Just not there.'

'I've already told Anton you're on the way.'

She recoiled as though he'd slapped her. 'What?'

'It's done.'

'It's not done,' she whispered, but tears filled her eyes and his gut rolled. He hated himself then, and the promise he'd made Anton.

'But I believe that facing your family and at least explaining to them—'

'You don't know what you're talking about.' She wrapped

her arms around her torso, shivering, her beautiful face radiating tension now. 'Imagine if your father was still alive and someone was taking you to him, telling you that it's always better to face your demons, to forgive and forget, would you?'

Despite the fact it was a hypothetical and he'd said he didn't deal in them, he blanched at the very idea.

'See?' she asked with a hollow laugh. 'Isn't that just the slightest bit hypocritical?'

'My father was a monster. Your family is not.'

'No, they're not monsters. They're wonderful, beautiful, loving, selfless people.' She stared at him for several long seconds so he thought she might be about to reveal something to explain why the hell she'd run away, what had motivated all of this. But instead, she shook her head slowly, looked at him as if he'd just slaughtered a cat in front of her, and left without another word.

CHAPTER SIX

FOR TWO DAYS, she ignored him. Two long days and nights. Every now and again he'd catch a glimpse of her, moving through the boat, going to get a book, or watch a movie, or to swim, but she never looked in his direction, even though she must have known he was there. It was as though she was going out of her way to avoid the briefest eye contact. She ate in her room—an unnecessary precaution because, having realised she wanted to avoid him, he would have given her the space necessary to do just that regardless.

After they'd slept together, he'd returned to his office to see a message from Anton on the screen.

You have no idea how relieved we are. I knew I could trust you with this.

The words had hit him in the chest like a grenade.

He'd agreed to help his friend without a moment's hesitation. Of course he had. Having heard only one side of the story, and never having met Amelia, he hadn't given her a second thought. His mind had filled out the facts necessary to make his peace with the whole concept and he'd set things in motion.

But she was under his skin now, a living, breathing, feeling human who had made it perfectly clear over and over again that she didn't want to return to her family.

He didn't agree with that choice. Regardless of Anton's request, he still believed it was better to face things head-on, particularly with people you loved. Knowing how he'd loved Sasha, understanding that there was nothing he wouldn't do for her, he recognised the pain Amelia's parents were feeling. He'd wanted to help.

But what authority did he have to control Amelia's life? She was right.

He didn't know anything about her circumstances. He had no idea what had motivated her to leave in the first instance. Forcing her home might make things ten times worse.

And if it did? Was it enough to be with her? Could he stand by her side as she faced whatever it was she feared? Could he offer her that at least? Was it a way of assuaging his conscience, just as she'd accused him of? And would she accept?

With a sense of determination that spurred him to take a step he'd never thought possible, he reached across his desk, picked up the photograph and moved through the ship, in search of Amelia and, he hoped, some form of redemption.

'Do you have a moment?'

Amelia startled, the sound of being spoken to directly after days of silence making her jump out of her skin.

The sight of Benedetto, whom she'd been forcing herself to avoid so much as looking in the direction of, made her skin flush and her heart race as a whole host of memories slammed into her. She blinked away quickly, staring instead at the dusk-lit ocean.

'There's something I want to explain to you.'

It was childish, but she still didn't speak. Partly because she didn't trust herself to. Her voice was hoarse from disuse anyway, but emotions were also crowding in around her.

She stood her ground though, jaw set mutinously, eyes focused ahead, and he remained standing at her side for several long seconds, then expelled a sigh, placing something down beside her. Despite herself, Amelia's eyes shifted, and she recognised the photograph from his desk, though she'd seen only the back.

Now that it was pointed towards her, she saw a smiling little girl looking back at her with dimples in her cheeks and eyes that seemed to sparkle with life and vivacity, so Amelia couldn't help smiling back. This child was, she suspected, the kind of girl who had that effect on everyone, even when rendered as a two-dimensional image.

'That's Sasha. Sash.' He cleared his throat. 'My daughter.'

She startled, jerking her gaze to his face. 'You have a daughter.'

'She died. Six years ago. After eighteen months of illness, treatments, the longest, slowest goodbye, and in the end, she was in so much pain that it was almost a relief when she— for her sake—but I was destroyed by it, Amelia.'

Amelia's eyes filled with tears and every shred of anger and rage and rightful indignation dropped away completely.

She stood up, wringing her hands in front of her.

'I'm not telling you for sympathy,' he responded gruffly, forestalling any effort she might make on that score, as if it would have been unwelcome anyway. 'I'm telling you because you need to understand. When she got sick, helping her became my sole focus. I pushed everyone away. I neglected my business. Lost most of my money, assets; it didn't matter. All I cared about was Sasha, and finding the right doctor, the best doctor, the treatment that would prove to be the miracle we needed.'

Silence surrounded them; the air pulsed with emotion.

Amelia stared at him, lost for words, full of feelings.

'And everyone left me.'

Her heart shattered.

'No one wanted to be near me; they didn't know what to say, what to do.' His voice was gruff, factual. Slow to form, the words dredged from the depths of his soul. 'Except your brother. Anton visited. Brought Sash toys. Came to stay with me at the end. Comforted me when she left. And afterwards, when I would have drunk myself into an early grave, he was the one who kept me tethered—just enough—to this world to fight back when I was ready. He was the hand reaching out for me, pulling me some of the way out of the worst grief I can describe, guiding me back to myself, my business. I owe him…everything.'

Pride and love for her older brother filled Amelia's heart, but there was also such hurt for Benedetto. She moved closer, picked up the photograph, looked at it. 'She has the most beautiful smile.'

'Yes.'

Benedetto's jaw was clenched, as though he was grinding his teeth, trying to control his emotions.

'So when he asked you for help, you agreed without hesitation.'

'I said I'd bring you home, whatever it took. I couldn't fail him. I can't.'

Amelia nodded slowly, wistfully, replacing the photo on the tabletop before pressing a hand lightly to Benedetto's chest.

'I had no idea—' his voice was gruff '—when I agreed to help, that it would cause you so much pain. You're nothing like what I thought you'd be.'

'Spoiled, selfish, thoughtless?' she prompted, because he'd made his assumptions abundantly clear.

'Maybe I wanted to think that, to make it easier to go through with this.'

'You're still going through with it though,' she said, gesturing to the ocean that surrounded them. 'Because of what you feel you owe Anton.'

He closed his eyes a moment. 'I want to help you too.'

'Oh?'

'I don't know what happened in Catarno to cause you to leave. You clearly don't want to tell me, and that's fine. I don't know what you're running from, but, if it helps, I can be there with you, when we arrive. I'll stand with you as you face your family. Whatever will make this easier, I'll do. I owe you that much, at least.'

A great big ball of feeling exploded in Amelia's chest. Sadness, relief, happiness, something else she couldn't identify—affection and gratitude and something shimmery that made her whole body feel as though it were tingling.

'Excuse me, Millie?' She was jolted from the wonder of those feelings by Cassidy's voice, from just a small distance away. 'Will you be eating in your room or do you want to sit out here? It's a gorgeous night.'

Amelia blinked, slow to compute.

Benedetto reached out, laced their fingers together. 'Have dinner with me.' But even as he said it, she felt the doubts in his voice, the hesitation, the unwillingness to surrender. Their attraction was something they hadn't foreshadowed, and it complicated everything, but that was worse for him.

Having heard what Anton meant to him, and why, she could well imagine Benedetto not wanting to sabotage their friendship by getting in a relationship with Anton's younger sister. And yet here he was, holding her hand, asking her to trust him.

Her heart stretched and thumped.

How could she?

How could she ever trust anyone again?

But this was just a meal. Dinner. It wasn't a lifetime commitment. And she didn't have to bare her soul to him just because he'd shared something so personal with her. Confident she could control this, Amelia turned to Cassidy. 'I'll eat out here.'

The ocean created the backdrop audio, a gentle lapping against the sides of the boat, rhythmic and seductive, soothing. When they were alone again, Benedetto gestured to the leather lounge that was at the top of the infinity pool, which was lit with stunning underwater lights, giving it a magical appearance.

Amelia allowed him to guide her to the seat, to pull her down beside him to rest back against him and listen to—and feel—the steady thrum of his heart, the intake of his breath, the good, solid, dependable movements of his body, his offer so exactly what she'd wanted from almost the first moment she'd met him.

'So you want to be my executioner and saviour,' she murmured, tracing invisible patterns on his knee.

'No one is going to want to execute you,' he said gruffly, pausing for a moment, and Amelia was quiet, waiting.

'When Sash was younger, before she got sick, she wanted to take a day off school. I can't remember why. She was fighting with a friend over something silly. She was only seven or eight.'

Amelia was still, listening, glad that he was speaking to her about his daughter, glad to hear about the beautiful child whose life had been extinguished far too young.

'Eight,' he said, snapping his fingers. 'Because her teacher was Mrs Fauci. I let her stay home. She had a nanny, a nice old lady who loved her like a grandmother, and I thought that was appropriate—the least I could do, really, as she had no one else to fill that role.'

'What about her mother?' Amelia asked softly. 'And her mother's family?'

'Her mother, Monique, was a woman I'd known for about three nights, when I was nineteen. She didn't tell me she was pregnant. The first I knew about Sash was when they turned up on my doorstep, Monique handing the baby to me telling me she didn't want anything to do with her.'

Amelia's stomach twisted.

'I didn't want a kid,' he said on a gruff laugh. 'Hell, my business was taking off, I felt like I was king of the world. And suddenly, I had to get a nursery ready, hire a nanny, work out how to fit a child into my life. And what if I turned out to be like him?' His voice sobered. Amelia turned a little, so she could see Benedetto better, rearranging herself so that instead of leaning back against him she was facing him, legs over his. He turned to look at her, a haunted expression in his eyes. 'It was my greatest fear. How could I know, until I had her in my life, that I wouldn't be just like my father? That I wouldn't lose it at the slightest provocation? That I wouldn't say things to her I couldn't take back?'

'You're not like him.'

'No, I'm not,' he agreed. 'You don't know how relieved I am to be able to say that. I raised my voice at Sasha only once in her entire life, and it was when she was two years old and was reaching for a pan that was filled with boiling water. She couldn't see above the stove, but if she'd got hold of it, if it had fallen on her—'

'That's a perfectly reasonable reaction,' Amelia responded.

'She turned to look at me with such surprise, and then giggled and ran into my arms. She was all that was good in this world.'

'She sounds amazing.'

He didn't reply at first, simply stared out at the ocean, one hand on Amelia's thigh. It was a balmy night, the kind Amelia loved. She'd always adored the heat, preferring it when she could sleep in just her underwear with a light sheet.

'So when she was eight, she stayed home from school,' he said, disorienting Amelia with his segue back to a conversation she'd forgotten about. 'Her nanny—Mary—told me later that they'd played Uno all day, Sasha had eaten well. She was happy that night when I tucked her into bed. But the next morning, she didn't want to go to school again. I insisted she go, she refused. It was rare for her to dig in her heels. Sasha was always happy and obliging and easy-going, so for her to get so worked up, I didn't know what to do. I let her stay home again. Mary told me they had another great day together. I don't know who enjoyed it more, honestly.'

Amelia smiled softly, pulling her hair over one shoulder as a gentle breeze rustled past them.

'The same thing, the next day. She just wouldn't go back. She wouldn't tell me why.' His eyes flicked to Amelia's. 'After a full week of this, we had a normal weekend, and then Monday morning came around. I was determined to get her to school. Again, she refused. I had no idea what was going on, so finally I called her teacher to see if there was something more at play.'

'And?'

'Nothing significant,' he said, lifting one hand palm up into the air. 'But then she explained how staying away from school can make even the smallest things seem like a huge deal. That our minds can build it up to be a bigger problem, that the longer we stay away, the harder it gets to go back. Mrs Fauci said the only solution was to bring her to school, even if she was in floods of tears. That within an hour she'd be over it.' He turned to look at Amelia, eyes scanning her face. 'She was right. On the Tuesday morning, I drove her to school myself, walked her to class. She was furious with me, glared at me, refused to give me a hug—completely unlike her—and I spent all day worrying that I was the worst parent in the world, that she would hate me for ever. She came home, smiling, with a story she'd written on bright green paper, and a card all her friends had made because they'd missed her so much.'

Amelia smiled, and her heart hurt too. 'You're a great dad.' She didn't know why, but she used the present tense, perhaps because she figured it wasn't a position you could lose. Even though Sasha had passed away, he was still her father and always would be.

'I got good advice from Mrs Fauci,' he replied. 'And was quaking in my boots going through with it.'

Amelia laughed. *'You?'*

'Oh, *sì*, absolutely. It was so unusual for Sasha to be angry with me, I was sure I was messing everything up monumentally.' He squeezed Amelia's thigh. Across the deck, there was movement—Cassidy was setting the table.

'I don't know why you left Catarno, but I wonder if the longer you stay away, the harder it's going to be to go back.'

She bit into her lip, surprised at how the comparison didn't reassure her. 'It's different.'

'Sure, the circumstances are, but what about the psychology? You've been gone over two years. Isn't that a part of it?'

On some level, he was probably right, but it wasn't so simple. 'I never planned to go back.'

'Never?'

I couldn't. She was so tempted to tell him the truth, but it was too awful, too shameful. Not just the truth of her parentage, but her idiocy in having shared her discovery with Daniel, putting herself in a position to be blackmailed. She couldn't allow history to repeat itself. She gulped, physically quashing that temptation, knowing she needed to take control of what was happening between them.

'I think we should talk about this,' she said, biting into her lower lip.

'This?'

'Us.'

She felt him stiffen and it was all the confirmation she needed that the conversation was imperative.

'You told me you don't do relationships.'

'*Sì.*'

'Well, I'm definitely not looking for a relationship either.' As soon as she said it, she felt the world tilt. It was so important to cling to that, to remind herself of what had happened with Daniel and why she'd been so careful ever since. 'I don't want this to get out of hand.'

'It won't.'

Her smile was wistful. 'You sound so confident.'

'Believe me, *cara*, as incredible as I find you, I will have no problems walking away from you after the wedding.'

She shivered inwardly. 'Because you don't do relationships?'

'Correct.'

'How come?'

'I could ask you the same thing.'

Amelia inhaled quickly. 'I…' She hesitated, aware that she was getting dangerously close to confiding in him. But surely she could offer a partial explanation, nothing to do with her mother's affair, but just a little insight into what had happened with Daniel? 'I suppose I learned my lesson,' she said haltingly. His eyes probed her face as he waited for more. Amelia sought the right words. 'I was dating a guy. I really cared for him; I thought we were in love,' she said with a lift of one shoulder, tilting her face to study the moon as it brightened in the sky. 'But he was just using me.'

'Why do you say that?' His question was calm and measured, as though drawing the information from her to assess its validity.

'It became apparent, when we broke up. He—' she broke off a moment, '—betrayed my trust, in the worst possible way. It made me doubt everything I knew about everyone. If I could be wrong about Daniel, who was I right about? I thought I knew him,' she said, shaking her head. 'I was an idiot.'

'No,' Benedetto contradicted. 'You just trusted the wrong person.'

She grimaced. He made it sound so simple, but it was a mistake that she would have to live with for the rest of her life. She'd never stop worrying about what she'd told Daniel. The power she'd given him to hurt her, and her family, would never go away.

'I won't make that mistake again,' she muttered.

'So it's easier to trust no one?'

She turned to face him, eyes unknowingly blanked of emotion, and nodded slowly. 'It's easier not to rely on anyone,' she amended. 'Whatever this is—' she gestured from her chest to his '—I want us both to be clear: it doesn't mean anything. It's not real, and neither of us owes the other anything. Okay?'

CHAPTER SEVEN

IT WAS A relief to hear her say that. The moment Amelia put boundaries around this thing, Benedetto recognised that a part of his misgivings had come from an anxiety around hurting her, leading her on.

'I'm glad to hear you say that,' he said, honestly. 'I didn't want to give you the wrong idea.'

A smile tilted her lips. 'That you're madly in love with me? Don't worry, you haven't.'

It was easy to return her smile, but he knew he owed her more of an explanation. 'It's not you. It's who I am.'

'I know that,' she said quietly.

'After Sash—even before Sash,' he corrected. 'I hated the idea of being in a relationship.'

'I guess your parents weren't the best example.'

'True.'

'So you've avoided commitments all your life?'

'Until Sasha,' he said, stroking his chin.

'Well, I'm not looking for commitment,' she said. 'As soon as I can, I intend to disappear from everyone all over again.'

'You can't do that.' He thought of Anton's family, of how much they loved Amelia, of how painful it was to lose a child, and hated the thought of her leaving them for a second time.

But Amelia only offered a wistful half-smile in response.

'So beyond this boat trip, we can forget we ever knew each other.'

Was that relief Benedetto felt again? She was making this so easy for him.

'But while we're here?' he prompted, watching her carefully, so he saw the way a delicate pulse point at the base of her throat sped up.

'While we're here,' she murmured, 'I think we should enjoy the ride.' She pulled her hair over one shoulder. 'It doesn't mean anything, Ben, but that's not to say we can't have fun...'

She moved a hand to his chest, pressed it there, her body sparking at the simple, innocuous touch. Their eyes met. She felt something stir inside her. Despite what she'd just said, and the important clarification she'd needed to make to protect herself and Ben from any possible complications, there was something about being so close to him, after their conversation about Sasha, that felt so intimate, as though she had a hotline to parts of his soul that were fundamental and raw. She moved closer instinctively, her lips almost meeting his.

'I like being friends, rather than fighting.'

'Fighting was fun too,' he said with a grin, but then he was kissing her quickly, as though magnetically drawn to her, and Amelia was moving too, urgently, needing him with all of herself, her body flooded with desire and pleasure and a thousand things she couldn't define and didn't recognise. He moved first, lifting her easily, carrying her against his chest, carrying her away from the deck, into the corridor and towards her bedroom.

Inside, they fell to the mattress together, and Amelia rolled over, straddling him, running her hands over his torso as he gripped the edges of her dress and lifted it, groaning when it came over her head, revealing her naked breasts. His hands roamed her body, cupping her, pulling at her nipples as she moved over his arousal, her underwear and his clothes unwelcome barriers to the coming together they both desperately needed, but even through the fabric she could feel his hardness and she rolled her hips, moaning at how close she was to feeling him, at how perfect it was to be this close. Torture and pleasure, all wrapped up inside her.

'God, Benedetto, this is so—I didn't know—'

He kissed the words back into her mouth, as if he'd said them himself or thought them. She arched her back and he moved to sit, his mouth finding her nipples, then seeking her lips once more, his kiss moving over her collarbone, his stubble dragging against the sensitive flesh. His hands cupped her bottom, moving her over his length, holding her down, lifting her up, separating her buttocks, inviting her, needing her, wanting her until finally he made a guttural noise and rolled her onto her back, stared down at her with breath hissing between his teeth.

'What is it?' She brushed her hair out of her face. 'Is something wrong?'

'You could say that.'

Amelia's heart thumped.

'I don't have protection. Tomorrow I'm stocking every damned room in this boat. But for now—wait here.'

'Oh.' Relief flooded her; she smiled. 'Okay.'

He was back almost immediately. 'You ran?' she teased, biting into her lip, his need for her the hottest aphrodisiac she'd known.

'A professional sprinter would have eaten my dust,' he agreed, pushing out of his trousers and rolling a condom over his length before coming back over her, kissing her, moving a hand between her legs, separating her thighs, bringing himself to her sex, pausing there a moment before entering her in one single motion, hard, fast, desperate, a thousand times more filled with need than the last time they'd done this when it had been new and different and they'd been exploring their attraction.

They'd agreed to the terms of this, and Amelia was glad, because it meant she could revel in the physical side of their attraction without worrying that it would get out of hand. They were just sleeping together. It didn't mean anything. It was simple, sensual, perfect...

But when the sun dawned the next morning, Amelia couldn't totally ignore the maelstrom of her feelings, so she was grateful that when she woke, Benedetto was no longer in her room. In another time and place, she would have wanted to roll over and lean into the nook of his arm, to rest her head on his chest, to kiss him awake. But that wasn't what they were.

This wasn't a real relationship, and he was the last man on earth she could trust. After Daniel, she'd been wary. Daniel had been a wolf in sheep's clothing.

At least with Benedetto, he'd been a wolf all along. She'd known from almost the first moment they met that he was her enemy, so at least there was no risk of a shock betrayal.

Nothing could change the fact that he was taking her home, even when he'd explained his relationship with Anton and why it had mattered to him so much to do whatever Anton asked of him. She was so angry with Benedetto, even when she forgave him completely, and none of it made any sense.

She could never accept his decision.

She'd thought she might be able to change Benedetto's mind in the course of the trip to Catarno, without disclosing the truth behind her disappearance, but, understanding what she did now, she knew that she'd never succeed. And weirdly, she wasn't sure she could even ask it of him. It shifted something inside her to recognise that she cared more for Benedetto's obligations to Anton than she did almost anything else. Why did that bother her so much?

Why did she feel such a deep sense of unease to recognise that there were few things that she cared about more than Benedetto's sense of duty? Was it because of how much he'd lost? Did she feel so sad for him that she was willing to sacrifice herself?

Of course not.

If she could escape, she would, even now, because her family deserved that. True, there would be a scandal attached to her no-show at the wedding, but it would be short-lived, and the royal family's PR machine would swing into action, coming up with some reason or other to explain it all away.

It would be better than the risks her return would bring. Unfortunately for Amelia, the chance of escape wasn't likely to occur, so she had to resign herself to her fate—in a matter of days, she'd be home.

'What is that?' Amelia asked from her vantage point on the deck, eyes focused on the land that was so close the beach umbrellas were visible.

Benedetto finished his strong black coffee before replacing the cup on the table between them. 'Crete.' The Greek island was not far from Catarno. It was almost time.

He turned to her, scanned her face. 'Have you ever been?'

'As a teenager,' she said with a smile of reminiscence. 'We used to sail the Med in the summer.'

The important thing was to get Amelia back to her family. It was his mission; he'd promised Anton. But the closer they got, the more inevitable their parting—and return to reality—became, he found himself wanting to stall. Just a little. 'Would you like to stop?'

She blinked across at him. 'Stop?'

Just a small delay. It wouldn't hurt… 'For lunch. You can get your land legs before we arrive in Catarno.' He contemplated that a little longer. 'We could stay here overnight.'

The second he'd said it, he realised how stupid the offer was. Where would they stay? A hotel? What were the chances her identity wouldn't be leaked by someone? Besides, wasn't there a risk she might run away again?

As soon as the idea occurred to him, he dismissed it.

She didn't want to go home, but, somehow, he was sure she understood why it was important to face her family. To be there at Anton's wedding. She wasn't a coward; he knew that much was true.

'Stay overnight, on the island?'

'Or the boat, but in port. For privacy reasons,' he said, relaxing into the idea of this. 'What do you think?'

What did she think? Amelia stared at him, her heart hammering, words hard to form. Was it possible he was trying to extend their time together? That he knew they were only a day away from Catarno, at most, and wanted to eke out their remaining time as long as possible?

But only yesterday, Amelia had promised herself that if she had a chance to escape, she would take it. Wasn't that exactly what was being presented to her?

Amelia chewed on her lower lip, totally lost, her heart stretching and twisting painfully in her chest, because she knew what she had to do but she couldn't make herself happy about it.

'Okay,' she agreed, forcing an over-bright smile to her face. 'Just give me a minute to get ready.' She walked towards the door that led to her rooms. 'Oh.' She snapped her fingers as if just thinking of it. 'Where's my camera backpack? I'll bring it in case there are some photos I want to take.'

'I'll get it,' he said without hesitation, which made her feel a thousand times worse, because the backpack also had her phone, and she knew she would need both in order to get off Crete.

'Thanks. I won't be long.'

* * *

They took the smaller speedboat into shore, Benedetto at the helm, looking every inch the devilishly handsome billionaire as the wind swept his dark hair from his brow and the water dappled across his shirt. Sun streamed across their path, warming them even as the breeze served to temper the heat of the day.

Amelia's heart was in her throat the whole way. She noticed a thousand tiny details about Benedetto, as if her unconscious mind was trying to commit him to memory, as if she needed to cement him into her soul before leaving.

Leaving.

Was she really going to do this?

Wasn't it her obligation?

Nothing had fundamentally changed since he'd scooped Amelia out of her life and brought her back here. She was still an illegitimate, secret daughter, the product of an extramarital affair that had the potential to destroy her family and undermine her parents' place on the throne. She was still a guilty secret. And Daniel was still out there with this knowledge, ready to blackmail her again.

Nausea rose in her throat and she blinked it away, gripping the strap of her backpack more tightly.

The ocean changed colour around them, going from a darker shade of blue to a turquoise so clear it was almost transparent, and gradually they were surrounded by other watercraft—boats, jet skis, holiday pleasure-seekers enjoying the sunshine and salt water.

Benedetto expertly steered them away, towards the marina, pulling them into a dock there and cutting the engine. His smile when he turned to her was completely without suspicion.

Her stomach squeezed painfully and before she could control her unconscious mind, she indulged a secret fantasy of pretending this was real. That they were two different people, with different pasts, who were willing to give this thing a real go, and see where it went…but it was an impossible dream.

'Ready?'

Her stomach dropped but she nodded. 'Let's go.'

A deckhand appeared from the marina to tether the boat, and once they were secured, Benedetto hopped out first then held out a hand for Amelia. She put hers in it, ignoring the spark that travelled the length of her arm, forcing a smile to her face. 'Where to first?'

They walked the ancient streets of the city, through narrow, winding cobbled paths with brightly coloured buildings on either side. Window boxes filled with geraniums and rosemary burst with brightness and fragrance, potted citrus plants decorated doorways, children played happily around them, and as they crossed the square, a group of old men in vests and caps began to sing happily, spontaneously, bowls of seafood in their laps, a card table set up with food and a rounded bottle of wine.

Amelia's chest hurt. This was so like her country, her culture, her people, that she felt such a wave of homesickness it almost paralysed her. She stopped walking, looked around, her breathing growing raspy.

'Amelia?'

'It's just…so familiar,' she said wistfully. 'It reminds me a lot of home.'

He reached out and squeezed her hand. 'You'll be back soon.'

He'd completely mistaken her feelings. Or perhaps he hadn't. She was homesick, she did want to go back, in a way. But missing home wasn't the same as being able to return. She was exiled.

Self-imposed, but no less binding.

They stepped into a very old church on the edge of the

square, admiring the architecture, the pillars, but always in the back of Amelia's mind was the knowledge that this would be the end. That this was when she'd escape. She *had* to escape. Didn't she?

But what if she didn't? What if she stayed with him? What if she agreed to let Benedetto support her—not in talking to her parents about the reason she'd left, but just by being her strength. By helping her get through it. What if he just acted as her friend, nothing more, nothing that would cause issues for him and Anton?

'You're distracted,' he murmured, brushing a hand over her hair.

Her heart slammed into her ribs and out of nowhere, she imagined them in a church filled with loved ones, his touch like this a deeper promise and pledge. Her heart trembled.

'Am I?'

'Hungry?' he prompted, still with no idea how deeply she was considering her next move.

'Yes,' she lied, for her stomach was far too knotty for food.

'I know a good place. Come on.'

She might have expected a fancy restaurant but instead he'd chosen an out-of-the-way seafood café with seating for about twelve people and views over the water. It was intimate, and the privacy of their booth meant she had no concerns about being spotted, so removed her hat and glasses.

They ordered something light, and some drinks, and Amelia imitated a relaxed pose, leaning against the leather banquette, looking out to sea. Their drinks came first, and while they waited for their food, Benedetto made easy small talk, telling Amelia about a project he was working on in mainland Greece, a package of three high-rises.

She listened, genuinely fascinated by his work, his world, his success. Their food arrived and they continued to talk, but in the back of her mind Amelia was angsting over everything. She couldn't decide what to do, but, ultimately, self-preservation had to win out.

When their plates were cleared and coffee ordered, she looked around with the appearance of nonchalance. 'Do you know if there's a restroom?'

'Through there.' He gestured to a double set of doors, bright red with portal windows.

'Thanks,' she murmured, reaching for her backpack casually, as though it were the most normal thing in the world, and excusing herself without a backwards glance. Her heart was racing so hard she thought it might give way as she slipped through the doors and into a corridor that had, she realised with relief, another door that led to a storeroom and then an alley.

Tears filled her eyes as she pushed through it and left the restaurant, her mind focused now on getting as far from Catarno as she possibly could.

But every step she took became harder and harder, heavier too, as if she were going in the wrong direction, wading through mud, pulling against elastic. Her lungs were burning with the force of breathing and her legs were shaking and as she pressed her back against a wall, waiting for her nerves to settle, she closed her eyes.

And saw him.

Benedetto, committed to memory perfectly, every inch of him, every beautiful, haunted, imperfect inch, and her heart stitched and her stomach rolled because the thought of never seeing him again was a torture she hadn't fully understood. She'd known it would be hard, but not akin to giving up breath or water. She'd thought she could control this. She'd thought she could spend time with him and not start to trust him, not start to want more from him. And maybe she could, but she wasn't ready to walk away from this yet.

'Damn it,' she muttered, dropping her head forward. What did that mean? She knew this would end. And soon—they were almost at Catarno. But she was running away again, and now she wasn't so sure it was the right choice. Everything was messy and confused, and it was all because of Benedetto. He'd got into her head and under her skin.

At first, he didn't think anything of it. He was more relaxed than he had been in years. Benedetto had always had an intensity about him, a wariness, courtesy of his father, and then their financial hardships. It was only a short time later he'd become a father, and that had probably been the only truly happy window of his life, a time when he'd gone from strength to strength professionally and had known, for the first time ever, uncomplicated, beautiful, easy love. He had loved his daughter with all of his heart, even when he would have said he didn't have a heart in the sense of feeling love. His had been just an organ responsible for pumping blood through his body until he'd met Sasha. Then he'd known what people were talking about. He'd loved her with all of himself, had known he would die before he let harm befall her.

And he would have.

If giving his life could have spared hers, Benedetto would have fallen upon the first sword he could find. But there had been no helping Sasha. He'd tried.

From that moment on, he'd been simply existing. Work had challenged him, had revived him, had brought him slowly back to life, and he'd taken a form of pleasure from succeeding, from rebuilding his fortune to the point of being one of the wealthiest men in the world, a Diamond Club member, welcomed into the most exclusive private club there was.

But everything had been about success. Not happiness, not relaxation, not enjoyment.

With Amelia, though, he'd felt a thousand things, not all of them good. He'd been aware of his conscience, he'd felt guilt, he'd felt shame, he'd felt frustration, even anger. But he'd also felt pleasure and joy, delight in another person's company. He'd felt things he couldn't quantify nor explain. And now, sharing a meal with her in a restaurant, which was such a normal activity, he'd felt relaxed despite what lay ahead for her, despite his worries for her and desire to shield her from any harm.

He'd let his guard down completely.

Which was why he hadn't noticed at first. He hadn't realised that she'd taken her bag. Hadn't been looking for anything out of the ordinary because he'd trusted her.

But just as he was starting to wonder why she was taking so long in the bathroom, his memory banged him over the head, reminding him of the image of her slipping through the door with the backpack over one shoulder. A backpack he hadn't even contemplated withholding despite the fact it had her phone, wallet and camera in it.

Because he trusted her.

Because he thought she felt—what? What did he want her to feel?

Had she expressed, at any point, a level of acceptance about going home?

Wasn't the opposite true? At every opportunity, whenever it came up, she insisted that it was wrong to go back. That she wouldn't forgive him for his part in it. That she couldn't face her family again.

He stood up quickly, reaching into his wallet, removing some money and throwing it onto the table before striding through the restaurant towards the doors to the restrooms.

The corridor was empty; a quick inspection of the stalls showed them to be likewise.

He felt as if he'd been stabbed in the chest.

He'd dropped his guard and Amelia had gone. Escaped. Left him.

Of course she had! He'd given her the perfect opportunity; could he blame her? The thought had even occurred to him but he'd dismissed it as ludicrous.

And if she wanted to avoid going home so badly, did he have any right whatsoever to chase her down again?

No.

He had no right.

He'd never had any right.

Amelia was a free agent. It was her life, her choice. She had to do what was right for her. Heart thumping hard against his ribs, he looked left and right, as if still hoping he might see her, before accepting that she had undoubtedly slipped far away from him already.

If she didn't want to be found, she wouldn't be.

They'd walked quite a way, and even with his long stride it was fifteen minutes before Benedetto made it back to the marina, to the boat he'd moored earlier that day with a strangely light heart. He grimaced as he stalked towards it and then stopped walking abruptly at the sight of the slim figure already on board, staring straight ahead. Frowning. Looking out to sea. Expression worried. Anxious.

His step quickened.

He stood short of the boat, staring at her, disbelief burning like acid in his gut. She turned to face him, her face mournful, confused, her eyes haunted, her cheeks stained with tears and he hated himself then for having anything to do with inflicting this pain on her.

'I'm sorry,' he said, moving quickly, stepping into the boat, crouching down before her. 'I should never have brought you here.'

She shook her head, evidently unable to speak. 'It's not Crete.'

'I don't mean Crete. I mean away from Valencia. I should never have got involved.'

A sob tore from her chest. He moved closer, cupping her face. 'You don't have to do this, Amelia. I'll take you home.'

'I don't know where home is,' she whispered. 'I don't know who I am.'

One of the deckhands approached their boat, looking to untether it, and protectiveness for Amelia, who was no longer in sunglasses or a hat, overrode everything else. He stood to shield her from view, slipped the deckhand a tip then sat beside her, ensuring she stayed out of view until they were alone again.

Even when they were, Benedetto remained where he was. 'Listen,' he said gently. 'This was a mistake. I didn't understand you, or the situation.' He put a hand on her leg, needing to feel her, to reassure her and also himself. He had to fix this. 'I'll take you back to Valencia.'

'You've already told Anton I'm coming.'

'I'll tell him I made a mistake. I'll tell him no one can force you to do anything you're not ready for. He'll be pissed—at me—but he'll get over it. Because it's the right thing to do. This should always have been your choice, Amelia. I apologise for not appreciating that sooner.'

She turned to look at him, her love-heart-shaped face so sorrowful that he groaned and pressed his forehead to hers. 'Please stop looking as though your world is ending. I made a mistake, but I'm going to fix it. It's going to be okay.'

'No, it's not,' she whispered, so haunted he wanted to stop the world and make everything and everyone in it do whatever was necessary to cause Amelia to smile. 'You don't know what you're talking about.'

He didn't. He had no idea what was going on, but he knew that forcing her to face it was wrong in a thousand kinds of ways. He could never be an instrument of pain to her. 'Come on,' he said softly, kissing her cheek with an odd, twisting feeling in the centre of his chest. 'Let's get you out of here.'

On the yacht, Amelia excused herself, numb to the core, needing to warm up with a shower. She stayed in there a long time, staring out of the darkly tinted window at the shore, imagining how things might have been now if she'd followed through with her escape. She'd formed a very quick plan as they'd wandered the streets, hand in hand, only hours earlier. She'd identified a travel agent, and located a bank, so she could access her trust fund.

There was no way to pull out money without revealing her identity but by the time any enterprising bank teller managed to sell the salacious information to a tabloid photographer, Amelia would have been long gone, booked onto a cruise ship off the island, where she would have stayed sequestered in her room until they put into port in a larger city, within reach of an airport.

And nobody would have been any the wiser.

But she hadn't been able to do it.

She missed her family. Even though she was terrified it might lead to heartbreak and pain for them, having come this close, the pull of Catarno and everything she'd walked away from was drawing her back, regardless of the risk.

And Ben? a voice in the back of her mind prompted. What role did he play in this? She tried to see through the wool in her mind, to understand. Their relationship still didn't mean anything. It was just temporary. But she would be lying to herself to pretend his offer to help hadn't lent strength to her. If the worst was to happen, was there anyone else she'd rather have at her side?

* * *

'What the hell do you mean?' Anton's voice came down the phone line with obvious surprise and Benedetto's hand tightened on the device.

'We're wrong to force her to come back.'

'You've got her on your boat, but you're saying you won't bring her to Catarno?' he repeated. 'Why the hell not?'

'She's adamant she can't come home.'

'This is where she belongs.'

'Then she'll come back of her own volition. It's not up to you or me to force her.'

'It's for her own good,' Anton snapped. 'You know the media circus that will erupt if she misses the wedding. Already the papers are full of speculation about it.'

'I know.' Benedetto nodded into the room. He'd seen the same reports. Not just the tabloids, even the broadsheets were running commentary on the likelihood of her return, speculating as to the work that was keeping her absent from royal life. 'And so does she. This has to be her decision, Anton.'

'You're serious?'

'I am.'

Anton swore softly. 'I trusted you.'

'And you still can. Trust me now—Amelia will always resent you if we do this. Would you rather she comes home for the wedding—and you lose her for ever—or that she returns when she's truly ready?'

'She will feel differently when she's here,' Anton said.

Benedetto closed his eyes. He owed Anton everything, but he should never have agreed to this. It was a family matter; Benedetto had no place getting involved. 'It has to be her decision, Anton. I'm not wrong about this.'

The Prince disconnected the call without another word.

CHAPTER EIGHT

HE FOUND HER in the underwater lounge room, staring out at the schools of fish, a book beside her, unopened, a cup of tea curled in her hands.

He hesitated in the doorway, not sure what to say, what to ask, what to do. It was an uncharacteristic uncertainty for Benedetto, and he resented it immediately.

'You turned the boat around.'

She'd clearly sensed him. He moved deeper into the room, then took the seat opposite her. 'Yes.'

Her eyes slid to his, pinned him to the spot. 'Why didn't I go through with it?'

He didn't pretend to misunderstand. 'I don't know.'

Her eyes glistened with unshed tears. 'I knew exactly what to do, how to escape, where to go. And then, I just couldn't do it. I couldn't.' A single tear slid down her cheek. She dashed it away quickly. 'Nothing makes sense.'

'Actually, I think things make sense for the first time all week. We're going back to Spain. That's the right choice. You can relax.'

Her smile was a shadow. 'Can I?'

'I've told Anton.'

Her brows shot up. 'What did he say?'

'Not a lot,' Benedetto responded truthfully. 'We had a slight difference of opinion on the matter, but he'll come round.'

'You're sure?'

'Yes, because I'm right.'

She shook her head slowly. 'You're right to leave the choice up to me, but I don't know what I should do. I hate the idea of going back, but how long am I going to stay away for? Am I really never going to see them again? And if I'm going to see them at some point, why not now?' She stood, teacup in hands, moving to the window, staring out at the fish without really seeing. 'I fought you tooth and nail but then today, when I could have left, I didn't. That has to say something about my subconscious mind, doesn't it?' Then, with eyes that were haunted and round like plates, she turned herself fully to face him. 'I miss them, Ben. I really miss them.' Another tear slid down her cheek, and he closed his own eyes, taking in a deep breath.

This was about her family, not him.

She'd come back for them, not because of Benedetto, and he was relieved because, despite the boundaries she'd insisted upon, a part of him was afraid that she was starting to want more than he could offer. Except she didn't. Nothing had changed.

'What do you want to do?'

That was a good question. She was standing on a precipice, and he was giving her the choice: to jump? Or not?

Amelia's eyes lifted to his and held, her throat shifting as she swallowed. 'I'm not who you think I am,' she said, eventually, so softly he almost didn't hear.

'What?'

Amelia pulled at a piece of invisible lint on her skirt and then she sighed heavily. Was she really going to do this? The truth had been like a ticking time bomb inside her for a long time. She twisted her fingers anxiously, speaking without looking at Ben. 'About two and a half years ago, completely by accident, I found something out about myself.' Her brow furrowed, and she looked at him, then shook her head. 'I can't believe I'm telling you this.'

'You can trust me,' he said, as though he knew she needed to hear that.

'Can I?'

'Of course.'

He was right, she realised. Ben had turned the boat around. He hadn't wanted to, but, ultimately, he was a good person. He was doing what he saw was the morally correct thing. He would never use this information against her. He wasn't Daniel.

It was like a weight being lifted off her shoulders. She nodded tersely.

'I was looking for a picture book my mother used to read me as a child. I wanted to take it with me to a hospital visit, to read to sick kids; the book was always one of my favourites,' she said, remembering the day as though it were yesterday. 'The attic is one of the best places in the palace. We're not really meant to go there,' she explained. 'But even as a girl, I loved it. It's where all of our memories are packed away, neatly into boxes, archived for posterity's sake. There are these windows near the top of the walls, round and old, that let in just enough light to see all the dust motes dancing in the sunshine,' she said, tilting her head to the side. 'But there are lifetimes' worth of artefacts stored, so it's not easy to find one particular item. I started with a trunk marked books, and kept going. Occasionally, I would find a book that interested me, pull it out, read a few pages, put it back.'

Her brow furrowed; Benedetto remained quiet, giving her space to explain.

'And then, I found a paperback novel that almost seemed not to belong with the rest.'

'Didn't belong how?'

She waved a hand through the air. 'It just wasn't the kind of book you'd keep.' She shrugged. 'I was interested in why it was with the old leather-bound hardbacks. And when I opened it, an envelope fell out.'

Guilt flooded her heart, her chest, her cheeks flushed pink. 'I should have put it away without looking, but I was curious.'

'What was it?' Benedetto asked, leaning closer.

Amelia squeezed her eyes shut. 'On the front, it said simply *"darling"*. I had no idea what it would mean. I suppose I was captivated by the romance of it. But I knew the moment I opened the envelope and lifted out the photo that I'd discovered something important. And wrong.'

Benedetto's eyes roamed her face.

'It was a picture taken some years ago—twenty-three, as it turns out—of my mother with the head of our stables, a man named Felipe Lamart. It was an intimate photograph.' Amelia's cheeks darkened from pink to red, her eyes not meeting Ben's. 'And in the letter, he asked if she planned to keep their baby.'

Benedetto's breath hissed out from beneath his teeth.

'I'm the baby,' Amelia whispered, needlessly. 'The King isn't my father...my brothers are half-brothers. I'm evidence of an affair that my mother clearly wants to hide. My real father is Felipe Lamart—a man who, I discovered, died when I was ten years old. He never tried to contact me. Evidently he didn't want anything to do with me.' She shrugged, blinking away.

'This is why you ran away?'

She shook her head. 'I...was in a state of shock,' she mumbled, the words tripping over themselves. 'I shouldn't have said anything to anyone, but I couldn't make sense of it. I needed to talk to someone, to ask for advice. Or maybe I just wanted to get it off my chest, I don't know. It was an immense thing to have learned about myself.'

'Who did you tell?'

Amelia's anguish was profound. 'My boyfriend at the time, Daniel.'

Benedetto's voice was carefully muted of emotion. 'That's a very normal response. What did he say?'

'Nothing important. Not then. I decided to get a DNA test, just in case it was somehow a mistake. Daniel helped me organise it. We sent away to a lab in America, using Daniel's address for correspondence, so it couldn't easily be traced back to me.'

Benedetto nodded.

'The test confirmed what I'd discovered. The King and I don't share any DNA.'

Benedetto lifted a hand to her cheek. 'I'm sorry, *cara*.'

Amelia's voice trembled. 'Things hadn't been great with Dan and me for a while, and, after this, I just needed to be by myself. We broke up. I thought it was amicable, but I'd misunderstood.' She pushed to standing, striding across the room now, so angry with herself. 'I knew he was socially ambitious, that he didn't have much money and was captivated by the palace and the lifestyle, but I still thought... I really thought he was with me because he cared about me. I was so stupid, Ben. So stupid.'

'What happened?'

'He blackmailed me,' she whispered, fidgeting with her fingers. 'He had a copy of the DNA results. He said that if I didn't give him two million euros, he'd sell the story to the highest-bidding newspaper.'

Benedetto swore in Italian, crossing the room to stand right in front of Amelia.

'And so?'

'And so,' she repeated, aghast, 'everything would have been ruined. I'd discovered this awful secret of my mother's, and mine, something that could ruin her life, her marriage, could change everything for my family, and then I'd told someone who saw me as a paycheque. I couldn't believe how stupid I'd been.'

'It's not your fault.'

'Of course it is,' she contradicted. 'I should have known better.'

'You were in a state of shock.'

'Yes,' she muttered. At least that much was true. 'But that's no excuse.'

'What happened with Daniel?'

'I paid him. He said it would be enough, "for now".'

Benedetto swore beneath his breath.

'I felt like I would never be free of him, Ben.' She groaned. 'And so I disappeared. I thought with me gone, the risk would go too. And it has. But if I go back...'

Benedetto felt as though he'd been punched in the solar plexus. He stared at her long and hard, as the pieces slotted into place and he understood, finally, why she'd run away, how selfless and courageous she'd been in taking herself out of the palace, away from her parents, to protect her mother, to disappear rather than risk any of this coming out. And how terrified she must have been, how heartbroken, after her bastard ex-boyfriend's advantageous betrayal.

Something uneasy shifted inside Benedetto.

A sense that Amelia was vulnerable, that she'd been badly hurt. That despite what she'd said, if Benedetto wasn't very careful, this could come to mean more to her than he wanted. Because no matter how much he desired her, Benedetto had no intention of staying in Amelia's life. Or any woman's. He would never risk that kind of attachment, permanence, connection. Not after what he'd been through.

Every cell in his body was committed to a lifetime spent on his own, relying on no one, depending on no one, loving no one. Never again. He had to make sure Amelia didn't mistake his sympathy for anything else, especially not now he understood what she'd been through.

He wouldn't become another man who let her down.

'My whole life is a lie,' she mumbled, wrapping her arms around her chest. 'How could I keep going to family events, dinners, birthdays, Christmas, festivals, all the things we do together, knowing what I know, and what I'd done? And my father, the man who raised me and taught me to ride a bike and bake and laugh at corny old movies, how could I look him in the eye again?'

'He's still your father,' Benedetto said, keeping a careful distance between them.

'I don't belong with them. I don't belong anywhere.'

'Listen.' He spoke sternly, needing to cut through her sadness. 'What you learned, and how you learned it, was devastating. There's no excusing nor ignoring that. But it doesn't change the fact that your family loves you. None of this is your fault. Don't you think you should at least discuss the matter with your mother?'

Amelia gasped. 'I could never!'

'Why not?'

'She'd be devastated to know I know. And furious with me for turning to Daniel, of all people.'

'He was your boyfriend,' Ben said rationally. 'Trusting him makes sense.'

'Not for us. We were raised to be more careful than that. I should never have told another soul.'

'This is not your burden to carry,' he said emphatically. 'Your mother had an affair. That happens. It was a mistake. Decades later, she and your father are still together, happy. They've raised a family, are on the brink of watching their oldest son marry, presumably soon to welcome grandchildren into the mix. Life is long, if we're lucky, and not always as we expect it. Your father would understand. Your mother would certainly not want something she did two decades ago to keep you away a day longer.'

Amelia dropped her head to his chest and sobbed properly now, her grief shifting to something else, to a cathartic release, so Ben found it almost impossible not to react. But this was a vital moment. He would support her, but he needed to make sure their lines didn't get blurred.

'I don't want to go back to Valencia,' she said softly, eyes searching his, looking for answers. 'I don't know what to do next, but running away isn't going to fix this. It's not going to solve it.' She pulled back a little, looked up into his face. 'Will you take me to Catarno, Benedetto?'

It was the right choice. She needed to stop running, to be back with her family.

'Yes.'

She held his hand when he would have stepped away to issue the command to Cassidy and Christopher. 'But, Ben?' Her eyes were huge, filled with sadness. 'When we get there...' she pressed a hand to his chest '...this has to stop.'

It was exactly what he'd been thinking, wasn't it? That they needed to end this... So why did hearing her say that so factually aggravate him?

'It's going to be hard enough, dealing with all this. I don't need to worry about someone finding out we're sleeping together. My life at the palace is an open book. It would be too risky...'

'That makes sense,' he rushed to reassure her, relieved that it was Amelia who'd said it first. 'I'm there if you need me though,' he added. 'As a friend.'

Her smile was tight, and dismissive. He knew then that she wouldn't call on him for help, and he wondered why that bothered him so much.

The biggest port in Catarno was Livoa, where there was a high-security section used by the Catarno military and, when in use, the royal yacht. It was not a surprise to Amelia when Cassidy steered Benedetto's boat past the others and towards the high-security gates. There was no checking of identities—the information had been sent ahead, the serial number of the boat verified by computer—and they were waved past the armed guards, into a section of the marina that was heavily fortified.

Amelia shivered as the boat was brought to a stop. Beside her, Benedetto seemed to stiffen as well.

'If, at any point, you want to leave, I'm at your disposal.'

Her heart twisted uncomfortably, because she knew he meant it. He was her saviour after all. The problem for Amelia was that it made Benedetto pretty damned perfect, and all the emotions of hostility and anger she'd felt towards him initially, which had inured her from feeling anything more for him than wild, overpowering desire, had faded into nothing, so it was almost impossible not to let her heart get involved in things.

But that would be well and truly stupid.

Benedetto had done an about-turn; he had shown himself to be noble and good, but that didn't change the fact that he wasn't interested in a relationship. And knowing what she did about his upbringing and his loss as a father, she could understand why he'd chosen a life of solitude.

It would be really dumb to fall for him.

Really dumb.

And so she'd ended things pre-emptively, knowing that to keep going as they were was a one-way ticket to Disaster-ville, for Amelia at least.

She looked up at Benedetto and he smiled reassuringly, his face changing, morphing into something beautiful and breathtaking, and inwardly she groaned because, despite her very best intentions, she was pretty sure the horse had bolted on the whole love front already. 'It's going to be okay.'

It probably wouldn't, but, somehow, his words comforted her a little anyway.

As the boat putted along, then finally drew to a stop, she saw a limousine waiting with two flags on the front—her brother's crest, and the flag of Catarno.

Her heart dropped to her toes. 'I can't do this.'

'Yes, you can.'

She expelled a shaky breath but stood her ground, and because Benedetto was at her side, it felt easier, more prac-ticable.

'Okay.' She nodded once. 'You're right. Let's go.'

Benedetto hadn't known what to expect. Flowers, serenades, her family lined up to greet her? Not this. The moment her feet connected with dry land, the royal guard formed a circle around her, separating Amelia from Benedetto, so she stared back at him wide-eyed, clearly terrified.

'Where are you taking her?'

None of them spoke to him and Amelia didn't say a thing in her own defence. The guards enveloped her so that, despite her height, she was almost invisible, and he understood—

there was the risk of photographers lurking. They were protecting her.

Anger at his impotence—an unwanted and unwelcome feeling that reminded him what it had been like as a young boy hearing his mother berated and insulted—crested inside him. He was furious and powerless all at once as she was shepherded into the waiting limousine. He stared after it, already reaching for his phone to call Anton and demand an explanation, to demand he have the limousine turn back.

'Ben.'

He spun at the sound of his name to find his closest friend standing at the edge of the dock, watching proceedings with a grim expression. But then, Anton laughed softly, shaking his head. 'You look like you're about to punch something.'

Benedetto grimaced, schooling his expression into a mask of calm. He was not his father. He would not surrender to anger. Ever.

'Your sister has done an incredibly brave thing. I intended to escort her to the palace, to make sure she was okay.' Even to his own ears, it sounded stupidly defensive.

'What for?' Anton's eyes narrowed. 'And brave how? She's come home, Ben, not to face a firing squad, but to be welcomed back with open arms by all and sundry. What in the world is she so afraid of?'

To that, Benedetto could not reply truthfully.

'Where are they taking her?'

'To my mother, who has not slept for two days, since I told her that Amelia was coming home. We deliberated a long time about the best way to effect the reconciliation and decided privacy was appropriate.'

Ben heard the subtext. This was a family matter.

'Come on.' Anton nodded over his shoulder, to where another car was waiting. 'Ride with me.'

* * *

A whole kaleidoscope of butterflies had taken up residence inside Amelia as the limousine cut through the streets of the old city and took the mountain roads to the palace. So familiar to her, so stunning and unlike any other part of the world. She could only stare out of the window—flanked as she was on either side by a guard, as though even now there was a risk she'd bolt—and allow the memories to consume her.

When the palace came into view, it was a moment of intense pain and exuberance. She made a guttural gasping sound and turned, seeking Benedetto, wanting to share it with him, but not able to, because he was no longer with her.

And that wasn't his fault.

The guard had descended too quickly, had taken her away, and she'd let them. She could have commanded them to stop, to wait for him, but part of her had been glad to separate, because she'd made the decision to part from him. Self-preservation instincts had kicked in.

Running away again? a little voice demanded, but she ignored it.

If she was running away, it was only because it was the right thing to do. Benedetto wouldn't want her to develop serious feelings for him—he'd sprint in the opposite direction if he thought there was any risk of that. Better to have ended it now, before it started to mean something to Amelia. Before she started to want him in her life, for always and for ever…

The limousine approached the palace gates, paused and entered at a snail's pace before picking up speed again. The trees to the west of the path were in full bloom, startlingly yellow and so beautiful her heart lifted despite the trepidation she felt. The palace itself was a sight she'd craved, and Amelia drank it in now, every stone face and gold-tipped turret, the wall that was covered in scrambling bougainvillea, the roses that grew rampant at the front of the palace. It was all so lovely, so utterly known to Amelia.

Nervousness besieged her but somehow there was also relief. She could barely keep her emotions in check as she stepped from the vehicle, looking around on autopilot for Benedetto. But of course he wasn't there yet.

She turned to one of the guards. 'Would you have a car sent to the dock to collect Benedetto di Vassi?'

'He has been collected, Your Highness.'

She physically recoiled at the use of her title. It had been a long time.

'Is he here?' She cursed her weakness immediately for asking the question.

'This way please, Your Highness.' Another guard spoke swiftly, a woman, gesturing towards the palace. Amelia compressed her lips, frustrated, but also impatient now, because she gathered where this was going. She was being brought home, to her family, to meet with them away from any risk of public scrutiny.

Her nerves jangled as the guard led her through the palace, as if she wouldn't know the way herself, to the doors of one of the morning rooms.

'Her Majesty is waiting,' the female guard said with a small bow before opening the door and ushering Amelia in.

And there was her mother, standing in the middle of the room, wringing her hands in the exact same way Amelia did when she was nervous, until she saw Amelia and let out a cry that was barely human and ran across the room, throwing her arms around her daughter.

'Oh, my darling,' she sobbed, burying her head in Amelia's shoulder, crying so much that her body was racked and her face wet. 'You're home. You have no idea how badly I wanted this, how much I have missed you. Oh, my darling, my darling girl, let me look at you,' and she pulled away only so she could study Amelia intently for several seconds before wrapping her up in another huge hug.

Amelia was numb and overwhelmed at the same time, an unusual combination but so it was. She'd missed her mother too, and she loved her so much, but she knew that she had to grow strong, to inure herself to this life, because it wasn't tenable for her to stay. She didn't belong here. She didn't belong anywhere.

Except on the boat, with Benedetto, that same dangerous little voice whispered in the back of her mind, imploring her to listen, to escape again, but this time, with him. This time with the proper goodbyes to her family, so they wouldn't worry. But that was a fantasy she couldn't indulge; it would never work long-term—he wouldn't want it, and she couldn't bear to ask it of him.

'My darling, tell me everything.' Anna-Maria Moretti wiped her tears and gestured to a small floral-covered sofa. They sat down as the door opened and a servant carried through a tray of biscuits and tea.

'"Everything" would take a while.'

'We have a while, don't we?' Anna-Maria asked, eyes roaming her daughter's face. 'You're not going anywhere, are you?'

Amelia couldn't quite meet her mother's eyes. 'Mum, listen,' she began cautiously. But what could she say? That she knew about the affair? About her parentage? That she'd been blackmailed, that someone out there knew their secret? She clamped her mouth shut.

'It's okay, it's okay. You're home now. We can talk about it later.'

'Okay,' Amelia agreed, uneasily though, anxious, stressed,

worried, of all people, about Benedetto. Who was more than capable of looking after himself.

She expelled a long, slow breath.

'Tell me about Anton's fiancée. Tell me what I've missed.'

Relieved that it seemed Amelia wasn't going to disappear immediately, Anna-Maria began to speak, a little too quickly, as though she too was uneasy, or nervous, but gradually she calmed.

'She's wonderful, you'll love her. We all do. She's been so good for Anton, so calming and steadying. She's made him a better man.'

'How did they meet?'

'At a hospital benefit. She's a paediatrician, you know. She'll give it up, once they're married, which is a great shame, but the constitution demands it.' Anna-Maria tsked her disapproval. 'Your father tried to change it but apparently he cannot. Sadly for Vanessa, she'll have to content herself with some volunteer work and becoming a patron of the charities she likes.'

'Is she okay with that?'

'I think it took some getting used to, which is one of the reasons she refused his proposal the first two times.' Anna-Maria's brows knitted together. 'She had a difficult upbringing, you know, to her, we are already like parents. I hope you like her, darling. I know it will mean so much to her to have you as a sister. She's been so looking forward to meeting you.'

Amelia's chest was hurting. She felt terrible for having disappeared, for having worried everyone, for having missed so much, and she also felt awful for being back, for the risk her appearance brought to them, for the possibility that just by being here she was exposing the family to a scandal from which they might not recover. She was a living, ticking time bomb, her very life the evidence of her mother's affair. Amelia was the evidence, but it was her mother who'd cheated, then lied, and as Amelia sat opposite the Queen, she couldn't help but feel a whip of anger at the base of her spine.

'I'm looking forward to meeting her too,' Amelia promised, distracted now.

Anna-Maria spent an hour going over everything else Amelia had missed and also some scheduling concerns, such as the dress fitting for the wedding, and the requirements for the next few days. Amelia barely paid attention.

'From tomorrow, the official events will commence. You arrived just in time, darling. Just in time.' Then, with a softening to her face and a hint of moisture back in her eyes, she said, 'I'm just so glad you came home. You have no idea how much I've missed you.'

'I've missed you too,' Amelia whispered, and, despite the complex emotions she felt towards her mother, she knew that was right.

As they hugged, the door opened and His Majesty King Timothy Moretti strode into the room, dressed formally, followed by his second son, Rowan. 'Good God, it's true,' Timothy said, wiping a hand over his eyes. 'You're home.'

A lump formed in Amelia's throat as she faced the moment she'd feared the most—seeing again the man who'd raised her, knowing he was not her father, that he'd been duped into the role. And though it had not been her lie, her betrayal, nor her fault, guilt curdled her gut and nausea rose like a tidal wave inside her.

She bowed, as was custom, but the King made a noise of frustration and pulled her into his arms, hugging her so hard she thought a rib might crack. 'Don't you ever, ever do anything like this again,' he said fiercely, but with a voice that shook. 'I forbid it. By royal decree, do you understand?' It was a joke, of sorts, but Amelia heard the strain in his voice and again the guilt at having run away and hidden herself from her family crashed into her like a tonne of bricks. What else could she have done though? She felt risk from every angle; it was stupid to have come back, but how could she have stayed away? Amelia felt as though she were caught between a rock and a hard place.

'I've missed you,' she said, simply, because she could not promise to stay, but had truly yearned for her family. A moment later, Rowan hugged her and her heart skipped because she felt closest of all to her middle brother, who'd had the privilege of growing up royal without the pressures.

'Ready to be one of us again?' he asked lightly, his eyes scanning her face.

Amelia swallowed quickly; she wasn't one of them, though. 'I'm glad to see you all.'

Rowan's eyes narrowed but he didn't push it, and Amelia was glad. There were some answers she just didn't have yet.

Benedetto had been to the palace before but now he saw it through different eyes. He saw it as the place where Amelia had grown up, the gardens she'd run through, the art she'd studied, the long, historic, beautiful corridors she'd skipped down as a child. The building that had housed her heartbreaks, hopes, that had finally borne witness to her awful discovery and the impact that had on her, the blackmail, the pain of that betrayal.

'You're not listening,' Anton said with a grin, a study in relaxed calm now that Amelia was back and Benedetto had taken his place at Anton's side.

'No.' Benedetto was unapologetic. 'Tell me again.'

'You're still worried about her.'

Benedetto's eyes flashed to Anton's. 'Yes.'

'You're being ridiculous. She's fine. Probably just being suffocated by my parents' many, many embraces.'

'Aren't you eager to see her too?' Benedetto asked, his voice carefully muted of emotion.

'I haven't seen her in over two years. I can wait a little longer.'

'You're angry with her.'

'It's my wedding in three days,' Anton said, but now Benedetto saw through the air of relaxation. 'I'm not angry about anything.'

Benedetto was too good a study of dark emotions though. 'Why?' he pushed.

Anton compressed his lips, gave up the pretence. 'Why do you think?' He spread his hands outward. 'She broke my mother's heart. And kept breaking it, every day she stayed away, every message she did not respond to, every time she refused to see us. Each Christmas and birthday she missed. She's selfish, Ben. Yes, I'm angry with her. But I can't think about that now, because in three days I'm getting married in a ceremony that will be broadcast across the globe, and viewed in person by thousands, including the heads of state of most countries in the world. So Amelia is the furthest thing from my mind.'

CHAPTER NINE

'LOOKING FOR SOMEONE?'

Despite her older brother's insufferable arrogance, she was surprisingly glad to see him. She turned to face Anton, not sure what greeting to expect from the sibling who was much older than her, far more serious, and incredibly dedicated to his duties.

'No,' she denied, only realising when Anton asked the question that she had been wandering the corridors of the palace in the hope of seeing Benedetto. Even though she'd ended things between them, she still wanted to *see* him, and she couldn't explain why.

'You put us all through hell, you know,' Anton murmured, standing in front of her, his autocratic face wiped of emotion.

She should have expected this from Anton. A lecture. After all, he had been the one to send Ben, to tell him everything about Amelia, and Ben had clearly thought the worst of her initially.

'It's good to see you too.'

He paused. 'I am glad you're home.'

'Well, you made sure of that, didn't you? At least I can add being kidnapped to the bucket-list items I've ticked off.'

'My understanding is you chose to return of your own free will, when the option was given to you.'

So Anton and Ben had discussed it? What else had they spoken about? Her pulse ratcheted up a gear.

'It seems as though my friend has become your knight in shining armour.'

Amelia's cheeks flushed a telltale pink but she worked hard to maintain a neutral expression. She wouldn't be drawn on what Ben had become to her. How could she answer that anyway, when she didn't even know herself?

'He told me what you did for him,' she said instead. 'When Sasha died. That was very kind of you, Anton, very decent.'

Anton stared at her long and hard. 'He told you about Sasha?'

Amelia stiffened. Had she inadvertently revealed more about their relationship than she'd intended anyway? 'A week on a boat is a long time,' she pointed out. 'We talked about a lot of stuff.'

'Sasha isn't stuff, she's— He doesn't open up about it. Ever. Maybe because you're my sister,' Anton reasoned, 'he presumed you already knew.'

Amelia let that settle between them, lifted her shoulder. 'Perhaps.' And something about his egotistical presumption endeared him to her, so she closed the distance between them, pressed a kiss to his cheek. 'I'm glad to see you, even though you drive me crazy.'

He lifted one dark brow. 'Do I?'

'Yes. Now, when do I get to meet your fiancée? I hear she's got the patience of a saint.'

At that, Anton laughed softly. 'I know you're teasing me, but in fact, you're right. Vanessa is—beyond compare. She'll be at dinner tonight.'

'Dinner?'

'Just the family.'

Amelia's heart sank. *I'm not family*, she wanted to scream. But how could she avoid this? What could she possibly say? And at least Benedetto wouldn't be there. For as much as she wanted to see him, from a distance at least, she wasn't sure she could trust herself to be in the same room as him and act as though he meant nothing to her.

Avoiding him was a far better idea.

As soon as Benedetto saw Amelia, he wanted to stop the clock and wind back time, he wanted to remove every last vestige of her princess life and return her to the wild, free spirit she'd been on his yacht, with hair all tousled and wind-swept, skin warm from the sun, face bare of make-up, clothes loose and floaty in concession to the heat, feet almost always bare. He wanted to go back to before she'd told him they should stop seeing each other and kiss the words right out of her mind. He just wanted to kiss her...

This Amelia was so different. Despite the fact it was a 'quiet family dinner', she was dressed to the nines. This was Her Royal Highness Princess Amelia Moretti, and she was every inch the princess indeed.

From hair that had been styled until it shone and pinned into an elegant bun low on her head, to the dainty tiara she wore, the suit—cream with gold buttons, she'd teamed a blazer with trousers and wore brown high heels that were the same shade as the small handbag she carried. Her face had been made up expertly, and at her throat she wore a simple necklace with a single diamond in the centre.

It was the first time they'd seen each other since being separated at the boat and curiosity had him staring at her intently across the room, waiting for her to notice him, but she was locked in conversation with Vanessa, who wore a pale pink gown with her dark hair loose around her face.

Frustration champed at Benedetto. He feigned interest in conversation with Rowan—who he usually liked and had a lot of time for. But at that very moment, all of his focus was absorbed by Amelia. She moved eventually from Vanessa to her mother, speaking in a low voice, smiling, laughing, and it was when she laughed that she tilted her head and her eyes met his.

Every muscle in his body tightened. The breath in his lungs caught and held. His lips parted on a short hiss of air and he had never before known a temptation quite like it: to storm across the room, throw her over his shoulder and run away with Amelia.

He forced himself to look away, back to Rowan, to nod at something he'd said, to actively listen to the conversation now, but he was conscious of her the whole time, and in the back of his mind he was planning ahead, attempting to work out how to peel Amelia away from her family, so he he could be alone with her.

Except he couldn't. Or shouldn't.

She was right to have put an end to what they were doing. He'd be crazy to pursue her now, here in the palace. Her life was an open book, as she'd said. That didn't stop him from wanting her though, and from needing to know she wanted him too...

Just being back with her family was exhausting. They were all making an effort to be accepting, no one asking her about her prolonged, unexplained absence, but she felt the questions, the judgement, the low-key anger and resentment from Anton. Or perhaps it was just the secret knowledge she held that she didn't really belong here, that she wasn't a real princess, that was playing on her mind.

Beneath the table, she fidgeted with her fingers, twisting the large diamond ring she wore, a gift from her grandmother, who had also clearly had no idea that Amelia was an imposter in their midst.

And the one person who had the power to make her feel better, to blot out all of this tension, was as far as physically possible across the table, and being monopolised in conversation by her father and Rowan. When their eyes had met, she'd felt a surge of awareness and known she couldn't look in his direction again. It would be too obvious. Surely someone would notice. And so she concentrated hard on being what everyone expected her to be, on smiling and nodding and ignoring Benedetto with every fibre of her being.

The night was long. Several courses, speeches, more food, and, finally, Anton signalled the evening was at an end by excusing himself and Vanessa. With immense relief, Amelia looked around, her eyes instantly latching to Benedetto's. He was watching her and the moment she felt his gaze on her, felt it connect with hers, her stomach squeezed and her heart stammered.

'Goodnight, darling,' her mother murmured, leaning over and placing a kiss on her forehead. Then, 'Tomorrow is going to be very busy, but if you'd like to join me for a walk in the morning, I'll be leaving from the West Gate at six.'

A smile pulled at Amelia's lips. For as long as she could remember, her mother had been conducting the same early morning walk through the gardens, past the stables, and down to the citrus grove. Amelia had often walked with her as a teenager.

'Thank you,' she said, without committing either way. 'Goodnight.'

Amelia stood, but rather than leaving the room, she moved deeper into it, pretending fascination with a painting on the wall. It was hundreds of years old, a Biblical scene with angels and clouds and women reclining with their long hair draped over their bodies.

Her heart raced as she studied the painting and listened as her family slowly filtered from the room, and she held her breath, waiting, hoping. She knew the smart thing to do would be to depart likewise. She'd ended things with Benedetto for a reason—it couldn't keep going on—but that didn't mean she had suddenly turned into a robot. She *wanted* to see him. She *wanted* to talk to him, to be alone with him.

The room was silent for such a long time that her heart plummeted, because Benedetto must have left too and the hope she'd nurtured all night of finally being alone with him withered into nothingness.

She turned, fidgeting with her ring, and then let out a small gasp, because he hadn't left at all. He was sitting at the table, staring straight ahead, a small coffee cup in his big, strong hands. Her heart skipped a beat and she moved to him as though being pulled by strings, gliding across the ancient carpets.

'Hello.'

He turned to face her, his expression inscrutable.

'How are you?'

It was a question laced with far greater meaning than the words usually asked for. He was asking how she really was. Not in the trivial sense, but in the deep emotional sense after all she'd been through today.

'It was tough,' she said, honestly.

'Are you glad you came back?'

She shook her head. 'I don't know.' Then, looking around the table, 'It wouldn't have felt right to miss it.'

'No,' he agreed. Then he stood, meeting her eyes, and her breath hitched in her throat, fear surging inside her. Was he going to leave? 'They care about you a great deal.'

'I know.' Her voice cracked. She didn't want to discuss her family. 'How's your day been?'

'Honestly?'

She nodded.

'Long.'

Amelia scanned his face. 'I presumed Anton was keeping you busy.'

'Yes, extolling the virtues of his fiancée, which I've heard about a thousand times, mind you.'

'He's madly in love.' Amelia smiled, but there was a strange hollowness in her heart as she spoke those words. Suddenly, not being able to touch him was a form of torture, and yet she'd done this to herself. 'Benedetto—'

'Amelia,' he returned, drawling her name with a hint of mockery.

She toyed with the ring she wore. 'This is weird.'

'Being back in Catarno?'

'Being here with you.'

His eyes flared. 'You are not with me.'

'No.' Her voice was ambivalent.

'You can't be,' he reminded her, or perhaps he was reminding himself too. 'It's too complicated.'

Amelia nodded, but frowned. 'Maybe it doesn't have to be.'

Benedetto was very still. 'Go on.'

'There's a way to my room through my office. You could come to me tonight.'

His nostrils flared. 'Sneak around behind your family's back?'

Heat flushed her cheeks. 'I know it's not ideal…'

'I'm not a teenager, Amelia, and neither are you.'

'My personal life is no one's business,' she said, tightly, but she was hurt, because he'd rejected her.

'You were the one who said your life here is an open book,' he pointed out.

'I know. It is. But—'

'There is no but,' he said, with a single shake of his head. 'We can't do this.'

'Damn it.' She stomped her foot, but at that moment a team of servants burst through the doors, intent on clearing the table. Amelia's eyes met Benedetto's, held them, her lips parted but what more could she say?

'Goodnight, Your Highness,' he said, with a dip of his head.

Amelia's heart turned cold. 'Goodnight,' she whispered, but Benedetto had already left.

If she hadn't told him about the discreet access to her room, he wouldn't have been lying in bed for hours, hard as a rock, staring at the ceiling, thinking of Amelia, craving her, wanting, wishing, needing.

But she had, and he was, and at some point in the small hours of the morning, tired of wanting and not having, he gave up on being noble and right, and decided to give into temptation. One more time. It still didn't mean anything. It was just sex. Like on the boat, but here. What did geography matter? So long as they both understood the temporary nature of this, what was the harm?

Benedetto dressed in a pair of trousers and a shirt, slipped his feet into shoes and strode from his room, down the corridor, towards the suite of rooms he knew, from previous visits, belonged to Amelia.

He concealed a bitter smirk as he approached her doors. One wrong turn and he might very well end up in Anton's rooms instead. How to explain that? he thought. But his memory was accurate. Silently, he pushed the heavy oak door inwards, taking in the details of Amelia's study as he went—the floral paintings, the pretty furniture, the large windows. He closed the door then looked around, for another way into and out of the room. At first, he missed it. This doorway was only three-quarter height, a relic from a different century, when people were smaller.

He moved to it, hand on the doorknob, as he contemplated turning back.

There were a thousand reasons to resist Amelia, namely, because he wanted to be able to look back and know that he'd acted honourably towards her. That he'd never done anything to risk her heart.

Which brought him back to the necessity of being honest with her *before* this happened.

So long as she understood, this would all be okay.

He knocked on the door lightly, then realised how stupid that was—she was probably asleep. So he probably shouldn't interrupt her. He should probably just go back to his room, stick to his original, much wiser idea, to ignore Amelia altogether.

'Yes?' Her voice was small, but audible.

His gut churned and his body tightened.

There was no way he was turning back.

He pushed the door inwards, frustration bursting through him. It was a frustration aimed mostly at himself, because he should have been strong enough to resist her. But it was also aimed at Amelia, because she'd invited him here. She'd weakened too.

'This is a terrible idea,' he muttered, striding across to the edge of her bed and staring down at her, wishing she didn't look so beautiful and innocent with her knees pulled up to her chest.

'What is?' Her eyes were huge in her face. It was dark in the room, except for the full moon's beam streaking through the window. He reached down, touched her cheek, felt his body galvanise with need.

He ignored her question. She'd asked him here for one reason; he'd come because of that.

'You understand—' He paused, scanning her face in the silver light. She looked up at him, guarded, careful, uncertain.

Benedetto cursed inwardly.

'I'm leaving as soon as the wedding's over,' he said. 'We won't see each other again.'

She was still. He waited, on tenterhooks. 'I know that.'

'You understand what I'm offering.'

Her lips pulled to the side in a gesture that was now intimately familiar to him. 'Sex,' she murmured, and then moved to kneeling, so their faces were almost at a level. 'The perfect, meaningless distraction,' she added as she leaned forward and kissed him, and Benedetto relaxed into the moment, because she *did* understand. There was no risk here. No complication. Just perfect, meaningless, satisfying sex, for a few more nights, and then he'd leave without a backwards glance, just like always.

Amelia woke early, stretching in the bed, frowning when she couldn't discern the familiar rhythms of the boat's rocking, then remembering the reason for that. She was no longer aboard *Il Galassia*, but rather here, in the palace, her home, with her family. And Benedetto.

Her skin flushed as she remembered the way he'd made love to her the night before, his desperate need, his body so strong and commanding, so capable, hard and perfect for her. The way he'd kissed her to muffle her screams, how he'd laced their fingers together and lifted her arms over her head to stop her from touching as he simply moved inside her, stirring her to a fever pitch, pleasing her again and again until she could barely breathe, much less speak or remember who or where she was.

Her body had felt both weak and strong afterwards, legs made of jelly, heart of steel. He'd turned to her, as if trying to ascertain something in her features, and then pushed to standing. Magnificent in his nakedness, glorious and sensual.

'You're leaving?'

He'd dipped his head once in silent agreement.

Her heart had felt momentarily hollow, but she concealed that reaction. 'It's probably for the best. There's no point letting anyone find out about this when it's so temporary.'

'My thoughts exactly.'

The air had pulsated between them. 'So it's our secret,' she'd said, a rush of excitement exploding in her veins.

Benedetto hadn't wanted to sneak around like a teenager, yet there they were, making exactly that sort of pact. 'Yes,' he'd agreed after a small pause. 'I'll see you soon.'

She'd wanted to ask when, but had, thankfully, stopped herself. She wouldn't reveal any kind of neediness to him. It was the last thing he'd want, and when the wedding was over and Benedetto was gone, and Amelia had moved on, she'd be proud of herself for seeming so casual.

'She's been very good for him, you know,' Anna-Maria said as they approached the crest of the hill and wound their way around the precipice, to reach a point with one of the most spectacular views of the valley. It was still early and the sun was only just cresting over the hills in the distance, casting the sky in the most spectacular oranges and pinks.

'In what way?' Amelia prompted, pausing to sip her water.

'He's far less serious. Oh, I love Anton, of course, but he can be a little intense sometimes,' Anna-Maria said with a wink.

'Mum!'

Anna-Maria linked her hand through Amelia's arm. 'You know what I mean. It's been hard for him, having the weight of his inheritance on his shoulders, knowing all his life that he would become King. Vanessa makes him laugh at himself, makes him laugh with the rest of us. And she helps him. She's very smart, an excellent sounding board for all manner of things. The public adores her too.'

Something like jealousy flashed in Amelia's gut and she turned away to conceal the bitterness from showing on her face. It wasn't the public who'd had issues with her though, but the press who'd seemed to delight in painting her as the misfit third child, who'd tormented her through their stories and lies. And the public had bought the papers and magazines, had believed so much of it. Amelia sighed softly.

Perhaps sensing the direction of Amelia's thoughts, Anna-Maria softened her tone. 'They never really gave you a fair shot, did they?'

'No.' Amelia flattened the hurt from her voice.

'I wish I'd known how to protect you better from that. At the time, I thought we were doing the right thing, by telling you to ignore it. But that wasn't fair. I should have done more.'

Amelia compressed her lips, neither agreeing nor disagreeing. Her parents had been in a difficult position—the royal family never commented on stories in the press. It was a policy of long standing. But the thick skin needed to cope with the onslaught of publicity was something Amelia had never really developed.

'Is that why you left?' Anna-Maria prompted gently.

'No,' Amelia murmured, sipping her water. 'But I'm not going to lie to you, the lack of press coverage over the last couple of years has been astoundingly nice. The silence has been wonderful.'

'I can imagine,' Anna-Maria agreed.

Amelia angled her face towards her mother's as they began to walk once more, arm in arm. 'You married into this lifestyle. Have you ever regretted it?'

'I always knew I would marry him and become Queen,' she said with a lift of her shoulders. 'Your father and I were betrothed when I was just a girl and he a boy. It was my destiny, and his, arranged by our parents to strengthen the throne and the royal family's place in the country's political system. My family was politically very powerful, his royal. It made sense.'

'I never knew that,' Amelia said with genuine surprise.

'You're saying your whole life you've been living in an ar-ranged marriage?'

'Well, yes,' Anna-Maria agreed, as if she too was a little surprised to have revealed as much.

'But you seem—I thought you guys had fallen in love. I knew your family was powerful, I just presumed you'd come to know one another by moving in the same circles.'

'And so we did.'

'But you didn't marry for love?' Amelia asked breath-lessly, piecing together an entirely different visage of her mother's life.

Her lips twisted. 'I married for love, in some ways,' Anna-Maria said hesitantly. 'I loved my parents, my country. I loved the idea of being Queen, particularly the jewels and gowns,' she added with another wink. 'And I liked and respected your father a great deal.'

Amelia's footing slipped a little at the mention of her fa-ther.

'But love took time with us. We fell in love on the job, so to speak.'

'So you do love him now?'

'Very much.'

'What made you love him?' Amelia pushed, her voice heavy with interest.

Was she imagining the way her mother's skin paled a little?

'Some time ago, when the boys were little and you were not yet born, a series of events led me to realise that I couldn't live without him,' she said. 'It was that simple. I had fallen in love without even realising it, and only when I thought about what I could lose, if I didn't face up to how I felt, did I finally comprehend the strength of my own feelings. I fell in love with him gently, softly, while I wasn't even paying attention, and for a thousand different reasons. I loved him for his passion for the arts—music, theatre, opera. His skill as a polo player. His body,' she added, knocking her hip into Amelia's, to signal a joke, but Amelia could hardly catch her breath, much less smile. This insight into her parents' marriage, given what she knew, was destabilising, to say the least.

'I loved how much he thought about everything. Your father is never rash, always considerate, he looks at a problem from every conceivable angle, sometimes twice, before responding. He's incredibly smart. And over time, he fell in love with me too.' Anna-Maria stopped walking, turned to face her daughter.

'You've been gone so long, I feel as though I have to get to know you all over again, in some ways.' She squeezed Amelia's forearm. 'Tell me, have you been in love, Amelia?'

'No,' she answered, but not entirely without hesitation. She'd thought she'd loved Daniel, but that had been a mistake. And since then, there'd been only Benedetto. While she lusted after him around the clock, that wasn't the same thing as love.

'Ah. I wasn't sure. I thought perhaps in Spain, you might have met someone.'

'No. No one.'

'That's a shame.'

'Is it?'

'Of course. But one day, you will find your other half, and you'll understand, when you love that person, that the idea of losing them suddenly becomes a form of torture. It wasn't just the thought of losing your father that made me realise how much I loved him, but the idea of jeopardising our family.'

'And so you realised you loved him, and then I was born,' Amelia said, studying her mother with every ounce of her concentration, looking for any hint of emotion that might betray the truth of Amelia's parentage.

But Anna-Maria smiled beatifically and nodded. 'You were a living, breathing testament to our love. A reminder every day of how much our marriage meant to us both, of why we would always fight for it, and each other.'

Amelia let out a soft breath. Was that true? Could she be both evidence of an illicit affair and a talisman to faithfulness? If what her mother was saying was true, and Amelia could read between the lines because she had a greater knowledge of the subject than her mother realised, was it possible that by cheating on the King, and recognising that her affair would potentially end her marriage, she decided to recommit herself to the King, to love him properly and fully? It made sense. In which case, Amelia supposed she could have been just what Anna-Maria had described.

'One day, you will fall in love, just as Anton has, and I will look forward to meeting the person who captures your heart.' She put an arm around Amelia. 'You are so special, darling. No matter what, don't forget that.'

CHAPTER TEN

'OH, WHAT A SURPRISE,' Anton remarked under his breath. 'Amelia's late.'

Something shifted inside Benedetto, an irritation, an impatience, a quickness to judge he'd never felt towards his friend. He tried to suppress it, but when Anton looked at Benedetto with a grin, Benedetto didn't return it. If anything, his expression was ice cold.

'She'll be here,' Anna-Maria said. 'And in the meantime, let's carry on.'

The rehearsal was long and involved and as Benedetto was to stand with his best friend as a groomsman, alongside Rowan, who was best man, he was an integral part of proceedings. But so was Amelia.

Where was she?

Far from taking the cynical tone of voice his friend had adopted, he felt worry begin to fray at the edges of his mind. She wouldn't have run away again, he was sure of it, but it also seemed strange that she'd be late for something as important as this. He gave the rehearsal about a tenth of his focus and spent the rest of his time looking at his watch surreptitiously and kicking himself for not having taken her phone number in exchange for giving out his own.

'This is where the bridesmaid will take the bouquet.'

'If she shows up,' Anton drawled, earning a sharp gaze

from his mother and a placating hand on the arm from his fiancée. At that exact moment, the doors to the chapel opened
and a clearly flustered Amelia jogged in.

'You've already started,' she said as she drew near the
group.

'Yes, an hour ago, when the rehearsal was scheduled for,'
Anton sniped.

'My schedule says three o'clock,' she responded tersely,
brandishing her phone. 'And I've literally just got out of the
dress fitting. Why did no one call me?'

They all looked at each other, but when Amelia's eyes
came to Benedetto, he hoped she could see how proud he
was of her for speaking up to Anton.

'Oh, dear.' Vanessa spoke first, moving to Amelia and
looking at her phone. 'You've been sent the old timetable.
I'm so sorry, that's our mistake completely.' Benedetto liked
Vanessa more and more. 'There have been so many changes
in the last week, everything's tweaked and you've received
the schedule that was valid up until a couple of days ago.'

'It's fine.' Amelia's manner softened immediately in deference to her future sister-in-law, and perhaps in response
to the obviously conciliatory tone in Vanessa's voice. 'I'm
sorry to have missed so much.'

'Oh, it's nothing complicated. I'll have a printed guide
sent to your room, but other than walking in with me, and
taking my bouquet, the main thing is to stand at my side and
smile serenely.'

'That I think I can manage,' Amelia replied. There were
smiles all round, except from Benedetto, who had a deluge
of unfamiliar emotions cresting in his belly.

After the rehearsal, when Benedetto wanted nothing more
than to leave with Amelia, and ideally whisk her back to the
boat for a few hours of actual privacy, he couldn't even get

close enough to her to speak. Frustration bubbled beneath his skin as he watched her disappear into a limousine, bookended by the King and Queen.

She suddenly seemed incredibly untouchable, and he hated that...

Amelia's feet were killing after a full day spent in heels, which she hadn't worn for the longest time. In fact, she'd barely worn closed-toe shoes at all since leaving Catarno. She flicked on the TV in her room, smiling at the footage that came up of Anton and Vanessa meeting well-wishers outside the palace. They were a very handsome couple and Anna-Maria was right—Vanessa was clearly an excellent match for Anton.

Amelia was on her way to the bathroom to fill the tub when a knock sounded at her door. Not the main door, but the smaller door from her study. With an unsteadiness to her legs suddenly, she crossed the room and wrenched it inwards, smiling instinctively at the sight of Benedetto on the other side.

His eyes flared with hers and before she could make a joke about the contortions he had to perform to get through the space, he was in her room and dragging her into his arms, kissing her hard, fast, slamming the door shut with his foot and fumbling the lock before lifting her, legs cradled around his waist, and carrying across the room.

She squawked as he dropped her onto the mattress then felt breathless when he simply studied her as though she were a piece of delicate artwork. Her pulse quickened.

She pushed up, reaching for him, as he came towards her, and their bodies melded once more, twisting together, legs, arms, lips meshed, hearts racing, clothes being shucked with so much urgency that something made a ripping noise and

Amelia laughed softly, but only for a minute, because then he was taking her, and it was more, so much more, than she'd ever known. His possession of her was so fierce and absolute, so breathtakingly swift, so full of hungry need that something powerful seemed to be emerging in her mind, with his every thrust and movement, a voice was sounding, a bell tolling, a knowledge forming that she couldn't quite grasp but knew better than to ignore.

It was all too hard to capture though. Passion was driving logic from her mind and as he moved, she pressed her nails into his shoulders, ran her fingers down his back, dug her heels into his spine for better purchase and then with a sound of frustration she rolled, moving him to his back so she was on top, in control, taking him in and arching, every part of her rejoicing in all of this, in all the perfection and pleasure that came from being with the man that she loved.

And there it was.

As pleasure exploded through her and she felt all the pieces of her fall apart at the seams, her brain forced comprehension to dawn on Amelia, so finally she understood exactly what her mother had been talking about that morning.

She loved him.

It had happened perhaps immediately, or maybe that had just been lust, but without Amelia realising what was going on, without her understanding the basis for her behaviours, and in contravention of everything she'd promised Benedetto, she realised it had all been about love.

That was why she'd felt panic at the thought of leaving him in Crete.

That was why she'd stayed. Because loving him made her brave and powerful, because, whether he was with her or not, knowing that she loved him made her strong, and whole. She hated the concept of needing any other person to be whole;

she'd certainly never felt it before. It wasn't that she'd been lacking in anything prior so much as, having met Benedetto now, she realised she would never be complete without him.

And the thought terrified her, because it was the exact opposite of what he'd said he wanted, what he felt about life and relationships and his future. How many times had he reminded her that this was just sex? That he was leaving after the wedding?

'Amelia?' His voice was raspy, his own explosion having coincided with hers, so his chest was racked with heavy, sharp breaths but his eyes were watchful, contemplative. 'Are you okay?'

What choice did she have but to answer that she was? She couldn't tell him how she felt. At least, not yet. The realisation was so fresh for her, Amelia needed time to interpret her feelings, to be sure she wasn't imagining this, because of her conversation with her mother.

There was no sense complicating everything, and before the wedding, when it might turn out to be nothing.

She smiled at him brightly, collapsed onto the bed beside him and stared up at the ceiling. 'I'm glad you came to see me.'

'As am I.' He caught her hand, lifted it to his lips. 'Anton was hard on you today.'

'He always is.'

Benedetto frowned. 'I didn't realise. In the past, when he's mentioned you—'

'You saw it from his perspective,' she said with a lift of one shoulder, then pushed up onto her elbow to see him better. 'That's because you're a very good friend.'

'As he has been, to me.' He hesitated. 'I didn't like the way he spoke to you.'

Her heart lifted. She cleared her throat. 'Why is that?'

'Because you don't deserve it.' He responded so quickly, she knew the answer was honest. 'It's not fair.'

'Ah. So your sense of justice is offended on my behalf?'

'You're laughing at me?'

'No.' She leaned forward, brushed his lips with her own. 'I just thought you might be being defensive of me, that's all. I don't think I've ever had a man, or anyone, be like that. I kind of like it.'

He frowned, and she realised she'd gone too far. 'You don't need me—or anyone—defending you. You are more than capable of defending yourself brilliantly.' He kissed her back.

Her heart thundered and she felt the sting of tears cloying at the back of her throat, but she pushed them aside. There would be time to understand her feelings later. For now, she just wanted to feel, and no one made her feel better, physically, than Benedetto.

He hadn't intended to stay the night. Not because he didn't want to, but because there was a greater potential for discovery if they started acting like that and they both knew this had to be kept secret.

Or was it, he wondered, early the next morning as he lay awake beside Amelia, naked and reluctant to leave her bed, that he didn't know how to define this, even to himself?

He'd known for as long as he could remember what he didn't want in life.

Even as a boy, he'd formed the strongest belief in a need to be on his own, never to put his life, heart, future in anyone else's hands, because that was where true happiness and freedom lay. And then Sasha had come along, and he'd experienced the wonder of loving someone—and the intense, awful vulnerability of losing them, and every lesson he'd ever learned as a child had rammed back into him at warp speed.

Nothing with Amelia changed his feelings on this score. If anything, she'd reinforced them all over again, because she was the one person he'd ever met he actually perceived as a threat.

She threatened him, with her very existence.

She made him vulnerable, just by being her.

Because if he let himself, he could really come to care for her. Not as he did now—as someone he felt protective of, someone he was incredibly attracted to—but as someone he simply wanted in his life.

The thought had him standing, pacing to the window, stark naked and unconcerned with his nudity, his gait long and athletic, as if the adrenaline coursing through his veins had energised him.

There was risk here, the kind of risk he usually avoided like the plague. With a spine of steel, and panic surging in his gut, he reminded himself how temporary this was. He was leaving, just as soon as the wedding was over. And yet, even the thought of that turned his blood to ice. Which only served to underscore the urgency of his departure.

'Good morning.'

Her voice wrapped around him like tendrils of silk, sending unwelcome sensations through his body and into his bones.

He turned slowly, steeling himself to look at her. 'Hello.'

She sat up, the sheet falling to her waist, revealing her beautiful breasts. Good intentions be damned, he prowled back to the bed like a bee drawn to a wildflower.

'You stayed.' She smiled, putting a hand to his chest, fingers splayed wide.

'I didn't mean to.' The words were unintentionally curt. 'I fell asleep.'

'I'm glad.'

'Are you?'

'Sure.' She pressed a kiss to his lips. 'This is my favourite way to wake up.'

He groaned inwardly. This was getting way out of hand. The sooner he left Catarno, the better. They both needed to get on with their lives and forget this had ever happened.

'What will you do, after the wedding?'

The question, as she sipped her strong black coffee, caught her so completely by surprise that her hand trembled and coffee spilled down her front. She swore softly, grabbing a napkin and dabbing at her robe. Benedetto reached over to do the same, but she batted his hand away.

'I'm fine. Just clumsy.' She replaced the cup carefully. 'Why do you ask?' Her pulse was racing, her heart bursting with such an intense hope she found it difficult to speak. Her insides seemed to be bouncing around all over the place.

'No reason,' he responded with nonchalance, sipping his own coffee in a far more successful manner. 'I'm going to fly out to Athens the following morning, spend a couple of days in my office there, then move on to New York. My boat, however, is still here, and can be put at your disposal, if you'd like to use it to get back to Spain.'

Amelia reached for the coffee cup so her hands would have something to do, so she could focus on something other than his words. There was nothing new here. He'd said again and again that he was leaving after the wedding, but that was so soon now, and she hated the thought of it. She forced a bright smile to her face. 'I hadn't really thought about it.'

She stood up abruptly, aware that she was acting strangely, that she was probably revealing far too much of her feelings and not able to care.

'You don't want to return to Valencia?'

'To do what?' she asked. 'Is there any point in running away again?'

'You had built a life for yourself.'

She nodded, digging her nails into her palms in an effort to control her rioting emotions.

'So you plan to remain here?'

She turned to face him, the sun streaming in through the window behind her, highlighting her hair with natural gold.

'What's in New York?' she asked instead, staring at him as though he were a stranger. Twenty minutes ago, they'd been making love as though they were one another's salvation, their reason for being, and now he was calmly discussing exiting stage left of her life in two days' time.

'A company I'm buying. I'll be there six months or so.'

You should come visit.

She waited for the invitation. Waited for him to say something, anything, that might suggest he was leaving the door open to something more happening between them. Even after his insistence that this was just sex, she hoped against hope, and it was then that she understood how desperately she really did love him. And how important it was to hide that from him.

CHAPTER ELEVEN

'AMELIA?'

Later that day she blinked across at her mother, realised she was probably scowling and tried to school her features into something resembling an expression of calm.

'Yes?'

'Something is troubling you.'

Amelia looked beyond her mother, to the window through which there was a view of the street beyond the palace. Crowds had been forming for days now, lining up with flowers and fake crowns and flags, all waiting out in the summer sun to wave and catch a glimpse of the family as they left for the ceremony. By order of the King and Queen, in deference to the heat, guards had regularly been handing out water and ice lollies—but nothing was getting in the way of the festive spirit below.

Amelia wondered, if she were to move close enough, if some of that spirit might not rub off on her.

'Amelia? Talk to me,' Anna-Maria implored. 'You hold so much inside yourself,' she said, moving to stand beside her daughter. 'You are like a closed book sometimes. I wish you would open up to me. I wish you would let me help.'

Amelia compressed her lips. 'I can't.'

'Why not?'

Amelia closed her eyes, the tangle of emotions in her chest rolling painfully through her. She couldn't talk about Benedetto. It was too new, too fresh, too confusing. She couldn't make sense of it herself, so how could she explain anything to her mother?

But there was the other matter that had been plaguing Amelia since her return: her reason for leaving, her mother's choices, and Amelia's place in the family. How could she plan her future without understanding more about her past?

'Mum,' she said on a soft sigh, moving back to the table, curving her hands around a chair, bracing herself. 'There's no easy way to say this.'

Anna-Maria paled. 'You're leaving again.'

Amelia shook her head. 'No. Yes. I don't know.'

Anna-Maria nodded but her lip trembled slightly.

Frustration, shame, pity, love, worry. So many emotions bubbled through Amelia, she found it impossible to contain them. 'I need to tell you something.' And as soon as she said it, she knew she was right. She couldn't keep running from this. The threat that Daniel might reveal something was still out there, but it was more than that. Amelia needed to be honest with her mother.

Amelia sucked in a deep breath. 'Please understand, I'm not bringing this up to hurt you.'

Anna-Maria became very still, watchful.

'I know.'

Anna-Maria's expression didn't shift.

'I know you had an affair.' She dug her fingernails into her palms. 'I know he's not my real father.'

Anna-Maria lifted a hand to her lips. 'Oh, Amelia.' She closed her eyes, her face pale. 'This is why you left?'

'In part.'

'How did you find out?'

'That's not important.'

'It is to me.'

'Because you want to stop other people from finding out?'

Amelia asked, the words hollow. She was angry with her mother but also guilty for betraying this secret to someone so untrustworthy.

'I found a photo and a letter. In a book in the attic. It was an accident but as soon as I saw it, I knew...'

Anna-Maria's hand fluttered to her mouth again. 'I thought I had destroyed everything.' She shook her head. 'You shouldn't have found out that way.'

'No, damn it, I shouldn't. I felt as though I'd been shot. How could you keep this from me?' She stood, frustrated. 'But it gets worse, Mum.' And now she'd started, she couldn't stop. 'I did something when I found out, something I shouldn't have done, and I—Oh, God.' She pressed her hands to her face. 'This is all such a mess.'

'Darling, darling.' Anna-Maria rushed to her daughter. 'What is it?'

'I told someone,' she whispered, scrunching up her face. 'Someone I thought I could trust. A boy I'd been seeing. I thought we were in love...'

'Daniel?' Anna-Maria asked, plucking the name from the recesses of her mind.

Amelia nodded. 'He blackmailed me. He has the DNA proof—'

'What DNA proof?' Anna-Maria asked, scandalised.

Amelia flushed. 'I got him to help me run a test.' She groaned. 'I thought I could trust him.'

Anna-Maria nodded without betraying any emotion.

'He said if I didn't pay him, he'd go to the press.'

'And so you ran away?'

'I paid him off first,' Amelia said. 'But I didn't think he was going to let it go so easily. I got scared. And I was so angry with you, and everything was so confusing, I just needed to get away. I couldn't be here, knowing my whole life is a lie...'

'It is *not* a lie,' Anna-Maria denied swiftly, urgently. 'The King is your father. In all the ways that matter, he is your father.' Anna-Maria pressed a hand to Amelia's cheek. 'Do you remember I told you about your father and me, how something happened to make me realise how much I loved him?'

Amelia nodded.

'That something was you. I was unhappy, darling, when the boys were younger. So was your father. We hadn't yet learned how to be together. I was young and foolish and when another man flirted with me, I was flattered and allowed my ego to tempt me. It was a brief, meaningless affair, and we both knew that. It was over almost before it began. But when I discovered I was pregnant, and your father couldn't have been the King, owing to his travel arrangements, I realised how stupid I'd been. What I'd put in jeopardy! And I realised then how much I loved him. I could not bear the thought of losing him, of embarrassing him, of ruining our family.' She sucked in a deep, shaking breath. 'But nor could I bear the thought of lying to him. Realising I loved him meant I needed to start our marriage with a clean slate, and so I told him everything. Everything.'

Amelia stared at her mother. *This* she hadn't expected. 'What did he say?'

'Nothing, immediately. He left the palace, for three nights, and they were the worst nights of my life, believe me, until you disappeared,' she added, shaking her head. 'But he came back to me, and, Amelia, if I hadn't already loved him, I would have fallen for him in that moment. Do you know what he did?'

'What?'

'He apologised to me. Your father apologised to me. For my infidelity! He blamed himself. He'd been ignoring me, he hadn't known, hadn't understood, how he felt for me either. He had seen that I was unhappy, but hadn't realised he could improve things for me. He said that if I would give him another chance, he would grab it with both hands. That he would love you exactly as he did the boys, perhaps even more, because you were the catalyst for us turning this corner. He was not angry. He was not threatened. And he has not once, not one day since, brought up my affair. He has never shown any hint of resenting me, of blaming me, of regretting the choice we made that night.'

Anna-Maria leaned closer, tilting her tear-stained face towards Amelia's. 'And what's more, he has loved you. Every day of your life, he has loved you. To him, you are his biological child. That's all that matters, isn't it? What's in a person's heart?'

Amelia bit down on her lip. Tears filled her own eyes, and love exploded in her heart, but it was more complicated for Amelia still. 'I'm different from everyone,' she said, shrugging. 'Half of me is made up of a man I never knew, a man who died before I could meet him, who didn't even want to meet me.'

'Yes,' Anna-Maria conceded. 'But all of you was shaped by your father. Your philosophies, your humour, your strength, your determination. These are things your father has taught you, by being in your life.'

Amelia closed her eyes, nodded.

'Oh, my darling. I'm so sorry you have carried this burden on your own for so long.' She shook her head. 'I'm even more sorry that you paid off that bastard.'

'What should I have done? I couldn't risk this coming out.'

'Why not?' Anna-Maria demanded defiantly. 'We are not ashamed, Amelia. We are not scared. You are our child—in our hearts, we know that.'

'But your affair—'

'Was a mistake, a lifetime ago.'

'I know. I just thought— I wanted to protect you all. I was scared.'

'Amelia, listen to me. Your father is not the only person to know about this. At the time, we recognised there was a risk of discovery. We have notified a select handful of people, including the president of the royal guard, the prime minister's office and a team of lawyers, engaged for just such a circumstance as this. But the most important thing for you to understand is that we love you. We always have and always will. We considered you to be a gift from heaven, and you have always been exactly that to us.'

It was purely by chance that the first person Amelia should see, when leaving her mother's suite, was Benedetto. And that he should be alone, for just about the first time since arriving in Catarno.

Amelia's heart gave a little thump before she could remind herself her heart had nothing to do with him, at least so far as he was aware. She walked towards him with the appearance of calm, his own expression impossible to read.

'Hi,' she said on a small sigh.

'Your Highness.'

Her heart trembled.

'I'm on my way to meet Anton,' he explained, though she hadn't asked.

But Amelia heard what he hadn't said: *I don't have time now.*

'Okay.' She looked up and down the corridor. People were milling about, but no one from the family, no one they knew. Still, she didn't feel she could tell him about her conversation with the Queen. Not here. 'I'll see you tonight?'

There was a beat of silence. 'I'll be with Anton,' he said. 'The night before the wedding, and all that. His groomsmen are staying in his suite.'

Amelia's heart dropped to her toes. 'Oh, right,' she said with a nod. Then, hating herself for sounding so needy, but at the same time truly needing to confide in him, 'Can you slip away briefly?'

His eyes bored into hers, and his jaw clenched visibly. It was the last thing he wanted. Her heart twisted. 'I doubt it.'

Amelia could feel tears threatening. She bit into her lower lip. 'Okay. But if you can…it's important.'

She waited for him to agree, to promise to come, but he simply smiled at her, in a way that didn't reach his eyes. 'Have a good day, Princess.'

And then he walked away.

It was almost midnight and she'd given up any hope of him coming. She knew she needed to go to sleep, or else she'd have enormous bags under her eyes that even make-up-artist wizardry couldn't disguise. But then, just as she was pulling back the covers, the small side door to her room opened and Benedetto came through.

Amelia's body responded immediately, every cell seeming to reverberate.

'Hi,' she said.

He dipped his head. 'I don't have long.'

'Anton's still awake?'

'And just getting warmed up,' Benedetto added with a grimace.

Amelia pulled a face. 'It's going to be a long night.'

'Yes.'

'I spoke to my mother,' she said quickly. 'I told her everything.'

Benedetto's brow quirked. 'Did you?'

She nodded. 'It went…well, actually.'

His jaw tightened. 'I'm glad for you, Amelia.'

But he was so cool. So formal! Her lips pulled to the side.

'We agreed not to mention anything to Dad, or Rowan and Anton, until after the wedding. But then, we'll talk to them.' She lifted one shoulder. 'No more secrets.'

Benedetto's eyes swept over Amelia's face and for a moment her heart stopped beating altogether. He looked at her with the same fierce possession she'd become used to. But he didn't move to touch her, and she wanted that so badly. 'You did the right thing.'

She nodded, awkward, and she hated that.

'And Daniel?' he prompted.

'I told her about him, too. She said they'd always been aware this might get out. They've made various high-ranking officials aware, there are contingencies in place for these sorts of things. If I hear from him again, I'll go straight to the palace police,' she said, the relief immense.

'Good.'

Silence crackled between them. Amelia felt as though she were being dragged over hot coals. She knew it was breaking all their rules to tell him how she felt, but at the same time, having seen the truth within her heart, she knew she had to be open with him about it.

'Talking to Mum,' she started, a little unevenly, 'about her relationship with Dad, and how they fell in love, got me thinking.' She hesitated. 'About us.'

She wasn't looking directly at Benedetto but she felt him stiffen. The very air around him seemed to throb with tension, but Amelia pushed on regardless, keeping her gaze carefully averted from his face.

'Mum was saying that she fell in love with Dad slowly, and didn't even realise it for a long time, until she almost lost him—because of the affair. It was being faced with what she stood to lose that made her face up to how she felt about Dad. And it made me wonder...' Her voice trailed off, her eyes darting quickly to his face and then away again.

'Wonder what?' Benedetto prompted, not moving.

'The wedding's tomorrow.' Her mouth felt so dry, she could hardly speak. 'Are you still planning to leave afterwards?'

Silence crackled.

'*Sì.*'

Amelia's brow furrowed. 'Is there no part of you that wants to stay?'

'What are you really asking, Amelia?'

That was so like Benedetto, to cut right to the chase.

'The thing is,' she said, toying with her fingers, 'I didn't understand how I felt until recently. I knew you were different, that wanting you physically as I do is new for me, but on the boat it was easy to put what we were doing into a box and contain it. But here, in the real world, it's different. My feelings for you are different. Or maybe they're the same and I just understand them better.'

'Amelia.' Her name was almost a curse. She could hear his anger. 'I have told you, from the beginning, what I could offer. And what I couldn't.'

'I know.' She nodded jerkily. 'But in the beginning, we were two different people.'

'No.'

'Yes. You changed me, and I think I've changed you. I don't think you want to walk away from me.'

His jaw tightened. 'Then you don't understand me as well as you imagine.'

She ignored the pain whipping through her. 'After Daniel, I never thought I would trust anyone again. I never thought I would love anyone again. But you showed me, every day we were together, how different you are, how trustworthy and dependable, how reliable and good.'

He shook his head. 'Even if this is true, that's not love. You're just grateful I'm not going to sell your secrets to the highest bidder.'

She recoiled a little at his reductive summation. 'You knew I was a princess but you've always treated me like a woman first, a human being. You're the first person in my life to do that.'

'Exactly my point. I'm different, and that's novel for you, interesting, but it's not love.'

'Please stop trying to tell me I don't feel what I feel.'

'But you don't.' Frustration was evident in his tone. 'You've deluded yourself, maybe because you need the distraction, because you were anxious about coming home, into thinking we're in the middle of some great romance, but I've been telling you all along, it's not that. It's sex. Chemistry. And at times, friendship, yes. But not love.'

'Are you so afraid to let anyone into your heart that you would actually try to tell me I'm imagining this?' She waved her hand from her chest towards his. His eyes were unreadable; he was totally closed off to her.

'Amelia.' Again, he said her name with utter frustration. 'Don't do this.'

She flinched. 'I think you're scared.'

His throat shifted, but he didn't answer.

'You're running away, just like I did. Well, let's both stop running, Ben. Let's stop running together.'

His nostrils flared. 'You ran away; I'm just getting on with my life.'

'And you don't want me in it?'

'Amelia—'

'Say it,' she demanded fiercely, moving closer, pressing a hand to his chest, so his eyes closed at the unexpected and incendiary contact. 'Tell me you don't want me.'

He lifted a hand, cupped her cheek, looked into her eyes, and everything stopped. They existed in a vacuum and a void, just the two of them. Amelia blinked up at him, her heart bursting to explode. Couldn't he feel this? Didn't he get it?

'I want you to be happy.' He drew his thumb across her lower lip, eyes following the gesture. 'I want you to live the life of your choosing. I want you to forgive your mother and father, to find peace with your situation here.' Her heart trembled. 'But no, I don't want you.'

It was like being shot. She almost stumbled back, but held her ground, right in front of him, one cheek in his hand, her hand on his chest.

'You're a coward.' She whispered the accusation as a tear fell from the corner of her eye. Except he wasn't. He'd been through the most unimaginable grief, he'd suffered intense emotional abuse as a child, had witnessed his mother's abuse, had grown strong from that, had gone on despite it, and then he'd known the worst loss a person could live through, the death of a child, and had still managed to somehow rebuild his life, to go on, one foot in front of the other, day after day. He wasn't a coward; he was brave, but everyone had their limits.

Or maybe he simply didn't love her.

Maybe this was a fantasy, built out of her inexperience and a hopeful heart. Maybe being stranded with him in those intensely emotional circumstances had simply heightened everything.

She stared at him, waiting for him to say something, waiting for there to be more, to understand, but he didn't. He pressed a kiss to her forehead, his lips lingering there. Her eyes feathered closed as her heart surged at the contact, and then he stepped back and the world turned ice cold.

'The sooner I leave, the better. For both of us. You'll realise, once I'm gone, that this was all just make-believe.'

She wouldn't, and he was wrong, but she couldn't keep banging him over the head with the truth. She'd told him she loved him, and he'd rejected the whole idea.

'Have you ever felt like this before?' she whispered, scanning his face, needing *something*. To know that this was special, that she was different. She hated herself for asking, but if he didn't love her, at least he could admit she held a special place in his heart and mind.

'This is what I do, Amelia,' he said, the words strangely weighted. 'I have short-term relationships and then I move on. That's the life I have chosen; it's the life I want. And not once have I lied to you about that.'

It was a form of torture. She took a step backwards, reeling, hating him then, as much as she loved him. 'So you feel this for every woman you sleep with?' she demanded.

'I'm not going to talk about my private life in this context.'

'God, Ben.' She wrapped her arms around her chest, shivering. 'You can't even admit I'm different, can you?'

Silence. Silence that pulsed and pulled and scratched at Amelia until she was almost completely raw.

'I'm truly sorry you feel this way,' he said, eventually, not moving.

Amelia tilted a glance at him, and her heart fairly shattered. He was the love of her life, of that she had no doubt. But he was also intractable and stubborn. He wouldn't change his mind. There was no point having this conversation—it would only hurt them both.

'You should go.'

'Amelia—'

'What?' She whipped around to face him, almost at breaking point. 'What more is there to say? I love you. You don't love me. You're the single most important person I've ever met in my life; I'm nothing to you. Is that a fair summation?'

A muscle throbbed in his jaw as he stared across at her. 'I don't know what you want me to say.'

'Yes, you do,' she whispered. 'But you're right, this isn't your fault; you've never lied to me. Not even now.' Her lips twisted in an awful approximation of a smile. 'Thanks for your honesty, at least.'

'I'm sorry.'

'Don't.' She shook her head. 'Don't apologise. You've done nothing wrong.' She pulled her hair over one shoulder. 'This was all my fault. My mistake.'

His eyes bored into hers, long and hard.

'I didn't mean to fall in love with you. I really thought I could control this. I thought, after Daniel, I was safe from ever feeling anything like this for anyone...' She blinked quickly to stem the threat of tears. 'Please just go, Ben. There's nothing more to say.'

Yet he lingered, watching her, and her nerves stretched and stretched until she couldn't take it any more.

'Go,' she shouted, pointing to the door, finally wiping at her eye just as a tear fell. 'I need to be alone.'

He hesitated before nodding once. 'Goodnight, Your Highness.'

She waited until the door was closed before letting go of the sob that was heavy in her chest.

Benedetto didn't go straight back to Anton's room. How the hell could he after that? He strode through the palace, his face a thundercloud, his body tense, as though preparing for war, his heart ramming against his ribs as though he'd run a marathon. He exited through a side door, found his way to a courtyard and moved to the edge of it, stood with his hands on his hips, staring out at the lights of the city, unseeing.

She loved him.

The world seemed to stop spinning. Sweat beaded on his brow. It was his worst nightmare. It was everything he didn't want.

What a fool he'd been, to think he could become involved with someone like Amelia and not have it get complicated.

She was so different from the women he usually slept with. Amelia wasn't sophisticated and experienced, she wasn't looking for a few nights of passion and then to move on. What was worse: she'd been in an intensely vulnerable position when they'd met.

He dragged a hand through his hair.

He'd told her at every opportunity that it was just sex, made sure she understood that he didn't do commitment and relationships. He'd been so honest and upfront about that, but what did that matter?

Wasn't the reason for his constant reminders to Amelia that he knew there was risk with her? That she was so different she wouldn't be capable of understanding, truly understanding, the way he chose to live his life?

She'd had her heart broken, her trust shattered, and had chosen to stay alone afterwards, but Amelia's heart was too good to be permanently on ice. She had too much love to give to withhold it for ever.

Whereas Benedetto had been broken in a way from which he would never recover. His heart belonged to Sasha, and always would. How could he allow it to beat for anyone else, knowing what would happen if he were to lose that person too?

He clenched his hands into fists by his sides.

He'd done the right thing by holding firm in the face of Amelia's declaration, but that didn't make it any easier. And it didn't mean he felt like less of an A-grade bastard.

The sooner the wedding was over and he could leave this country, the better. Then they could both start getting on with their lives and forgetting this had ever happened.

CHAPTER TWELVE

AMELIA WALKED BEHIND VANESSA, holding the elaborate train of her dress, her features serene and impenetrable, her eyes focused on nothing and no one, even as Benedetto stared at her and willed her to look his way.

She didn't.

She wouldn't.

Her gaze was angled steadily ahead, her eyes on the front of the church.

She looked beautiful, but Benedetto could see beyond her mask, to the grey beneath her eyes, the tightening around her lips, and he knew he was the cause of that.

Had she not been able to sleep, in the same way he couldn't sleep?

Had she replayed their conversation with the same sense of frustration, because it was the exact opposite of how she wanted things to end between them?

Benedetto had known he would leave, but he had hoped they could part on good terms. That they could both look back on their time warmly.

Warmly?

How insipid, he thought with growing frustration. Suddenly, he wanted the entire congregation gone. He wanted to scoop Amelia up and take her somewhere private, with just the two of them. He wanted to be alone with her again, to finish the conversation, but to do it better this time.

Better how? What would he say? That she was special? Different? And give her false hope that their relationship might have a future after all? The more special and different she was, the more Benedetto wanted to run from her.

Her eyes flicked to Anton, and Benedetto narrowed his gaze, needing her to look at him so he could pierce her with his eyes, to smile at him and reassure him that she was already feeling better, but she didn't. Her eyes stayed on Anton's face, a smile crossed her lips—but not a smile like Benedetto had seen her give. This was practised and poised. A smile for the cameras, he thought, because the wedding was being televised. And of course Amelia, having grown up in the spotlight, was all too aware of not putting a foot wrong. She was totally in control of herself, in complete command of her emotions, outwardly at least.

She was an impeccable, beautiful princess.

His chest felt as though a load of cement were pressing down on it; his gut churned. He blinked it away, ignoring those feelings, ignoring the questions in the back of his mind. He had no doubt that leaving was the right thing, but he'd never wanted to defy his instincts more.

It had been the performance of a lifetime.

Amelia's cheeks hurt from smiling, when inside her heart was torn to shreds. She had stood beside her new sister-in-law throughout the proceedings, as Anton and Vanessa had declared their love for one another, as they had pledged to live and love for the rest of their lives, to honour and respect, and she'd known that only a few feet away from her was the only man she'd ever want to say those same words to, to make those same promises to, and yet he didn't want her. The knowledge had been like a hammer in her head and heart throughout the entire wedding. Somehow, she'd kept her cool, listening as the words were spoken, smile pinned in place, and when, from time to time, her eyes had sheened with tears, she'd known it didn't matter, because people would presume they were tears of happiness, instead of what they really were: an expression of absolute dejection.

Outside the chapel, everyone was full of joy, and Vanessa and Anton were the stars of the show, the couple everyone was looking at and adoring, so it was easy for Amelia to slip away a moment, to step through a narrow opening at the side of the ancient church and find her way through a path to a small courtyard with a fountain at the centre and a seat at the edge.

Checking the seat was clean, she sat down, and stared across the courtyard at the stone wall, eyes misting over.

She was tired. Exhausted. The act of a lifetime had cost her. She just wanted to curl up into a ball and sleep. Her eyes traced the old grout lines between the stones, seeking calm in its disordered sense, in the way the stones differed in sizes and shapes yet still somehow made up uniform lines. It was a warm day. She stretched her legs out in front of her, so the sun caught them in a triangle formed by the shape of the walls surrounding her, and she closed her eyes, trying to be still, to calm her racing mind and aching heart.

He was leaving.

There was nothing to be done about it, no more she could say, no further argument she could make. It was his life, his choice, and when she'd offered herself to him, all of herself, he'd politely, steadfastly declined. He didn't love her.

Except, she couldn't quite believe that. He'd said it, he'd been so confident, but, in her heart, Amelia suspected a love like she felt couldn't exist without reciprocation. It had been born from what they shared, from the way they'd made love, the secrets they'd revealed, the deep, abiding trust they'd built, the care they had for one another. For a brief time, all too brief, she'd walked in lock step with another person. For the first time in her life, she'd had a true partner.

What did her hopes and beliefs matter though? He'd been adamant. He didn't love her.

With a heaviness in her gut, she prepared to open her eyes and become Princess Amelia once more, to rejoin the wedding and the festivities. She sighed, then blinked, because she was no longer alone. Benedetto stood across the courtyard, in his stunning suit, looking too gorgeous to bear, and the last vestiges of Amelia's heart splintered and cracked. She was preparing to resume her act, she just wasn't quite ready yet.

Quickly she stood, turned away from him, did her best to assume the mask she knew she had to wear.

'Your brother asked me to find you,' he said quietly. 'The cars are leaving.'

She didn't turn to face him. 'I'll be right there.' Damn it, her voice wobbled.

A moment later, he was at her side. 'Amelia,' he murmured, reaching out, putting his hand on hers. She flinched away.

'I'm fine.' Her chin jutted defiantly, but her eyes were moist.

'Listen, about last night—' She heard the tormented apology in his voice, and her chest seemed to split in half. This was all about guilt, obligation, the feeling he'd done the wrong thing.

She'd imagined everything.

'There's nothing more to say.' She stared at him, and even then, she hoped. 'Is there?'

He thrust his hands into his pockets.

'You didn't lie about your feelings? What you said last night, you meant it, didn't you?'

He was quiet for a beat and then he made a gruff sound. 'Yes.'

She closed her eyes on a fresh wave of pain. 'If you care about me at all, please leave me alone. I have to get through today, tonight, I have to be what they all expect—I don't have the capacity to feel *this* and to be that.'

His eyes raked her face and then he nodded. 'Your car is ready.'

Grateful for the return to business, she spoke curtly. 'Thank you. I'll be right out.'

He left without a backwards glance.

In the morning, Amelia awoke with a sadness in her chest that was deeper and darker than any she'd known. Benedetto would leave today, and she would never be the same.

She wouldn't see him again.

He would manage that carefully, ensuring that if he visited Anton, Amelia wasn't present. She just knew he would avoid her, to avoid hurting her again, to avoid the risk of anything more happening between them.

Accepting the reality of that, knowing he was out of her life for good, was incredibly counterintuitive.

He was the love of her life, but she had to accept his decision. Suddenly, she couldn't bear to be at the palace for all of the post-wedding activities, the necessary farewells. She couldn't bear to see Benedetto again. If they were to go their separate ways, then she wanted it to be now. Like the ripping-off of a plaster, she would never see him again. It was what he wanted.

It was still early, and she suspected everyone else would be asleep after the festivities of the night before, so Amelia took advantage of the slumberous palace and dressed quickly, washing her face, pulling her hair back into a ponytail and slipping out of a side gate, moving towards the garage.

The chauffeur startled to be disturbed but rallied quickly. 'Your Highness.' He dipped his head. 'Good morning. Where would you like to go?'

'Nowhere in particular. Just…away from here for the morning.'

If he thought it was strange, he didn't reveal as much. 'The kingfishers have taken over Anemon Lake. It's supposed to be an incredible sight. Would you care to see them?'

'Yes, thank you,' she murmured with relief, slipping into the back of the car as he held open the door for her. Amelia took great pains not to look over her shoulder at the palace as the car slipped elegantly through the gates.

Benedetto hadn't been relishing the goodbye, but he had at least expected to be able to make it. He'd wanted to see her, one last time. Things between them had ended badly, and he hated that, but he still wanted to do this part, at least, properly.

Only, upon arriving at Amelia's apartment, it was to find it deserted. A question to one of the housekeepers revealed that she was 'out'.

He waited as long as he could, but after several hours cooling his heels, it dawned on him that she considered they'd already said their farewells. That there was nothing left to say—just as she'd said, after the wedding.

She'd come to him and literally offered her heart; he'd immediately declined. Her face and eyes had shown her hurt. Her surprise. But why should she have been surprised?

His gut twisted as he strode into the sunshine-filled courtyard. With Anton on his honeymoon, and Benedetto having already issued brief farewells to the King, Queen and Rowan, there was nothing for it but to leave.

Except, as Benedetto approached his car, the door held open by a chauffeur, he hesitated, pausing, inexplicably, to look back at the palace, his eyes chasing the windows, as if he might catch a glimpse of her, even now. His hand clenched into a fist at his side.

He knew what he had to do, and yet leaving felt strangely wrong, particularly leaving without seeing her again. He stood in the triangle formed by the open car door, at war with himself.

His head said leave, but there were other parts demanding he stay.

His head won out. He'd learned that it was much safer to trust his head, and so he sat heavily in the car and looked forward, towards his own future, and a life without Amelia Moretti anywhere near it.

The emptiness was pervasive. He hadn't expected that. After all, he'd known her for only a short time, and yet arriving in New York, after a week in Athens, Benedetto couldn't ignore the heaviness in his chest any longer, the feeling that something vital was missing from his days, from his life. He disregarded the feeling. Or rather, he compartmentalised it, as he'd learned to do as a boy, boxing away the hurt, the confusion, the disappointment and fear and stacking that tightly sealed box into the recesses of his mind, allowing him to function unimpeded.

As he'd learned to do when Sasha had become sick, when she'd died, and he'd had to co-exist with the heavy, pervasive grief of having lost her.

Except Amelia had done something to that grief. When they'd spoken of Sasha, he'd smiled, because he'd remembered all the happy, good, warm things about his daughter. And sharing that with Amelia had felt so right, as if he was bringing Sasha where she belonged—into the light. He hadn't spoken of her in so long, because no one else had tempted him to, in the slightest. But with Amelia, it had all been so easy.

He buried himself in work, taking solace in the very familiar form of denial. He spent twenty hours a day at his office, becoming master of this domain again, reading and negotiating contracts, hiring staff, micromanaging every aspect of his business. And even then, she crept into his mind when he wasn't firmly concentrating on control, allowing her to slip past the guards, and fill his thoughts, his body, so he would breathe in and swear he could taste her.

'Damn it,' he cursed, in the early hours of one morning, staring out at the glittering skyline, eyes bleary from lack of sleep. But it was sleep he feared, because in sleep, the vice-like grip on his self-control was weakened. His dreams were always filled with her.

'It's not because you're different, you know,' Anton, a month after his fairy-tale wedding and having returned from his honeymoon days earlier, sat beside Amelia in the pretty sun-dappled courtyard.

She turned to face him, her face pale, features tight, eyes, unbeknownst to her, lacking all their usual light and spark.

Anton was, for a moment, worried, though he didn't show it.

'What wasn't?' she murmured.

'The reason for us clashing. It's not because you're different. In case you think that somehow I knew, all this time, that he's not your biological father.'

Her smile was mournful; she turned away from him. It was enough to alarm Anton even further. 'I didn't think that.'

'You've always been so much better than me, Amelia.'

She frowned without looking at him. Worry for his sister stirred through Anton. Why hadn't anyone told him she was like this? She was a shadow of her former self, in terms of joy and vitality. She clearly wasn't coping with being home.

'That's not true. Has Vanessa put you up to this?'

An attempt at a joke was good, but still Anton's concern grew. 'You are so much more patient, kind, wise, willing to listen to other people before making up your mind. In that sense, you are the most like Dad of all of us,' he added. 'Biology isn't everything, you know.'

'I know.' Tears sparkled on her lashes.

Anton stood, needing more answers than he was going to get from his sister. But before leaving, he reached down, put a hand on her knee. 'Is it Valencia?' he prompted. 'Are you so desperate to go back?'

She lifted her face to his, eyes hollow, so unlike the Amelia he'd grown up with. 'No.'

A simple one-word answer that told him nothing.

'Is it being here?' Anton pushed. 'Do you hate it?'

She shook her head. 'I just need time, that's all.'

He nodded, but a sense of uneasiness was spreading through him, and there was only one person he could think of to speak to, only one person he trusted with all his innermost thoughts, besides his new wife.

He reached for his phone as he strode from the courtyard, Ben's number on speed dial.

CHAPTER THIRTEEN

BENEDETTO LISTENED TO his friend with an impassive mask. Despite the fact there was no one else in his office, he didn't want to let his guard down. But his insides were far from unaffected by the phone call.

'I'm worried about her.'

'Why?'

'She's not happy.'

Benedetto gripped the phone more tightly. 'Why do you say that?'

'She's my sister. I can tell.'

Benedetto's eyes closed.

'Did she tell you anything about her life in Valencia? About what she was doing there? Is it possible she had more going on than we realised? A serious relationship? Something important she couldn't leave? But if that's the case, why not go back? No one's forcing her to be here. Did she say anything to you, Ben?'

'No.'

'I want to help her, I want her to be happy. I just don't know where to start.'

Benedetto ground his teeth together. Guilt slammed into him. He'd messed everything up.

'She's been through a lot,' Benedetto said.

'I know. But this isn't like Amelia. I've never seen her like this.'

Benedetto leaned back in his chair, his mind conjuring an image of Amelia with ease, her beautiful, happy face on the boat, her laugh, her sun-kissed smile.

'So she didn't say anything to you?'

Benedetto dragged a hand through his hair, not answering the question directly. 'In my experience, no matter the problem, time's the solution. Your sister is right. In time, she'll be herself again.'

He disconnected the call as quickly as he could, hoping he was right.

But if having Amelia permanently moored in his brain had been hard before, it was almost impossible now that he imagined her miserable. Now that he saw her face as it had been after the wedding, when he'd found her staring at the fountain as though it held the answers to the universe. He imagined her sadness and ached to draw her into his arms, to hold her, to kiss her until she smiled against his mouth, until she laughed, or cried out in ecstatic euphoria, whichever came first. He ached to swim with her, to travel with her, to simply co-exist at her side. Five weeks after he last saw Amelia, and he began to suspect he was wrong: perhaps time wasn't the answer he was looking for. So what was?

She wasn't sure why she'd come back. Only when she'd woken that morning and gone through the motions of pretending everything was fine, that her heart wasn't breaking over and over again, and her mother had asked what was on Amelia's schedule, she'd heard herself say, without putting any thought into it, 'I'm going to Crete.'

Only in uttering the words had she realised that she'd been thinking of that day with yearning for weeks now. In Crete, they'd walked hand in hand through narrow laneways, admired brightly coloured buildings, he'd picked a geranium flower and handed it to her—she still had it flattened in between the pages of a book. In Crete, she'd stopped running: from her family, but also from the love she felt for Benedetto. In Crete she'd accepted she couldn't go in a different direction from him. And even though he'd subsequently left her, the need to be back on those streets, to exist in the midst of memories that were so tangible and real, had called to her.

'Oh, lovely, darling. What will you do there?'

'I have a few things in mind,' she'd responded vaguely. 'I'll see you later today.' She'd pressed a kiss to the top of her mother's head, bowed in the vague direction of her father, then walked from the room with more purpose in her step than she'd had in over a month.

Benedetto couldn't have said if it was courage or stupidity or a strange kind of sadism that had led him to set up a news alert on Amelia's name. Morbid curiosity? Or a desire to reassure himself that she was okay? That the press wasn't hounding her as it once had? And what would he have done if that had been the case? Flown to Catarno and rescued her? As if he had any right.

Whatever his reasons, when an email came through some time after midnight with Amelia's name in the headline of the article, he stopped everything he was doing and clicked into the link, breath held, eyes furiously scanning his tablet, reading everything, before he saw the photograph of her in a familiar setting, and every part of him froze.

His finger hovered over the photograph, but that jerked

the article closed. He swore, reloaded it, forced himself to look but not touch.

Princess Amelia Moretti enjoys a break at a local restaurant. That was the subtitle that accompanied the photo.

But he knew which restaurant she was at—one they'd been to together. Where they'd sat and talked, and the sun had filtered in through the window and Benedetto had felt happy and relaxed and— He frowned, searching for another word to describe the elusive emotion that had coloured every moment of that day, until she'd run away. Then he'd gone from sunshine to shadow, feeling as if he'd lost everything in the world.

Until he'd arrived at the marina and Amelia had been waiting for him, and it had been as if he could breathe again; as if everything had been restored.

There was no sunshine for him now, only a heaviness he could hardly live alongside, a true absence of pleasure in every moment.

When Sasha had died, it had been truly awful. He had grieved her because he'd had to.

This was different.

Amelia was still here, alive, well, in another country. He was separated from her by choice, which made it harder to grieve her, to accept how much he missed her.

He flicked back to the photo, studied it, looking for any kind of sign that she was doing okay. Looking at her face, trying to understand her. Listening to the photo as though he might be able to hear her speak, hear her thoughts, learn something from the picture beyond the fact that she'd gone to the restaurant in the first place.

His instincts were pulling on Benedetto, telling him to stop fighting this, to go and see her, to talk to her, to just work everything out later, because suddenly nothing mattered more than at least being in the same room as her. He didn't know what the future held, but he knew he could no longer live at this great distance from Amelia. She was in his soul, weaved into all the fibres of his being, and he was starting to realise that she always would be.

He called Anton from the air. The conversation was brief and businesslike—the content made that a necessity.

Benedetto and Anton were men cut from the same cloth: both private, proud, not quick to trust. Neither wanted to jeopardise their friendship, but Benedetto recognised the necessity of honesty with his friend, now that he stood on the brink of—he didn't know what. But he at least needed to explain to Anton, as a courtesy, that things were more complicated than anyone had realised. That he was coming back to see Amelia, and, finally, that he needed Anton's help. In a voice that could only be described as moderately shell-shocked, Anton agreed. 'Of course I'll help. But if you hurt her, Benedetto, if you hurt her—'

Anton didn't need to finish the sentence. They both knew what was at stake.

'I'm not really in the mood.'

'Would you do it as a favour?' Vanessa asked, a smile playing about her lips that spoke of some secret or another.

Amelia sighed softly. 'Does it have to be the marina?' She hated the thought of going back there, of seeing the boats but not Benedetto's. She hated the memories that she knew would flood her, hard and fast.

'I cannot possibly go onto a naval boat at the moment.' Vanessa leaned forward, confidingly, looking around the dining room to assure herself that they were alone. 'I already feel as though I am fighting seasickness all day and night—

standing on a boat, I would be likely to be sick everywhere. Can you imagine the photographs?' She winced and concern eclipsed Amelia's feelings of self-preservation.

'Are you not well?'

'Oh, I'm very well,' Vanessa contradicted, then quite obviously pressed a hand to her still-flat stomach. 'It's the hormones.'

'Oh!' Amelia stood up, feeling her first flush of joy in a long time, truly delighted for her sister-in-law and brother. 'What wonderful news!'

Vanessa smiled. 'We're thrilled.'

'I'm sure you are. How absolutely lovely. A baby!'

'Yes,' Vanessa whispered, looking around quickly. 'But we have not yet told anyone.'

'My parents?'

'In a week or so,' Vanessa said with a nod.

Amelia was honoured that her sister-in-law had chosen to share this secret with her. 'I won't say a thing.'

'Thank you. Now, regarding the boat opening?'

'Of course I'll do it,' Amelia agreed immediately, hating the idea of a ribbon-cutting of any sort, because of the necessary publicity that would ensue, but knowing she had to rise to the occasion. She was not the same young woman she'd been when she'd fled Catarno, nor the girl before that who'd been hounded while at university and made to feel as though everything she did was wrong. Amelia had grown up a lot in the last two years, and, vitally, had learned who she was, away from the palace and her role in the royal family.

Dressed in a striking navy-blue suit with a crisp white collar, and almost at the marina, she admitted to herself that she wasn't dreading this half as much as she'd thought she might.

Until the car came to a stop and she looked around, eyes automatically gravitating towards the berth that Benedetto's boat had occupied, expecting to find it empty, only to see that *Il Galassia* was still in port.

Her chest rolled.

She felt as though she might be sick. Butterflies danced through her central nervous system and little tiny lights flickered in her eyes. She gripped the door of the car, closing her eyes and giving herself a stern talking-to. So his boat hadn't left. That meant nothing. It wasn't even necessarily the case that Benedetto's crew was on board. Perhaps they'd flown somewhere else, to do something else, leaving the boat here to be maintained until he needed it again. Or perhaps Cassidy and Christopher were on board. Perhaps if she went to them, after the opening, they'd let her step inside. To sit for a while in the underwater lounge room and remember what it had been like to spend a week with him. Maybe even to pretend that she'd slipped back in time and they were still together, on the boat.

Her heart twisted painfully and she blinked open, eyes landing on the deck again.

The car door swung open and she knew she couldn't indulge these feelings any longer. She was on display, here representing the royal family. She had a job to do, and Amelia was determined to prove to everyone how much she'd changed.

'This way, Your Highness,' one of the members of the royal guard said, then bowed and gestured towards the docks. There was only one other boat in sight and it was not new. She looked around, wondering if perhaps there was a larger craft further out at sea that she was to be taken to.

But the guard led her, not to any naval boat, but rather towards *Il Galassia*, and each step brought more confusion, not clarity, so that when they reached the plank that led to the back of the boat, she stopped walking, memories slamming into her now, hard and fast.

'I'm sorry, there must be some mistake.'

'No, Your Highness.'

A numb sort of curiosity had her moving forwards, her mind refusing to allow her heart to hope, concentrating impossibly hard on not imagining anything, on simply walking, one step in front of the other, until she was on the boat.

The guard didn't follow. She looked around, frowning, then continued to move forward. 'Hello?' she called out. No answer.

Lips tugging to one side, she moved up the stairs, to the next deck, then around to the front of the boat, eyes widening when she saw that, instead of the pristine white deck with which she was familiar, there were tens of thousands of red rose petals scattered like a carpet, everywhere she looked.

Her eyes squeezed shut, as if to clear the image.

When she opened them, Benedetto was standing there. He wore a suit, but the jacket had been discarded and the shirt sleeves were pushed up to his elbows, one side had come untucked. He looked so incredibly good in this dishevelled state. Though he would have looked good to Amelia no matter how he presented because it was six long weeks since the wedding and every day had been filled with a yearning for Benedetto that had taken her breath away.

Nonetheless, she stayed exactly where she was, the hurt of the past impossible to ignore, and it served as a shield now, making her cautious.

'What's going on?' she asked.

Benedetto didn't move at first either and then, slowly, he crossed the deck, stopping when he was just a few feet away from her. Close enough for her to see every detail of his face, to touch him.

She crossed her arms quickly, to prevent her from doing anything quite so stupid.

'You went to Crete.'

It was the last thing she expected him to say.

'How do you even know that?'

'I saw an article.' Was she imagining the slight darkening on his cheekbones? A blush, from Benedetto? 'Why did you go back there?' His voice was so gruff.

She angled her face away, staring out at the sea, trying not to react, trying not to feel. 'Why shouldn't I?' she said, eventually, aware that she was hedging the question. 'I'm more interested in why you're here now. In what all this is about.' She gestured to the boat.

'I don't know,' he said, moving a step closer, so she flinched. She had to be strong, but she was so tired, and had missed him so much. 'Or is it that I know, and cannot put it into words?'

'Well, why don't you try?' she snapped, frustrated and in so much pain she couldn't believe it. 'Because I'm going to walk off this boat in about one minute.'

'I don't want to do this any more.'

She narrowed her eyes. 'Do what? You're the one who came back, who brought me here.'

'I mean I don't want to do this without you.' His voice was a low rumble, like thunder. 'Life. I have been miserable since I left here, miserable with missing you, wanting you, needing you, aching to talk to you, to see you, to hear you, to just be with you. I was so sure I could conquer those feelings, that it was better for me to stay away, because I don't want what you want, because you deserve better than the future I can offer you. And yet here I am, discovering that, for you, I would do anything, go anywhere, be anything.'

Amelia's lips parted in wonder and surprise, but her brain

was there, quickly tamping down on her excitement, because surely there was the possibility that she was misunderstanding him in some vital way.

'I have never been in love. I've never even really witnessed it. My parents were at each other constantly. I've avoided relationships of any meaning. But you are everywhere I look, including deep down in my soul, always in my thoughts. You are in my dreams, and everything I see and do seems a little worse when you're not there to share it with. Is this love, Amelia? Is it love to crave a person to the point you would do anything to see them, just one more time? Is it love that makes me know I would give my life to save yours? Is it love to know that I could spend every minute with you for the rest of our lives and it would still never be enough? Is it love to want to protect you from any force in your life that might do you harm even when knowing you are strong enough to protect yourself? You are the best person I have ever known,' he said gruffly, cupping her face then, staring down into her eyes. 'I don't want to fight this anymore.'

She closed her eyes, inhaled him deeply, her heart exploding.

'I hate that I hurt you. I hate that it took me so long to wake up to what I was feeling. I hate that I had to hurt us both before I could see that the only future I want is one with you in the very centre of it. Most of all, I hate that when you told me how you felt, I didn't understand my own feelings enough to shout from the rooftops that I love you too.'

She pressed a hand to his chest, struggling for breath, let alone words. 'Oh, Ben,' she whispered, tears on her lashes. 'It's okay.'

'No.' He was adamant. 'It's not. I've been such a stupid, selfish bastard, and I cannot forgive myself for that. But if you are generous enough to let me back into your life, to tell me you still love and want me, then I will never give you any reason to doubt my feelings again.'

And she knew he wouldn't. 'Even that night, I didn't really doubt them,' she said. 'I knew that loving someone like I did you wasn't, couldn't be, one-sided. Every memory I have on the boat is about *us* falling in love, not just me. This is a partnership.' She reached for his hand, linked their fingers together. 'We always will be.'

'Yes,' he said with such a sound of relief that she couldn't help but smile. 'We always will be.' And in the middle of the deck, surrounded by so many rose petals she half wondered if a whole country had been denuded of flowers, Benedetto di Vassi broke the promise he'd made himself as a young boy to always be alone, and instead begged Princess Amelia Moretti to be his other half, always and for ever.

And she agreed, in an instant.

It was much later that day, when the sun was almost gone and the stars had come out, that Benedetto explained the process that had finally brought him to heel. He told Amelia about the news alerts, about how desperately he'd sought out even the smallest hint of information about her, but that there'd been nothing—*because I was hiding out in the palace*—until the day she went to lunch, and then it had hit him like a meteor, right between the eyes.

He loved her.

He had to be with her. There was no question of choice or free will, it was simply as inevitable as breathing.

He explained to her that he'd known their relationship and happiness had to be secured but that he'd known that happiness would always be slightly lessened if it came at the cost of Anton's happiness, of their friendship. Benedetto relayed the conversation with Anton, in which he'd very succinctly explained that he'd fallen in love with Amelia and intended to propose to her, that he knew Amelia too well to ask anyone's permission for her hand in marriage—*'I'm my own person and I'm glad you understand that!'*—but that he nonetheless felt the courtesy of a heads-up was appropriate, given their friendship.

'And what did he say?'

'There were some threats,' Benedetto drawled.

Amelia laughed softly.

'But then he told me that I deserved to be happy, and so do you, and that if we can make each other happy, there would be no greater supporter of our relationship than him, except perhaps Vanessa. Apparently she suspected something was going on between us.'

'I'm not surprised. She's very observant.'

'I didn't want to ask anyone for permission but once he'd accepted how things were between us, it was like the last piece fell into place. I knew I had to do this. I just hoped, with all my heart, that I hadn't ruined things between us completely. I was so worried you would have stopped loving me. That you'd have realised you couldn't love anyone who'd put you through this.'

'I was upset,' she agreed softly. 'But I don't think love is quite so transient as that. Certainly not the love I feel for you.'

'Nor I for you,' he promised, leaning closer, pressing a kiss to her lips. She sighed happily and snuggled into his arms.

Royal tradition dictated that Amelia should have a full, elaborate wedding, and so she did, but twenty-four hours before the ceremony the world was invited to attend via the news cameras positioned throughout the abbey, Amelia and Benedetto said their own vows privately on the deck of his boat, surrounded only by her family, and Cassidy and Christopher.

It was an intimate ceremony imbued with all the love they felt for one another, and each and every guest in attendance felt that heavy in the air—it was an evening of magic, of love, and of happily ever after, just as the bride and groom deserved.

EPILOGUE

Six years later

'THEY'RE GOING TO get someone killed.' Vanessa groaned, pressing a hand to her forehead, and earning a laugh from Amelia.

'Nonsense. Teeth might go missing though,' she said, as their two oldest children—a pair of boys born only a year apart and so alike they were sometimes mistaken for twins—tore through the palace garden, a tangle of legs and arms and high-pitched laughter as they raced for the big oak tree, to see who could touch it first.

'I can't bear to watch,' Vanessa said, reaching for her tea and taking a sip.

'Then don't watch. The less we see, the better.'

'I don't know how you can be so sanguine about it.'

'I had two brothers,' Amelia pointed out.

'Hmm, that's true. I can't imagine Anton ever running around like this, though.'

'Oh, he wasn't always so boring,' Amelia responded, with a wink.

Vanessa laughed. 'You really are so bad to each other.'

Amelia lifted a hand in silent surrender. 'I'm pretty sure he started it.'

'Started what?' Anton appeared at that moment, and Vanessa's whole face showed happiness.

'Our all-out war,' Amelia joked.

'Yes, and I intend to win it,' he warned, then grinned, turning to his wife. 'The twins are awake.'

'Ah. Duty calls,' Vanessa said, standing, putting an arm around Anton's waist. 'I'll see you later?'

Amelia nodded, watching them walk away, smiling, because their happiness was so familiar to her. She sighed as she turned back to the boys, who, having reached the oak tree, were now busily trying to work out how to climb it. Even Amelia felt a slight twinge of alarm at that, but before she could intercede Benedetto was there, hoisting their son, Peter, onto his shoulders before scooping Anton and Vanessa's son into his arms and spinning him around. The laughter grew higher in pitch, and he carried them away from the tree and back to the grass, where he placed them both down and neatly pointed them in the direction of the football. It worked—for now.

Amelia exhaled a sigh of relief, then a sigh of something else, something delightfully warm and intoxicating, as her husband drew closer and placed a kiss on her forehead. Her heart, as always, pumped harder, and she reached out, her hand curling into his.

'Hello.'

He squeezed her hand. 'Hello.'

'Thank you for saving them from the tree-climb adventure.'

'Saving them? I promised I'd help them build a tree house later.'

'Oh, no,' Amelia chortled. 'You'd better include safety harnesses.'

'They're more capable than you give them credit for.' He reached for a strawberry and bit into it. 'Where's Valentina?'

'She's reading with Mum and Dad.' The King and Queen

had taken to the role of grandparents with aplomb. They delighted in their five grandchildren and spent as much time as possible with them. Valentina, the only granddaughter, was doted on by all.

'She's so like you were!' the King would marvel. *'I never thought we would be so lucky to have a chance to do this all over again.'*

And Amelia, who had never really had cause to doubt her father's love for her, felt it radiate through her.

But there was one other child who was very much a part of their world, even though she was no longer with them. Sasha was spoken of often, brought into the light by Amelia and Benedetto, particularly with their children. For Benedetto, it had been imperative for Peter and Valentina to know about their older sister, to feel connected to her, and so he told them stories about her, showed photographs, and, in doing so, he felt those last stitches of grief begin to come together in his heart.

He would never get over losing Sasha, but he knew what a privilege it was to have loved her, and to have the chance to love Peter and Valentina. Loving, it turned out, was the greatest gift he had, and he was so grateful he'd recognised that, finally.

Amelia had run away from Catarno in fear. She'd been so afraid of not belonging, of everyone discovering that she wasn't who they thought she was. She'd been afraid of her secrets being sold to the press, and, in the end, it had all been for nothing.

Daniel did not reappear in her life.

She heard, some years later, through a mutual acquaintance, that he'd moved to London and married a wealthy aristocrat's daughter. Given his primary aim seemed to be living comfortably and working little, she presumed he'd succeeded in his goals and wouldn't likely bother her again.

But if he did, she wasn't worried.

It all seemed like such a long time ago, the feelings she'd had when she'd learned of the affair totally foreign to her now. She knew exactly who she was, and where she belonged, and with whom. She didn't fear exposure—though it never came. If it had, she wouldn't have worried, because it changed nothing. She was Amelia di Vassi, a princess of Catarno, and she was happier, she suspected, than anyone else on earth.

The next morning, with their children happily installed in the palace with grandparents, cousins, aunt and uncles, as well as a team of nannies primed for the havoc of the royal children, Amelia and Benedetto kissed everyone goodbye, as had become their annual tradition, to celebrate their wedding anniversary on *Il Galassia*.

Some years, they had been able to leave for only a night, when the children were young, and that hadn't mattered because, wherever they were, their life was full of romance and love. But now, as the children were older and very comfortable staying with family, they had a whole week to look forward to. A week on the boat that had started it all, a week together, just the two of them, more in love with every day that passed, more in sync, more convinced that they were perfect for one another than they had ever been.

* * * * *

STRANDED
AND SEDUCED

EMMY GRAYSON

MILLS & BOON

To Mr. Grayson, Mom and Dad. This book
would not have been finished without your support.

To my editor Charlotte.
I'm a better writer because of you.

To my darling children.
This book would have been finished a lot sooner
if you would sleep through the night.

CHAPTER ONE

GRIFFITH LYKAOIS TRACED a finger over the scar that cut through his right eyebrow, skimmed the corner of his eye and sliced over his cheek. Another scar stretched from the side of his mouth down to his chin, surprisingly smooth to the touch. Still a visible angry red slash even when he combed his beard to cover it. As he sat in the leather high-back chair by the balcony doors, a glass of whiskey within reach, he could picture his ghoulish visage in his mind as if he was looking in a mirror. The past eleven months had faded the scars to dull pink. But time hadn't dimmed the memory of the first time he'd seen himself. Stitches crisscrossing the fresh wounds. Eyes bloodshot and unfocused from the medication they'd pumped into him.

Monstrous.

Her horrified voice had slithered through him, that word burying under his skin, as he'd drifted in and out of consciousness that first day.

Not even his status as the son of a wealthy shipping magnate, with millions in the bank, had been enough to make Kacey Dupree want to stick around. Not when her boyfriend had looked more like a beast than a man.

Surely you must understand, Griff.

Her voice had sounded like nails on a chalkboard, digging into his brain like sharp talons as he'd tried to wrap his mind around the fact that his father had been killed and he'd been left scarred.

All because he hadn't been paying attention. Had been focused on himself, as his father had just accused him of, before the world had been tossed upside down with a bone-wrenching jolt and screeching metal.

The word echoed in his mind as he dropped his hand from his face and grabbed the glass. A sip of the whiskey, straight and tinged with spice, burned down his throat. He avoided getting drunk. Too easy of an out.

But he allowed himself just enough to dull the pain.

Monstrous.

Kacey had visited him the second day in the hospital, her glistening blond hair twisted into an elegant chignon that had displayed her pale, heart-shaped features perfectly. A beauty that hadn't even registered as he'd fought against pain and grief. She'd laid her hand on his shoulder, then snatched it back quickly, her plump red lips twisted into an expression of disgust when she'd seen the blood seeping through the bandage.

Rage had simmered beneath the dressings. His father had just died.

"Surely you must understand, Griff."

"Give me the necklace."

Her mouth had dropped open. She'd switched from placating to furious in seconds, raging at him for daring to take away the one thing that would leave her with memories of what they'd had before the accident. It had only been when he'd threatened to sue her for theft and ensure the news made it into the papers that she'd taken off the four-million-dollar ruby necklace and hurled it at him before rushing out in a fit of tears.

That his first thought had been *Good riddance* said more

about their six-month relationship than he ever could have. It had hurt more that it hadn't hurt much at all.

With one hand still wrapped around the glass, his other came up, fingers touching the tiny moon-shaped scar on the left side of his face. The only visible injury to that side. The thin scar high on his left temple from where his head had slammed into the doorframe had been covered by hair.

But he could feel it. Feel it when he combed his hair. Feel it when it throbbed at night with a pain that felt as deep and fresh as the moment he'd heard his father shout his name before everything had turned black.

Kacey had been right about one thing. He *was* a monster. Inside and out.

He took another sip of whiskey. Aged sixty years in the wilds of Ireland, one of the hand-painted bottles fetched over one million dollars at Sotheby's New York location. A year ago, he would have been on top of the world with one of Europe's most coveted models sitting across from him, the finest jewels his money could buy around her neck, and the whiskey in his glass.

Now it was merely a means to an end. A good-tasting whiskey that eased his discomfort and helped pass the time.

Fate, he'd discovered, had a very cruel sense of humor. For the past ten years he'd been consumed by money and image. When he'd first heard of the Diamond Club four years ago, envy had been an ugly shadow dodging his steps. The clubhouse, a casual name for an opulent town house in London, offered refuge for the ten wealthiest people in the world. Rumors had spread like wildfire of the amenities: a helipad on the roof, columns fashioned from Calcutta marble and suites designed to its residents' particular tastes.

Now, as he stood and walked through the suite his father had had decorated, he no longer felt envy.

He just felt sick.

Three months after the accident, when his spinal fractures had been declared healed enough for him to remove the back brace, a lawyer had visited him at the family estate in Kent. His father had branched out over the past few years, investing in everything from real estate to technology. Those investments had resulted in a fortune worth billions.

Enough billions that the lawyer's visit had been shortly followed by an invitation. The cream-colored envelope had been delivered by a woman in a black suit that matched the limo she arrived in. She had inclined her head and handed him the envelope as she told him Mr. Raj Belanger cordially invited him to take his father's place at the Diamond Club.

Once one of his loftiest goals, now achieved. At the expense of his father's life.

Yes. Fate was very, very cruel.

He hadn't been able to bring himself to leave the safety of Kent, the familiarity of the gleaming wood floors, the antique furniture he'd once scoffed at. Now he understood his father's inability to get rid of the chesterfield sofa with its worn arms where he'd once sat with his mother as they watched old movies. His refusal to sell the faded Persian rug in front of the fireplace where Griffith had sat in the winter and opened Christmas presents.

Too late, he saw the value, saw the wisdom of his father's words, understood the caution urged upon him not to get too caught up in opulence and bank statements. With both his parents gone now, the pieces of furniture were no longer old heirlooms he wanted to replace, the home no longer old and lacking the polish he preferred in his purchases. Now the sofas and rugs and chairs inspired memories of times he could never get back. The home welcomed him with open arms, despite all the disparaging remarks he'd made.

Much as his parents had.

Kent had become a harbor, a place to hide. The familiarity of his surroundings, the warmth of a place he'd once called home, had given him the kind of solace none of his ritzy penthouses and expensive town houses had.

But his refuge had been ruined a week ago when he'd been out walking along the shores of the private lake and a light had flashed in the trees. The next day, a picture of him looking down at the ground had appeared on the front of a tabloid magazine. The picture had been a touch out of focus, enough to blur the worst of his scars. But it was evident that the man who had once been lauded as one of the handsomest in Europe was no longer so.

The story had included a full recounting of the car accident that had claimed the life of his father, Belen Lykaois. It had also revealed that the head of Lykaois Shipping had been worth far more than hundreds of millions of dollars. He had been worth billions.

Billions that had been left to his sole surviving heir, Griffith Lykaois.

The phone calls had started less than an hour later. The vultures had descended, including invitations to charity galas, private yacht vacations, dinner parties and of course more investments, scams, people clawing for a piece of his wealth.

Wealth he had once dreamed of. Wealth he could barely now stomach the thought of possessing.

Kacey's call had been the final straw. He'd just gotten off the phone with his secretary in London who had been fielding calls for interviews, events and the like. His private cell phone had rung, and he'd answered without checking.

Kacey had greeted him with that nickname he'd loathed— Griff—and told him she missed him and could she see him please to apologize—

He'd tossed the phone out the window into the pond below without a second thought.

Security had caught two more paparazzi later that evening. His sanctuary tainted, he'd taken his limo down to London, to the one place he knew would be as secure, if not more so, than Buckingham Palace.

The Diamond Club.

He'd walked into the lobby from a private back entrance off the mews and been greeted by a portly man with a beak-like nose and one of the most elaborate silver moustaches he'd ever seen. Lazlo, as the man had introduced himself with a deferential bow, had led him across the marbled floor of the grand hall and up a sweeping staircase. The hallway had been covered in silk carpeting that masked the sound of their footsteps as they'd walked to a black door with a gold number eight.

He'd been here for six days now, stalking around the suite like a caged animal. That Griffith's father had had it decorated not for himself, but for his son, had been obvious. Soaring windows with black trim on one side, an accent wall of red brick, and creamy-colored paint elsewhere balanced warmth with the industrial look Griffith favored. After his mother's death, he'd grown to detest the old-world charm of their estate in Kent. The style he imagined his father would have selected if he'd decorated for himself. But Belen had chosen gleaming metal and glass, the style Griffith preferred that, as Griffith had argued numerous times, signified progress.

Whenever Griffith looked around, at the leather furniture, at the original artwork on the walls, he didn't experience any pleasure. Just shame. Shame and a deep-rooted self-loathing that he had rejected everything his father stood for, kept him at arm's length for so long while Belen had continued to love him from afar. He'd even eschewed his own preferences as he decorated the Diamond Club suite for his ungrateful son.

Griffith had everything he'd talked of wanting, only to find that he was missing the one thing he'd had all along and never appreciated. The last conversation he'd had with his father, more of an argument than a discussion, had been an old one. Belen had been concerned about...well, everything. Griffith's long work hours. His relationship with Kacey. His spending.

"I don't spend your money," Griffith had snapped as he stopped at a light. "I spend the money I earn. You yourself just acknowledged I work my ass off for this company."

"And for what?" Belen retorted. "Rolex watches? Paintings and sculptures you stash away in one of your numerous penthouses?"

"You own beautiful things."

"Yes, and I enjoy them. I don't just buy them to have them. Your grandfather built Lykaois Shipping from nothing. My early years were poor. Your grandfather lived most of his life poor. To have the wealth we have now—"

"Is earned, not a right," Griffith finished. The edge in his voice widened the growing chasm between them.

Belen had sighed, a sigh that cut straight through Griffith's anger and lodged in the part of his heart that would always be a boy seeking his father's approval.

"There's more to life, son, than things."

"Things are like trophies. Evidence of success. The result of hard work." His hands tightened on the wheel. "Tangible."

Griffith shoved the memory away before he could relive what had followed. He moved to the balcony, leaned his forehead against the cool glass. Plush chairs surrounded a glass fire pit. Wrought iron fencing rose up just high enough to interrupt prying eyes from nearby buildings. Black lanterns fixed to the fencing gleamed bright as gray clouds rolled across the sky, growing darker with impending rain.

What was he going to do? Lykaois Shipping, his grandfather's pride and the legacy that had elevated their family from poverty-stricken resistance fighters in World War II to the upper echelons of the world's wealthy, was being run by an efficient team in his absence. No one had questioned his request for a yearlong sabbatical. Between his extensive injuries and his father's death, not to mention the international scrutiny, the board had vocalized complete support in the virtual meeting he'd conducted. He'd kept his camera turned off.

Not because they'd wanted to be rid of him. No, as his executive assistant had shared, they wanted him to rest so that he would come back stronger than ever. After he'd been put in charge of the British division of Lykaois Shipping five years ago, everything had soared: the company's share of container traffic, accuracy, profits. The board wanted him to do the same for the entire company. Even if they had to wait a year for him to bury his ghosts and adjust to his new reality.

Griffith stepped out onto the balcony, moved to the edge and gazed out over London, the blend of old and new. A cool wind whipped across the rooftops. A few miles away lay the London office of Lykaois Shipping. What had once energized him, given him a reason to get up in the morning, now felt hollow.

An icy-cold raindrop fell on his face. Before he could turn away, the clouds unleashed a downpour that soaked him before he could make it to the door.

Perfect.

He stepped inside, shaking raindrops off like a dog, just in time to hear the quiet buzz of his private line.

"Yes."

"Sir." Lazlo's voice, deep and proper, rolled through the line. "There's a young lady to see you."

If anger could manifest into something physical, steam would rise from his clothes.

"You can tell Miss Dupree that she can ride her broomstick back to wherever she came from or go straight to hell. I don't care which."

"As enjoyable as that would be, sir, it's not Miss Dupree."

Griffith frowned.

"Who is it?"

"Rosalind Sutton of Nettleton & Thompson."

The firm that had handled all of his father's estate planning. A firm that dated back over two hundred years and managed the assets, wills and trusts of CEOs, politicians, even the occasional royal. They wanted him to sign the papers that would officially transfer his father's fortune to him. This woman, Rosalind Sutton, had certainly been tenacious, from calling his private number to showing up at his various offices and even his home in Kent. Thankfully, he'd been gone that weekend. Otherwise, she might have found herself a guest of the local constabulary for the night.

He knew at some point he would have to cave. Would have to sign the damned papers and acknowledge that his father was gone.

But not today. He wasn't ready.

You'll never be ready.

Ignoring that nasty little voice inside his head, his next words were terse. "Tell her I'll contact her later."

"Of course, sir."

A rustling sound eclipsed Lazlo's voice.

"Miss Sutton—"

A feminine voice, strong yet muffled, replied, "Give me the phone. I need to—"

Griffith paused. He knew the voice, had heard it on the one voice mail he'd listened to before deleting it and blocking the number. Cool and professional. Yet this version of the voice was vibrant, feminine with a brash confidence that awoke something inside him.

Lazlo's exasperated voice cut through once more. "Miss Sutton—"

The line went dead.

CHAPTER TWO

GRIFFITH STARED AT the phone. His previous irritation with Miss Sutton's inability to take no for an answer morphed, shifted into admiration for the woman who had somehow managed to get into one of the world's most exclusive clubs. The American accent hadn't even registered when he'd listened to the voice mail. Now it intrigued him, made him want to know more about the tenacious woman who worked for one of the most exclusive law firms in London.

It had been a long time since anything had interested him.

His lips quirked. Imagining Lazlo fending off a woman trying to wrestle the phone away brought him as close to a laugh as he'd gotten in nearly a year.

He returned the phone to its cradle and started for the stairs, which led to the second floor of his suite where a massive king bed waited for him. Then he stopped as curiosity warred with encroaching exhaustion.

Curiosity won.

He walked out into the main hall, the walls tastefully decorated with a mix of contemporary and classic paintings by legendary artists. Sconces provided light all the way down to the top of the grand staircase. The marble marvel swept down to the main hallway, a large room lined with columns and a soaring ceiling that boasted a tiered chandelier crafted from diamonds.

The expense and beauty were lost on the people down below. Lazlo stalked out of his office, the figure at his side mostly obscured by his broad body. He moved with purpose across the hall.

"You are not welcome here again, Miss Sutton." Lazlo's voice, usually polite and refined, dripped with icy command.

"Aren't you supposed to be serving your clients?"

The same husky, feminine voice Griffith had heard on the phone drifted up, wrapped around him with a surprisingly strong grip. He moved closer to the top of the stairs.

Lazlo turned and guided Miss Sutton toward the double front doors where two security guards waited. It gave Griffith his first glimpse of the tenacious attorney who had been badgering him these past few weeks.

His first impression was curls. A riotous mass of dark brown curls cascaded over her shoulders and down her back. She wore a tan trench coat that skimmed the back of her knees and navy rain boots.

"Yes. Mr. Lykaois doesn't want to see you."

"But if he doesn't see me, he'll risk—"

"Might I suggest calling his secretary?"

"I have. Multiple times. I've also driven to his offices in Liverpool, Portsmouth, Southampton…"

As if sensing his presence, she suddenly whipped her head around and looked up. Their eyes met. She held his gaze even as Lazlo continued to move her forward.

A current of emotion arced between them. The anticipation of two adversaries finally coming face-to-face charged the air. Yet something deeper wound its way through, added a dark, hypnotic power just before desire slammed into him. Vivid images filled his mind, carnal thoughts of a slender body arching beneath his as he tangled his fingers deep into those curls, kissed her bare throat as she curved against him—

Shaken, his hand shot out and gripped the banister, his fingers digging into the marble with such force it was a miracle he didn't leave indentations in the polished stone.

"Mr. Lykaois?"

His chest tightened as he forced himself to stay in place. He was in the shadows. She couldn't see him clearly. He couldn't even make out any defining features, aside from an oval-shaped face framed by those unruly curls. But it didn't stop the voice from slipping beneath his skin, wrapping around his taut nerves and teasing, coaxing, urging him to stay just a moment longer, to look his fill of the woman who had set his body on fire.

"Mr. Lykaois, please. I need to speak to you about your inheritance."

The last word snapped him out of his reverie. Cold flooded his veins as his hands tightened into fists at his sides. He turned his back on Rosalind Sutton and returned to his suite, ignoring the fading sound of her voice calling out his name.

With each step he took, he grabbed the errant strands of his self-control and wove them back to order. If he had thought Rosalind Sutton a mere nuisance before, one who was pushing him to accept something he didn't want to, he now saw her in a far different light. In the span of a heartbeat, lust had taken over, gripped him with a ferocity he'd never experienced before. That it transcended his previous hedonistic exploits, that just the sound of her voice had inspired him to act on impulse and go out to the lobby to get a glimpse of her face, were warning signs he couldn't afford to ignore.

He had worked hard the past eleven months to correct his lifestyle. To listen to his father's words, even if it had been too late for Belen to see the results of his tireless support and love for his only child.

Rosalind Sutton threatened it all. That he could not allow.

He stalked back into his suite and walked up the stairs, pausing on the landing to stare out the window that overlooked the street below. London was now awash in dark gray, the people below pummeled by sheets of a rain too cold for the beginnings of summer.

Just below him, an umbrella opened. It caught his eye because of the almost painfully bright yellow material. It moved amongst a sea of black and crossed the road, covering its owner from view.

He knew, even before he caught a glimpse of the navy rain boots and trench coat flapping in the rain, that Rosalind wielded the colorful parasol. The umbrella moved down the sidewalk and away from the Diamond Club at a brisk pace.

How had she managed to brazen her way into the club? Into Lazlo's private office? The woman had guts, he'd give her that.

But she also wanted him to face a reckoning. To her, it was a simple signature, one last bit of business.

To him, it would be the final acknowledgment his father was gone.

He would need to sign the papers eventually. Alone, in a location of his choosing, with Rosalind far, far away. He could not risk another face-to-face meeting with a woman who tempted him to sin with her mere presence. Angry as he was at his reaction to her, it wasn't her fault. His anger needed to be directed fully and completely at himself.

It would be easy, preferable even, to place the blame for his unnatural reaction on her. But that would also be indulging in his old ways. Not taking responsibility for himself, for his actions and the consequences incurred by his selfish nature.

He turned away, firmly dismissing her from his mind as he continued up the stairs. Eventually he would deal with the damned inheritance. But right now, he wanted peace.

Needed it if he wasn't going to go mad. Kent was no longer safe. While the Diamond Club offered refuge, the longer he stayed the more his guilt pressed on him, tightening until he could barely breathe.

Yet every property he owned outside of England was the opposite of peaceful. A penthouse in New York City, a beach house in California, and an apartment in Tokyo he'd acquired weeks before the accident. Luxurious, expensive and surrounded by people.

He paused at the top of the stairs, glanced down at the sumptuous furniture laid out on the floor below him. Thinking of the beach house made him think of another beach, one he hadn't been to in over thirteen years. His heart twisted in his chest, sharp and vicious, then released as he forced the emotions away and focused on the practicality. It was certainly remote, unlikely to attract the attention of anyone who would care.

Relief eased the edges of the tension straining his body. He'd always sworn he'd never go back to the far-flung coast of Normandy, to the chateau his mother had poured her heart and soul into right before her death. But not only would it serve as the perfect hiding place, it would also be just punishment.

He walked into the bedroom, ignoring the bottle of pain pills on the nightstand as he stripped off his clothes with harsh movements that made his right arm and leg burn. Then he sank down onto the bed, closed his eyes and slept fitfully, his nightmares plagued by breaking glass, squealing tires and a yellow umbrella darting to and fro amidst the chaos.

CHAPTER THREE

One week later

WHITE OAK TREES towered on both sides of the lane, their thick branches creating a canopy so thick only the smallest slivers of sunlight pierced the ground. But in those little pockets of sunshine, the crushed seashells covering the drive glowed white.

Rosalind Sutton stood and stared, one hand clutched around her briefcase, the other around her umbrella. Beyond the trees there would be a gate, and beyond the gate lay the castle.

Not castle, she mentally corrected herself, *chateau*.

She'd learned that from Bonar, the kind, elderly man who'd given her a ride from the village and shared his extensive knowledge of the Chateau du Bellerose as his clunky truck had sputtered along a dirt road flanked by rolling hills.

The stone bridge that separated her from the trees linked the chateau to the rest of the world. A river cut through the gorge that separated the plateau the manor had been built on, providing the only way in or out. Key, Bonar had said, to defending the manor house when it had first been built.

And now providing sanctuary for one very stubborn, very rude billionaire who had a contract to sign.

The memory of that moment in the hall of the Diamond Club crept into Rosalind's mind. She'd felt someone watching her, had taken a guess as to who spied on her just beyond the light from the diamond chandelier. She had only seen his legs, hands hanging at his side. The rest of his body had been masked by darkness.

When she'd said his name, something had arisen between them, pulsed. A jolt of energy, a shock of sensual awareness.

Awareness that had evaporated as soon as she'd said the word *inheritance*. She had felt the anger, seen his hands tighten into fists.

And known that whatever battles she had fought so far, from sitting outside of his office in the pouring rain to calling in a number of favors just to determine the address of the elusive Diamond Club, were nothing compared to the war she would have to wage to secure that signature.

Instinct, along with extensive research, had prompted her to keep tabs on the Lykaois private jet at Heathrow Airport. A flight plan had been filed the morning after she'd been escorted out of the Diamond Club. A short trip from London to Le Havre on the Normandy coast. A quick review of the Lykaois family properties in France had netted several results, including a penthouse in Paris and a villa on the shores of the French Riviera.

But there had been only one in the Normandy region: a centuries-old manor just outside of the small village of Étretat.

One train and two taxis later, she was finally here. No henchmen in Savile Row suits to toss her out. No stone-faced secretaries telling her to stop coming by unless she wanted to be arrested.

Yet still she hesitated. Part of her wanted to turn around and follow the dirt road down to Étretat. To walk through the streets lined with homes constructed of timber and brick, to relax with a glass of wine at a beachside restaurant and gaze at the white chalk cliffs. To seize a moment's peace.

Later. She made herself that promise as she forced herself to walk across the bridge toward the shadowy tunnel created by the trees. After securing Mr. Lykaois's signature, she would enjoy the remaining days of her cottage rental. Maybe she would even take an actual vacation, spend a week in Paris or Rome.

Yeah, right.

Once she secured this promotion, her already demanding schedule would become even more so. Late nights, long weekends, holidays. The price to pay for working her way up at a prestigious law firm.

She'd been working toward this promotion ever since she graduated law school and accepted a position as a junior associate at Nettleton & Thompson. Her ascension from a small town in Maine to being offered a job in London had made her parents so proud. It had been her mother's dying wish to see Rosalind reach even further, achieve even more, than anyone in her family had ever dared to dream.

Sometimes, Rosalind wondered if she should have told her parents how much she would have preferred a smaller firm, an organization dedicated to helping people who needed her services versus the ones who could pay a small fortune.

But then she remembered her last conversation with her mother, the pride that had rang in Jane Sutton's weakening voice.

It wasn't just her version of the dream that mattered.

The next step of that dream was within reach, so close it nearly drove her mad that one man held the power over her career with Nettleton & Thompson.

Unbidden, the one glimpse she'd gotten of that man rose in her mind. Cloaked in shadow, there had been no reason for her body to respond to the glance they'd shared.

Tension tightened her muscles, her breath quickening as she remembered the sudden burst of heat deep within her belly, a heat that had spread and made her body languid even as sparks had skipped through her veins.

Utterly ridiculous.

So why couldn't she forget it? Why had she woken up every morning for the past week tangled in her sheets with her heart pounding, tendrils of sensual dreams she'd never experienced before lingering with her throughout the day?

She paused halfway across the bridge. Morbid curiosity drew her to the edge and she leaned over. The drop down to the thin line of water at the bottom of the gorge was dizzying. She sucked in a deep breath, knew she was secure behind the solid wall of stone. But her heart beat a little faster as she continued on.

On toward the one man who had stirred inside her a carnal curiosity that, despite her best intentions, she couldn't ignore.

It had been easy to resist the attentions of overly hormonal teenage boys when she'd been so fixated on earning money for college. Then, once she'd reached Chicago, dating had fallen low on her priority list. One girl in her dorm, Louisa, had accused her of having impossible standards. Of building up what her first time would be like to impossible heights no man could meet.

Perhaps, Rosalind thought as her shoes scraped across the stone underfoot, Louisa had been right. Perhaps she'd never let her dates go beyond a kiss because she'd been afraid. Afraid that her fantasies of her first time, of intimacy and sex and the man she would share her body with, would fall far short of her desires.

Except now everything she'd ever dreamed about in the safety of her own bed and her own flat was coming to life at the worst possible moment.

Not to mention the worst possible man.

Her phone rang and yanked her out of her immature

thoughts. Cursing when she saw who was calling, she answered.

"Yes, sir?"

"Where are you?"

Robert Nettleton's voice, smooth as whiskey and cold as ice, snapped through the line.

"France, sir."

"Making progress, then?"

"Yes, sir."

Kind of...sort of...not really.

"Good. I needn't remind you of what rides on the completion of this contract, Miss Sutton."

She gritted her teeth.

Only every other time we've talked the past six weeks.

"No, sir."

"Good. The deadline is eight days away."

"I have a flight booked back to London for Tuesday, sir."

"Be in my office by Wednesday morning at nine a.m. with the signed contract, Miss Sutton. I want to see it with my own eyes. Daily updates are encouraged."

She rolled her eyes. It was as if her hard work the past few years had been wiped away over one damned document.

"Yes, sir."

"Your future at this firm—"

A burst of static made her wince as she moved off the bridge and into the shadows of the trees.

"Sir?" The static faded, followed by a single beep. "Great." Rosalind shoved her phone in her pocket. While she wasn't upset at her conversation being cut short, she didn't care for the lack of reception as she prepared to walk into the proverbial lion's den.

Walk to the chateau. Get the signature. Get out.

Cool air kissed her skin as she moved beneath the trees. Quiet descended, save for the soft crunch of shells beneath her feet and the occasional trill of a bird. The tension she'd been carrying slowly drained away, replaced by the peace she had desperately been seeking ever since she'd had the unfortunate luck to be assigned to the Lykaois case.

The research she'd conducted on the new CEO of Lykaois Shipping, the third generation to hold that title since the company was founded, had been fascinating. Griffith Lykaois was known to indulge in pleasures most people couldn't even dream of. Six-figure bottles of wine. A contemporary painting that would have paid for two dozen students from her tiny hometown to go to college. Black truffle and caviar dinners at the most expensive restaurants in the world. And of course, as evidenced by the numerous photos taken over the years, a revolving door of glamorous women on his arm. Even when he had finally settled down for more than a week with one woman, it had been a supermodel famous for sporting the world's largest diamond during a photoshoot...and little else.

Yet despite his predilection for obscene luxury, he also had the rare distinction of showing up to his office and working. The British division of Lykaois Shipping had soared under his guidance. He played hard, yes, but he worked just as hard.

Or at least had until a drunk driver had T-boned Griffith's Lamborghini, killing his father and leaving Griffith with severe injuries and a patchwork of scars. Some theorized a plastic surgeon would ensure that only the tiniest wounds would be visible. Others whispered that the reason Griffith had taken a leave of absence for an entire year had been because he was too ashamed to show his face in public.

The interview his ex-girlfriend Kacey Dupree had given less than two weeks ago certainly hadn't helped squash those rumors.

Whatever had happened, Griffith Lykaois had left behind his life of vice and hedonism for isolation.

She did feel sorry for him, had felt a kindred pain of loss

when she'd read about the accident, seen the photos of twisted wreckage and bits of glass scattered across the road. But even if he wasn't engaging in decadent endeavors, he was still making selfish choices. Choices that had made her life hell, from the veiled threats from Mr. Nettleton about her future at the firm to the embarrassment of being escorted out of the Diamond Club.

She shook off her frustration and focused on the bittersweet, earthy scent of oak that filled the air, the occasional flash of warmth when a sunbeam fell across her face as she walked. She had been so driven for so long, so intent on working hard to get out of the town her parents had told her over and over was too small for what she was capable of, that she hadn't stopped to just breathe.

Or think about what I *wanted.*

Uncomfortable at the path her thoughts had taken, Rosalind shifted the strap of her bag to the other shoulder. It wasn't her parents' fault they had wanted the best for her. It wasn't their fault she had never gotten the courage to tell them she wanted something else. How could she, when they had looked at her with such pride? With hope that she would continue down the path they'd set for her.

You'll be a senior lawyer at Nettleton & Thompson one day. I know it. You won't give up on that, will you?

I won't... I'll make you proud, Mom.

Her parents had married young, scrimping and saving to buy a tiny house with a constantly leaking basement and three small bedrooms they'd crammed themselves and four kids into. Rosalind's older brother had been destined to follow in their father's footsteps as a lobster fisherman. Her two younger brothers had been adamant about going straight to work after high school, to make their own way.

It had fallen to Rosalind to achieve her parents' dream of having a child graduate college. A dream that had surpassed their wildest expectations when she'd been accepted into law school in Chicago, followed by the internship and then the job offer.

She'd never questioned herself before. Had simply accepted the praise they'd heaped on her, preened at the knowledge that her parents thought her so capable and merrily gone after each goal they encouraged her to reach for.

Her mother had lived long enough to see Rosalind try on her cap and gown the month before she graduated from law school, to learn about the job offer from Nettleton & Thompson. Rosalind was on track to do exactly as her mother had wanted.

So, why didn't she feel excited by that?

All too soon, the lane curved and she emerged from the trees and turned to find herself in front of the gate. Constructed of wrought iron, and flanked by two stone pillars topped with statues, it certainly put the little white picket fence back home to shame. Her eyes traveled up, landing on the figures atop the stone pillars guarding either side of the drive—women garbed in dresses that reminded Rosalind of ancient Greek statues. Both statues had tumbling hair threaded through with what looked like stars. One woman held a rose clutched to her chest, while the other held a thorned flower up to the sky, as if offering it to the heavens.

A few hundred meters behind the gate lay the chateau, a sprawling manor house with rows of arched windows gleaming in the sun and topped off by a steep roof. Even at this distance, it exuded elegance. The kind of place her mother had described when she'd tell tales of princesses and princes, palaces and dungeons, enchantresses and beasts.

A brisk wind tore through the bars of the gate. She put her head down and shivered at the sudden coolness as heavy gray clouds scuttled across the sky and chased away the summer blue. An even bigger cluster of clouds loomed up behind the manor. Bonar had mentioned a storm moving in from the sea. But he had said it wouldn't hit until that evening.

She headed through the gate. She would get in, make her pitch and walk out with Lykaois's signature, and be back in Étretat before the storm really got going. Bonar had told her to call him if she needed a ride back to the village. Given how Lykaois had behaved so far, she doubted he would be so kind as to offer her a ride himself.

Rosalind took in more of the chateau as she got closer to it. Mr. Lykaois's New York penthouse sat on Billionaires' Row at the southern end of Central Park. It had been featured in a luxury real estate magazine, all glass walls and gleaming metal. The California beach house, fashioned in the shape of an L and colored gray, presided over a private beach and included a saltwater infinity pool that overlooked the Pacific. The Tokyo apartment overlooked Tokyo Tower and included access to a library, bar, spa and a private dining room serviced by international chefs.

So why had he chosen a centuries-old manor to hide out in? It was beautiful, yes. Expensive? Absolutely. Sweeping stone staircases trimmed in black railing framed either side of a three-tiered fountain. The steps curved up to a long terrace and massive double doors constructed of golden-brown wood with an arched window just above. The house had been maintained with not only great care but devotion to the original design. The final result was stunning.

But a very different feel from what Griffith Lykaois otherwise seemed to prefer. New, modern, flashy. Not historic and elegant.

Rosalind gripped the handle of her bag as she reached the stairs and started up. She needed to get her emotions under control. She'd had a strong reaction to him in the Diamond Club. But, as she'd told herself repeatedly in the days since, it had been understandable. Emotions had been running high.

A lot was riding on her finally coming face-to-face with him and she'd read enough about the man, watched enough interviews from before his accident, to feel like she'd met him, knew him. Finally seeing him had pushed those emotions over the edge.

It made sense, too, that with her limited experience she would have a stronger response than the average woman. How often was anticipation better than the actual event?

Besides, she had other things to think about other than her hormones. Things like getting the contract signed and finally being promoted to midlevel associate attorney.

The thought of going back to London, of presenting the signed contract to Mr. Nettleton, should have buoyed her. Instead, it quickened her steps, as if she could outrun the restlessness that had been growing these past few months. Outrun the question that had been haunting her for months.

Do I want to keep doing this?

The strap of her bag pressed into her skin, the weight of her decision growing heavier with each step. She liked her work, liked hearing people's stories and what had become important to them over the course of their lives. Yet as time had gone on, the once dignified atmosphere of Nettleton & Thompson had started to feel more like a prison.

She had always considered herself a happy person. Even on days she'd slogged through thirteen hours of paperwork and client meetings, she'd been able to find the positives, like successfully navigating a will with a difficult client or watching the moon rise above the nearby Buckingham Palace.

But now...now she just felt exhausted.

The one positive in the struggle of reaching Mr. Lykaois was that she'd been able to put off confronting her dissatisfaction with her job just a while longer. To figure out if she wanted to work for the firm she had once thought she would retire from, or if she had the nerve to finally stop burying herself in work and make her own decision about what she wanted to do with her life. Live a little outside the walls of her office.

She shoved the questions away. Not the time to be having a personal crisis.

Now was the time to do her job.

She stopped in front of two massive wood doors.

Here goes nothing.

She raised the heavy knocker, a round loop of metal topped off with a sculpture of what looked like a rose, and let it fall.

No one answered.

Wind howled over the top of the manor, followed a moment later by scattered rain. Hunching her shoulders against the storm, she tried peering into one of the windows, but the curtains had been drawn tight. She went back to the door and knocked with her fist. One of the doors quivered, then slowly swung in.

She stood on the threshold, her hand tight around the handle of her briefcase. Technically no one had invited her in. But the door was open. And she'd come all this way after over a month of chasing the dratted man down.

Besides, it was starting to storm. Surely Mr. Lykaois would allow her to at least take shelter until the rain passed.

With a deep breath, she pushed the door wider and walked inside.

CHAPTER FOUR

Rosalind's mouth dropped open.

Mosaic tiles swirled into a stunning pattern of deep blues, vivid greens and elegant reds beneath her feet, contained by white stone edging the room. A matching stone staircase, wide enough to fit four people across, hugged the wall and spiraled up. The chandelier had been fashioned in black like the railing outside and hung from the ceiling a good fifteen feet above her head. Thankfully it was lit and kept the encroaching gloom from the storm at bay. The walls, painted a creamy ivory, caught the light and made the room glow. A long, thin table hugged one wall. The dark wood gleamed as if it had been freshly polished. Beautiful but bare, as if it were waiting for a bowl of fresh flowers or an antique vase.

The overall emptiness of the room struck her, made her sad. A stunning house with much to offer but left empty and alone.

She started to move about, too jittery to stay in one place. A painting caught her eye, one of the few adorning the walls of the hall. Well over four feet tall, it depicted white-capped waves surging onto a beach. The strokes that had captured the dark blue of an ocean at twilight had been fierce, the slashes depicting water churned up by the hint of dark clouds on the horizon. A cliff jutted out into the sea, proud and immovable against the water's wrath. The wildness spoke to her, sent a frisson of energy through her that rejuvenated her flagging spirits. It reminded her of the autumns of her childhood, with her nose pressed against the glass as she watched storms lash the Maine coast just steps away from her home. Fury and power, nature reminding man what it was capable of.

One lone figure had been painted on the small beach, a simple black shadow made strong with a tilted-up chin and shoulders thrown back, as though the person was confronting the ocean itself. It was tempting to reach out, to touch the character and encourage them to keep fighting.

A small smile flitted about her lips as she breathed in deeply. Whether she was projecting or not, the thought gave her a much-needed boost of determination to see her mission through.

A twinge settled between her shoulder blades. Awareness made her skin pebble as her breath caught in her chest. The same sensation she'd experienced in the Diamond Club right before she'd caught a glimpse of Griffith Lykaois lurking in the shadows. She hadn't seen his face, not clearly. That hadn't stopped the shock that had stolen her breath, the heat that had appeared out of nowhere and burned her skin.

The same heat now creeping over her, a fever that could only be assuaged by one decadent act she'd never experienced before.

She whirled around.

There was no one there.

"Miss Sutton."

The voice—deep, harsh, yet surprisingly melodic—rang out through the hall. It washed over her, slid under her skin and reverberated through her body like a deep roll of thunder.

Startled, she looked up. A man stood on the first landing of the grand staircase. A very tall man, his torso and face covered in shadow.

"Mr. Lykaois?"

"How did you gain entrance to this house?"

She tilted her head but couldn't make out any features. She had heard the rumors of his scars. One of the law clerks had even shown her the blurred photo published in last's week gossip magazine. But whether it had been out of focus intentionally or by accident, it had been hard to see much detail.

Curiosity nipped at her, but she quelled it. His scars, or lack thereof, were none of her business.

"The door was open."

One hand tightened on the railing. "So you trespassed."

Frustration reared its head. "Sir, I need to—"

"No." He stepped down onto the top stair, the shadows shifting up but still shielding his chest and head. "What you need to do, Miss Sutton, is leave before I call Nettleton & Thompson and tell them to fire you."

"For what?" she snapped.

Knowing he could do exactly as he'd threatened and that Mr. Nettleton would probably acquiesce in a heartbeat made her angry. She had worked hard, very hard, to get here. Regardless of her own doubts, that was the truth. She had tried to be nice, to be patient. But this man, who had the world at his fingertips, had thrown obstacles in her way at every juncture.

Determination lent strength to her voice. Irritation added an edge. "For doing my job? Going above and beyond by tracking you down across two countries?"

"If going against your client's wishes and stalking them is considered your job, then I'll take my business elsewhere."

Helplessness was an uncomfortable feeling. Helplessness coupled with anger was even more unpleasant. She could feel the words bubbling up in her throat, tried to stop them.

And then decided she didn't care anymore. If this was truly

going to be the end of her career with Nettleton & Thompson, which at this point seemed inevitable no matter what she did, then she might as well go out in a blaze of glory and leave this spoiled playboy with a hint of the damage he'd caused.

"Until you sign this contract, my client is your father, or rather his estate." She reached into her bag and yanked out the thick sheaf of papers. "Since you haven't signed it, I don't care where you take your business. In fact," she added as she stepped forward and flung her head back, "I'd sincerely prefer you not do business with Nettleton & Thompson because you have been nothing but a pain in my butt."

Silence fell, save for the furious thudding of her heart in her chest.

Then, in a firm voice tinged with reluctant amusement, he said, "Really?"

"Really."

"And if you get fired?"

"If you don't sign, I'm fired. If you call Nettleton & Thompson, I'm fired." She threw up her hands in the air, barely keeping a grip on the contract. "So congratulations, you have me over a barrel."

"Over a barrel?"

She rolled her eyes. "Helpless. At your mercy."

"You don't sound helpless, Miss Sutton."

The heat trickled back in at the hint of admiration in his tone. Heat that only upped her irritation. How could she possibly be attracted to such an infuriating, self-absorbed man?

"I'm not helpless. I'm not a damsel in distress. I've continued forward through five canceled appointments, numerous hang-ups by your oh so efficient secretaries, and traveling over five hundred miles trying to track you down with my boss breathing down my neck and putting the future of my career in your hands. If I can survive that, I can survive anything."

Her chest rose and fell as she stared up at his shadowed face. She'd probably already signed her future away with her outburst. But God, it had felt good to finally vent her anger at his arrogance, at her career being reduced to her ability to get one simple signature.

She ran a hand through her curls and looked longingly at the partially open door before she turned back to him.

One last time. Try to explain just one last time.

"Do you not understand? If you don't sign, you'll lose everything—"

"I've already lost plenty, Miss Sutton." Cold suffused his words, all traces of amusement and admiration gone. He started walking down the stairs with slow, measured steps that made her chest tighten with dreaded anticipation. "My father. My girlfriend. My looks. My ability to walk in a crowd without scaring small children." The shadows crept up, revealed broad shoulders and a strong neck, the skin marred by one thick scar tinged pink. "What makes you think I give a damn about money anymore?"

And then he stepped into the light.

Rosalind pressed her lips together to stem her gasp. The scars on the right side of his face were made all the more distinct by the lack of damage to the left side. One scar started at his hairline and stabbed downward through his eyebrow. Miraculously, whatever had caused the wound had missed his eye, but just barely, judging by the way it slashed to his temple before traveling down over one carved cheekbone. Still another scar, a larger patch of red, was visible beneath his trimmed beard, snaking from mouth to jaw and then farther down.

Jarring, yes. But the way the tabloid had played it up, including a lurid description from his former girlfriend, had made him sound like a beast or Frankenstein's monster.

To her, he looked like a man who had suffered, yet survived, a horrific car accident.

"If you don't want the money, then I need your signature on a different document relinquishing any claims on the inheritance."

Surprise flitted across his face. Had he expected her to run away screaming?

"Did you not hear me, Miss Sutton?" He raised his chin even as he managed to look down his still-aristocratic nose at her. "I'm not signing it. Any of it."

Fine. If the man wanted to refuse billions of dollars, money that people like her parents and her neighbors back in Maine could have used to do so much with, then that was his choice. That he would prefer to throw it away rather than put it to good use angered her further and added acid to her next words.

"Then use it for something else. Drawing. Writing poetry. Perhaps making paper airplanes. My nephews get a kick out of that sort of thing."

"Do I look like the kind of man who writes poetry?" he growled.

"No."

She took a risk as she moved to the bottom of the staircase and looked up at him. He stood a few stairs above her. The light from the chandelier highlighted the left side of his face from the unblemished warm ivory of his skin to the sharp line of his jaw. Dark golden hair, thick and slightly tousled, fell over his broad forehead.

Her anger bled away. It almost seemed crueler to leave him with half of his former face. A constant reminder of who he had been.

Their gazes collided. Her heart stuttered in her chest. The heat returned, spread throughout her body and made her limbs heavy, drugged her with desire.

She blinked and stepped back, trying to get her bearings, to summon something akin to professionalism after her eruption. The scar by Griffith's mouth twisted as his lips curled back into a sneer.

"Then what kind of man do I look like, Miss Sutton?" He came down until he was just one step above her, only inches between them. "A spoiled bastard who got what was coming to him? Or maybe something simpler? A monster, perhaps?"

The last words, raw and guttural, stopped her anger in its tracks. Her gaze moved over him, registered the taut cords of muscle in his neck, the tension in his jaw twisting his scars. And behind the patrician gleam of disdain in his eyes...pain. Deep, horrible pain.

The remnants of her anger dissipated, slipped away, left her wanting to reach out and offer something, anything, to lessen the burden of such profound agony.

"No. You look like someone who's hurting."

His face twisted into an expression of disgust that made her feel small and insignificant. He stared at her, chest rising and falling, a pulse pounding in his throat. She could almost feel his heartbeat, feel the anguish that kept him in an iron grip.

Her eyes traveled from his throat up to the scarred, handsome face, her breath catching as his glittering gaze ensnared her.

"I said no. I'm not signing."

For a moment she just stared at him. Dimly she heard a howl of wind, the deeper rumble of thunder warning that the storm was getting closer.

Finally, the cold words registered and snapped her out of

her reverie. Her fury returned, eclipsing her surroundings as she let go of any hope of keeping her job.

"I would be curious to see how a man who's had everything handed to him on a diamond-encrusted platter would handle throwing out a mere mortal like myself. But no matter," she continued as his lips parted on a retort. "I've literally traipsed hundreds of miles, stood out in the pouring rain and argued with your employees the world over to just get one signature. And I'm done."

She held up the contract. Common sense whispered for her to stop, to hold back, but no. She was done playing nice with such a selfish man.

She let go, savored the thump when the file hit the table as much as she enjoyed the widening of his eyes, the thinning of his mouth.

"Have a good day, Mr. Lykaois."

She shot him a megawatt smile, inclined her head to him and then walked out of the chateau.

CHAPTER FIVE

GRIFFITH STARED AT the open door. He couldn't recall the last time someone had walked away from him. That she had done so with an attitude, acting as if *he'd* wronged *her* when she'd been the one to stalk him across the Channel and trespass on his land, had him stride across the hall to shut the door on Miss Rosalind Sutton once and for all.

He reached the door, then glanced back at the contract on the table. A seemingly innocuous stack of papers that he wanted nothing to do with. Signing them would bring an end to this mess. Stop Miss Sutton's relentless campaign.

Although if her parting words were any indication, she had no intention of seeing him ever again. Which should make him relieved.

But it didn't. Instead, the emptiness of the house pressed in on him, as did the roar of the storm growing outside. The thought of never seeing Rosalind again, a woman who had made such an incredible impact in a matter of minutes, sent an unexpected pang through the hollowness of his chest.

Damn it.

Lightning pierced the sky, followed seconds later by thunder that rattled the windows. Griffith stopped in the doorway. In the few minutes since he had come downstairs to confront Rosalind, the encroaching storm had darkened the summery landscape. Wind howled around the corner of the chateau and tore at the tops of nearby trees.

He might be a selfish bastard. But he couldn't send the lawyer away in this, could he. It was a long way back to the village and an image of her battling the wind and the rain, fighting to stay upright, came to mind. Going after her was the right thing to do, he didn't need to like it.

Griffith started down the steps, his eyes sweeping over the freshly mowed lawn, the neatly trimmed hedges bordering the front yard, the dry yet still elegant fountain, for any signs of a caramel-colored trench coat or mahogany brown curls.

Nothing. Aside from the whimsical fairy that perched on top of the fountain, he was alone.

Had she double backed and found another way into the house? Or discovered the covered patio on the north side of the house?

Movement caught his eye. His lips parted in surprise as he saw a distant figure moving toward the avenue of trees.

"Miss Sutton!" he bellowed. "Rosalind!"

The wind snatched away his words as Rosalind disappeared into the trees. Cursing, he hurried down the steps. As soon as his feet hit the drive, he ran.

He'd been a runner before the accident, had hopped back on the treadmill as soon as the doctor had cleared him. But the machine, useful as it was for letting him run while avoiding prying eyes or paparazzi, was nothing compared to the freedom of being outside, of feeling the cool whip of the wind across his face as blood pumped hot in his veins.

Alive.

He'd taken so much for granted. Lost so much.

Not this. Not yet.

He should let her go. Let her walk away.

Not yet.

Cold raindrops fell on the back of his neck. Light, but the pace picked up as he entered the avenue. Up ahead, Rosalind continued moving at a brisk pace toward the bridge.

"Miss Sutton!"

She turned, a frown appearing between her brows. She stopped and faced him, the hem of her trench coat flapping about her knees. For one wild moment, he saw her as something more, something magical and mysterious. With the wind grabbing her curls and whipping them about her beautiful face, the stubborn tilt to her pointed chin, the sparkle of life in her dark green eyes, she reminded him of an enchantress or a mischievous fairy.

"Making sure I actually leave?"

"Come back until the storm's over."

She stared at him, her lips slightly parting.

"Excuse me?"

He could barely hear her over the wind, the thunder that clashed far too close for comfort.

"It's too dangerous for you to walk. The nearest petrol station is over three kilometers away."

"You told me to go. I wouldn't want to stay where I wasn't welcome."

"That was before I realized how bad the storm was."

She shook her head even as she squinted against the shrieking wind whipping down the avenue. "I have no interest in being around you, Mr. Lykaois. I can make it to the road, call my ride and be gone before the storm gets worse."

"The storm is coming too fast. Don't be foolish."

Her eyes turned molten with anger. Before she could utter a retort, lightning flashed above their heads, spearing down through the canopy and striking the trunk of one of the trees. Thunder followed, deep and fierce. It nearly covered the sharp crack as bark splintered and the tree shifted.

He lunged, wrapped his arms around Rosalind's waist and tackled her to the ground as the towering oak shuddered and fell. They landed on the crushed shells of the drive and rolled. He kept her body pinned to his, planted his feet and stopped so that he lay on top of her.

The ground shook beneath them. He raised his head. The oak lay just a few feet away.

He turned his attention back to Rosalind. She lay beneath him, face white, eyes wide as she stared at the tree.

"Are you all right?"

Slowly, she nodded. She looked at him, then down at their bodies pressed together. A blush stole over her cheeks. The sight summoned the desire that had invaded earlier as she'd stood in the hall, beautiful in her kindness, frightening in her perceptiveness, stunning in her defiance.

He quickly shifted, rolling off her before she felt the evidence of his arousal. Standing, he held out his hand and pulled her to her feet.

His eyes followed hers to the fallen tree. Before they'd even set eyes on the house, his mother had fallen in love with the towering oaks. His father had joked they didn't even need the house, just the trees.

Centuries. The tree had stood for centuries, withstood war and changing seasons, birth and death in the manor just beyond.

Now it lay on the ground, chunks of bark scattered across the seashells like dark wounds.

A vise clamped around his heart, squeezed. His gaze moved over the leaves still clinging to the branches, then down to the jagged edges of where the tree had split from the trunk, portions of it blackened by the lightning's fury.

Foolish to get sentimental over a damned tree.

He turned his back on it, focused his attention on the woman who had drawn him out into the storm.

"Miss Sutton—"

The clouds unleashed their fury, the rain turning from a spatter to a downpour. It was impossible to see more than a few feet ahead. He grabbed her hand and yanked her forward. When she resisted, tried to pull away, he tightened his grip and tugged her close until her body pressed against his.

"We need to get back to the chateau." His lips nearly brushed her ear.

"I'm not five," she retorted. "I can make my own—"

"And get separated in this rain? Tumble into a ravine? Catch pneumonia?"

"Are those possibilities or personal fantasies?"

"My fantasy is to be warm, dry and not worrying about whether you're wandering my property or lying under a tree."

He pulled her forward again. She followed, keeping pace with his long strides as he kept his eyes on the seashells. He followed the path, catching glimpses here and there of familiar shapes beyond the rain.

Then, at last, light pierced the darkness. The lanterns on the front wall of the house glowed gold in the deluge. They stumbled up the stairs and into the grand hall. Griffith slammed the door behind them.

And immediately realized he was trapped in a hell of his own making.

Rosalind stood in the center of the hall, water dripping from her trench coat onto the tiled floor. A leaf clung to one wet curl. Mud coated her knees and streaked her calves. She stared at him with intense dislike, her lips pursed as if she was trying to hold back one of her pithy insults.

And he had never wanted a woman more than he did in that moment. A woman who had ensnared him with just the sound of her voice and her fierce tenacity in the face of adversity. Adversity he had created to keep her and everything she represented at arm's length.

Instead of faltering, she'd hit back stronger and harder. Then, when he'd resorted to petty threats, she'd stood up to him and told him exactly where to stick it.

He didn't want to like her. Didn't want to admire her. Didn't want to imagine stripping off that coat, leading her upstairs and into his palatial shower, leaving a trail of wet clothes as he pulled her beneath a steaming hot spray and—

Stop!

Indulging in those kinds of thoughts would only make this more difficult.

Although, he realized as he glanced around the hall, the situation was about as difficult as it could be. From what he'd been able to see, the tree had landed on the bridge. He would go down after the storm had passed to confirm his suspicions. But if that were true, they were stranded at the chateau until next week when the housekeeper, Beatrice, and her husband journeyed up from their village to bring food and clean.

A hard knot formed at the base of his spine as a headache began to pound away at his temples. When he'd contacted Beatrice and told her he was coming for an extended stay, she'd reminded him the chateau didn't have internet and had very unreliable cell phone reception. He'd told her those conditions would work perfectly for the isolation he sought.

Except now it had left him alone with a woman as tempting as she was infuriating…

"I'll show you to a room so you can change."

"If you just tell me—"

"No!" The thought of a stranger wandering through the house—his mother's house—filled him with anger.

Rosalind watched him from her place by the door. She

didn't tremble, didn't look away. The longer she watched him, *stared* at him, the angrier he became. Angry at her being in his house, the one place that was supposed to be safe. Angry at himself for displaying such raw emotion. Angry at the world for constantly taking, punishing, driving him closer and closer to the edge.

"Follow me," he growled.

He knew he was overreacting, despised himself as much as he despised her seemingly calm demeanor. She'd walked into a fierce storm, nearly been crushed by a tree and now followed a scarred, hollowed husk of a man up a staircase into a strange house. A man who had threatened to have her fired and, by her account, made her life miserable. Not once had she cried or complained. Up until twenty minutes ago, her name had been synonymous with irritation. The uptight, overzealous lawyer with a ridiculous umbrella who couldn't leave well enough alone.

But now...now he saw more of what he'd glimpsed that day in the Diamond Club. Confidence, strength, resilience.

No. He had survived the past year without sex, without extravagance, without anything from his old life. Too little, too late, but at least he was doing something to honor Belen. To be the man he should have been instead of the indulgent bastard who had kept his father at arm's length.

His lust for Rosalind threatened his self-imposed punishment. A whim that he would not allow himself to satisfy.

He stalked down the hallway and stopped in front of a white door trimmed in gold filigree.

"Here." He twisted the knob and opened the door. "Power should stay on with the generator—"

"Oh!"

Her breathless exclamation cut him off midsentence. She moved past him into the room, spun around in a circle with wide eyes and parted lips. Her wet hair framed her face, delicate in its shape but countered by the narrow, strong point of her chin. Rain dripped from the hem of her trench coat onto the plush wool and silk Persian carpet. She looked nothing like the sophisticated, discerning women he had dated over the years.

He shouldn't want her. Couldn't want her. Didn't deserve to want her. He could hardly stand to look at himself in the mirror, share his bed with a woman. Indulging his own whims, his own desire, was out of the question.

Rosalind shot him a huge smile, one that made her eyes crinkle at the corners and a tiny dimple appear on one side of her mouth.

"This room is incredible." Her eyes softened. "Thank you, Mr. Lykaois. For saving—"

"Don't."

The smile faded from her face. A part of him mourned the loss, wanted to do something to bring back the radiance.

But that would only prolong the torture.

"You're staying here so you don't get killed on my property and someone sues."

The words tasted sharp, bitter. The brief flicker of surprise and pity in her eyes drove it home.

"Of course." She turned her back to him then, dismissing him. "I'll be gone as soon as the storm clears."

She didn't even look at him as she turned and moved to the window, pulled aside the filmy curtain to gaze out into the wall of rain.

Griffith strode out, managing to refrain from slamming the door behind him as he headed for the stairs. Miss Sutton had already stirred up his emotions, piqued his curiosity. She hadn't flinched at the sight of his face, true. But what would she do if she saw the worst of the wounds that cut over his ribs, snaked along his thigh and down his leg?

It didn't matter. She would never see them. He wouldn't allow himself to surrender to the inferno raging through him. Not with the woman who wanted him to acknowledge that his father was gone, her actions rubbing salt in the wound of his culpability.

If I would have been paying attention...if I wouldn't have been angry...

It didn't change anything. Never would. His father wasn't coming back.

He entered the library and set about making a fire. The rough scrape of the wood on his palms, the scent of smoke, grounded him, gave him something to focus on beside thoughts of Miss Sutton moving about on the floor above.

He hurled the last log onto the fire. Sparks shot up, glittering red and orange and crackling up into the air before falling back down. Some littered the edge of the hearth, pulsing with a hypnotic glow.

Rosalind was the kind of woman he had always stayed away from. The kind of woman who wanted compassion, affection, love. Things he was incapable of giving. Her enthrallment with her room, her gratitude and, most telling of all, her perception of his pain before she'd walked out into the storm, told him all he needed to know. Fierce but kind. Determined but empathetic.

She deserved someone who could fulfill her needs, not just physical but emotional. When he'd withdrawn into himself following his mother's death, latched on to the solidity of his vices, the immediate distraction and pleasure they brought, he knew he'd been turning his back on the traditional things: a wedding, marriage, children. Now, even if he wanted to change that, he'd lived a life of isolation for so long he couldn't feel much of anything except the rawness of grief and intensity of self-loathing.

He stopped in front of the window, stared out at the wind-tossed sea. Then saw his reflection in the glass. His hand came up, touched the ugly ridges of the largest scar that snaked down his face. Scars that had disgusted Kacey, caused more than one person in his life to look away, unable to meet his eyes without staring.

Rosalind hadn't. She'd faced him without flinching. He hadn't missed the answering flicker of desire in her own eyes. What would she do if she knew the extent of his own lust? The almost animalistic need to claim her body, which had seethed beneath the surface ever since he'd seen her in London?

Miss Sutton had nothing to fear from his visible scars. It was the cold, dark bastard who lurked inside him who should frighten her most of all.

CHAPTER SIX

ROSALIND AWOKE TO a faint glow behind the curtains. She lay still beneath the comforter, luxuriating in the feel of actual silk against her skin.

When she'd walked into the room the night before, it had been like walking into a fairy tale. Hardwood floors with streaks of gray and tan had gleamed beneath the light of an actual chandelier hanging from the tall ceiling. Antique furniture in various shades of blue and trimmed in toffee-colored wood, from the navy chairs situated in front of a white stone fireplace to a periwinkle blue fainting couch arranged in front of the massive windows, had been polished to perfection. Paintings adorned the walls, all of them featuring various seascapes or the surrounding cliffs.

And the bed…the glorious bed had sat on a raised dais with actual curtains gathered with gold ropes at the corners. The number of pillows would have made her father and brothers roll their eyes.

But it had been perfect. Even with the ocean obscured by the rain and the gloominess of the man who had escorted her upstairs, it had eased the iron grip that tension had kept on her chest since she'd dropped the file on the table and left the chateau.

It had also been a much-needed balm for the chaos that had scraped her heart raw in just one hour. She'd lost control and insulted the highest profile client she'd ever worked for. Then, when she'd been so close to freedom, she'd almost been crushed by an ancient oak.

And rescued by the very man she'd offended moments before.

She pulled a pillow over her face and groaned into it. Yes, it had been terrifying to realize how close she'd come to getting hurt or even killed during the storm. But she'd lived through her fair share of nor'easters and even the occasional hurricane growing up on Maine's rugged coast. She'd learned resilience at a young age.

What unsettled her more was her reaction to Griffith and his unexpected bravery. The man had gone from selfish bastard to selfless hero with one act. It had confused her, made some of the respect and curiosity she'd experienced when she'd first researched him resurface.

His anger, too, had intrigued her. Not that she was going to put up with being his emotional punching bag for whatever issues he was dealing with. But his reaction to her being in the chateau, to her appreciation for the room, had seemed rooted in something other than simple selfishness. As she'd told him before she had—yes, foolishly—walked out into the storm, he seemed like he was in pain. Not just grief, but something more, something deeper.

Frustrated with herself for ruminating on him, she sat up and tossed a pillow across the room. What was the point in thinking about him? Wasting time and energy theorizing about his hang-ups when he had made it clear he wanted her gone as soon as she was able to? Honestly, she thought as she threw back the covers, it was a good thing he'd left her alone last night. She'd been vulnerable, susceptible to her feelings of gratitude and attraction. Yes, the man was ridiculously handsome. But she had held out this long on having sex. Had rebuffed advances from men far kinder as she waited for the right one, the one she felt both an emotional and physical connection to. When she finally took a lover, it would be someone she could potentially see a future with.

No matter how intriguing or exciting Griffith Lykaois was, he was the exact opposite definition of a long-term boyfriend. He would tempt a woman to indulge, enjoy, lose herself in pleasure.

And then he'd be gone just as quickly as he'd arrived.

What she needed to do now was get up, gather her things and get out of here. Make a plan for how she would drop the news to Mr. Nettleton about the unsigned contract. Make a contingency plan in case he decided to fire her or in case Griffith had already called to demand the same thing.

She stopped her runaway thoughts. Breathed in deep.

You had a bath in an actual claw-foot tub last night. Focus on the positives.

Her stomach rumbled. She had eaten a late lunch in Étretat before she'd set out for the Chateau du Bellerose. The chaos of the afternoon, including dealing with Griffith Lykaois and nearly getting squished by a centuries-old oak, had driven any thoughts of hunger from her head. After she'd gotten out of the tub, exhaustion had enticed her into bed.

She slipped out from under the sheets and the pleasant weight of the down comforter. Cool air kissed her bare skin. It had been odd sleeping nude, but her clothes had been soaked, from her favorite coat down to her underwear. She pulled a light, airy blanket off the corner of the bed and wrapped it around her body as she moved to the windows. She drew back the curtains.

And caught her breath.

Behind the house lay an incredible garden, one full of winding paths made of what looked like the same crushed seashells as the drive and encircled by a towering ivy hedge. There were occasional trees, including a willow with long strands of leaves that flirted with the surface of a pond. Benches had been added, too, and an occasional statue.

But the pièce de résistance was the roses. Hundreds and hundreds of roses in varying shades of red, pink and white. Crimson blooms climbed over a stone archway. Softer colored flowers that reminded her of ballet slippers spilled from a stone urn. Ivory roses adorned row after row of bushes.

Grief slid in, quiet at first. But it grew, slow and steady, until her body was heavy and her joy disappeared.

She moved to the windows and leaned her head against the cool glass. It had been two years since she'd gotten the first phone call from her father. Her mother had come down with a mild but persistent fever just a month after recovering from what had seemed to be a mild bout of pneumonia. She'd video-called home, seen Mom propped up in bed and rolling her eyes as Dad had fussed over her. Her mom had asked her about her classes, if she was dating anyone, the mother-daughter railroad trip they had planned for the summer that would take them from Italy to Monaco.

It had all seemed so ordinary. Just a simple fever.

Then the second phone call had come at two in the morning. The tension in her father's voice, the hint of panic underlying his thick Maine accent, had set her nerves on edge before he'd even told her that her mother's fever had spiked and she was in the hospital. It was the first time her mother had been to a hospital in over two decades, the last time for the birth of Rosalind's youngest brother.

Rosalind had hung up and started packing as she purchased a ticket home. She'd been walking into the airport when her phone had rung again.

"Rose…"

Goose bumps had covered Rosalind's arms as her mother's raspy voice descended into a coughing fit.

"Mom?"

"Darling… I'm so proud of you."

"I know, Mom."

"Never stop living your life to the fullest. Reaching for… reaching for those goals."

Another hacking cough came over the line, sending cold fingers of fear down Rosalind's spine.

"You'll be a senior lawyer at Nettleton & Thompson one day. I know it. You won't give up on that, will you?"

"I won't." Her fingers tightened around the phone as her heart hammered in her chest. "I'll make you proud, Mom. And when we go to Italy this summer we'll—"

"Italy…" Her mother's voice turned dreamy, as if coming from some faraway place. "Such a fun trip."

"Mom…"

"Yes, darling?"

She stood in the middle of Chicago's O'Hare Airport, passengers streaming by, tears pouring down her face as she clung to her phone, like if she held tight enough she could keep her mother tethered to this earth through sheer will.

"I love you, Mom."

"I love you, my baby girl. My pretty rose."

Rosalind closed her eyes against the hot sting of tears. Time had softened the sharpest edges of her grief. Yet there were times like now, moments she knew her mother would have embraced with a delighted smile and a hearty laugh, that brought it rushing back as if it were yesterday.

She'd known when her father had taken the phone from her mother, had told her that things weren't going well, that she wasn't going to make it. That hadn't stopped her from boarding the flight and paying the extra charge for Wi-Fi to stay in touch with her brothers as she'd flown north.

The plane had been just south of the Great Lakes when she'd gotten the message. Her mother, her biggest champion and her best friend, had passed. She'd spent the rest of the flight with her face turned to the window, tears streaming silently down her cheeks.

She opened her eyes and stared out at the sea. The weeks she'd spent at home had passed in a gray haze, with many hours spent on the dock that jutted out into the bay, sometimes crying, other times just staring at the horizon. Always awash in grief, an aching loss that haunted her every waking moment.

She'd always been able to see the good in everything, to focus on the positive, just like her mother. But this…it had shaken her foundation, introduced true sorrow into her life. Moving to London, to her internship at Nettleton & Thompson, had been the lifeline she'd desperately needed to pull her out of her heartache. She'd thrown herself into her work. Knowing that she had made her parents proud, that she had achieved everything her mother had dreamed for her, had kept her going for the past two years.

And it had sustained her. At least to start with. It hadn't stopped discontent from starting to creep in, to fester, especially in the last month or so. A feeling that in her quest to be a responsible, mature individual, to do everything her parents had expected of her, she'd missed out on something crucial.

She was liked well enough at work, occasionally shared lunch with her coworkers. But she didn't go out with them for dinner, to clubs or on weekend trips to the Continent. She rarely dated. When she did, it was someone she had met through work. Conversations inevitably turned to the legal field and the dates ended up feeling more like a job interview than something romantic.

Even the one thing she did make time for, reading, had become a chore instead of a source of relaxation as she'd prepared herself for a potential promotion. Instead of romances and cozy mysteries, she'd read legal briefs, case studies and samples of wills until she could recite them in her sleep.

She was good at finding the happy things in life. But when was the last time she had enjoyed a long lunch? Said yes to a coworker's invitation to go out or traveled outside the comforts of London?

A year. Maybe more.

Past the garden lay a meadow of tall grasses swaying in the breeze. Then a cliff, and beyond that the ocean, the same deep and mesmerizing blue as the pillows on her bed, the throw tossed over one of the chairs by the fireplace.

Her brows drew together. Someone had gone to a great deal of trouble to maintain this house, keep it in working order. Yet from what she could tell, Griffith Lykaois was the only person in residence. He hadn't been here in the past month. Did he pay to have someone keep it like this? If so, why? Did he come here often? Why this place and not one of his other properties?

She shook her head. It didn't matter. Griffith Lykaois's intentions and preferences were his own. The only choice she cared about was whether or not he signed for his inheritance.

A thought came as she turned away from the window and the spectacular view, one that filled her with resolve and cautious hope. As much as she could have done without the almost getting flattened by a tree, she could see the storm had been a blessing. It had given her a second chance to catch her breath, refocus her attention and secure his signature before she left.

Concentrating on business had the added benefit of shifting her attention away from the memory of Griffith's brooding stare and the decadent desire he could inspire with a single glance.

She padded into the bathroom. Another work of art, she thought with a small smile, and larger than her childhood living room. The claw-foot tub she'd soaked in last night had been installed before a bay of windows, which, by the light of day, she could now see also overlooked the rose garden and the sea. A shower made of black tile and a wall of glass with not one but two waterfall showerheads in the ceiling took up most of the back wall. Marble counters and gleaming silver fixtures shone under the glow of elegant wall sconces.

A distant knock pulled her out of her reverie. She walked out into the bedroom just as the door swung open.

"Wait!"

"Miss Sutton…"

Griffith's voice trailed off as his eyes landed on her blanket-clad figure.

Shock froze her in place. His gaze moved from her face down to the thin material she clutched to her breasts.

The atmosphere shifted, heated as his eyes sharpened, traveled down over her legs and bare feet before moving back up to her face. Her nipples hardened into tight points and pressed against the fabric. Mortification and desire clashed, melded into a heat that spread throughout her body.

Their gazes met, locked. In the bright light of day, his scars were more vivid. Most were paler in color, but the one that cut through a thick brow and around his eye was still red.

The wounds didn't detract from his sheer handsomeness. They added complexity, depth to the chiseled features. The cleft in his chin interrupted the nearly perfect line of a strong jaw covered by a well-trimmed beard.

And his eyes…right now they glimmered, a dark blue that somehow burned as he watched her.

A voice whispered in her ear, dared her to do something outrageous like let the blanket fall. To place the ball in his court and see what happened next. She'd been waiting her whole life for the right man, the perfect man, to share her body with. Each man she'd gone to dinner with, kissed, had fallen short somehow. Some had simply not been a good fit. Others had been cordial, kind, interesting.

But none had done this. Set her body aflame with a single look.

"I knocked."

"I didn't hear you."

God, was that her voice? Breathless, husky?

"The tree fell onto the bridge."

She blinked and just like that, the fire was gone from his eyes. The cold, controlled man from the night was back, his voice authoritative and sterile.

"What?"

"The tree," he repeated, as if she was a child not paying attention. "It fell onto the bridge."

Unease fluttered in her stomach.

"So…what does that mean?"

"It means until someone can come up here and remove the tree and test the bridge, make sure it's safe, you're to remain here."

She stifled her alarm, took in a deep breath.

"Okay. I understand. When will someone be by?"

"Probably a week."

Her mouth dropped open.

"A week?"

"Yes."

"But…why so long?"

"Because that will be the first time Madame Beatrice and her husband will be back to restock the kitchen and any missing supplies."

"Why don't we just call someone?"

"No reception." He arched a brow. The scar added a dangerous, almost thrilling edge to the gesture. "Surely you noticed last night?"

"When I was walking up, yes, but I assumed you'd have reception here."

"No. Eventually I'll have something installed out here for phone and internet."

Unease morphed into dread.

"I can't just stay here."

"Unless you plan on climbing down into a one-hundred-foot gorge before scaling the other side, or swimming around the cliffs to the nearest beach, you're not going anywhere."

"What if there's an emergency?"

He shrugged. "It was supposed to be just me."

The part that went unsaid, that he appeared to care less whether or not something happened to him, stirred her sympathy. They'd both lost a parent, but he was now alone in the world. No brothers to call and tease him, no father to send small gifts from back home.

"I'm sorry."

He blinked, as if surprised by her apology.

"Too late now."

Her sympathy evaporated.

"Are you always this charming?"

"Always."

Her eyes narrowed. Could that have been a hint of humor in his voice?

It doesn't matter.

She had seven more days to get the contract signed and

back to London. If the housekeeper and her husband made it up in six days, that left her one day. One day for the tree to be removed, the bridge deemed safe and for her to get back home.

Her mind scrambled, tried to find a solution that wasn't foolish or unsafe but didn't cut it so close to her deadline.

And came up with zilch.

"Okay." She squared her shoulders. She'd faced down bickering relatives and bloodthirsty rivals in the legal world. She could handle one week at a remote chateau with a less than friendly host. "What do we do?"

He shrugged. "I don't care what you do. You may use the common spaces and the grounds. Help yourself to what's in the kitchen. But," he said, his voice dropping into something dark and almost menacing, "stay off the third floor. My office and private quarters."

"I'll have no trouble with that," she grumbled under her breath.

"And don't expect me to entertain you."

"I have no desire to be entertained by you," she shot back with a sweet smile. "The only thing I desire is your signature on one contract or the other so that after this unfortunate week is over, we can never see each other again."

A laugh escaped him, dry and rough, as if he hadn't used his voice for such a purpose in a very long time.

"You're trying to discuss business while you're wearing nothing but a blanket?"

She narrowed her eyes at him. "It certainly beats my only alternative at the moment."

No sooner had the words left her mouth than his eyes slid down again to her breasts. The tension returned, so hot and heavy it was a wonder she didn't start sweating. His hands clenched, unclenched by his sides. It wasn't the only sign that he was affected by what she'd just said. Her own gaze wandered over the dark gray sweater that clung to his broad chest, the hint of hair curling at the base of his throat, then farther down still to the noticeable bulge beneath his black pants.

She swallowed hard. She wasn't a stranger to what happened when men grew aroused. The last time she'd gone out and her date had pulled her close for a long kiss goodnight, she'd felt how much he'd wanted her pressed against her lower belly. The weight of his desire had sparked nothing but a mild curiosity. She certainly hadn't been curious enough to take things further.

Now, though, just the sight of Griffith's hard length straining against his pants had her own thighs growing damp with arousal.

"Don't you have something else to wear?" he snapped.

She lifted her chin up in the air. He was the one who had invaded her privacy.

"Once my dress is dry, yes."

He turned and walked out, slamming the door behind him. She released a pent-up breath.

What was that?

A shudder moved through her body, delicious and slightly wild. Never had she been tempted to do something as audacious as seduce a man. Let him see all of her. Let him see how quickly and easily she had been turned on by his presence. That had been part of the problem—really *the* problem—with the men she'd dated. None of them had made her feel the way she wanted to feel with her first lover. They checked the boxes of kind, attentive, thoughtful. But the physical attraction, the desire, had never appeared.

Her roommate in college had told her on numerous occasions her expectations were too high. Her mother had told her to trust herself. That when she found the right man, she would know.

Not someone like *him*. Brooding, solitary and downright rude. Although, she thought with a twist of her lips, he had at least done her the favor of showing her what was possible.

A carnal image appeared in her mind, of Griffith yanking the blanket from her hands, scooping her up in his arms and lowering her to the bed, before standing back and peeling his sweater away from chiseled abs—

Three loud knocks sounded on her door. He was back.

She waited for Griffith to storm back in, to renew their argument, but he didn't. Silence reigned.

Finally, she walked across the room and cracked the door. A trunk—an actual steamer trunk—sat in front of the door. It had been painted an olive green and trimmed in black leather with gold accents. But there was no sign of Griffith.

Keeping one hand firmly on the blanket, she grabbed hold of one black leather handle and pulled the trunk inside, casting one more glance up and down the hall before closing the door and locking it. She undid the latch and pushed the lid up.

A rainbow of material greeted her. She reached down, ran a finger over red silk, periwinkle linen and daisy-yellow cotton. One by one she pulled out dresses, skirts, shirts and a pair of pants, until nearly twenty garments lay across the bed. All of them still had tags attached, all sporting the same floral design and the name of a designer she knew only by reputation. The kind of designer with a storefront on Bond Street in London's high-end Mayfair district.

Did Griffith keep clothes around for potential visiting lovers? She should be thankful he had anything for her to wear at all, but the thought made her surprisingly irritated. Pushing it aside, she settled on a forest green dress with matching buttons running from the sweetheart neckline over the cinched waist and down to the hem of the full skirt. Simple yet luxurious as she dropped the blanket and pulled the dress on, the linen caressing her skin.

She moved to the full-length mirror by the fireplace. Spun in a circle and grinned as the skirt flared out.

It was not how she had planned on spending her time in France. But with a trunk full of designer clothes she'd never get to wear again, a stunning bedroom overlooking the sea and nearly a week to convince Mr. Griffith Lykaois to sign, things were certainly looking up.

With that encouraging thought in mind, she turned and picked the blanket up off the floor. The feel of the fabric in her hands made her remember Griffith's heated gaze fixed on her breasts, his jaw tight and his fingers curled into fists at his sides, as if he could barely hold himself back.

Her hands tightened on the blanket before she balled it up and threw it into a corner. She could have a good week, could make it into something positive, if she kept her erotic imagination under control.

A walk, she decided. She'd go for a walk first.

And hope the cool sea air would knock some sense into her, starting with the fact that she had a job to do and Griffith Lykaois was the last man on earth she should be fantasizing about.

CHAPTER SEVEN

GRIFFITH'S FINGERS TIGHTENED around his pen as the sound of a door closing drifted in through the open window. Unless a ghost had taken up residence, it could only be one person.

He would prefer the ghost. Perhaps it would haunt him less than Miss Rosalind Sutton.

He hadn't seen her in two days. Not since the morning she'd walked out of the en suite bathroom clad in nothing but that gauzy blue blanket that had clung to the curves of her breasts and wrecked his control.

Never had he wanted a woman as badly as he'd wanted her in that moment. Sunlight had pierced the thin material, highlighted the nip to her waist, the flare of her hips, her long legs. Her curls had had a mind of their own, spreading around her head like an auburn-colored halo.

And those eyes...large, framed by dark lashes, innocent.

The answering heat that had flickered in the green depths had catapulted his lust into something so fierce and reckless he'd had no choice but to leave. His self-control was resting on a knife's edge. Retreating was the only option. It was what he was good at. Keeping himself out of emotion's way.

Surprisingly, she had left him alone. It was for the best. At least that was what Griffith told himself as he tried to focus on anything but the woman whose mere presence tormented him.

Fortunately, he had plenty to do, even without the modern

wonders of technology. He had brought printouts of finances, shipping routes and summaries from each of the members of the executive boards, which he'd requested a month ago. Summaries that included what they had achieved during his sabbatical, what they wanted to change and, most importantly, what they wanted to see in the future. His father had done the company proud, had celebrated success even as he'd kept a constant eye on opportunities to grow. A continuation of the legacy Griffith's grandfather had started when he'd turned a few shipping boats into an empire. A legacy Griffith was determined to follow.

You don't deserve to lead. You're not even half the man they were.

He smothered the intrusive thoughts. He hadn't been deserving before. But he would be. He would never make the same selfish mistakes ever again.

Having work to focus on would also help him maintain control.

With that resolution in mind, he'd sat down at the oversize walnut desk, three levels of bookcases soaring up to the ceiling in front of him and the large windows overlooking the rose garden at his back. An ideal environment to jot down notes and make the most of his sudden desire to be productive.

Except every time he sat down to work, thoughts interfered. Thoughts of dark bouncy curls framing an angelic face that hid a surprisingly strong character. Thoughts of a slender body clad only in a blanket, the material following curves his fingers itched to touch, and long legs that he had envisioned, more than once, wrapped around his waist as he drove himself inside her.

Cursing, he stood and threw the pen down on the desk. It was only understandable, he reassured himself, that he was entertaining thoughts of himself and Rosalind tangled up in his bed. It had been well over a year since he'd had sex.

Was that why the attraction he was now feeling for the feisty and determined lawyer was so strong? So all-consuming.

He stalked to the window. Not only did he want nothing to do with her damned envelope full of papers, with resolving his father's estate, but he also wanted—no, *needed*—to keep his distance from her and the temptation she presented. Jumping into bed with a woman he'd just met would be repeating his past sins. Placing pleasure above more important things like taking up the reins of Lykaois Shipping.

Or serving out his punishment for the way he'd lived for the past thirteen years. Focusing on hedonistic pursuits and material goods instead of maintaining a relationship with a father who had experienced his own loss.

A punishment that seemed all the more just when he allowed himself to remember how things had been before Elizabeth Lykaois's death. Yes, he'd been raised in luxury, traveling frequently between his mother's native England and his father's home in Greece. But he'd never once doubted his parents' love, had been secure in a way he knew few children were. He'd been drawn to the finer things in life. Belen had even cautioned him about his preference for new cars and dating around in his first couple of years at university. The tone then, however, had been one of paternal warmth, of sharing words of wisdom with a boy turning into a man.

Not the cold disappointment that had followed as Griffith had spiraled out of control after Elizabeth's swift illness and shocking passing. Once he started, once pleasure eclipsed anguish, it had been impossible to turn back.

And every time his father had reached out, every time Griffith had been tempted to sit down and have a heart-to-heart with his father, he'd backed out of it, unable to bear it. His father had represented love, family. Things that demanded he open his heart and deal with his pain.

So he'd run. Run in the opposite direction and welcomed anything and everything that would distract him. And ignored, to his detriment, the small part of him that wanted to reconnect with his father. To grieve with his father.

A part he now realized he should have paid more attention to.

His lips twisted into a grimace. It was awful to have a life-changing realization after it was too late to do something about it.

Griffith glanced out the window at the gardens. They had been his mother's pride and joy. When one of his father's solicitors had shared the real estate listing for the chateau, his mother had fallen in love with it. The black gates had been rusted and falling off the hinges. The roses had grown wild, tangling over the sidewalks and up the walls. The mosaic in the grand hall had been chipped, some of the tiles missing. Even then he had been drawn to the modern, the contemporary, seeing more value in the designs of the future rather than getting stuck in the past. His father had been a mix, appreciating aspects of both history and the future. But his mother, while she had appreciated innovation, had been in love with history.

Nowhere was this more evident than in the chateau and all the loving work that she had put in to restoring it to its former glory. The year before she'd gotten sick, she had spent almost every waking hour at the manor, working alongside bricklayers and restoration specialists, learning the craft and pouring in as much of her own blood, sweat and tears as she expected from the workers.

At the time, he had been proud of her, with her dust-covered face and big happy grin as she stood in a pair of overalls. She'd held a paint roller in one hand and a glass of wine in the other as she'd celebrated the completion of the painting of the great hall with her husband and son.

Yet as his grief had taken over after her death, he'd come to resent the chateau. It had started small at first, wondering if she hadn't been so caught up in the restoration if she might have noticed the little signs of her illness sooner. Then his father had invited him down to tour the finished home just a few months after the funeral. It had been too soon. He had declined, seen the hurt in Belen's eyes. By not going, he had started a snowball effect that would affect his relationship with his father the rest of his life.

But he hadn't been able to bring himself to step a foot back into the house that he associated with her. The house that should have brought joy and instead only served as a reminder of what would never be.

It had been around that time that he had thrown himself into what his father had described more than once as a self-indulgent lifestyle. The never-ending carousel of trips, luxury cars, yacht parties and one-night stands. By the time he'd hit thirty and realized that his way of life could only be sustained by buying more, doing more, to fill the always present chasm his mother's death had carved out inside him, he hadn't known any other way to exist.

And, he admitted to himself as he stared out the window at the roses, now tamed and flush with summer beauty, the thought of trying something new, of putting effort into overcoming his grief, had seemed insurmountable.

Coward.

A movement caught his eye and tore him out of the past. Rosalind walked down the steps of the patio and into the garden. She wore a creamy blouse tucked into a dark blue skirt that circled her waist and fell in soft folds past her knees. He did a double take as he realized that her feet were bare.

When he had realized that she had no clothes except the

dress she'd worn, he'd gone up to the attic. His mother had never been able to resist supporting aspiring artists and designers, ranging from painters and sculptors to aspiring fashion moguls. Many of them had found their success under her patronage and had sent her gifts, including their own work, as thanks. He had recognized the label on one of the trunks, now an international fashion powerhouse. Knowing his mother had never even seen the garments had helped him steel himself against the sudden onslaught of emotion.

Also knowing that Rosalind would be wearing clothes instead of that damned blanket had helped as well.

She wore them well, he thought as he watched her move about the gardens, wandering along the stone path, stopping here and there to smell a flower. Casual, but elegant, they brought out her natural beauty. Her curls lent her a youthful air. But the confident set of her shoulders, the delighted smile on her face as she smelled a rose the same pale orange as the sky at dawn, made him all too aware of the fact that she was a woman.

She ran one finger over the petal of a rose. The sight made him hard in an instant.

You're a grown man, not a prepubescent teenager.

His body ignored the lecture from his rational mind as blood pumped through his veins. He should turn away, needed to get back to work.

One more second. Just one.

She stopped, frowned. Threw one last look of longing at the flowers before she moved back to a table on the patio and sat down with a sheaf of papers. Working, no doubt. Trying to figure out how to convince him to sign those damned papers.

The woman wouldn't know how to have fun if it bit her.

You could show her.

No, he couldn't. That part of his life was over.

The sound of a chime drifted up through the open window.

He saw her glance at her phone, could sense even from here the sudden tension that gripped her. The occasional phone call or text message would still occasionally slip through.

Who was reaching out to her? Her boss? Her parents? Perhaps a boyfriend? Just the thought of another man talking to her, kissing her, touching her, filled him with an unexpected pulsing rage.

Cursing, he turned away from the window and went back to his desk. Was he so desperate for connection, so starved for physical affection, that he had taken to spying on a guest, no matter how unwelcome she was? To creating imaginary lovers to vent his frustration and anger on? Succumbing to jealousy, an emotion he'd never experienced before?

He managed to refocus on a proposal from a board member about expanding their shipping routes to include the Northwest Passage the following summer. A move that would save ships currently navigating through the Panama Canal thousands of miles, not to mention time, fuel and money.

The proposal, well written and well-thought-out, drew him in. So deeply engrossed was he in reading that it took him a moment to realize someone was knocking on his door.

He looked up just as the door swung open. Rosalind stood in the doorway. Her fingers plucked at her skirt as she hesitated on the threshold of the room he'd told her to avoid.

Shocked that she would defy a direct order, furious that she had done so, he remained seated. Let the silence stretch between them.

"I…" A deep blush crept over her cheeks. "I need to speak with you."

"I told you to stay away from my office."

"I know. I—"

"But you decided to invade?" He stood then, a thin thread of humor beneath the quiet anger in his voice. He slowly circled around the desk like a predator stalking its prey. "Tres-

pass? Ignore any and all common decency because you
wanted something and damn anyone else who might get in
your way?"

She swallowed hard as he prowled toward her. But she
didn't back down. He hated that he liked her for that. Hated
that even with fury pounding through him he noticed details
he shouldn't, like the swell of her breasts pressing against her
shirt, the rapid pulse dancing at the base of her neck.

"I need to talk to you."

"So you said. And I told you I had no interest in speaking to you."

Her eyes narrowed. "Did you ever stop to ask me what I
wanted? Or do you just toss out orders and expect people to
obey them without question?"

"Yes."

"That's not how I operate, Mr. Lykaois. I talk to people,
ask them what they want, engage with them."

"Then you're in the wrong business, Miss Sutton."

Her lips parted as something flickered in her eyes. She
glanced away, then back at him so quickly he would have
missed it if he hadn't been looking right at her.

"I'm good at what I do."

He walked back around the desk, put much-needed distance and a physical barrier between them.

"Apparently not good enough."

Instead of bursting into tears or responding with fiery
words of her own, she merely cocked her head to one side and
pinned him with that mossy green gaze that saw far too much.

"Does it work for you?"

"What?"

"This impenetrable shield you've got going on."

She stepped closer. The muscles in his back tensed. Suddenly he felt cornered, with the windows at his back and fiery
temptation in front of him.

"You snap at people. Say horrible things to push them away." Another step closer. The faint scent of jasmine reached him, teased him with its alluring dark floral fragrance. "But I think there's something else going on."

"I didn't realize you had a degree in psychology, too."

"No, just good people skills. You keep people at arm's length because then you don't have to try."

His mouth dried. "Excuse me?"

"When you're rude to people, you set a precedent. No need to try, no need to make nice when people don't expect it of you. Then you can hide in your Kent estate or your secret London club or wherever and just…" She threw her hands up in the air, as if trying to physically grab onto the words that eluded her. "Just wallow in your pain and misery."

"Wallow?"

If she caught the dangerous edge to his voice, she didn't show it as she held his gaze.

"Yes. I lost my mother a few years ago. I know it's hard to move on from—"

"You know nothing."

He ground the words out, watched as her eyes widened in alarm. She saw too much, made him want too much, feel too damned much. She had the perception, the power, to rip away every wall he'd built and leave him with nothing except the pain he'd managed to keep at bay for thirteen years.

She threatened his very sanity. He needed her gone, out of his office, out of his life.

Now.

"Don't try to build a bridge between us, Miss Sutton. There is no common ground. Yes, we both lost our mothers. But that is where the similarities between us end. If you think sharing the *woe is me* details of your life will somehow make me sign that contract, then think again."

Too far.

He'd gone too far. She didn't cry, didn't yell, didn't even blink. But he could feel the change in the air, the cold creep in as her heart hardened against him and his reckless words.

Ashamed, his eyes flickered to the side, caught sight of his reflection in the glass of a painting hanging on the wall. The scars twisting down his face, distorting his once handsome visage into something unnatural and beastly.

Monstrous.

That was what Kacey had called him. And she was right. The way he acted could be monstrous. But how else could he protect himself?

"No, I don't know your whole story, Mr. Lykaois, or what losing your mother was like." The compassion beneath her cool words only deepened his guilt. "I think you're punishing yourself." A board creaked. The scent of jasmine grew stronger, sweet yet seductive. "But have you ever stopped to think, for even one moment, that you're punishing everyone else around you, too?"

It was as if someone had reached down his throat, wrapped their hands around his lungs and squeezed every ounce of air from his body. He couldn't speak, could barely think, as the shocking weight of her words penetrated and left him adrift in a new reality.

One where, once again, he had made himself the center of it all.

He recovered just enough to say what he should have said the moment she came to his office door.

"Get out." The icy calm in his voice belied the storm raging inside him.

With the faintest rustling of her skirt, Rosalind turned and did exactly that.

CHAPTER EIGHT

ROSALIND PAUSED LONG enough to pull on a pair of slippers she'd brought downstairs before she hurried out the door onto the patio. Heart pounding, eyes aching with unshed tears, she rushed down the stairs and into the garden.

She'd gone to Griffith's office to bring up the contract again. She knew it was wrong, knew he'd told her to stay away. But a text Mr. Nettleton had sent yesterday had come through, demanding to know why she hadn't sent him a daily report. It hadn't been too hard to imagine the barrage of missed calls, texts and emails that would be waiting for her when she finally got back into an area of full service. It had galvanized her to action.

The last two days had been spent distracting herself with work, reviewing documents she had thankfully packed in her briefcase for the new clients she would take on after she completed the Lykaois contract. She had told herself she just needed to give Griffith time to adjust to her being at the chateau. That one day she would come down and he would at least be in the hall, the kitchen, somewhere other than hiding away.

This had marked the third morning she'd come down to an eerily empty house. Nettleton's text, combined with her exasperation over Griffith's immature behavior, had spurred her on as she'd climbed the stairs to the third floor. It had been long enough since their last encounter over the contract. Surely, he could take five minutes and listen to his options.

Except he hadn't. And then he'd been cruel. Like a wounded animal lashing out. His pain touched her empathetic nature, tugged at the strands of her own grief of losing her mother.

But it had also done what he'd intended it to do. Hurt her until she had no choice but to turn away before she let him see just how deeply his words affected her. How his insinuation about her career path chipped away at her already eroding self-confidence. How his accusation that she would use her mother's death to connect with him and entice him to sell struck at her heart.

As she walked down the path, she glanced to her left. A small tunnel of ivy beckoned to her, curving just a few feet ahead so she couldn't see what lay at the end.

Needing something, anything, to distract her, she stepped inside. Coolness enveloped her as the thick netting of ivy shut out the sunlight. She followed the twists and turns of the tunnel, running her fingers over the thick, smooth leaves.

Slowly, she became aware of a dull roaring. Anticipation built as the sound grew louder and the ivy began to thin. She turned another corner, saw the sunlight up ahead and, beyond that, the beautiful blue of the sea.

She emerged onto a plateau thick with wild grasses and flowers. Wind rose up over the nearby cliffs, tumbled across the plain and stirred the stalks of grass into a frenzy.

Mindful of the cliff's edge, she walked until she was twenty feet or so away from it. Being unfamiliar with the terrain, she had no desire to end this eventful journey with the ground suddenly giving way and falling into the ocean.

A glimmer of white caught her eye. Turning, her breath caught.

A couple kilometers down the coast, the ocean curved into a shallow bay. The plateau jutted out far enough that she could see a sandy beach backed by soaring white cliffs and topped with green grass. The cliffs nearest to her jutted out into the ocean and formed an arch. Beyond that, at the far end of the beach, a single pillar of white jutted up from the waves, the top narrowing into a point.

The setting from the painting. Even though the painting had been stunning, it didn't hold a candle to the view in front of her.

It was odd to see the cluster of buildings beyond that. To know there were people so close and yet so far away.

Her lips curved up. Even if she lost her job, lost the respect of her family and friends back home, she would have moments like these to remember from her chaotic adventure. Moments that made her feel…content. Peaceful. Like herself.

She wrapped her arms around her waist. If the worst happened and she did lose her job, the hardest part would be telling her father. It had been her parents' dream for her to go to college, to travel and see the world. Since Rosalind had entertained those dreams herself, it hadn't bothered her much that her parents had been so adamant about certain things. Her ability to find the good had helped, too. Even when something hadn't felt quite right, had felt more like a wish of her parents' rather than her own, she hadn't known what she wanted enough to take a different path.

But now, as she faced the truth that she wanted something far different than what her parents had envisioned for her, she was also confronting the very real possibility of letting her father down. Of seeing his face crumple as he realized his daughter wouldn't be a powerful attorney at a distinguished law firm in London. That she might very well own a hole-in-the-wall office helping single parents and grandmothers instead of wealthy CEOs and political powerhouses. Barely scraping by but being fulfilled by the good she was doing.

She'd never disappointed her family before. Didn't want to.

But she also didn't want to keep living like this. Working hard, then harder, then harder still, all for something far in the future and missing the present.

She glanced back at the chateau, at the numerous gleaming windows and polished stone. The kind of place she would have described as a fairy-tale castle.

Right now, though, it seemed little better than a gilded prison.

A shudder passed through her. If Griffith Lykaois wanted to hide here from the media attention, that was his choice. He was punishing himself. For what, she had no idea. The news reports had all stated that Griffith had had a green light. That the driver, whose blood alcohol level had been triple the legal limit, had torn through the intersection and only applied the brakes a second before the crash.

His mother had passed from some sort of illness. Something also out of Griffith's control. Yet based off the articles she'd read, his indulgent lifestyle had started a few months after his mother's death.

She sighed. Slid off the flats she'd found in the trunk and savored the feel of cool earth and soft grass beneath her bare feet as she'd chosen to in the rose garden earlier. It grounded her, gave her a moment of much-needed pleasure as her mind tried to piece everything together.

None of it was her business. Just like going into his private domain had been none of her business, she realized that. Yes, she'd been angry. And growing bored. But there had been books scattered throughout the house. Other rooms she could have explored. Garden paths she hadn't ventured down. A beautiful kitchen with plenty of food and ingredients. She had chosen work, as always, over taking time to relax, to do exactly what she had been saying she wanted to do and enjoy herself.

And then she had given her dratted boss even more power by letting his text get to her and spur her to action. Instead of waiting, of hanging out in the kitchen or one of the main rooms Griffith would have to pass through eventually, she'd violated his request and intruded on his privacy.

She sighed. Four days to go. If she left Griffith alone, gave him space the next few days, perhaps by the time the bridge was repaired they would both be in better places to at least have a conversation about the contract.

You're in the wrong business...

Had he seen how much those words had twisted her up inside? How much they'd torn at her rapidly growing doubts?

No, she wasn't good at working with clients like him. Big clients with big reputations and even bigger bank accounts, the kind who brought prestige to a firm like Nettleton & Thompson. She preferred working with the grandmother who wanted to divide up her assets fairly among her grandchildren. The parents who worried about providing for a son with health concerns once they passed. The husband confronted with his mortality too soon who wanted his wife and children to be financially stable.

Those were the people she wanted to work with. The people she loved working with.

Once she became a midlevel attorney, those types of clients would be rare. Even rarer still when she became a senior attorney.

A bird flew overhead. She watched it soar, swoop down before it arced back into the sky. Entranced, she stepped forward as it winged out over the edge of the cliff and flew above the waves.

"Stop!"

Startled by the loud voice behind her, she whipped around. A sharp, stabbing pain shot through her foot as something pierced her skin. She sank down into the grass, clutching at her leg.

"What in the hell do you think you were doing?" Griffith demanded as he reached her side.

"What are you talking about?" she asked as she gritted her teeth against the pain.

"Do you have any idea how unstable the ground is around here? How close we are to the cliffs?"

"Yes," she groused as she looked down and spied a thorn sticking out of the sole of her foot, "dangerous territory."

"If you hadn't come traipsing about out here, you wouldn't have gotten hurt."

"If you hadn't ordered me to get out of your office, I wouldn't have been out here in the first place."

He dropped down next to her and took her foot in his large hands with a surprisingly gentle touch.

"If you hadn't come into my office when I told you not to, I wouldn't have asked you to leave."

Her lips curled back over her teeth as another bolt of pain shot up her leg at his probing.

"You know, I think I have something that trumps all of this."

He arched a brow as he glanced up. "Oh?"

"If you would have just signed the contract or the refusal, we wouldn't be in this position right now."

He stared at her for so long she wondered if he was just going to leave her out amongst the grasses. Instead, he did something even more unexpected. He scooped her into his arms, held her tight against his chest and stood.

"What are you doing?" she shrieked.

"Carrying you back to the house."

She thumped a hand against his chest. "Let me down. I can walk."

"Not with a thorn that size in your foot."

"Hobble, then," she amended.

"I'm more than capable of carrying you."

Through her pain she detected the offense in his tone.

"I'm not saying you're not physically capable," she said quietly.

His hold on her tightened. It startled her, made her want to relax into his embrace, savor the novel sensation of being carried by a man who obviously took good care of himself.

Dangerous. The warning whispered through her mind. Griffith, and her attraction to him, were very dangerous. She had never got to know a man well enough to feel comfortable taking a relationship beyond a good-night kiss. Thought that was what it would take to want to take things further.

Then Griffith had appeared in her life. She didn't know him at all. Comfortable was the opposite of what she felt when she was around him. The instantaneous attraction was both thrilling and overwhelming.

Yet it had also set off warning bells. How could something so sudden be real?

No matter what she felt, he was off-limits. Yes, technically his father's estate was her client, not him. But Griffith was involved. Sleeping with him could derail the career she'd worked so hard for.

Satisfying a simple burst of hormones was not worth that risk. It couldn't be, could it?

The rest of the trip back to the house was made in silence. Once inside, he took her into the kitchen and sat her down on one of the chairs. She watched as he moved about from the state-of-the-art refrigerator and freezer hidden behind wood paneling to a cupboard that contained stacks of neatly folded cloth.

"How does it feel?"

"Painful," she ground out through gritted teeth.

He sat in the chair across from her and made a motion with his hands for her to bring up her leg and rest it on his knee. She did so, even though it stung her pride.

"Hold still."

"I'll try."

"If you yank back, I may not be able to keep a hold on it and it could break off in your foot. It could cause an infection."

"I have three brothers. I helped my mom patch them up enough times to know about pulling out things. Thorns, glass, porcupine quills."

His lips lifted a fraction. Not much, but just enough to count as an almost smile.

"Porcupine quills?"

"It always amazed me," she forced out as pain pulsed in the bottom of her foot, "how something with such a cute face could be so menacing."

"I've wondered the same thing."

Her eyes came up to meet his and she realized with a jolt of surprise that he was teasing her.

"You're saying I'm cute?"

"Perhaps."

Shock rendered her speechless. He thought she was cute? She would have preferred beautiful or sexy. But she could make do with cute, too, especially from a man like him who maybe offered a compliment once or twice a year.

"I think the last time I was called cute," she finally managed to say, "was in middle school by Henry Dorsey."

"And you and he didn't live happily ever after?"

"My brothers scared him off. As they—"

With a sudden yank, he pulled the thorn out of her foot.

"Ouch! You could have warned me."

"Which would have made you tense up and made it all the more likely that the thorn would have broken off in your foot."

She managed to keep her lips pressed together as he cleansed the wound and wrapped her foot.

"Thank you."

His head snapped up. "What?"

"Thank you," she repeated. "For taking care of me."

He blinked, as if he didn't know what to make of her gratitude. His lips parted, then came back together before he finally managed to say, "You're welcome."

Tension still lingered between them, but her accidental sojourn into the wild rose bushes had created a temporary truce between them.

A truce she needed to avoid. A truce meant the potential for her attraction to him to flourish. To tempt her closer to crossing a boundary she needed to keep in place.

"There."

He lowered her foot to the floor, then stood up and moved away from her quickly. Relieved, she braced her hand on the table and started to stand.

"What are you doing?"

"Going up to my room."

And as far away from you as I can get.

"Don't put pressure on that foot, at least not for a few hours. It was a good-size thorn and it's likely to be pretty painful."

"Okay," she said slowly. "If I'm going to be off my feet for a couple hours, I'd rather not do it in the kitchen. Besides, as I said, before I'm very good at hobbling. I can make my way upstairs—"

He moved forward. She started to step back, winced as her foot made contact with the floor. The pause gave him enough time to sweep her into his arms once more.

"Or I could just carry you."

"You've really got to stop doing that."

"What? Playing Prince Charming?"

She threw back her head and laughed. When he glanced down at her one brow raised, it only made her laugh harder.

"Not handsome enough for Prince Charming?"

"Oh, it's not that," she hastened to reassure him. "You're actually too handsome."

He shook his head slightly. "Too handsome?"

Embarrassed, she looked away.

"You said it."

"I wish I hadn't."

"Why not?" he asked as he walked out into the main hall and headed toward the stairs. "Say more if you like. I haven't heard a compliment about my appearance in…well, you can guess," he said with a sardonic smile.

"What else is there to say?" She could feel the heat creeping up her neck and moving through her cheeks. "You're handsome."

"Handsome enough to be Prince Charming?"

"Yes," she practically growled.

It was his turn to chuckle, a sound that hummed in his chest and stirred her skin. As the pain in her foot resided, she became aware of how snugly he held her body against his, of the sheer strength in his arms as he gripped her tight. She snuck a glance at him from beneath her lashes, her eyes traveling over the sculpted line of his jaw beneath his beard, the scar that cut down the left side of his face.

"Ask."

"Excuse me?"

"The scars." His lips thinned into a line. "Everyone stares, but no one has the guts to ask."

What would it be like to have everyone know the details of your life? To know almost every horrific thing and still want to know more, to take every bit of knowledge as if it were their own?

"I didn't really have a question. More of an observation."

"What's that?"

They reached the top of the stairs. As he moved down the hall, he spared her a glance.

"That it's very unfair that people won't leave you alone."

This time his laugh was short, harsh. "For once, Miss Sutton, you and I agree. I didn't used to mind the spotlight. As I'm sure you know, I embraced it."

She thought back to the hours of meticulous research she had performed preparing to accept this challenge. To try and get inside the head of Griffith Lykaois, renowned shipping magnate and consummate playboy.

"I know."

He reached her room and walked in through the open door, then sat her down on the long midnight blue sofa in front of the fireplace. As he released his hold on her, she knew a sense of loss, one that affected her body as much as it did her heart.

He moved over to the fireplace, turned his back to her as he braced his arm against the mantel.

"You think me spoiled."

She thought for a moment, tried to find a way to be diplomatic. And then decided that the best course was truth.

"Yes."

"I am," he replied simply. "I'm spoiled and I like nice things. I also have the kind of money that can buy the kind of things that attract a lot of attention. Coupled together with…"

He gestured at his face. "What I used to be, it attracted a lot of attention."

She frowned. "That's not all everyone focused on. I read a number of articles about the advancements you and your father made—"

"Stop." The order snapped out, wiped away any of the intimacy that had developed between them in the kitchen. Her body tensed as she watched the tightening of muscles in his back beneath his shirt, the cords of his neck tensing.

"Don't talk about my father. Please."

"Okay."

She wanted to say more, to offer some sort of comfort. His behavior, everything he said, convinced her more and more that while he might have selfish and indulgent tendencies, the man in front of her was a man in pain. A man with hidden depths, given the level of care he had administered to her just minutes after their argument.

He faced her then. Sadness bloomed in her chest at the frozen expression on his face. The mask had slipped back once more.

"Can I bring you anything?"

"No. I had some of the frozen crepes and fruit for breakfast. And there are bottles of water here in the guest room."

One corner of Griffith's mouth quirked up. "Beatrice lives in constant hope that one day I'll return to the chateau. Bring someone here who I could share it with."

A vision filled Rosalind's head, of Griffith in the rose garden, a baby bouncing on his knee, a toddler running about. It was hard to imagine any of the women she'd seen pictured on his arm out here amongst the historic elegance. They seemed more suited to the city, to the nightlife and luxury shops that abounded in cities like London. But Griffith… Surprisingly, she could picture him here.

"Well, when you see her, please thank her."

The stilted conversation stole her remaining energy. She leaned back into the couch.

"You could use some rest." Griffith inclined his head to her. "I'll check on you later."

"I should be able to be up and about on my own in a few hours."

"I'll check on you all the same."

"You would have made an excellent doctor," she said as she failed to stifle a yawn.

"I sincerely doubt that," he replied dryly. He hesitated, then nodded his head, as if he'd made a decision. "Tomorrow."

"Tomorrow?"

"We'll talk about the contract."

Confusion cut through her fatigue. Why the sudden change of heart? Had her accident stirred up some emotion? Perhaps guilt?

Does it matter? Just say yes!

"Okay. Thank you."

He nodded once more. "Get some rest."

As she shifted down to stretch out on the couch, she heard his sharp inhale, turned her head to see what he was about to say. But he was moving toward the door, not even looking in her direction. She waited until the door clicked behind him before she let her eyes drift shut.

Never in a million years would she have pictured a man like Griffith tending to her. It had made him seem almost human. And, she thought as she drifted off to sleep, it made her attraction to him all the more treacherous.

CHAPTER NINE

GRIFFITH KNOCKED ON Rosalind's door the following morning. He steeled himself when he heard her footsteps, stayed strong when she opened the door wearing a navy blue shirt and a vivid red skirt, her curls caught up into a loose bun that left her neck bare to his gaze.

Then lost his grip as he imagined trailing his lips from jaw to shoulder, then lower still—

"Good morning."

"Good morning."

Rosalind blinked and stepped back at the growl in his voice. He started to explain, then stopped. He just needed to get this conversation over with. When he'd suggested it yesterday, the offer had been rooted in guilt and curiosity. Guilt for the way he'd treated her not just the past few days, but the past few weeks. Curiosity about the woman who didn't give up, who couldn't let herself enjoy more than a few moments in a rose garden.

Who made him crave not just sex but something more. Something that carried a power he'd never experienced before.

Dangerous. Yet so tempting he couldn't resist spending just a little bit of time with her.

Chances were these few minutes would finally relieve him of some of the attraction he felt. Take away the mystery, the anticipation, and he would be left with a beautiful woman who wasn't a good match and, after this week, would be out of his life for good.

That was his plan. And that plan should not be unsettling him as much as it was.

"My office."

She blinked at the command in his voice, but simply nodded. He turned and walked out. A moment later he heard her footsteps behind him. If he was going to do this, to concede to her and listen to something that threatened to rip out what was left of his heart, then it would be in the one place in this massive house he felt in control.

He gestured to a chair in front of his desk as he circled around and sat. She leaned over and handed him a thick bundle of papers in a leather folder before taking her seat.

"Your father's estate is currently valued at approximately one billion, four hundred million dollars."

A number Griffith had aspired to for years. To officially wield the title of billionaire. A number that, as he opened the folder and stared at the figure, stirred nothing but sorrow. Sorrow that his father had worked so hard while spending the last years of his life widowed and estranged from his only child. Sorrow that Griffith had been the reason for that estrangement.

"I have my own fortune." He closed the folder, set it down on the desk. "I don't need the money."

"You have several options. You can accept the estate in its entirety. You can accept part of it. You could reject it all."

"What happens if I reject it?"

"Then it goes to the next family member. A distant cousin living in Greece."

He frowned. He knew the cousin she spoke of, a decade older than him with a predilection for alcohol and drugs.

He sighed.

"So I have no choice."

She tucked a stray curl behind her ear. "May I make a suggestion?"

"I'm surprised you even asked."

She arched a brow at him. "I read a lot about your family when I was assigned your father's estate—"

"Why were you assigned to it?" Griffith interrupted.

"Excuse me?"

"This is a rather high-profile account for a junior associate to take on."

She sighed. "It is. My boss had it. When you declined to meet with him for so long, he put it on me, too. I think he thought I could either succeed where he hadn't or, if it all fell apart, he could blame it on me. Either way he gets the win."

Disgust slithered through him. "And you never get any of the credit."

"He's brilliant when it comes to law. Unfortunately, he only cares about the law as it benefits Nettleton & Thompson." She looked at him then and narrowed her eyes. "Back to the estate. Your parents were both involved with a number of charities and start-ups."

"Yes. My mother invested quite a bit of her time and money supporting independent artists, fashion designers, photographers."

"And your father, if I remember correctly, financed scholarships for underprivileged youth in his home country of Greece."

"He grew up extremely poor. My grandfather founded Lykaois Shipping when my father was a teenager. He started off as a dockhand and worked his way up."

"You must be proud of them." She glanced at the papers, then back at him. "What causes are important to you?"

He blinked. "What do you mean?"

"Causes," she repeated. "You know, charities, philanthropies."

"I maintain donations to all of the charities and trusts my parents set up."

A wrinkle appeared between her brows. "Is there nothing you care about personally?"

Uncomfortable with the direction the conversation was taking, he shrugged.

"I continue to support the causes my parents championed. I ensure alterations to match inflation. I'm not capable of more."

She frowned. "Not capable or you don't want to open yourself up to more?"

He flashed her a cold smile. "Monsters aren't capable of giving much, Rosalind. I give money. That's my limit."

Her frown deepened. "You really believe that, don't you?"

"Yes." He pointed to his scars. "Inside and out."

"I don't believe that."

The quiet conviction in her voice hit him. Made him, for the first time in years, want to be something more than the shadow he'd turned himself into. Drifting in and out of life, marking time until it was all over.

More temptation. More yearning. He didn't want to end their time together just yet. But he couldn't stand one more moment of talking about the damned contract. Talking about his life and all of his failings.

"Let's talk about you."

Her eyes narrowed as her nose wrinkled.

"Me?"

"Yes. You intrigue me. Tell me more about Rosalind Sutton. The woman who let her boss walk all over her without question."

She shrugged as a pale blush stole over her cheeks.

"Not much to tell."

"What do you do for fun?"

"I work a lot." Embarrassed, she stood and started walking around the room. Pacing like she was caught in a trap. "Sometimes I read."

"Fairy tales?"

That surprised a small laugh from her. "Sometimes. I do love the happier ones. Romance and cozy mysteries if I'm not reading briefs or final testaments."

"What about family? You mentioned three brothers."

"They're wonderful unless they're being terrible," she said with a grin. "Always looking out for me."

"What about your parents?" Too late, he remembered what she had said about her mother. "Disregard that."

"It's okay." She smiled at him, a truly kind smile meant to reassure. "It happened so fast."

"Were you able to be with her?"

"I was in Chicago at school. I didn't make it back in time."

She swallowed hard, grief evident in every subtle gesture, every slight movement of her body. Never before had he been so in tune with someone, read every single one of their emotions. Grief, regret, a lingering sadness. It all echoed his own. Everything he never allowed himself to feel, never allowed another soul to see.

"But you came back to England?"

"I did. My parents were very proud of me getting the internship. When my mom heard about the job offer, my chance to live abroad…" She looked back at him and smiled. "I don't think I ever saw her so excited."

"What about you?"

"What about me?"

"Were you excited?"

She blinked, as if she'd never been asked such a question before. Irritation flickered inside him. She spoke about her family in glowing terms. But what kind of family relentlessly foisted their own dreams on their children? His parents had made it clear that his path forward would be his own. His father had told him multiple times that, while he enjoyed the idea of his son taking over as he had done for his father, it was always Griffith's choice.

"I mean, yes. Not many people make it out of the small town I grew up in, let alone all the way to London."

"What about your work? Did your parents push you into that, too?"

She scowled. "They encouraged me to get a degree and move out. Take advantage of opportunities they didn't have."

He dialed back his frustration. If it didn't upset Rosalind, it shouldn't upset him. Only it did. It bothered him that everything she'd worked for, everything she should be proud of, came second to her parents' happiness.

"And you chose law."

"I took a career exploration course my first year in college. I enjoyed the legal unit we did and excelled at math, reading legal documents. A professor recommended I look into estate planning." She smiled. "And here I am. I like helping people, and the stories they bring into my office. They're interesting. Helping them navigate that stage of life, and giving them peace of mind to enjoy the rest of their days. Never something I saw myself going into when I was younger, but I really love it."

"And you like working for Nettleton & Thompson?"

There it was. That same flicker of emotion he'd witnessed down in his office when he'd lashed out at her.

"I do."

"But?"

"Sometimes the prestige... I'm just not always sure that Nettleton & Thompson is the place I'm meant to be."

"Then why continue with it?"

"Wanting to see it through. I promised my parents I would." Her fingers traced a circle on the surface of the table. "Maybe I'll do something else later. Open my own firm."

He heard the faint, dreamy note in those last words. Started to ask more, but she interrupted him.

"Anyway, back to business. What if you donated your father's estate? Contributed to causes they believed in, and some that you believe in, too?"

He sat back in his chair. She sat up straighter, squaring her shoulders as if readying for a fight.

"I'm not talking about the contract. I'm just pointing out that you seem removed from everything in your life. Let's take you right now, in this moment, with a wealth few have. Why don't you find something you care about? Something personal? Donate the estate so you don't have to worry about it, but do something good with it, too?"

"I had something I cared about," he shot back. "Now it's gone. I do the bare minimum, which when it comes to my personal situation, still means millions of dollars every year getting funneled into charities and organizations around the world, not to mention paying some of the highest salaries in the shipping industry. Take the stars out of your eyes, Rosalind. I do more than enough with what I have. Just because I don't get my hands personally dirty doesn't lessen the impact I'm making."

"Perhaps if you were to get more involved, you could find something else you care about."

"Why are you pushing me on this, Rosalind? Surely, this is beyond your legal duties," Griffith warned her. This conversation was taking a turn he had never intended. Had not permitted. And yet, she still persisted.

"I don't know you," she admitted. "But I see a man who has so much potential, that could be so much."

"Because I'm rich?"

"It's not just about the money. There's this whole other man beneath the harsh exterior, but you've got him locked away so deep down inside that I don't think even you know who he is. Maybe you did once, but not anymore."

The accuracy of her statement hit home. Anger welled inside him as he stood, his chair scraping against the wood.

"And what about you, Miss Sutton?"

"What about me?"

"Do you know who you are? Or are you simply the woman everyone else wants you to be?"

Her lips parted, closed, then parted again as she stared at him.

"What?" she finally gasped. "I just told you how I went after my career—"

"Yes, at a school your parents pushed you to. A job you accepted because it would make your parents happy."

The more he talked, the angrier he became. He was a lost cause. But this woman, so full of life, so full of potential, was wasting it all on someone else's dreams. The anger also helped to restore his sense of control. Anger he understood, an old friend that kept his heart guarded and hurt at bay.

Except once again, she didn't turn around and walk out. Didn't capitulate or surrender. She faced him, fierce and furious.

And gorgeous. Gorgeous with her eyes snapping emerald fire and color high in her cheeks. Her determination had drawn him in that day at the Diamond Club. Now it harnessed his anger, fanned the fires of his fury into something hotter.

Her eyes darted down, rested below his waist. The blush deepened as her chest rose and fell. He saw the blink, the sharp intake of breath, the desperate attempt to regain control of her own desire.

Seeing the naked lust in her gaze yanked him back to that edge. But right now, with his blood roaring and his body pulsing, the boundaries didn't seem like something to avoid. No, he wanted to take her in his arms and hurtle over the edge, wrapped up in each other.

Her tongue darted out, touched her lower lip.

"Sometimes we do things for people we love." Breathy, husky, her voice wound through his veins, a siren's song he could no longer resist. He took a step toward her, his body thrilling when she didn't retreat.

"I wouldn't know."

"Surely you must have loved someone once."

"Once." He stopped just inches away, stared down into her eyes. "Not something I plan on repeating."

"When you love someone, you'll do something for them even if it's not what you want for yourself."

He leaned down, left a whisper of space between their lips, imagined he could hear the frantic beat of her own pulse as she tilted her head back. The seduction came naturally, a skill he hadn't used in what felt like ages, but that was easy to summon.

The desire, however...that was beyond his control. And right now, he didn't give a damn.

"I'll take your word for it, Miss Sutton."

With that pronouncement he laid a hand on her waist, the other sliding into her hair as he tilted her head back farther still. He heard her sharp intake of breath, felt the warmth of her skin beneath his hands.

And then his lips met hers and his world exploded.

For a moment she didn't move. When she came alive, he knew he'd made a mistake. She didn't shy away, didn't pull back and call him a monster.

She returned his caresses with a fervor he hadn't antici-pated, couldn't get enough of. Her lips pressed against his. He reached up, pulled at the band securing her hair and thrilled to the feel of curly silk cascading down, a strand whisper-ing over his scarred cheek, his neck. She trembled as his hands moved up and down over her arms. When her fingers threaded through his hair, tugged, he groaned. His hands moved to the waist of her skirt, pulled the hem of her shirt free. He touched the bare skin at her waist, knew he was lost when just brushing her with his fingertips brought him to the edge.

His tongue slipped inside her mouth, deepened the kiss. Her answering moan, the way she met him with strokes of her own, drove him mad.

His hands slid higher, over her ribs, his knuckles grazing the silk of her bra.

He wanted it gone, wanted to touch her bare skin.

He reached around, fingers settling on the clasp. It wasn't until he heard her whisper his name, felt the eager press of her body against his, that it hit him just what he was doing.

Stunned by his loss of control, he pulled back so quickly she stumbled. She stared at him, eyes wide, breasts rising and falling as she sucked in a shuddering breath. One hand drifted up, as if she were moving through a dream, her fingers settling on her swollen lips. With her shirt wrinkled and her curls pulled free of the bun, now hanging in wild disarray about her face, she looked ravished. Seduced.

Aroused.

No. Her wanting him, returning his desire, was the last thing either of them needed.

"Griffith…"

He shook his head. "Rosalind… Miss Sutton… I'm sorry."

"No…" Her eyes were wide, luminous.

Wanting.

"Don't be sorry."

Her breathy voice curled around him, smoky seduction and tantalizing temptation.

It also had a surprising effect on Rosalind. She blinked, as if waking from a trance. Her fingers wrapped around the top of her chair. Something primal inside him howled, reveled in the effect he had on her even as he hated himself for surrendering to his base instincts.

She bit down on her lower lip. "I... I have to go."

She grabbed the leather portfolio off the desk, turned and walked out.

Oh, Theé mou. At least *she* had come to her senses. That would make keeping their hands off each other easier over the next few days.

Liar.

It made nothing easier. Now that he'd tasted her, felt her answering passion, his need had become so intense it physically hurt.

How long could he spend with Rosalind before he dragged her down, too? Took that beautiful, optimistic light and squelched it with his own selfish needs and grief?

Is it worth the risk? Worth hurting someone else, hurting her?

He knew the answer. Knew the answer and hated it as much as he hated how he had very nearly lost control.

He moved to the bank of windows behind his desk. The gardens behind the house lay before him in all their glorious summer splendor. Roses swayed back and forth in the breeze. The benches and archways scattered throughout, providing havens for readers, explorers and lovers.

He turned his back on the gardens. Refocused on his office, the sanctuary of his own company, even as he ignored how his footsteps echoed off the walls and amplified the void inside his heart.

CHAPTER TEN

ROSALIND SAT CURLED up in a burgundy wingback chair in front of a massive stone fireplace, a book lying on her lap. She could imagine it filled with burning logs in the winter, fire crackling over the wood as thick snowflakes fell outside.

She'd tried, and failed, several times over the morning to focus on work. After realizing she had read the same page of a client profile four times and not retained a single word, she'd shoved the papers into her briefcase and made her way to the library.

Every creak, every little noise, had made her heart pound. She had no idea what she would say to Griffith when she saw him again. She should apologize for her glaring lack of ethics, her unprofessional behavior.

Except she didn't want to. For so long she had been pushing her own wants and needs to the side. Had thought in the beginning that she needed to keep her attraction to Griffith buried, convinced that giving in to someone like him would only leave her heartbroken, would take her focus off work.

She had told herself to stay away from Griffith on a personal level. To keep her attraction to him in check. But the more she contemplated a future without Nettleton & Thompson in it, the more she thought about breaking off and finally going after something she wanted, the less she worried about the professional implications sleeping with Griffith would carry.

And the more she imagined his body on top of hers, what it would feel like to be filled by him, to have him move inside her...

Her skin tingled at the memory of his lips on hers, the way his hands had slid into her hair, exuding strength and yet such exquisite tenderness it overwhelmed her. She'd surrendered without a second thought.

An affair between them wouldn't lead to marriage. Of that, she had no doubt. They moved in different worlds. He was determined to keep everyone away.

But he obviously found her attractive. What if, she wondered as she closed the book and got up, they could come to some other arrangement?

The idea of an affair, of having a man like Griffith introduce her to sex, excited her. But it wasn't something to be taken lightly. She'd always thought the first man she'd sleep with would become her husband. This was very much not going to be that.

Taking a moment to let her chaotic thoughts settle, she wandered about, taking in the details of a renovated eighteenth-century library. From the soaring cases fashioned out of dark, gleaming walnut to the windows that stretched up three stories high, it was truly the personal library of her dreams. Luxurious, brown leather chairs were arranged about the room. Two sofas and two love seats, the color of a deep, fine wine, had been placed in the middle of the room on top of a plush Persian rug. The faint scent of wood polish, coupled with the fragrance of old books, was almost a seduction in itself.

Which brought her right back to Griffith. To the glimpses of the man he was beneath his pain. The feelings he stirred inside her. The way he desired her, like she was a craving he couldn't satisfy. It made her feel beautiful, empowered, alive.

Think this through.

Irritated at her mind's less than enthusiastic response, she grudgingly trudged back to her room, even though every cell in her body screamed for her to go upstairs and tell him. Ask him to be her first.

She felt no fear. No second thoughts. Only desire.

But was it worth it? Mixing something so intensely personal with the biggest contract of her career? Worth sharing her body with a man she knew she had no future with?

With her nerves on edge and her body unsatisfied, she needed to do something to relax. She had touched herself before. But as one friend had once so depressingly put it, it had been the equivalent of scratching an itch. Short, hurried sessions that had always left her frustrated and feeling vaguely disappointed.

But not tonight. No, tonight she was embracing the passion Griffith had awakened in her.

Slowly, she unzipped her skirt, imagining his hands on the zipper, fingertips grazing her back as the material parted. The skirt pooled at her feet with a sensual whisper of fabric that sent a delicious shiver over her skin, followed a moment later by her shirt. Her hands came up, cupped the weight of her breasts as she closed her eyes and let her head fall back.

What would it be like? To have his hands on her, teasing her, stroking her? Her eyes drifted shut as her fingers grazed over her own nipples, a gentle touch that teased them into hard buds and made her breath catch. Would he be gentle, tender? Or would he take charge, pushing her to the limits of what they could both handle as he dominated her body?

With a languid sensuality winding through her, she moved into the marble bathroom and turned on the claw-foot tub's hot water. A black end table standing next to the tub offered an assortment of soaps and a bottle of rose-scented bubble bath. As steam drifted up, she poured herself a glass of red wine from the minibar, pulled a plush robe from the closet, and found a box of matches in one of the drawers. Minutes later, she sank beneath the bubbles. A candle flickered on the counter. She'd dimmed the lights, creating a dreamy atmosphere that seduced almost as much as the desire she had finally surrendered to.

She took a fortifying sip of wine before setting the glass down on the window ledge next to the candle. Leaned her head back on the plush pillow at the back of the tub. Then let her arms drift down below the surface of the water. One hand wrapped around her breast, squeezed gently, tugged. The other moved lower, over her belly and down to the apex of her thighs. Her fingers stroked the sensitive skin, up one side and down the other, before lightly resting on her clitoris. She pressed, gasped at the sensation that spread, an electric current that lit up her entire body. Her mouth curved up into a shocked smile as she continued to tease, touch, exploring herself in a way she never had before.

Her passion built. Her hips arched against her own hand. Even as the pleasure spread, too, it made her acutely aware of the ache between her thighs. Images of Griffith filled her head, the thunderous expression on his handsome face before he'd crushed his lips to hers, the way his scent had wrapped around her as he'd kissed her to the point of madness on his desk.

"Oh, God…"

She found her release, stronger than she'd ever experienced before. But the pleasure did nothing to assuage the ache Griffith had stirred in her.

She sighed. Even if Griffith said no, she wasn't going to

head back to London and go in search of a random one-night stand. No, she needed some kind of connection to make that leap. And she sorely feared that, after the incredible desire Griffith had stirred in her, she wasn't going to find anyone like him ever again. Even someone who could offer her all of the future dreams she eventually wanted.

She breathed in. Exhaled. Thoughts swirled in her head, some louder than others, all of them chaotic and demanding attention.

Through the storm, one constant remained.

She wanted Griffith.

Her thoughts quieted. Peace reigned even as anticipation made her pulse beat faster. She wanted Griffith to be her first lover. She wanted everything she'd experienced these past few days: the excitement, the passion, the tenderness mixed with a primal lust that nearly made her come apart in his arms.

She dried herself off, applied a minimal amount of makeup, and contemplated the dresses in the trunk. What did one wear, she thought with a wry twist of her lips, to ask someone to take her virginity?

Settling on a simple sleeveless black dress with a V-neck that teased a peek of her cleavage and a full skirt that swayed just above her knees, she moved out the door with a confident set to her shoulders. This time, as she climbed the stairs to the third floor and walked down the hall to his office, it wasn't dread that pounded through her veins. There were no thoughts of contracts or inheritances or promotions.

Only Griffith.

She knocked on the door. A moment passed. She knocked again.

Dimly, she heard footsteps. Then the door swung open. Griffith stared at her. She returned his gaze with one of her own, taking in the tousled hair, the long-sleeved tan shirt and dark pants that followed the lines of his muscular physique.

"Why are you here, Rosalind?"

"Because I want you."

He blinked. Once, twice.

"What?"

"I want you, Griffith." Her heart climbed into her throat as she pushed herself to the edge of her limits, reached out with both hands for something she wanted with a desperate passion. "I want you to be my first lover."

He stepped back, his face contorting with shock. "First?"

She silently cursed herself. "That didn't come out right."

"Either you're a virgin or you're not, Rosalind?"

Intrigue dripped off every word.

She tilted her chin.

"I am."

He let out a melodic string of Greek, the harsh sting of his tone making it clear he was cursing.

"A virgin?" he repeated.

"Yes. I understand we're a rare breed past a certain age, but it does happen."

He turned away, groaning as he scrubbed a hand over his face.

"Rosalind, I need you to leave."

"No." She stepped forward, planted herself in the doorway so he couldn't slam the door in her face. "I won't go away unless you look me in the eye and tell me you don't want me, too."

"That's exactly why you should go away." He turned on his heel then, stalked back across the room until a mere whisper separated them. "Because I want you. I want you so badly I ache for you. It physically hurts not to touch you."

Her chest rose and fell, desire twisting and twirling through her veins with such ferocity it made her feel faint.

"Then why not?"

"Because that's all I can offer you." He stepped back then. "Physical pleasure. With whatever time you have left here. Nothing more."

"Did I ask for more?"

His raspy laugh sounded torn from some place deep inside him. "Not now. But a woman like you, Rosalind, you shouldn't even have to ask. A man should look at you and know that you deserve more than one night. More than a few pieces of jewelry."

Her lips parted in shock. It meant something that Griffith saw her like that. Despite her insistence that this would only be a physical thing, she knew that she was risking, and would most likely lose, part of her heart to this man. This man so convinced of his own hideousness that he couldn't see the moments where his humanity shone through.

Was it worth it?

Yes.

"And I want those things. Eventually. A husband. Marriage. Kids. But not right now."

His hands tightened into fists at his sides. "You know the twisted part about all of this? Just the thought of you being with someone else, sharing your body with another man, makes me want to rip his head off." He looked away. His sharp profile caught in the light streaming in through the windows. "But I can't give you any of that, Rosalind. I'm not capable of offering anyone that kind of emotional depth."

"And I'm not asking for it."

"You should." He placed his hands on her shoulders, his fingers tightening on her skin. "You should ask for the world, Rosalind. You should not settle for what you think you can get because you're stuck out in the middle of nowhere with a man who can't control his own lust. Look at me."

He craned his neck to the side so that she could see the full scarring along the side of his face. He grabbed the collar of his shirt and yanked down, revealing the continued path of the scars as they snaked down his neck.

"Do you know what my ex-girlfriend said when she first saw me in the hospital? 'Monstrous.'" He released the collar, let the fabric creep back up over his scars. "And she was right."

Rosalind stared at him, her heart aching.

"Then she wasn't the right woman for you."

Griffith threw back his head and laughed, harsh and grating.

"Obviously."

"I said it before, and I'll say it again. There is nothing repulsive about you."

"Then perhaps you haven't looked close enough. You said you loved fairy tales. Don't most of those talk about the beauty within? About the importance of who someone is on the inside?" He moved toward her. "I do not have any beauty within. There is no love in my heart. I am not capable of it."

"I'm not looking for love. Not with you."

Did she imagine the flicker in his eyes, the flash of something dark?

"You're just looking for a quick lay to finally see what sex is all about?"

"Not too quick."

Instead of lightening the mood, her quip made his eyes turn molten. He swallowed, his hands clenching, unclenching.

Sensing that his resolve was weakening, she moved forward, savoring the burst of feminine power that wound through her as he watched her with carnal hunger.

"I want you to be my first lover. I've never felt this way before, Griffith. Never wanted someone like this before."

She stopped in front of him, slowly leaned up on her toes and brushed a kiss against his mouth, felt him shudder even as he kept himself still.

"I need time to think."

Thrilled that she had at least gotten him to reconsider, she stepped back.

"All right. I'll be in my room."

She had almost reached the door when his voice rang out.

"Rosalind." She turned back. "Could you truly accept an affair? Just an affair? No strings, no emotional attachments?"

She hesitated. There would be no coming back from this. She would be crossing a line, not just professionally but personally. Already she knew there was more to her attraction to Griffith than simple physical lust. She was courting danger, risked her heart, risked everything she had worked her whole life for.

Once she did this, once she gave in to indulgence and put her career on the line, would she ever be able to go back to life as she'd known it?

But I don't want to go back to how things were.

"I know you make me want. I want things with you I've never wanted with another man. I want you so much I..."

Her voice trailed off as self-consciousness chilled her ardor. His eyes darkened.

"You what?"

Be brave. Bold. Confident.

One more moment of hesitation. And then she stepped off the ledge and flung herself into fantasy. She raised her chin. "I touched myself and imagined it was you."

A growl emanated from his chest, rumbled up his throat as his jaw tightened.

"This is my choice, Griffith. I choose you. I hope you'll accept that."

"Mori."

The word sounded torn from deep within him. And then he was in front of her, sweeping her into his arms as he kissed her with that incredible passion that sent flames licking over her skin and a deep, pulsing need straight to her core.

"I'll be damned tomorrow." His voice rumbled against the sensitive skin just below her jaw as he trailed his lips down her neck. "But tonight, Rosalind…" His hand tangled in her hair as it had the first time he'd kissed her, arched her head back and bared her throat to his mouth. He knew just where to kiss, to nip, to drive her wild until she was panting and wet.

"Tonight," he repeated as he brought his lips back to hers, "you're mine."

CHAPTER ELEVEN

How had he ever thought her straitlaced? Buttoned-up? Because the sensual creature in his arms was anything but staid. She moaned, gasped, met him touch for touch as he explored her with his lips and tongue.

She'd touched herself. Thought of him while bringing herself pleasure. Despite his scars, what he'd shared, she still wanted him. Her desire for him, coupled with their undeniable chemistry, stripped away the last of his misgivings.

He leaned down, slid an arm beneath her knees and lifted her into his arms. Unlike their adventure out on the plains, where he'd barely been able to resist from tasting her, he now feasted. He carried her next door to his bedroom. He stopped next to his bed, his fingers sliding the zipper of her dress down. When the material pooled at her feet and his hands came up to cup her breasts, he nearly lost it when he realized she was completely naked.

"Rosalind…"

"There wasn't any underwear in the trunk," she said with a smile that turned into a moan as he stroked a finger down the slope of one breast. Her sharp inhale was music to his ears. He kissed her again as he continued to stroke and touch. He took everything she had to give, demanded more.

Selfish.

And he couldn't stop. The only thing that could have made

him stop was her, and she responded to every touch with a need that made him so hard it nearly hurt. He teased the seam of her lips with his tongue. She opened to him, gasped into his mouth as her fingers dug into his hair. Pressed her body against him. Deepened the kiss.

He stopped by the bed and lowered her down onto the silken cover. Reveled in her moan of protest as he straightened.

And stared.

His eyes consumed the sight of her. The swell of her breasts. The slope of her stomach, the flare of her hips, the dark curls, the curves of her thighs.

Her skin, still pink from the heat of her bath, darkened as a flush spread over her body. But she didn't move to cover herself. No, his tenacious beauty shifted, slowly arched her back and looked right into his eyes.

"Are you sure, Rosalind?"

She nodded. The trust she placed in him, the desire that flamed in her forest green eyes as she looked him up and down, pierced his armor in one fell swoop. That she trusted him with something so important, that she still wanted him despite his scars, touched him in a way he'd never experienced before, enhanced the desire pulsing through him.

What if she knew it all? Would she still want you then?

He pushed those thoughts away. She knew how things stood between them, that what they were about to do wouldn't go further than the chateau. When they both left, that would be the end of anything personal between them.

His fingers closed around the hem of his shirt.

"Wait."

Disappointment felt like a cold fist around his heart. A sensation that disappeared almost immediately as she stood and reached for him, her hands tentative but her eyes luminous. Her fingers settled over his, slipped beneath his shirt and grazed his stomach. His eyes drifted shut as his breath escaped in a harsh exhale. She pulled his shirt off.

Then froze. He uttered a silent curse as he suddenly remembered.

The scars on his face paled in comparison to the marks down his left side. One scar stood out from the rest, an angry slash over his ribs down to his waist. Smaller scars branched out from it, some faded and pale, others more visible.

Slowly, she reached out, laid a hand on the most prominent scar. At his sharp intake of breath, she snatched her hand back.

"Did I hurt you?"

"No." Not even close. Feeling her touch had been...wonderful. A deep part of him wanted to beg for her to touch him, just once more. "No one other than the doctors and nurses have touched me there since the accident."

She reached out again. He held his breath, only releasing it on a harsh exhale when her fingers trailed down over the scar.

"Griffith..."

He tensed. "Yes?"

"I want you."

He kissed her. Raw, sensual, commanding, yet vulnerable, he took everything she offered and demanded more. She gave and gave as his hands roamed over her body, cupped her hips and pulled her tight against his hardness, caressed her breasts until her nipples puckered once more beneath his touch.

Her bare breasts grazed his chest, nearly drove him insane as the light touch stoked him hotter, higher than he'd ever been with a woman.

Then her nimble fingers settled on the waistband of his pants. His eyes flew open and he captured her hands in his.

"But I—"

He kissed her, a deep kiss that coaxed a response with

strong, sure strokes of his tongue, which she answered with excited passion.

"If you take my pants off, I may not make it to the bed."

Delight filled her face, giving him another glimpse of the dreamer she'd suppressed for so long.

"You want me that much?"

"More."

He kissed her again, edged her back toward the bed until her knees hit the mattress and she tumbled back.

"Damn it. I don't have a condom."

"I'm on the pill." At his arched brow, she frowned. "I planned on having sex one day. I wanted to be prepared."

He chuckled. "And I've never been happier to hear that. I haven't been with anyone since the accident."

"And I haven't been with anyone. Ever," she added with a naughty grin.

His smile disappeared as he looked at her again, his eyes lingering on every inch of her body.

"Show me."

"What?"

"Show me," he repeated in a voice raspy with need, "how you were touching yourself."

She watched him for a long moment, her beautiful breasts rising and falling, her lips parted.

One hand moved. Fingers trailed over her face, down the curve of her neck to her breasts. When she cupped herself, uttered a soft gasp as she tugged on the hardened peaks, he nearly lost it. He was so hard it hurt.

Then her hand slid lower. He widened his stance, imagined chains wrapped around his ankles keeping him anchored to the floor so that he didn't interrupt this, didn't stop one of the most arousing and beautiful things he'd ever seen. To see a woman like Rosalind, tenacious and intelligent and yet so innocent, take charge of her pleasure entranced him more than he had ever thought possible.

His breath caught in his chest. Desire tightened, squeezed the air from his lungs as her fingers slid into the dark hair at the top of her thighs. Her eyes drifted shut as she touched herself. Her hips moved, her legs shifting restlessly as her breathing grew heavy. He curled his hands into fists even as he moved forward, using his own legs to gently nudge hers apart where they draped over the edge of the bed. Imagined himself sliding into that slick, wet heat. Hearing his name on her lips when he took her for the first time.

Not yet. Soon, just not yet.

For nearly a year he had denied himself pleasure. He could survive another minute.

And then she arched up, her moan filling the air between them.

"Rosalind."

She opened her eyes, panted as her gaze moved up and down his body.

"Griffith. I need you."

He shucked off his pants and covered her body with his. Moans filled the air as his chest pressed fully against her breasts. Their hands moved, caressed. He kissed her mouth, the tip of her nose, grazed his lips over her temple. He trailed his lips down over her cheek, her jaw, her neck, inhaling the faint fragrance of rose that clung to her skin.

Then he shifted, pressed kisses with gentle grazes of teeth along the slopes of her breasts. She cried out, her fingers digging into his hair, as he sucked one tight nipple into his mouth. He wanted more, to move fast, to satisfy himself.

But something else drove him farther down her body, a need to make this moment intimate, special for a woman who had trusted him enough to choose him.

His hands settled on her thighs. He spread her legs, the scent of her arousal making blood roar in his veins.

"Griffith…"

He heard the hesitation in her voice, looked up even as his fingers pressed down on her skin.

"I want to taste you, Rosalind." He turned his head, pressed a kiss to her inner thigh that made her tremble. "But only if you say yes."

Slowly, she parted her legs even more, her fingers trailing over his face, moving with the same gentle caress over his scars and unmarked skin. Her touch, her lack of fear or disgust, made his throat tighten as he lowered his head.

The first touch was a brush of his lips against swollen, sensitive flesh. Her answering moan made him smile. He teased her with kisses and licks and nips along her thighs, the skin just above her mound.

But when he kissed her again, he tasted her desire.

And had to have more.

Gentleness disappeared as he devoured her. Her thighs clamped around his head. Her fingers tightened in his hair as she cried out, urged him on as she bucked against his mouth, incoherent sobs barely registering past the roaring in his ears.

Her body tightened, stiffened. She screamed his name as she peaked before sagging onto the bed.

He moved, slid up her body as he dropped a kiss on her hip, the slight swell of her stomach, the dip between her ribs. She lay still, her breathing shallow, her face turned to one side.

"That…"

"That what?" he prompted.

Her eyes fluttered open. She turned her head and smiled lazily at him.

"That was amazing."

"I'm glad."

He said it with no small degree of masculine pride. But beneath his own satisfaction lingered the tenderness that had surprised him in those first few moments, that had guided his actions as he had made love to her body with his hands and mouth.

Her eyes widened as he moved his hips, his hard length pressing against her thighs.

"Oh."

She shifted, the action making her slick skin rub against him. He groaned, breathed in deeply to steady himself.

"Are you ready?"

She nodded. He placed himself at her entrance. Slowly, he eased inside. Her body closed around him, tight and hot and so wet he nearly came right then. She tensed as he came up against the barrier. He slid a hand into her hair, cradled her head and kissed her as he pushed deeper, swallowing her small cry of pain.

When he was fully inside, he stopped. Let her get used to the sensation of him inside her.

Even if it nearly killed him not to move.

"Thank you."

Her whispered words swept over him. Prompted by a rising tide of emotion, he leaned down, kissed her. The kiss was gentle, warm, affectionate. A chance to savor the moment, the monumental change that had just occurred.

She wiggled. He groaned.

"Don't do that unless you're ready."

She arched a brow as the corners of her lips tilted up. "Do what?" She moved again. Her eyes widened. "I can feel you getting bigger."

"That tends to happen when a man is aroused."

She slid her hands up his back.

"Show me what happens next."

He pulled out, reveled in the shocked wonder in her eyes as he slid back in. He started slow, long strokes that drew out the sensation, gave him the chance to notice things he'd never paid attention to with previous lovers. The flush that spread up from her breasts to her neck, the hitch in her breathing when he sank himself to the hilt.

Their pace quickened. She started to meet his thrusts, her fingernails scraping across his skin as she moved beneath him.

"Griffith. Oh, God, Griffith, I can't…"

"Don't hold back, Rosalind." He kissed her. God, he couldn't stop kissing her. "Do you trust me?"

"Yes."

Pressure built. He couldn't have stopped it if he had tried.

"Then give it all to me. Everything."

She surrendered, her body clamping down on him like a vise as she came apart in his arms, his name uttered over and over. He found his own release a moment later, shuddering as an intense pleasure wracked his body.

He eased himself down onto her body. Enjoyed the comforting feel of her beneath him, her fingers gliding slowly up and down his back.

For the first time that he could remember, he wanted to stay.

Which was why, after letting himself have just a moment longer, he rolled off and got up.

"Griffith?"

He looked back and inwardly cursed. She lay on her back, her slender body looking even smaller in the vastness of the bed where he had just taken her innocence. Taken an incredible gift, used it and was now abandoning it.

Because he was scared. Frightened of what she stirred in him. What she made him want. He had thought the simple temptation of her was dangerous enough.

But these unexpected bouts of tenderness, of romance, were even more perilous. He needed safety, not risk. Isolation, not emotion.

Except that meant focusing only on what he wanted and needed right now.

Classic Griffith.

"I'll be right back."

He went to the bathroom, ran a hand towel under warm water. When he came back, Rosalind frowned, then glanced down at her legs. A blush burned in her cheeks.

"Um... I can do that—"

"Do you remember what we just did?"

"I was there."

Her feisty reply gave him the chance to kneel on the bed, to slowly wipe away the traces of their lovemaking and her first time.

"You gave me something tonight. The least I can do," he said as he tossed the towel into a hamper, "is give you something in return."

"You did. Twice."

He threw back his head and laughed. "Then we're even."

Her brows drew together. Another curse rose to his lips. He'd been clear about how things would stand between them. But did he have to make their interlude sound transactional? Especially in the moments after she'd just been with a lover for the first time?

"I..."

She stopped. He saw the insecurity flash across her face, the doubt. This was the moment he could break the pattern of holding himself back, and let himself connect with someone beyond a mutually shared pleasure.

Except the words couldn't come. That he had been moved to do something as intimate as care for her after sex, that he was even contemplating inviting her to stay, were signs he needed to reverse course and reintroduce distance between them.

So he said nothing.

"Thank you, Griffith."

Before he could retreat, she leaned over and kissed him on the cheek. A simple action, chaste compared to what they had just done to each other in his bed. But the sweet gesture stabbed deep and wrapped around his heart. Made him want things he didn't want to risk wanting. Things that would require emotion, risk, sacrifice.

She rolled away and stood, plucked her dress off the floor and walked to the door. Did he imagine her hesitation as she grasped the handle? The shudder that passed through her as she turned it?

Then she was gone, the door closing behind her with a soft click. Alone, he leaned back into his pillows, closed his eyes, didn't even bother to keep his demons at bay as they came for him, ripping him apart with guilt and self-loathing.

Yes, she'd asked. He'd given her pleasure, paid attention to her needs and wants because he had wanted to, not simply because of masculine pride.

All things he could argue he did for her that made the situation slightly less horrible.

None of them justified the glimpse of pain he'd seen in her eyes when she'd rolled away from him.

It's better this way, his demons whispered. *She'll never want you now.*

CHAPTER TWELVE

ROSALIND WANDERED INTO the kitchen the next evening. She'd slept well past her usual rising time, a pleasant ache between her thighs. And had stayed in her room for the rest of the day. Not quite daring to leave, not quite knowing what she'd do if she ran into Griffith.

Her emotions were still all over the place.

You've brought it on yourself.

Griffith had asked her right before he'd invited her into his room if she could handle a simple affair. He'd been nothing but honest with her about what this was, where it was headed. Yet during their lovemaking, the tender way he'd touched her even as he'd worshipped her body like he could barely stand not touching her, followed by the gentle way he'd cleaned her after… He was a practiced lover doing what he did best.

She knew that. Or at least her mind did. Her heart, however, had other ideas.

"Good evening."

Startled, she turned to see Griffith framed in the doorway. Her heart beat a frantic rhythm against her ribs as she forced what she hoped was a relaxed smile onto her face.

"Good evening."

His eyes roamed over her, as if he was trying to discern what she was thinking. Apparently finding nothing amiss, he advanced into the kitchen. Dressed in a white V-neck shirt

and navy pants, he looked ridiculously handsome for someone dressed so casually.

"I trust you've had a good day?"

She smirked at him, dug deep for a confidence she didn't
feel. "Very."

His eyebrows drew together. She didn't respond, simply
watched and waited. Even if she didn't feel casual and care-
free about their time together, she would not show him the
turmoil inside her. Partly pride, partly embarrassment.

Perhaps a little bit of heartbreak, too, her devious mind
whispered.

She saw him hesitate and sighed.

"Griffith, I don't want things to be awkward. Last night
was fun, but I'm not trying to stalk you. I just came down
for some food."

"I didn't think you were." He nodded toward the refrigerator. "Join me?"

"You don't have to—"

"I know I don't," he said as he moved past her and opened
the fridge door. "You're hungry. I'm hungry. Join me."

Put like that, there wasn't a good reason to refuse. The
"dining nook," as Griffith had called it, was bigger than the
kitchen and dining room in her small apartment put together.
Set in a large alcove off the kitchen, the massive windows
offered soothing views of the rose garden.

"How do you not spend more time here?"

He glanced out the window. Tension tightened his face for
a moment before his expression smoothed out.

"Too far away from my work."

The lie hurt. Ridiculous, she told herself as she speared a
bite of peach covered in zesty dressing. They'd had sex once.
He'd made it perfectly clear that after she left the chateau,

they wouldn't have anything else to do with each other on a personal level.

Except that when he'd made love to her, there had been moments, numerous moments, when she'd sensed something more from him. A sweetness that had not only relaxed her but also enhanced the experience of sharing her body with a man. An intimacy that had gone beyond the physical and into something that had rocked her to her core.

Perhaps, she brooded as she stared down at her panzanella salad, it had all been in her head. An intimacy born from years of built-up expectations and fantasies concocted from her readings. What had seemed like true love in the dark of night had more than once turned out to be a simple case of lust.

Not that I'm in love.

That was ridiculous. Griffith might be an incredible lover. But not only had he made it clear he had no interest in any type of actual relationship, he wasn't the kind of man she wanted to build a life with. Cold, selfish, no interest in a family of his own.

You had great sex. Let the rest go. Move on.

She turned the conversation to something she was far more comfortable with: business.

"I saw your company announced your return date next month."

"No work talk." Before she could apologize, he leaned forward. "Tell me more about you."

Flustered, she swallowed, then coughed on the peach. She took a large sip of sparkling wine.

"Are you all right?"

"Yes. Just…not the question I was expecting."

"Why not?"

Now she saw just why this man had been such an authori-

tative figure in the shipping industry. He could charm someone with that direct gaze of his. He might think his physical
scars had marred his features to the point no one would want
to look at him. But even with the jagged mark that cut down
the left side of his face, the fading nicks and cuts on his cheek
and jaw, he was still handsome. Handsome with an innate
power that filled a room.

"Um…" She tucked a stray curl behind her ear. "I'm not
that interesting."

His eyes sharpened. "You're an American living in London and working for one of the most prestigious firms in estate law. You somehow talked your way into the Diamond
Club. You're very interesting."

She barely stopped herself from preening. "Oh. Thank
you."

No one had thought her interesting before. Her parents had
constantly complimented her hard work and initiative. Her
teachers had sided with them, encouraging her to apply for
scholarships, to get out of town before she got stuck.

No one had stopped to ask what she wanted. If she was unhappy living in their village by the sea. If she wanted to stay
in the community she'd grown up in. Instead, they'd heaped
their own unfulfilled and forgotten dreams on her shoulders.

"How did you end up in England?"

"An international internship program. In my second year
of law school, we had to secure an internship. One of my
professors recommended me for Nettleton & Thompson."

He tilted his head to one side. "You didn't want it?"

"I didn't say that."

"You didn't have to."

She took another sip of wine. She'd never told anyone
how she'd really felt as her career had progressed at lightning speed.

Who better to tell than a man you'll never see again?

"I was excited about the internship. About living and working in London for a summer. But it was just supposed to be one summer." She smiled slightly. "My mother flew over for a long weekend the summer I had my internship. She was so excited for me." Her smile faltered for a moment. "Probably more excited than I was," she admitted softly, not wanting to meet his eyes. To admit he'd been right. With a quick inhale, she continued. "We crammed so much into those three days. Tower of London, the British Museum, Buckingham Palace. We were supposed to go on the Eye, but it was closed for a private event."

Silence descended.

"What happened to her?"

"An infection. The February after my internship, she caught pneumonia. We thought everything was okay. But four months later she had a lung infection." She swallowed hard. "She didn't make it."

A hand settled over hers. Startled, her head snapped up. Griffith gazed at her with something akin to compassion in his eyes.

"I'm sorry, Rosalind."

He squeezed her hand before releasing her. She took a moment to work past the lump in her throat before she spoke. "I had gotten a job offer from Nettleton & Thompson the month before she passed. Everyone in my town was so excited for me, including my mom. I think because I enjoyed the internship everyone just assumed I would be equally excited about the job offer."

"But you weren't."

"I just never imagined myself working somewhere like that. Or with clients who could afford a place like Nettleton & Thompson."

"But you didn't want to let your parents down."

"No." She pushed a tomato around her bowl with her fork. "Especially after my mom died, doing something else felt like a betrayal. My parents worked hard to save up for me to go to college."

"What would they have said if you had told them you wanted something else?"

Surprised by the question, she set the fork down and leaned back in her chair. She stared out over the garden, over the silver light of the moon casting a glow over the roses, the shimmer added to the water splashing down from the fountainhead into the pool.

"I don't know. They would have encouraged me to go after my dreams. But," she added as she looked at him, "they would have been disappointed. It sounds so simple. Do what you want, accept your parents might be sad or not fully accept your choice."

"It's not simple."

Griffith's voice whipped out, harsh and guttural. She didn't take it personally. She had a pretty good idea of where his pain lay, of the reason behind his hurt.

"No. It's not simple at all."

"So all work and no play for Miss Sutton?"

"Hard to advance in your career if you're off playing."

"Is that why you are...were," he corrected as one corner of his mouth lifted, "a virgin?"

"Pretty much." She sighed. "I dated. But never long enough for me to feel comfortable with things going to the next level. And then I just decided to wait until..."

Her voice trailed off. She'd been about to say she had decided to wait until she found a man she thought she might spend the rest of her life with. That wouldn't have gone over well.

"Until what?"

"Until I found someone I was very attracted to."

The look on his face told her he saw right through her lie. But given that he had lied to her about his reasons for not spending more time at the chateau, she shoved her guilt away.

"I don't regret waiting. But I do wish I had... I don't know, lived a little more. Had more adventures."

"Having fun isn't all it's cracked up to be."

The darkness in his tone caught her, stopped her from saying the joke that had risen to her lips.

He trailed two fingers up and down the stem of his wineglass, his gaze turning distant as he retreated into the past. "Indulging for the sake of indulgence. Buying things because they're expensive. Attending parties because of who will be in attendance and not because you want to go." His fingers tightened on the wineglass. He tilted it up, drained the contents, then set it back down with a precision that belied the seething grief and fury she saw in his eyes. "Living in a constant state of working hard and playing just as hard to avoid dealing with something hard."

He leaned back, angled his body so that even though he was looking at her, he physically shut himself off from her. She felt the loss as acutely as if he'd stood up and walked away.

"So perhaps you did yourself a favor. Working hard and staying focused."

The last words dripped with bitterness and self-loathing.

"I doubt someone who increased the value of his family's business as much as you did didn't work hard," she said gently.

"I did work hard. I just played harder. Bought new properties, spent only one night in each of them, sold them the next day. Went to auctions at Christie's or Sotheby's and bought the entire lot because I could. Slept with women whose names

I didn't know because they wanted me. Wanted a piece of the millionaire shipping heir, and I wanted sex." His head snapped around, his eyes hard as rock. "Fun is fun until it leads to death. Destruction."

Her heart shuddered, cracked. She wanted to reach out, soothe the anguish from his face and offer him comfort.

A comfort she knew he wasn't ready to receive.

His chair legs grated on the floor as he stood. He collected their plates and carried them into the kitchen. She stayed at the table, turned his confession over in her mind as she watched him out of the corner of her eye.

"Did you always indulge like that?"

A plate clattered in the sink. He stood with his back to her, the muscles in his back tense and pressing against his skin.

"Most of my adult life, yes."

"When did it start?"

"Does it matter?"

He turned then, leaned back against the sink and crossed one leg over the other as he tucked his hands into the pockets of his pants. His broad shoulders, bare to her gaze, slowly dropped, as if he was forcing himself to relax, to appear cavalier.

"I think it does."

He shrugged. "I don't. It was a way of life for me. Now it's not."

"But it still seems to bother you. Like you were living that way of life but not really enjoying it. Like you were doing it for another reason and now regret it."

He pushed off the sink and stalked toward her.

"Maybe I was." He grabbed her hands and hauled her to her feet. "Maybe I wasn't." He looped an arm around her waist, yanked her against his body. "But I can tell you I don't regret last night."

"Griffith—"

"We only have a few days. Let's make the most of it."

The words cut her heart. She knew why he'd said them. To remind her this was nothing more than sex, a short affair that would begin and end at the Chateau du Bellerose.

Terms you accepted. Terms that were worth both the pain and the pleasure.

He cut off her next words with a searing kiss that reawakened her desire. She hesitated, then pushed her wavering aside. She'd asked for this. Demanded it. If she only had days to experience this level of need, then she was going to take them and enjoy every single, passion-filled second.

Armed with her newfound confidence, she rose up on her toes, met him this time as an equal as she nipped at his lower lip, drew back a fraction when he tried to deepen the kiss. Glorified in the growl that sounded like it had been ripped from his throat before he took her mouth again.

As his hands slid beneath her bottom, pulled her hips against him, discomfort flickered through her. Was he using sex to distract her? To keep her attention on the pleasure coursing through her body and off him?

I can't offer you anything but sex.

He'd been clear. Laid down the rules. No matter how curious she was, how much she yearned to know him on a deeper level, she had no right to ask more.

With that, she let go of her questions and surrendered to the passion he offered. Let go of thoughts of tomorrow, a week from now, a month. Indulged in the intoxicating sensation of enjoying the now.

Seized by a brazen boldness she'd never experienced, she broke the kiss, slid down his body and dropped to her knees. Satisfaction wound through her as his eyes widened.

Her fingers gripped his waistband and pulled down. When

she wrapped her fingers around his length, he shuddered. She stroked him, watched the fire in his eyes burn even hotter as she lowered her head. She took him in her mouth, moaned at the intimacy, at feeling him pulse against her tongue.

She experimented, moving slow and steady, then fast. He hardened, thighs tensing beneath her hands as his head dropped back and he groaned.

"Enough."

He barked the command as he reached down and grabbed her arms, hauled her to her feet.

"I want to be inside you when I come."

Thrilled by his words, by the fever descending over her skin, made all the more potent by their previous intimacy, she didn't protest. Simply gave herself up to his passionate kiss. His hands slid down to her legs, lifted her up. She wrapped her legs around his waist and moaned into his mouth as his shaft pressed against her still-sensitive flesh through the thin material of her robe.

He whirled around, set her down on the kitchen island. The coldness of the marble served as a sharp contrast to the fever ravaging her body. He kicked his legs free of the pants, pulled the robe up over her hips, and pushed inside her.

"Oh, my God!"

The exclamation burst from her lips as he filled her. He stopped, dropped his head to her shoulder.

She dug her nails into his back. "Don't you dare stop."

He pulled back, thrust deeper as she kissed his neck, his jaw, the scars on the left side of his face. His rhythm slowed.

"Griffith." She clutched his face in her hands, nearly broke at the pain in his gaze. "I want you. All of you."

His fingers dug into her hips. He plunged deeper. She hung on, met his thrusts and arched into him, pressed her lips to his mouth as delicious pressure built, pushed her higher until she couldn't stand it anymore.

"Griffith!"

She came apart on a scream, thrashed as he gathered her in his arms, held her close as he followed her moments later. They soared into oblivion, bound by mutual hunger and a need for pleasure, for connection.

They drifted back down. His breath fell hot and heavy on the tender spot at the base of her neck.

Somewhere deep inside, her resolve weakened, cracked. She couldn't imagine finding a physical connection like this again. But with every tender touch, every time he prodded her for her true wants and desires, saw past the mask she'd worn for everyone else in her life, the more she wondered if she would ever find a man who saw her as intimately and completely as Griffith did.

Not falling for him was becoming harder with every passing hour.

CHAPTER THIRTEEN

ROSALIND TRAILED HER fingers over the spines of leather-bound books as she explored the second level of the library. After their rendezvous in the kitchen, Griffith had walked her back to her room. He'd left her with a searing kiss.

But he'd still left.

He'd spent the rest of the evening in his office and the night in his room, and she in hers. The way it should be, since they were indulging in a simple, short affair. But she was coming to realize, there was nothing simple about this. The more she got to know Griffith, the more her suspicions were confirmed that his selfish tendencies were not an inherent part of his character. Rather, they were a shield, even a weapon, against the pain of loss.

She hadn't liked the man when she'd first started researching him. But she had respected the professional, the leader who had taken his family's company and elevated it to new heights with strategic decisions and a firm hand. Through the news articles, the occasional interview and, of course, the tabloid stories, she had formed an image of Griffith Lykaois long before she had walked into the chateau.

An image that had been turned on its head when he had picked her up off the grass and swept her into the house with such infinite tenderness. The bits and pieces he'd revealed of himself since had only strengthened her belief that he was a man who, like so many others, had sought a way to alleviate a deep grief.

He had alluded to his so-called hedonism that first day in his office. Had given her a little more insight last night. And yes, she thought with a wry smile, there had been plenty of photographic evidence of his lengthy and varied dating history. But he had still managed his duties, still led, balancing profits with the well-being of his employees. That had been a source of confusion as she fought through his constant rebuffs.

Now that they had indulged themselves, perhaps they would be returning to their previous arrangement where they stayed out of each other's way until she could return to civilization. A prospect that just only thirty-six hours ago, would have been a relief.

But now it just made her feel unsettled. Even a little sad that her time with her first lover would be so brief.

She pulled a book from the shelf. The soft whisper of leather on leather calmed her, as did the quiet crackling of the spine as she opened the book. The delicious scent of old paper drifted up. Her lips curved as she read the words of the familiar story about a man and a woman determined to keep each other at arm's length despite the passion building between them.

She leaned against the shelf, her fingers tracing over the words. She had been so sure giving in to her desires would send her down the path to ruin. Yet even by the light of day, she couldn't regret what had happened between them. It had been too pleasurable, wonderful.

It had also left her with a sense of languid relaxation that was carrying her through the morning. Instead of turning her attention immediately to business, she'd enjoyed a muffin on the back terrace, a cup of white tea as she'd strolled through the rose garden, and was now wandering through a massive library instead of reviewing wills, financial documents and lists of personal possessions for other clients.

It was fun, getting to know herself again. To see what activities she was drawn to when she had the rare luxury of a little free time.

A shrill ring cut the silence. Startled, she dropped the book. It took a second for her to realize that the ringing was coming from her pocket. She'd gotten used to the lack of cell reception, the fact that no one could reach her here. Her good mood dissipated when she pulled out her phone and saw who was calling.

"Yes, sir?"

Mr. Nettleton's voice snapped through the line.

"Why haven't you been answering my calls?"

"The reception is terrible here."

"You're still in France? Has he signed?"

"I'm here, but no—"

Before Rosalind could tell her boss about any on the discussions she'd had with Griffith, a squawk of indignation cut her off, followed by a burst of static.

"…no problem removing you from this firm."

Her chest constricted as her fingers tightened around the phone.

"Excuse me?"

"I said I will remove you not only from this case, but from this firm if you don't succeed."

Her heart dropped to her feet. "What?"

"I thought removing the opportunity for promotion would be sufficient incentive to motivate you to get the job done. Obviously, I was wrong."

Before Rosalind could respond, the call dropped.

Slowly, her hand came down. Blood thundered in her ears as the sunlight streaming through the massive windows turned from a comforting glow to glaring brightness. She sagged against the bookcase, blinking rapidly as she tried to process the bombshell Nettleton had just dropped on her.

Years of hard work. Of pursuing the dream her parents had for her. Of tucking her own hopes away as she'd foregone any type of social life to work harder, do more, be more.

All brought down to one contract the senior partner didn't have the guts to tackle himself.

"Rosalind?"

His voice slid over her, deep and firm, unexpected kindness in his tone. He stood below her, hands in his pockets, his handsome, scarred face tilted up as he watched her.

"Good morning."

"Good morning. Are you all right?"

"I—" She started to tell him, wanted to confide in him. Had always imagined being able to share her life, from the positives to the challenges, with a lover.

But she couldn't. Not when Griffith had explicitly laid out the terms of their arrangement. Even if their relationship was based in affection, how could she put the weight of her career on his shoulders? Whether she liked his decision or not, it was his choice.

"Yes." She forced a smile. "Just an uncomfortable conversation with my boss."

"About the contract?"

She slid the book back onto the shelf, debated how to reply. "About business." She walked down the spiral staircase. "I'll be okay."

She started to walk by him. His hand shot out, closed around her wrist.

"Walk with me."

She shook her head as she tried to pull her hand back. "No, thank you. I've wasted a lot of my morning and I—"

"Wasted how?"

He tugged her closer. Her hands came up, rested on his

chest, his heartbeat a steady pulse against her palms. She stiffened and started to pull back. But when he slid a finger under her chin and tilted her face up to his, she found herself holding his gaze. Taking comfort from his presence, despite the intensity of their eye contact. It was as though Griffith was trying to see right through her, into her soul. It was unnerving and exhilarating all at once.

"I've been reading instead of working."

"How dare you?"

His dry comment startled a laugh from her and eased the tension from her shoulders.

"Let's go on a walk. Get out of the house. Clear your head."

"I have work—"

"Do you ever give yourself one day, Rosalind? One day to enjoy yourself."

He took her hand in his, held it with a tenderness she hadn't anticipated, tugged her toward the door.

I should say no.

And instead she followed him out into the great hall where they'd officially met for the first time. As he led her toward the front doors, she stopped in front of the painting.

"Where did you find this? It's very well done."

He stared at the painting, his eyes moving over the ridges and edges created by the artist's knife.

"I was at a museum in early spring." He spoke quietly. "An oil painting exhibition. The museum does an up-and-coming artist feature, a booklet where they put together paintings by local artists. I saw this painting and knew it. Knew the style. It had belonged to a painter my mother hosted from Brazil. I dismissed him as an amateur. Even before her death, I had started to gravitate toward wealth. Reputation. Selfishness." His eyes centered once more on the lone figure on the beach. "Buying it seemed like righting two wrongs. Honoring my mother and all the work she did for artists like him. And a way of atoning for how I dismissed him. I had it shipped from Kent when I decided to spend some time here."

Rosalind entwined her fingers with his. He wouldn't listen if she pointed out that the simple act spoke volumes about the man he was becoming.

But she saw it. Saw and knew there was far more to Griffith than he let himself see.

Maybe one day...

"It's a beautiful painting."

He glanced down at her. The kiss he brushed across her forehead was unexpected and tender. It stirred something inside her chest, a yearning for more moments like this. Not just the wild, passionate desire they'd indulged in, but times when they just enjoyed each other's company, drew strength from one another as they faced their demons.

Dangerous.

The word echoed in her mind once more. But this time, as she followed him out into the sunlight, she felt like the danger Griffith presented was no longer as simple as a threat to her career.

Now he was a threat to her heart.

They walked down the stairs into the bright French sunshine. When he'd notified Beatrice he'd be staying at the chateau, she'd immediately hired over a dozen people from her village to trim the grass, tidy the gardens and clean the house from top to bottom. It hadn't been an insurmountable task. Belen had hired Beatrice to keep the house and grounds maintained when Elizabeth had passed, as if she might suddenly reappear and walk back through the gates. At the time, Griffith had thought it unhealthy at best, a downright obsession at worst. But when he'd driven up twenty-four hours later, he'd been grateful for the cleanliness, the care and attention that had created a peaceful haven. His only thought had been to have nothing to do besides prepare for his return to Lykaois Shipping and savor the silence.

But now, as he and Rosalind walked down the drive, surrounded by velvety green grass, manicured bushes and lush flowerbeds, he was glad she saw the chateau at its finest. As they walked, the tightness eased from her jaw and her usual sunny demeanor returned.

He'd heard enough of the conversation to guess what had happened. And it was his fault. His fault for not being able to sign a damned piece of paper. Before Rosalind had arrived, he'd seen that contract as the last thing standing between him and finally having to accept that his father was truly gone.

He hadn't realized it was affecting more than just him. Not just affecting, he corrected, potentially ruining her career.

Resignation dragged down his own mood. He would have to have another conversation with Rosalind. A proper conversation about what his options were. Before she left, one way or another, he would have to sign.

He glanced at her out of the corner of his eye. With a slight smile playing about her lips and her bright eyes looking skyward, it gave him a chance to watch, to savor the sight of her happy and content.

When was the last time he had felt happy and content? Had he ever?

He heard her sigh when they walked past the entrance to the lane of oaks, suppressed one of his own when they saw nothing but the felled tree blocking the bridge.

One more day. Just one more day.

Their walk took them through the empty fence posts that his mother had one day envisioned as the beginning of a vineyard, through an apple orchard with trees already laden with growing fruit.

They ended up back on the cliff tops, staring out together

over the ocean. He glanced down, noticed a smooth, round rock the color of snow.

"Here."

She smiled as if he'd given her all the jewels in the world. "It's beautiful. Limestone?"

"Yes. Same as the cliffs. Although I don't normally find one so smooth."

She slipped it into her pocket as she stared out over the sea. "It's odd to think that on the other side of this ocean is where I grew up."

"Do you miss it?"

"Sometimes." She sighed. "Living in London, though, is a dream come true. My mother loved my father, loved being a mom. But she told me that she wished she would have traveled more, especially in college. Seen more of the world before settling down."

He heard the wistfulness in her voice, sensed the want coursing beneath the surface.

"That's something you wanted, too."

"Yes. It's why when my parents encouraged me to go to college somewhere else and pursue an internship abroad, I didn't question it too much."

"Why not travel more?"

"I should. I just never have the time." She breathed out. "Sometimes I feel like I've put myself into this box. A really tiny box that grows tighter every year. Like I'm giving up on some things I shouldn't."

"Why keep doing it, then?"

"Partly because of ego. When people learn I work for *that* Nettleton & Thompson, or when I hear my father bragging about me or think about how excited my mother was…" Her voice trailed off. "It's hard to let go of having a parent be proud of you. I worry about disappointing them."

An image of his father flashed in his mind, that last look

of defeat on his face moments before the crash. The more he thought about that last look, about how different things could have been if he would have let his walls down, just once, the deeper his regret grew.

"I understand that."

She started, looked up at him. "I'm sorry. I—"

"Don't be. Just because I pushed my father away doesn't mean I didn't want his approval." He followed the path of a seagull as it arched up into the sky, then dove down out of sight beyond the cliffs. "I just told myself I didn't want it."

"I tell myself the same thing sometimes." She leaned her head against his shoulder in a natural gesture that touched him. "I like looking at the bright side of life. But sometimes I think I focus so much on finding the good in a bad situation that I don't realize it's just a bad situation. One I need to get out of."

They stood there, watching the white-capped waves rise and fall in the distance, each ruminating on their own circumstances.

"Life isn't perfect." She sighed. "I forget that sometimes. Try to paint everything as perfect, to find the good so much I don't accept that sometimes things will be hard."

So had he. He'd been so used to living a charmed life that the loss of his mother had devastated him. He hadn't known how to cope. Distraction had become his therapy, indulgence the balm to his pain. No matter that it had to be constantly reapplied, with increasing frequency and excess. It had been better than falling back into the black void he'd lived in for weeks after his mother's death. A nothingness that had pulled him deeper until he'd wondered if he would ever surface.

They returned to the chateau. She thanked him for the walk and started to go upstairs. Even with just a few steps separating them, he felt her loss. It wasn't simple desire but something deeper, something that made him want to spend time with the woman he was coming to know. He'd never wanted someone this way before. It unnerved him. But unlike the affairs he'd conducted before, his feelings for Rosalind felt…healthier. Stronger. Something more than just satisfying a sexual urge.

Something he wanted to explore, to savor in the precious little time they had left.

"Are you hungry?"

She paused, one hand on the railing. "Yeah, actually. I didn't even realize I was until you said something."

"Let me surprise you."

She smiled even as she tilted her head to the side. "Surprise me? With what?"

"That would ruin the definition of *a surprise*."

She laughed. "I suppose it would."

"I'll meet you on the patio in ten minutes."

"All right. I'll just grab—"

He took the stairs two at a time, gently but firmly reached for her hand and stopped her.

"No work, Rosalind."

"But—"

"If you were caught up on absolutely everything and had ten minutes to yourself, what would you do?"

Her lips quirked. "Well, after yesterday…"

"Besides that," he said even as his body went hard. "I'm not opposed to a repeat performance. But food first."

She ducked her head almost shyly. "I would read."

"Then grab a book from the library and a glass of wine from the kitchen and go read on the patio while I prepare lunch."

"Wine?" she laughed. "At lunch?"

"You're in France. A glass of wine at mealtimes, savored with good company, is acceptable."

She reached up, smooth a lock of hair back from his forehead. Her fingers brushed the top of one of his scars. He didn't flinch.

"Thank you."

He made quick work of making, heating and packing food into a wicker basket he'd seen tucked in a cabinet. He added a couple more things before walking out onto the patio where Rosalind reclined on a lounge with a book and a glass of rosé.

"What's this?" she asked with a huge smile as she sat up.

He held up the basket and, for the first time in months, he returned her smile with a genuine one of his own. "We're going on a picnic."

They traipsed back out onto the grassy plain at a safe distance from the cliff's edge. He laid out the red blanket he'd filched from one of the guest bedrooms before setting out the food and the bottle with the remaining rosé. They dug into the salad, enjoying the contrasting flavors of sharp feta with sweet watermelon and cherry tomatoes. The creamy polenta and seasoned shrimp brought about exclamations of pleasure from Rosalind. Watching her enjoy her meal, how she lingered over a bite, drew out a sip of wine, made him think of the countless meals he'd had at five-star restaurants around the world. He couldn't remember one he had enjoyed more than this picnic by the sea.

"That was incredible."

Rosalind lay back onto the blanket, sliding her hands beneath her head as she watched the sky.

"What dishes do you enjoy back home?"

"Lobster is a big one in Maine. Clams. Anything to do with seafood."

"Would you go back home if you didn't work for Nettleton & Thompson?" The thought made his chest tighten.

She hesitated, then finally said, "I don't think so. It was my home at one time. But even though I followed someone else's dream to get here, I really do love London."

"What would you do, then?"

She was silent for a long time. "I've thought about opening my own firm."

"Why don't you?"

She sat up and picked up her glass of wine, swirled the blush-colored liquid inside.

"I worked so hard to get into the international internship program. So many people coveted the spot I got. And when I was offered a full-time position, only a fool would have turned it down. I've learned a lot from them."

"But it's not what you love."

She slowly shook her head. "No. I got interested in estate planning when my mom helped out our elderly neighbor, Mrs. Carr. Her son and his wife had passed away in a car accident, leaving her with full custody of three grandchildren. She was grieving, terrified that she didn't have enough to take care of them, especially because she wondered about how much time she had left.

"Mom and I were over at her house helping her clean an attic room when an estate lawyer came to visit. Local man, nice enough when I saw him around town. He sat down with her and answered all these questions, helped her make a plan and then a plan for the plan." Her lips curved. "By the time he left Mrs. Carr was…peaceful. It was still a horrible situation, but she was able to move forward." She looked at him then, with her hair gilded by sunlight and the smile on her face content. "I realized I wanted to do that. Help ordinary people find peace and enjoy the rest of their lives."

Floored by the depth of her kindness, unsettled by the stark difference in how they fell into their respective career paths, he watched as she looked out over the gardens. Even though his parents had always stressed leading Lykaois Shipping was his choice, he'd slipped into his various roles with little more than his father's recommendation. When it had been time to take over his current position, he hadn't questioned if he would or would not get it. He'd done good work. Hard work. But he was also a Lykaois. He'd expected it.

He followed the direction of Rosalind's gaze. More oaks had been planted around the perimeter of the garden, their leafy tops soaring above the garden walls. Once he'd recovered from most of his injuries and the pain had subsided to a manageable level, work had been a saving grace. A much healthier distraction than how he'd dealt with things before. Even though he'd taken an official sabbatical, he'd kept his eyes on the company from afar, reviewing the data and reports on a daily basis. He'd grown to appreciate the inner workings, the details he'd thought himself master of that, when applied to an international scale, were far more complex and intricate.

Details he was now responsible for. A duty he had not taken lightly. It was, he realized as he watched the treetops sway in the breeze, something good to come out of tragedy. Something he would give up in a heartbeat if it would bring his father back. The money, the prestige, the company, all of it.

But he couldn't. What he could do, however, was continue on this path, one of responsibility and leadership. One he realized he deeply cared about.

His eyes drifted back to Rosalind. To the serenity on her face, the slight smile about her lips. He'd never been bothered to think past the surface, to see light in darkness. But the woman at his side had inspired him to do just that.

Something shifted in his heart. Something deep that he would have to deal with later.

Much later. Not now, not when he was enjoying himself too much to stop and think and dissect what was going on inside him.

"Your clients are fortunate to have you."

"Some are even grateful."

She laughed when he arched his brow at her. He reached into the basket and pulled out a small container of fudge. When Rosalind bit into a piece, her eyes drifted shut as she let out a moan that shot straight to his groin.

"This is incredible." She looked at him, happiness radiating from her face. "I wish I lived like you did. Turning something simple into this incredibly decadent experience."

Her words hit him. He'd always seen the way he'd lived his life as an escape, a way to keep himself isolated. It was why he'd punished himself with deprivation the past year.

But to hear Rosalind do what she did, find the good in something, unsettled him. Disturbed the way he'd thought about things for so long. Made him remember a time before his mother's death when his parents had also indulged in the finer things in life, albeit in a much more moderate way. But they had instilled in him an appreciation for both the large and the small, the things they had earned and the things they benefited from because of their station in life.

When had he lost sight of that? Bastardized it for his own selfish needs?

"The way I've lived my life is not something to admire."

"Not all of it, no." She shrugged as she took another generous sip of wine. "Doesn't take away the fact that there are good things. I read some of the interviews you gave two years ago. You know your company. The way you talked about operations and some of the things your departments were working on. Not just big projects, but smaller ones, too." She smiled at him. "Unless it has a six-figure inheritance attached to it, Mr. Nettleton doesn't bother to get involved with smaller clients. But you do. I like that about you."

I like that about you.

His breath caught in his chest as her words slid through him, warming him with their simplicity and sweetness.

The possibility that he could be the kind of man she saw him as, the kind of man who could live a better life, was something he had never contemplated before and suddenly desperately wanted.

"Thank you, Rosalind."

"You're welcome, Griffith."

Would he ever tire of hearing his name on her lips? The tenderness and heat in her voice as she spoke?

"The first time you called me Mr. Lykaois, I wanted to hear you say my name."

A delightful crinkle appeared between her brows.

"When I called you?"

"The second time," he amended with a slight smile. "In the lobby of the Diamond Club."

She laughed. "When you watched me get thrown out?"

His smile evaporated. He cupped her cheek, his thumb tracing the delicate line of her cheekbone as he stared into her eyes.

"I did. It was wrong. It was selfish."

"Selfish?"

"I needed you to leave."

Her lashes swept down, then back up as she pinned him with her frank gaze.

"Why?"

"The first time I heard your voice," he murmured, leaning over to kiss her forehead, "I didn't think anything of it. I was too wrapped up in my pain, so angry at what you were trying to do, that I didn't pay any attention." He trailed his lips over her temple. "And then I heard you in Lazlo's office. The feisty American who faced off against the guardian of the wealthiest people in the world."

"Didn't get me far."

Her tone was tart, the underlying breathlessness making him smile in pure masculine satisfaction as he dipped his head.

"It caught my attention." He kissed the curve of her ear, scraped his teeth over her lobe and savored the hiss of her breath escaping.

She pulled back suddenly, leaning away as she stared up at him.

"Did you feel it?"

"Feel what?"

"That day. In the Diamond Club. When I looked up at you, I felt…" She paused. A blush stole over her cheeks. "Never mind." She turned away and set her wineglass down. "It's silly."

He hauled her back against him, buried a hand in her hair. "Tell me."

Blood rushed to his groin as she bit down on her lower lip. "Like there was a…a connection."

He swallowed hard. The unknown lay before him, shrouded in darkness and pulsing with potential. Potential pain, heartbreak, loss.

But then there was Rosalind. Here, now, alive and vibrant in his arms, looking up at him with desire and hesitancy. He'd put her through so much these past few weeks. And still she put herself out there, risked his rejection, with more bravery than he had mustered in over a decade. Admitting that she hadn't been alone in what she'd been feeling that day. That it had shaken him to his core, that he had escaped the country because of it. Admitting that would be his own act of bravery.

"I felt it, too."

Her eyes widened. Before she could say anything, he surrendered himself to his desire and took her mouth in a kiss.

Griffith slanted his lips across hers, swallowed her moan of pleasure. His hands moved over her, pressed against her back and urged her closer. Her fingers moved over his face, over his scars.

He tensed.

She grabbed his face in her hands. His own came up, covered hers, the intimacy of his palms on her fingers driving her wild.

He moved so quickly he startled a gasp from her as he eased her back onto the blanket.

"Griffith—"

He kissed her again, claimed her with deep, possessive strokes of his tongue. Her murmurs of delight, his answering moans of passion, fed her, slipped into her veins and heated her blood.

And then there was nothing but sensation, pure and unadulterated sensation as her head dropped back and he set his lips to her jaw. He kissed his way down to the hollow of her throat, laved the sensitive skin with his tongue as she moaned. His fingers undid the buttons on the bodice of her dress, pulled the material down and divested her of her bra with one quick move.

"Not fair." She nodded at his shirt. "You're overdressed."

He grinned and stood, yanking his shirt, pants and briefs off, tossing the clothes somewhere onto the grass before he rejoined her on the blanket. She pushed herself up onto her elbows and stared at him in the sunlight. His well-defined muscles, from his toned arms to his chiseled abs, spoke to the physical discipline he held himself to.

And the scars that covered the left side of his body, trailing down over a muscular thigh all the way to his ankle, spoke to the trauma he had overcome, and survived.

Griffith, her heart cried out, *do you not realize how incredible you are?*

She stretched out a hand. He pressed her down onto the blanket as he kissed her again. His lips moved farther down, over the swells of her breasts and her taut nipples, sucking first one rosy peak and then another into his mouth. She cried out, arched against him as he drifted lower still, pulling the hem of her dress up and groaning when he realized she wore no underwear.

He placed his mouth where he had just a day ago. He coaxed her to new heights of pleasure with long, leisurely kisses that drugged her body and sent her spiraling toward pleasure.

She peaked, cried his name. Went limp.

Then came alive again as he moved up over her body. She felt his hardness probing her most intimate flesh. Instinct had her parting her thighs, running her hands up over his back as he pressed inside her. He moved, long strokes that built her up and made her soar. The warmth of the sun, the soft kiss of the wind on her bare skin, the sensualness of making love in broad daylight, all of it heightened the incredible pleasure of Griffith moving inside her, claiming her with every thrust. Sensation built, so bright it was almost painful as she reached her peak. She cried out his name, felt herself come apart as he groaned hers.

And knew as he cradled her close that she had lost her heart to the man who called himself a monster.

CHAPTER FOURTEEN

SUNLIGHT WOKE HIM. Rosalind's warmth pressed against his side, one arm thrown across his chest and her curls spilling over his shoulder.

He breathed in her scent, allowed himself the luxury of running his fingers through her hair, gently gliding down her back. She murmured in her sleep and her arm tightened around him. The gesture struck him squarely in the heart.

He'd awoken next to lovers before of course. But never had he looked down at their sleeping faces and felt such contentment.

Rosalind's lashes lay dark against her cheek. Her lips were slightly parted, her breathing heavy and even. Satisfaction curled through him. Given how many times they had made love the day before, exploring each other's bodies, indulging the desires they'd both fought for days, he was surprised that he had awoken refreshed and alert.

Especially after their final interlude on the balcony in his room as night had fallen. They'd spent the rest of the day lounging on the blanket, dozing beneath the sun and engaging in another round of lovemaking. By the time they'd returned, the sun had been setting.

As they'd eaten, she'd asked about the third floor of the chateau. He'd taken her up and given her a tour of the sectioned-off attic, along with his office and his private chamber. He'd shown her the incredible view from his balcony and left her there to go downstairs for another bottle of wine. He'd returned and gone hard at the sight of her naked as she leaned against the railing. The smile she'd shot him as he'd walked out had been daring with a touch of shyness. The intoxicating mix had pulled him in. Instead of leading her back inside, he'd slid his fingers into her curls and anchored her head as he'd plundered her mouth, drinking her moans like a man dying of thirst.

Then he'd turned her around, placed his hands on her hips, and slid inside her. He'd nearly come right then as she'd pushed back, taking him deeper and embracing the wildness of their lovemaking beneath the moon.

Just as he had embraced the connection between them, surrendered to the temptation to show his feelings of tenderness.

When she'd started to roll away, he'd reached out, grabbed her wrist and pulled her back against him. Wide-eyed, she'd stared at him as he'd cupped her face.

"Stay."

He couldn't think of a more beautiful sight than the sweet smile she'd given him before sinking back down against him as he'd pulled the sheet over their naked bodies.

Now she stirred again, murmured something in her sleep, and curled tighter against him. He smiled slightly as he leaned over to kiss her forehead before climbing out of bed. As he walked toward the bathroom, he glanced back over his shoulder. She had already moved to the middle of the bed, arms and legs splayed with her face buried into a pillow. His body stirred at the curve of her bare back, the slope of one naked thigh tangled in the sheets. With the glow of morning lighting the room and her soft snores, he couldn't remember the last time he'd felt this content. The last time everything had seemed perfect.

He froze.

She did look perfect. Here, in his room, in his bed. In all his years of sleeping with women, he had never brought one back to his bedroom. He'd made do with guest rooms, the sofa, even a hotel room. But his bedroom had been his private sanctuary.

Yet he'd brought Rosalind up last night without a second thought. Because he had wanted her to see the view from the balcony. Had wanted to worship her body in the space he felt most comfortable. Safe.

Had wanted more than just sex.

He took a quick shower, turning the water to arctic. The cold momentarily knocked some sense into him, long enough to get dressed and slip out instead of sliding back into bed with Rosalind and pulling her into his arms.

At first, he wandered down the drive aimlessly, eyes roaming over the estate. When his parents had first bought it, he'd enjoyed coming here, watching the house evolve under his mother's dedicated care and his father's bottomless bank account. It hadn't been his style; even though he hadn't fully descended into his hedonistic lifestyle, he'd preferred modern and contemporary.

And after his mother's death…anything that reminded him of her had been too painful. Looking ahead, to the future, had kept him from delving too deeply into what had been.

Yet now, as seashells crunched softly underfoot, he felt a new appreciation for the chateau. That the estate had withstood the tests of time—war, human capriciousness and greed—touched him in a way it never had before.

Because of Rosalind.

He blinked and glanced back at the house. The suite he'd taken as his was on the back side of the house. He wouldn't see Rosalind in one of the many windows, wouldn't see the balcony where she'd arched against him and cried out his name as he'd shuddered and come apart inside her.

With her, he felt freer than he had in years. Even when he'd indulged his wants and vices to excess, when he'd wallowed in his precious possessions, there had been a chain about his neck. With each purchase, the satisfaction had been fleeting. If he waited too long to go out and seek the next best thing, the ache would start. Dull at first, but quickly growing until grief flirted at the edges of his mind and threatened to pull him under.

So he'd bought more, each purchase delaying the inevitable reckoning of his mother's death.

After his father's death, his desire for things had evaporated. The one thing he had desired above all else—to see his father again—was out of reach.

But now, when he asked himself what he wanted above all else, the answer was immediate and clear.

Rosalind.

As he neared the entrance to the lane of oaks, he scrubbed a hand over his face. He'd known her less than a week. Had spent the first two days avoiding her entirely. Their sexual chemistry was explosive, their conversations engaging. And she was an incredibly beautiful woman.

It's more than that.

Impossible as it seemed, he had developed something that went far deeper than simple affection for Rosalind. A woman who challenged him, pushed him, yet also supported him in ways no other woman in his past had.

He cared about her. He cared very much.

You care for her too deeply.

He *was* in too deep. He'd overstepped a boundary of his own last night by bringing her to his room. Had told himself he could keep his emotions back, that sleeping with her would get this obsession out of his system.

Except it hadn't. The longer he was stranded here, the more time he spent with her, the more he risked wanting what he couldn't have. At some point, he would falter. Would make a mistake and drag her down. His track record when it came to managing and processing grief was abysmal at best.

He hadn't tried to lift himself out of his misery for his own father. Why did he want to now? Because his connection with Rosalind went beyond sex, because he truly cared about Rosalind? Or was he tired of living in his self-imposed state of isolation?

Could he even answer that question? Did he want to? He'd spent a lifetime punishing himself, eschewing emotion and connection. He didn't know how to sustain either. And he knew he couldn't have Rosalind without those, it wouldn't be fair to her. Wouldn't be fair to a woman who craved both.

The sound of a saw cut into his thoughts. His head snapped up. Realization hit him hard in the chest before he rounded the corner and entered the shadow of the oak trees. At the end of the lane, a crew worked diligently to cut up the once mighty tree that had been felled by the storm.

Chateau du Bellerose would soon rejoin the outside world.

He didn't know how long he watched. But as a path was finally made for a smaller truck to drive through, he started walking toward the bridge. Each step reverberated through him, pushed the thoughts and possibilities that he'd been considering back as reality set in.

Cocooned out here in their own slice of heaven, it had been easy to enjoy her, to indulge her, to allow vulnerabilities to show and secrets to be shared. To imagine himself the kind of man she dreamed about. The kind of man he wanted to be, both for her and for himself.

But that was here. Not London, not the everyday where the demands of life would tug and pull at them. How many people had he known who had jetted off to a romantic getaway, convinced they'd saved their relationship on the white sands of the Caribbean or the lush forests of Bali, only to return to reality and realize that there wasn't really anything left to save?

We could give it a little time.

He could hear Rosalind's voice in his head, picture her wide, hopeful eyes. A part of him wanted to do just that. Give whatever they'd started here some time and see if perhaps he was ready for something more.

The image in his head altered, changed to Rosalind with tears glistening on her cheeks. At some point, his selfishness would rear its head again. He'd revert back to his old ways when things got hard. That was just who he was. He couldn't contemplate dragging out what they'd started here when he knew he couldn't give her what she wanted.

He knew what he had to do. Knew what the right decision was.

Knowing that didn't lessen the pain that clenched around his heart and twisted as he turned to walk back toward the chateau. But he would harden his heart to it, it's what he always did. He was a master at it.

He had to say goodbye to Rosalind Sutton, once and for all.

Rosalind awoke to the soft creak of a door. She opened her eyes just in time to see Griffith closing the door.

"Good morning."

She smiled at him as she brushed her curls out of her face. The sheet fell to her waist as she sat up and bared her breasts to his gaze. A touch of shyness still persisted. But the pleasant drowsiness that lingered in her limbs made her confident as she threw back the covers and walked to him.

"You're up early."

She went up on her toes and brushed a kiss across his lips. He didn't reciprocate.

He grabbed her by her arms and held her away from him.

She blinked as she saw the reservation in his eyes.

"Are you okay?"

"I have something for you."

She smiled and let one hand drift down his chest. "If it's what I'm thinking—"

He caught her wrist, stopped her exploration. "It's not."

Stung by his dismissal, she took a step back. Worry pooled in her stomach.

"Griffith, what's wrong?"

He picked up an envelope from a nearby table. He'd clearly brought it into the room with him. Cold slithered up her spine as her fingers closed over the packet.

"I signed it this morning."

"I thought…"

She stared down at the envelope, at his name written at the top and the date she'd received her assignment. Over a month and a half ago. How had she gone from despising the man in front of her to…

To what? Sleeping with him?

"I thought you weren't ready."

"I'll never be ready. You helped me see that."

Alarm bells still clanged. He wasn't the same Griffith Lykaois she'd met when she'd first ended up stranded at the chateau. But the camaraderie they had developed over the past week, not to mention the intimacy they'd shared over the past couple of days, had disappeared.

"There's a crew working on the bridge."

He said it so casually it took a moment to penetrate. When

it did, the relief and happiness she'd expected didn't surface. No, it was disappointment.

"Oh."

"Beatrice tried to come up this morning and saw the tree blocking the bridge. She sent a crew from the village to remove the tree."

"And the bridge?"

"So far it looks all right. I was able to make a call. An inspector is arriving this afternoon and will confirm if it's safe to drive on." His expression remained placid. "But given that half a dozen men were on it this morning, it appears safe to walk across."

She forced a smile. "That's great."

"I've arranged for you to fly back to London on my private jet. There's an airfield near here—"

"Wait." Her head spun. She held up a hand. "You just… you made all of these plans? Without even talking to me?"

"Your boss will be pleased." He gestured to the envelope. "The documents are signed. You can go back to London and present this to your superiors. It's what you wanted."

"It was. It is." She stood. Suddenly conscious of her nudity, she moved to the bed and grabbed a shirt he'd thrown on the footstool the night before, hastily buttoning it up to cover herself before she turned to face him again. "But what about us?"

The sigh he released tied her stomach into knots so tight she could barely breathe.

"Rosalind."

He said her name so gently, as if he were talking to a child. Before he could continue, she turned away.

"I see."

She'd known this was a risk. Had accepted it when she'd decided to take the leap and share her body with Griffith.

How many times had she fought her attraction, told herself that she shouldn't let herself get carried away?

The sight of the ocean waves rising and falling drew her to the windows. She crossed her arms over her chest, watched the familiar sight with a desperation that made her feel weak, fanciful.

Foolish.

She'd let her body rule, let her heart take the lead, instead of listening to her brain, to her instincts warning that while she might thoroughly enjoy her time with Griffith, he would ultimately break her heart.

"Rosalind," he said again. "We talked about this. About the differences between us and what we want."

"I know." She sucked in a steadying breath, reached for an inner strength that eluded her. "I just…" No matter what he'd said, she knew something had shifted between them. Knew what had started as pure sex, pure hedonistic enjoyment, had morphed into something else.

Her voice trailed off as her mind raced. Did she tell him what was in her heart? What she had realized last night as they'd made love under the stars?

That she had fallen in love?

It was too much too soon, she knew. Especially to be in love with a man who believed himself incapable it. A man who hid behind this monster persona to keep himself protected from the grief life inevitably threw in one's path.

Yet hadn't she dealt with her own grief in an unhealthy way? Pursuing a career that, from the beginning, she'd had misgivings about? All in some misguided way of honoring her mother's memory when she knew, deep in her heart, that her mother would have been devastated if she would have realized how unhappy her daughter had become.

Yes, Griffith had work to do. So did she. Didn't everyone?

But behind the hurt was the man she'd glimpsed, the one who had cared for her, loved her body, taken her on a walk to calm her mind, encouraged her to follow her dreams…

"Will we see each other again?" One hand fluttered in the air between them. "Obviously I don't have much to go on, but this, what happened between us…that meant something to me."

"It meant something to me, too."

He said the words, but the lack of inflection, the flat tone, said differently, twisted the knife in her heart.

"We could—"

"I can't give you what you want, Rosalind." Suddenly Griffith stood before her, eyes glittering with pain and anger. "Not because I don't want to, but because I can't. I will inevitably mess up. If I couldn't be the kind of son my father deserved, what makes you think I could even come close to being the kind of man worthy of you?"

"Do you even believe half the things you tell yourself?"

He blinked. "Excuse me?"

"You told me you weren't the same after your mother's passing. Everyone responds to grief differently. Would it have wrecked you so much if you hadn't cared about her? What about your father? Would you be this upset, this wrecked, if you didn't love him? The company you work so hard for, the one you never let down even when you were spending like crazy and dating slews of women?"

"Obviously I didn't care enough. If I had, I wouldn't have kept my father at a distance until it was too late."

The words hung in the air between them, wiped away her moment of anger as pain surged forth. She started forward, to lay a comforting hand on his arm, to soothe away his anger and fears.

But once again he moved out of her reach, quelled her

motion with a single glare that gave her a glimpse of the reputation that had supposedly made grown men quake in the boardroom.

"I know that I can't offer you what you want, Rosalind. We can't all live our lives with such an overly optimistic outlook. Us. Your career."

"My career?"

"Yes, your career. You're continuing with this charade that you want to reach the next level with a prestigious firm instead of examining your life and deciding what you really want."

Anger punched through the hurt.

At a loss for words, she turned away, ran her hands through her hair as she tried to think, tried to make sense of the jumble of thoughts clamoring for space inside her head. Pain took front and center, that he would be so dismissive of her feelings, of what they had shared. Yet hadn't he told her, repeatedly, he was too selfish to engage in anything beyond what little time they had been given? Had she been so captivated by their physical chemistry that she had let herself mistake attraction for something more?

Doubt hovered at the edges of her pain. She wondered if she had let herself be swept up in the romance of her first lover, in the novelty of their glamorous seclusion, instead of seeing things for what they were.

And now doubt that she was even capable of separating fantasy from reality. Even before she'd set foot inside Chateau du Bellerose, she'd questioned her future with Nettleton & Thompson. But she'd brushed aside her misgivings, focusing on living as much as she could, on achieving the loftiest goals, to do her mother proud.

She swallowed hard before turning back to face Griffith.

"You make a good point." He blinked, as if she'd surprised

him. "And that is something I'll have to deal with. Sometimes people don't respond the way that they should to loss," she added quietly. "I don't think either of us dealt with our grief in a good way. It doesn't mean that's the way we have to stay."

"No, it doesn't."

He let out a shuddering breath. Closed his eyes. When he opened them, she saw his answer in his eyes.

And it broke her heart.

She moved then, walking toward him with an outward confidence she didn't feel. She reached up, ignoring the barely perceptible flinch as she laid her hands on his cheeks.

"I do sometimes look at things unrealistically. With too much optimism. Sometimes I do exactly as you suggest and turn a situation into a positive when actually it sucks and needs to be fixed. Sometimes I avoid discomfort." She blinked rapidly, willed herself not to cry. "But isn't that better than embracing misery. Not allowing yourself to feel anything else."

He tried to step back. She held on for just a moment, leaned up on her toes and gently kissed the scar that cut over his cheekbone. His sharp intake of breath nearly undid her as she pulled away.

"I think what's truly the saddest of all," she said as she moved to the door, "is that you can't see yourself as I do."

"With rose-colored glasses?"

"No." She glanced back over her shoulder. He stood, framed in the morning light, body tense and poised as if he would run away at any moment. "As someone who made mistakes, realized he made mistakes and is trying not to repeat them. You're not perfect, Griffith, and you never will be. And maybe you will never want what I want out of life. But that doesn't mean you can't be someone you could be proud of. Someone who does good with all of his money and influence."

"Or perhaps," he said, his voice low and bordering on a growl, "I'm exactly the man I told you I am and you're just not listening."

She nodded toward the gilded mirror on the wall, the one they'd stood in front of last night as he'd undressed her, worshipping her body with such care it had warmed both her body and her soul.

"Take a good long look at yourself, Griffith. I hope one day you'll realize you're the only one who sees yourself as a monster."

With that final pronouncement, she grabbed the signed contract that she'd come here for all those days ago, stepped out into the hall and closed the door.

CHAPTER FIFTEEN

"CONGRATULATIONS, ROSALIND."

Rosalind blinked and refocused on the couple seated on the opposite side of the massive walnut desk.

"Thank you."

Mr. Robert T. Nettleton nodded, his smile wide and bright. At sixty-three he was still an attractive man. His silver hair was cut just long enough to be combed back from a broad forehead touched with only the faintest wrinkles that made him look distinguished rather than old.

Ms. Kimberly Thompson sat to his right. Sharp angles and a strong jaw went against traditional standards of beauty. But it was an arresting face that, coupled with her quiet confidence and *Mona Lisa* smile, made one look twice.

Nettleton slid the signed contract out of the envelope. His smile broadened as he stared down at Griffith's signature. Rosalind waited for a sense of victory, of accomplishment.

Nothing. Nothing but the persistent numbness that had settled over her like a shield when she'd walked away from Griffith's room.

"You've always been an asset to this firm, Rosalind."

Really? Even when you threatened to fire me?

"Thank you, sir."

"Which is why we'd like to offer you the position of mid-level attorney."

His words washed over her. The words she had been working toward for the past two years.

In a flash, she saw the next five years. No weekend jaunts to Europe as she worked longer hours. The couple of trips she took home every year becoming fewer and further between even though she would be making more money to cover the cost.

No pleasurable afternoons reading on a patio. Indulging in a sun-drenched picnic.

It hit her all at once.

This isn't what Mom wanted. She wanted you to do what made you happy. She thought this would, that's why she pushed you so hard. She wanted you to have the financial security to do whatever you wanted. Whatever made you happy. To have options.

"Rosalind?"

She looked up to see Nettleton watching her, the smile still in place but a faint crinkle between his brows.

"Sorry, sir." She shook her head. "I just…"

Temptation flared, bright and blinding for one spellbinding moment. To take the safe choice.

And then it disappeared. Where had it gotten her before? Lonely. Overworked. Heartbroken.

"This is what I thought I wanted. But recently, I've come to realize that I've been trying to be someone I'm not."

Robert sputtered. "You're quitting."

"Yes." Rosalind smiled. "Yes, sir, I'm submitting my notice."

"You can't just quit the most prestigious—"

Kimberly silenced her colleague. She gave Rosalind a slight smile before shooting Robert a cold gaze that made his continued objections fall silent. "What will you do now?"

"Take a break. Go to Maine and visit my family." She glanced out the window at the clouds scuttling over the

London skyline. Even on stormy days, England had become home. "Then come back and start my own firm."

Kimberly blinked. And then she smiled, a true smile that stretched from ear to ear.

"It'll be a lot of work."

Robert muttered something under his breath, but Rosalind ignored it.

"It will be. But I'll get to work with the kind of clients that got me interested in doing this." She grinned. "And I'll get to call the shots."

She walked out of the office with her head held high. Each step she took buoyed her confidence, until she was fairly brimming with it.

Was she scared of the uncertainty, worried about what the next phase of life had in store for her? Absolutely. But she would get to tackle it on her own terms with her own dreams leading the way.

She should call her father. Tell him she was coming home for a visit. Tell him in person about the momentous decision she had made.

Two weeks.

Two weeks and she'd be free. Free to take on the next phase of her life on her own terms.

She reached into her pocket for her phone. Her fingers brushed something smooth and cool. Her heart twisted as her hand closed around the small white stone Griffith had given her on their walk. She'd nearly left it behind but at the last second had tucked it into her pocket when she'd changed back into the clothes she'd worn to the chateau. Then forgotten about it as she'd drifted through a haze of heartache as she'd traveled back to England.

She pulled it out now, let it lay flat on her palm. The man could have bought her rare paintings, diamonds, a private jet.

But the rock, a simple token that had made him think of

her, meant more to her than anything else in the world he could have bestowed upon her. The urge to call him, to tell him he had been right, that she had finally broken free and decided to take the risk of being herself, nearly won out.

Until she remembered his face when she had walked away. The cold hardness in his eyes, the resoluteness in his clenched hands. She truly hoped he would find peace. Would come to terms with who he was and who he could be.

But he wasn't ready. Not for his past and not for his future. Which meant he wasn't, and might not ever be, ready for her. Self-doubt had her wondering if she wasn't enough, if her love wasn't enough.

Except she knew it had nothing to do with how much she loved him, even if she hadn't told him so directly. Until he could accept himself, love himself, nothing would ever be enough.

Sadness wrapped bitter fingers around her heart and squeezed. She clenched her eyes shut, let herself experience the grief for a heartbeat.

Then pushed it away. Now was not the time for mourning.

She tucked it into her pocket before continuing on to her desk. Nostalgia hit, memories flickering through her like an old movie reel. The plant on the corner of her desk, the first thing she'd added on her first day. Meeting her first client as an associate attorney. Calling her parents after her first win in court.

Her lips curved into a sentimental smile. She wouldn't regret her time here. But in two weeks, when she would walk out of Nettleton & Thompson for the last time, she would be looking to her future.

Griffith stared out the window at the London Eye. The massive structure, white against the deep blue of a summer sky, slowly rotated. He'd ridden it plenty of times before, had even reserved a luxury dinner for an actress he'd enjoyed a weekend fling with.

But now, as he watched it turn, all he could think about was Rosalind and the ride she'd never gotten to share with her mother.

In the first few hours after she left, he had managed to focus on business, returning to the reports he had neglected in the days they had indulged in their brief but wild affair. But when he'd slipped into his bed that night, her scent had assailed him, drifted up off the pillowcase and summoned memories of her body wrapped around him as he'd driven himself deep inside her.

He'd ended up in a barren guest room on the second floor. But even glancing at the window as he'd fallen asleep, seeing the moonlight stream through the glass, had reminded him of her naked body awash in silver as she waited for him on the balcony.

Realizing that almost every room held some memory of her now, he'd made arrangements to leave for London the following day, walking across the bridge and to the edge of the road where he managed to get enough of a signal to reserve his private jet. It had been then that he had learned Rosalind had never shown up for her flight the day before. She must have purchased her own ticket back to England. It had stung, even if he understood why she had done it. Admired her for it.

He had known their separation would be painful. Had mentally prepared himself for it.

But no amount of preparation had kept him safe from the constant barrage of memories: a sip of wine on the plane reminding him of their cliffside picnic; the site of a rosebush making him think of the tender way she had stroked the rose petals in the garden, and her slow smile as if she had realized for the first time there was more to life than work, more than chasing after others' dreams instead of her own.

Time, he told himself. He just needed time. His relationship with Kacey had been his longest to date. But his time with Rosalind had been the most emotional, the most he'd ever allowed himself to get involved.

A few days had felt like a lifetime of knowing her. Of course, it would take time to let go.

Except instead of getting better, it was only getting worse.

He managed to get through the days. He returned to the office a week after arriving back in London. The meeting with his executive board had gone better than he had anticipated, with only a couple casting curious glances at his scars. A few of the staff members had had stronger reactions to his new face. Widened eyes, quickly looking somewhere else, even a gasp from an intern. He'd mostly ignored it, and in the case of the intern, had surprise himself by offering the young woman a slight smile and a comment of *It is a little jarring when you see it for the first time.* She'd stammered out a quick apology. Then they'd moved on.

It had been a little strange to discover that he had missed the daily interactions that came with being in the office. He'd been steeped in grief and isolation so long that he hadn't realized how much he enjoyed casual greetings, small talk with his secretary and the myriad of meetings that filled his day.

The nights, however, were hell. It was at night, in his penthouse in Knightsbridge, where his mind inevitably turned to Rosalind. What was she doing? Who was she with? And, the most pervasive: Was she happy?

Three weeks after she had walked down the drive and out of his life, he'd received a call from Mr. Nettleton directly, thanking him again for working with the firm and offering to represent Griffith's estate as the firm had represented his father's. Griffith had agreed to a meeting, surprising Nettleton when he had declined the attorney's offer to come to him and instead making the trip down to the law firm. It had been there that Griffith had discovered Rosalind had quit.

Even as he silently cursed Rosalind's decision to leave, mourned the chance to see her one last time, pride surged inside him. Whether she had taken his words to heart or discovered what she'd needed to make the decision on her own, she'd done more in the three weeks they'd been apart than he'd done in over a year. She'd taken charge of her life, made some hard decisions and moved on.

And what would he have done with that last meeting anyway? Apologize for how he'd ended things? He'd thought it would be the pain in her eyes that would haunt his dreams. The stricken look on her beautiful face when he'd taken the special moments they'd shared and ended them, swiftly and ruthlessly.

Except it hadn't been the pain. No, it had been that one aching moment when she'd looked at him with unabashed longing and resignation.

You're the only one who sees yourself as a monster.

A knock sounded on his door.

"Come in."

Alicia Hunter walked in. Even though she was nearly sixty, Alicia still commanded attention whenever she walked into a room, including the executive board she had served on for over thirty years, most recently as chair. From her trademark pant suits in vivid, jewel-toned colors to her short cap of silver hair that showcased her smooth dark skin and polished cheekbones to perfection. Her leadership and knowledge of shipping were legendary but so was her signature style.

That she had also played hide-and-seek with him when his father had brought him to the office as a child had added an amusing touch to their working relationship.

"Welcome back, Griffith."

"Thank you."

She tilted her head to one side. "You look good."

He arched a brow. "Really?"

"Yes." Her eyes narrowed as her gaze swept him from head to toe, assessing with a touch of maternal warmth. "Word is you're actually talking to people."

"I talked with people before."

"Not like this. You were always respected around here."

"But not particularly well-liked."

She shrugged. "It wasn't a matter of liking. You just didn't do much to get to know the people who worked for you."

Because he had been focused on other things. Namely himself.

"Something I'm working on."

"It suits you." She moved to his desk and set her tablet down so he could read the screen. "The press conference is in twenty minutes. Daniel and I will be onstage with you," she said, referencing the chair of the board of directors.

"Good."

The public relations department had recommended a formal press conference to announce Griffith's official acceptance of his position as CEO of Lykaois Shipping after returning from his sabbatical. An event made more crucial after the media circus following Kacey's interview.

He'd known that something like this would be coming, had resisted the idea almost as much as he had resisted signing the contract accepting his inheritance. But now, as he glanced back out over London, he felt something deeper. Determination.

He'd experienced an unexpected sense of homecoming when he'd walked into the lobby on his first day back. He'd wondered if his emotional investment in Lykaois Shipping would change once he was surrounded by people again, by the company that bore his father's mark everywhere he looked.

Thankfully, he'd discovered that while there were still

currents of grief and regret beneath the surface, they didn't weaken his resolve or his feelings. He did care about this company. *His* company. The people who worked for it. The legacy his father and grandfather had crafted.

As he'd assimilated back into the environment over the past few weeks, his determination had only grown. On the few occasions he had experienced uncertainty, he'd squelched it. He could, as Rosalind had said, wallow in his own fears and misery. Or he could do something about it. And at least with the company, there were tangible measures of success he could look to, numbers and reports to create a foundation he could build from.

He slid some written notes over to Alicia. "Thoughts? Public Relations approved it. But I'd appreciate your eyes on it."

She picked up the paper, read through it quickly. "It's good."

"But?"

"You don't talk about your father a lot."

He looked down at his desk, splayed his fingers across the surface. The same desk his father had worked from. His grandfather before him. Months ago, the significance would have been lost on him. But now he recognized it for what it was, the meaning embedded in the faint scars, the streaks in the polished wood.

If he applied himself enough, focused on the company instead of himself, he would be at least half the leader his father had been.

"I don't think he would care for being included in any speech of mine."

The silence felt thick, heavy. His eyes flickered up to find Alicia watching him.

"What a thing to say."

Anger shimmered through him.

"Excuse me?"

"He was proud of you, Griffith."

He barked out a harsh laugh. "Yes. Proud of his overindulgent son."

"He blamed himself."

Stunned, his head snapped up. "What?"

"Your father blamed himself for how you dealt with your mother's death." Alicia sighed, her shoulders drooping as if she'd been carrying a heavy burden for a long time and had finally let it go. "He told me that his family didn't talk much about their feelings. More of a soldier-on attitude."

Griffith remembered that well. He'd never doubted his father's love for him, for his mother. But he had overheard, more than once, his mother encouraging him to talk to her, to share the bad along with the good.

"I still made my choices."

"Yes. And he let you. He didn't try to talk to you, get you counseling, anything."

"I doubt I was in a place to listen."

"Eventually, no. But I remember those first few months, Griffith. You were obviously grieving and depressed. And Belen, as much as he loved you, didn't know what to do. He just assumed you'd buck up. By the time he realized how bad it was, you'd...found another way to cope."

A delicate way to put it, he thought in self-disgust.

"He loved you, Griffith. Even when you were at your most self-centered, you never let that bleed into your professional life. You accomplished a lot at a young age." The look she directed his way made him feel like he was five and had just been caught sneaking into the conference room to play with the projector. "Think. Do you really believe your father would have left you the fortune he did, or an international company, if he didn't think you were capable?"

Before he could reply to that astonishing bit of logic, an

assistant from the public relations department arrived to walk them down to the conference.

Minutes later Griffith was outside the front door of Lykaois Shipping, stationed behind a podium on an elevated stage as dozens of cameras flashed.

Instead of pushing the world away, retreating into his isolation, he stood and faced them.

He read his official statement. He paused at the end, took a breath.

"I hope to not only serve my employees and our clients, but to do my father proud." The improvised words, torn from his heart, were rough with emotion. "To honor the legacy my family has created."

Alicia placed her hand on his shoulder, squeezed. He acknowledged the gesture with a slight nod in her direction before turning his attention back to the reporters. Tried to stop looking for Rosalind amongst the sea of faces.

And failed.

He hadn't thought she'd be there. Why would she be? He'd pushed her away. Had told her in no uncertain terms they were done, that he didn't want to see her again.

Yet a foolish part of him had still hoped he would find her watching, encouraging him with that beautiful, confident smile of hers.

The first few questions were routine. Plans for future expansion, the exploration of adding a route through the Northwest Passage. One bold reporter asked about Kacey, a question Griffith deftly handled by arching a brow and replying with "I don't see what that has to do with shipping," much to the amusement of the others in attendance.

"Mr. Lykaois, what are you looking forward to in the coming year?"

His lips parted. Several answers would have been more

than appropriate. But none of them felt right. None of them *were* right.

Because when he thought about the next year, his thoughts had nothing to do with Lykaois Shipping. They centered around a woman with unruly curls and a sunny smile who had fought her way through grief and still managed to find the good amidst the bad. Memories slipped into dreams of mornings spent on the patio of the chateau, afternoons exploring the neighborhoods of London he'd always avoided because they had never been wealthy enough to catch his interest. Dreams of a wedding, a ceremony that had never interested him but now made his heart twist at the thought of gazing down into her face and saying vows that would join them forever. And dreams of the life after: children, supporting Rosalind a she pursued her goals, hands joined through the ups and downs of life.

The crowd quieted. Whispers rippled through the crowd. Cameras clicked. The world watched as the answer became clear.

Rosalind.

He loved her. He loved her and he wanted to be with her. When he'd thought about the possibility of a future with her, it had been clouded by pain, by the habit of avoiding emotion for years, by his fear of hurting a woman who had seen the best in him even when he couldn't.

But when he stripped away all of that, when he answered the simple question with the simplest answer, it was Rosalind.

"There are several new initiatives we hope to focus on in the coming months. Some I can't speak to as the…details have not been hammered out yet. I will say that, as has been reported in the news, my father…" His voice caught. The lights flashed. "My father worked hard and, as I'm sure you've heard, left me with a substantial fortune. I'll be exploring ways to put that money to good use."

"No more champagne and caviar?" someone from the audience called out.

Griffith's chuckle cut through the mix of shocked murmurs and awkward laughter.

"Yes. But in moderation." He paused, then smiled. "Someone recently showed me there are more important things in life."

The questions came, fast and hard. He deflected, smiled as he stepped back from the microphone, ignoring the barrage of shouts as he allowed the assistant to guide him, Alicia and the other representatives from Lykaois Shipping back into the building.

It was only a few minutes later, even though it felt like hours, that he walked into his office and closed the door.

And finally confronted the realization that had nearly knocked him off his feet during the press conference.

What happened between us...that meant something to me.

His time with Rosalind had meant something to him, too. More than anything else in his life because he was in love with Rosalind. He loved her and wanted a life with her in it. Couldn't picture an existence without her in it.

And he'd forced her out of his life.

He quelled his panic, reined in his fear. Yes, she might reject him. That was her choice. But if he didn't ask the question, if he didn't tell her how he felt, what he wanted, he would never know.

He thought about calling, showing up at her flat.

No. Rosalind deserved something more. Something worthy of a fairy tale.

He picked up his phone, dialed his executive assistant.

"I need you to make a reservation."

CHAPTER SIXTEEN

ROSALIND STARED AT the cryptic invitation in her hand before her gaze moved to the towering white wheel in front of her. In all the years she'd lived in England, she had yet to ride the London Eye. It was one of the tallest Ferris wheels in the world and offered views of Buckingham Palace, Westminster Abby and Big Ben. One of the senior attorneys at Nettleton & Thompson had even been proposed to at the top of the wheel.

Another glance at the simple yet elegant card that had appeared in the mail a few days ago yielded few clues. The wheel normally closed at six o'clock. But her ticket indicated she should arrive at eight in the evening.

Her mind, along with her foolish heart, had immediately thought of Griffith, then dismissed him just as quickly. She'd heard nothing from him since they'd parted in France nearly five weeks ago. After her last day at Nettleton & Thompson, she'd gone home to Maine for a much-needed visit that had seemed to end almost as soon as it started. As she'd waited for her flight back to London, she'd given in to temptation and typed Griffith's name into her online search bar. An article had mentioned an upcoming press conference announcing Griffith assuming his father's role as CEO of Lykaois Shipping.

She'd been happy for him. But she'd also mourned that he had returned to England and made no attempt to see her.

Just like he said he would.

She breathed in deeply as she craned her neck back to look at the top of the Eye. Over thirty capsules with floor-to-ceiling windows were anchored to the wheel. At its height, the monument soared to well over four hundred feet. Her father and oldest brother, Jordan, had made plans to visit in the fall, and she planned to bring them here. Jordan would enjoy the ride while her father marveled over the engineering of the massive wheel.

A sentimental smile crossed her face as she approached the ticket booth. Her time in Maine had been not only a wonderful reprieve from the chaos of the previous weeks, but it had been a much-needed solace for her battered soul. She'd made more than one trip to the cemetery to lay flowers on her mother's grave. She'd also been surprised and relieved when her father had responded to news of her resignation and future plans with excitement and encouragement.

Part of her regretted the time she had spent chasing after something that had been tied to whom she thought she should be. Yet she couldn't regret the experience she'd gained, the people she'd met or how it had prepared her for the next step of operating her own firm. There would be long hours, yes, especially in the first year. But they would be spent doing what she loved. And as she grew, added to her staff and found success on her own terms, she would carve out time for the things she loved instead of just observing the good from afar.

Branches formed a leafy canopy overhead as she approached the main entrance. The queue lines were empty, the wheel immobile.

Frowning, she glanced down at the invitation again. It had come from the director of the Victoria and Albert Museum in Knightsbridge and suggested that she had been invited to a private ride on the Eye to discuss an upcoming exhibition.

Believing it a prank, she'd called the museum directly. The director's secretary had assured her the invitation was genuine. The director, the young woman had shared, had heard that Rosalind was starting her own firm, and was actively recruiting up-and-coming London business owners to be a part of a new exhibition.

Be a part of was usually code for sponsorship. And while she'd saved up plenty of money working for Nettleton & Thompson and living in her tiny flat, the rent on the office space she'd decided on wasn't going to be cheap. Nestled between the neighborhood of Camden's vibrant market and social streets and its quieter residential area, it would be the perfect place to meet with the kind of clients she enjoyed working with.

Still, when the director of a world-famous museum sent her a private invitation, how could she say no?

Another glance at the ticket confirmed the date and time were correct. She'd suddenly realized that there was no one else there. Had she been the only one invited? Surely not. She looked around.

"Hello?"

"Good evening!"

A woman emerged at the top of the ramp leading up to the platform where guests boarded their capsule.

"Miss Sutton?"

"Yes."

"My apologies. I was getting your capsule ready. My name is Sara and I'll be your host this evening."

"It's nice to meet you."

"And you, ma'am. The rest of your party is ready."

"Oh. I'm sorry, I thought the invitation said eight o'clock."

"It did," Sara said with a reassuring smile. "The other guest arrived early."

Rosalind frowned. The museum secretary had made it sound like there would be a group of people, not just the director and her.

"Only one?"

"Yes, ma'am." Sara's eyes fairly sparkled. "This way."

Rosalind followed her onto the platform as she wracked her brain. She couldn't recall meeting the director before, or doing anything that would have drawn his attention.

"Here we are."

She looked inside the empty capsule. "There's no one else here."

"They'll be just a moment, ma'am."

Stifling a sigh, Rosalind walked inside and moved to the far side of the capsule. The water of the River Thames rippled as boats cruised by, from a long double-decker boat crowded with tourists to smaller sailboats that glided along the surface. The setting sun's rays turned the puffy clouds dotting the blue sky from white to shades of rosy pink and glowing orange.

Some of her uncertainty disappeared as she looked up once more. No matter what this meeting was actually about, at least the view from the top would be spectacular.

The wheel began to move, so slowly at first she almost didn't notice it. Surprised, she turned just as a man walked into the capsule.

Her heart began to pound in her chest, so fiercely she grasped one of the rails to steady herself.

"Griffith?"

"Hello, Rosalind."

Sara appeared in the doorway behind him, her face wreathed in an enormous smile. "Enjoy your ride!"

She shut and locked the door behind him, leaving Rosalind alone with the man she loved.

* * *

Griffith's eyes devoured the sight before him. Rosalind stood on the other side of the capsule, her chin lifted slightly, her eyes sharp and fixed on him. She'd regrettably pulled her hair into a loose chignon at the base of her neck. A few stubborn curls had managed to escape. The dress she'd worn, a simple sleeveless dress in forest green with a flared skirt and tantalizing V-neck, gave her a sense of class while mercilessly teasing him with a view of her long legs.

How had he gone over a month without seeing her? Without hearing her voice?

"Unless you took over as the director of the Victoria and Albert Museum, you owe me an explanation."

He bit back a smile at her tart tone. God, he'd missed her. She'd been one of the few people in his life to hold him accountable, to not let him get away with excuses.

He loved her for that.

"I may have made an arrangement with the director."

"May have?"

"Did," he admitted. "I did make an arrangement with the director. But," he added as she opened her mouth to interject, "it does involve a new exhibition. He just omitted that he would not be present at this first meeting."

She rubbed at her temples, as if staving off the beginnings of a headache.

"You could have just asked to see me, Griffith."

"Yes. But then I couldn't have surprised you."

She glanced over her shoulder as the capsule began its ascent. A small smile played over her lips.

"It is beautiful."

"I'm glad you like it."

When she turned back to face him, he had set the silver bucket he'd kept behind his back on the oval-shaped bench in the center of the capsule. The sound of her laughter, light and surprised, filled him as nothing else had since he'd left France.

"Champagne?"

"Yes. To celebrate the opening of the Victoria and Albert's new exhibition next spring."

He popped the cork and poured two glasses of bubbling golden liquid.

"What exhibition?"

He handed Rosalind her glass, savored her sudden inhale as their fingers brushed. Blood pumped through his veins at the sight of the blush that crept into her cheeks.

At the very least, she was still attracted to him. Perhaps he hadn't waited too long.

"Recovery."

Her brows drew together as one corner of her mouth kicked up into a confused smile.

"Recovery?"

"Artwork made by recovering alcoholics."

She paused with the glass halfway to her lips.

"What?"

"It's a form of therapy. I didn't know it existed until…" He paused, tried to gather his thoughts as his heart started to pound. "Until I took someone's advice and started digging deeper into causes my parents cared about. Causes I could put more of myself into."

He turned away from her then. Even now, after everything that had happened the past two weeks, he still felt angry. Not as acute, but certainly persistent.

"One of the art schools my mother supported was trying to start up a therapy program for a clinic that treated alcoholics." His laugh was short, rough. "At first it felt like a cruel joke considering the accident. I wanted to walk away."

The soft rustle of fabric sounded behind him. He sucked in a breath a moment before she laid her hand on his back.

"But you didn't."

"No. I wanted to."

"My mother told me that doing the right thing when we didn't want to made it even more important."

"I would have liked to have met her."

"She would have liked you, too, Griffith."

He turned, caught her hand in his and brought it to his lips. He savored the flutter of her eyelashes as she looked down, the deepening of her blush.

"I'm working on believing that."

The smile she gave him nearly broke his heart. Sweet, kind, supportive. Fear kicked in, blazed bright for a moment.

And then he crushed it. Fear didn't have a place in this moment.

He kept his grip on her hand, led her to the bench and sat down. Their thighs brushed. His fingers tightened around hers as need built inside him. Not just a need for her body, but for her and everything that made up the incredible woman he'd fallen in love with.

"I listened to what the director of the program had to say. Why it was important. I agreed to a tour of the clinic."

Tears glimmered in her eyes. "Oh, Griffith."

"It was hard, Rosalind." He faced her, squared his shoulders as he surrendered control and shared his deepest fears. "It was even harder meeting the people who had made mistakes just like the man responsible for my father's death. To not redirect the anger I'd harbored toward myself onto them. But," he said quietly, "the clinic is trying to help them. So is the art school. And as someone reminded me, I could use some of my money to help make the world a better place."

"Griffith…" She reached up, laid her hand on his face as a

tear slid down her cheek, followed by another as she dipped her head. "I can't... Saying I'm proud of you doesn't seem enough."

"It's enough. More than enough." He took her champagne glass from her and set them both down before grabbing her hands in his. "I love you."

Her eyes rounded as her lips parted.

"What?"

"I love you, Rosalind Sutton." He cupped her face, ran his thumb over the line of her cheek as he watched her. "I started to fall in love with you the moment I heard you bossing Lazlo around in his office."

She huffed. "I was not—"

He silenced her with a kiss. For one heart-stopping moment, she froze.

And then she bloomed in his arms, throwing her arms around his neck with abandon as she kissed him back. He groaned her name, thrilled to the sound of her answering moan. He pulled her onto his lap. Pressed her closer. Slid one hand into her glorious curls.

She pulled back, her arms still looped around his neck, her smile so bright and luminous it rivaled the sunset behind her.

"I love you, too."

His throat tightened. He leaned forward, rested his cheek against hers and breathed in her scent.

"I almost let you go. Almost let us go."

Her fingers moved across his back in soothing circles.

"What made you come back?"

"I accepted my past for what it was and borrowed a page from your book by looking at how I could turn some of those traits into something good for the future." She started to say something, but he lay a gentle finger on her lips. "I'm afraid I'm going to fail myself. I'm not used to trying. To putting myself out there. Most of all," he admitted with a harsh exhale, "I worry that I'll fail you. That the man you think I can be won't stand the test of time."

"Oh, Griffith." She rested her forehead against his. "You'll make mistakes. I will, too. I made my own. I quit Nettleton & Thompson because you helped me realize that I was trying to be someone I wasn't. You showed me how to live. How to take joy from the simple things. How to make myself a priority instead of only living for others."

His arms tightened around her. "You deserve a life you love, Rosalind. Although I do appreciate your optimistic outlook." He leaned down, brushed a kiss across her temple. "You saw the potential in me when I couldn't."

"I do like looking at the sunny side of things and thinking hard work can solve anything." She let out a slow breath. "But it can't always be that way. You ground me."

"Just as long as I don't stop you from dreaming."

"No." Her smile took his breath away. "You encouraged me to take my own risk. To go after what I truly wanted and what I'm good at. For all my talk about looking at the sunny things in life, I wasn't letting myself live."

"I'm glad. And I'm proud." Surprisingly, his next admission was the hardest one to make. "The exhibition…"

"Oh!" She laughed, snuggled into his embrace. "I completely forgot. Tell me everything."

"When I dropped by last week, they gave me a tour of the studio. Right now, it's just a spare room, but come spring they'll have a new addition to the clinic." He smiled slightly. "There was an older woman in the back corner of the room when I visited. She wasn't done, but her canvas was partially covered by a field of flowers. Square ones, diamond-shaped, rectangles and all sorts of colors that shouldn't work. But they did. She told me how she started drinking after her husband passed away. How she was painting the field where he proposed and how the art helped her process her husband's death. Helped her stop drinking. It got me thinking. Maybe other people would like to see their artwork, too, hear their stories. That maybe I could do more to help. *Recovery* will open with featured artwork from members of the clinic's art therapy program. Admission fees will fund treatment. Artists can be anonymous, but most are sharing their names. They have the option of keeping their work when it's over, or having it auctioned off at a gala to celebrate the end of the exhibition."

"Griffith…" Her tremulous smile made his blood sing.

"It's a step. Maybe one day I'll be able to forgive the man who hit my car. Forgive myself for all the years I wasted not dealing with my mother's death."

"You don't have to do it alone."

He slipped an arm under her legs and the other behind her back as he lifted her up, held her tight for a moment and then set her on the bench next to him. Before she could move, he slid off the bench and got down on one knee.

Her eyes widened. "Griffith…"

"You make me want to be a better man, Rosalind. You make me want to be the best I can be. And while I'm terrified I will let you down, I want to try. I want to go to bed with you every night and wake up to you every morning. I want to hear your thoughts, live with you in our chateau by the sea with five or six kids running around."

"Six?" she asked with a laugh. "How about three?"

"Four." He kissed her again, simply because he could, and then reached into his jacket pocket. When he flipped the lid open on the white velvet box, she gasped.

"This was my mother's." The yellow pear-shaped diamond winked up at them, set on a gleaming silver band and surrounded by smaller jewels. "Rosalind, would you do me the honor of becoming my wife?"

The words had barely left his lips when she flung her arms around him.

"Yes! Yes, Griffith!"

Laughing, he pulled back long enough to slide the ring onto her finger before sweeping her into his arms and carrying her to the far side of the capsule. The sun hovered just above the horizon. The timeless landmarks of London, from the sprawling walls of the Houses of Parliament to the dome of St. Paul's Cathedral, lay below them.

He set her on her feet and pulled her snugly into his side.

"We missed almost the entire ride to the top."

Rosalind held out her hand, the ring glinting in the evening light.

"I'm not disappointed."

He cut her laugh off with another kiss.

"How soon will you marry me?"

"As soon as you want me to."

"I can bribe a justice as soon as we reach the bottom," he said. Then, seeing her pointed look, laughed and said, "All right, a week?"

"How about long enough for me to plan my dream wedding?"

"You don't already have it planned?" he teased.

She smiled up at him. "Bits and pieces. But I was missing the most important part. Until you."

EPILOGUE

Rosalind sighed and wiggled deeper into the embrace of the plush egg chair in the garden. Spring had finally come to France, ushering in warm temperatures and budding blooms. Exhaustion and a vague sense of nausea had kept her inside the past week. But when she'd seen the green in the rose garden, heard the faint whistle of a bird outside her window, she hadn't been able to resist going outside.

She had nearly fallen asleep when a shadow fell across her. She opened her eyes and smiled when she saw her husband standing above her with a cup of tea in hand.

"Hello."

"Hello." He leaned down, kissing her warmly before pressing the mug into her hands. "You looked like you could use this."

"Thank you." She stifled a yawn as she noticed the package in his hands. "Did it come already?"

"Delivered by Beatrice and Jean this morning. Would you like to unwrap it?"

She laid a hand over his. "Thank you. But I think you should."

He nodded once, breathed in deeply and set about unwrapping the brown paper package tied up with string.

"Griffith…" She stared at the painting in his hands. "It's beautiful."

A sandy beach glimmered beneath a blazing sun. White chalk cliffs stood guard, including a familiar-looking arch that plunged into the deep blue sea just off the coast. The waves had been textured with a palette knife so that they rose up, almost as if they were about to swell off the canvas. A couple stood on the beach holding hands.

"Mary did well." Griffith held it up. "In the library? What do you think?"

"Perfect."

Rosalind smiled. The woman Griffith had spoken to on his first tour of the studio had grown from acquaintance into friend over the months. Seeing Griffith support her through her recovery, from taking her out for coffee to accepting her invitation to stand by her side at the unveiling of the exhibition, had made her even prouder of how far her husband had come in such a short amount of time.

"How is she doing?"

"Good." He smiled, pride evident in his voice. "She's been sober for ten months. She's still in counseling, but she said they've made a lot of progress. If things continue this well, her daughter said she'd like Mary to move in later this summer. Her and her husband are talking about trying for a baby this fall and want Mary to be involved with her grandchild."

"That's wonderful."

"She's volunteering at the clinic on Thursdays, too."

Rosalind didn't bother to hold back her smile of contentment. The nine months since Griffith had proposed to her had been a whirlwind. They'd celebrated an October wedding in the rose garden of the chateau, with Griffith flying her father and brothers over for the ceremony. The designer whose clothes she'd worn during that incredible week they'd first spent together had custom designed her wedding gown. The full skirt was colored the same pale blush as the pink

Hermosa roses that had bloomed just before their wedding ceremony. Sparkling beads and light blue flowers threaded as the skirt and the sleeve that had covered one arm. The other arm had been left bare, adding a touch of sexiness that had made her feel all the more beautiful as she'd walked down the makeshift aisle to Griffith.

He'd also made headlines in his role as CEO, from expanding Lykaois Shipping's routes to his generous contributions to clinics, treatment programs and volunteer organizations. His philanthropy, especially in light of his father's passing, had been lauded.

Few knew how much those first steps had cost Griffith, how hard it had been to start down the road to forgiveness. A road that hadn't been entirely smooth, either. The first time he'd opened a letter from the man who had crashed into his car, he'd only made it a couple paragraphs in before he'd tossed the letter on the table and gone out for a walk. It hadn't been until after Christmas that he'd managed to make it through a whole letter.

Progress was progress. A phrase she told him as often as he needed to hear it, especially when he vacillated between the raging emotions of loss and the expectations he now set for himself.

And, she thought to herself with a small smile, a phrase he repeated back to her as she worked to get her firm up and running. Griffith had repeatedly offered to finance it, everything from payroll to office supplies. She'd turned him down flat on the money. She had, grudgingly at first, accepted his offers to help in other ways, including painting the walls of her new space and filing all the necessary paperwork to get started. Old habits, including the need to prove herself, had been hard to break. Yet as the months passed and her client list grew, she had come to recognize his support as the strength it was instead of a weakness on her part.

"How much did you pay for it?" She nodded toward the painting.

"A gentleman never tells."

Recovery had been an astounding success, running through the month of March with record numbers of guests paying the extra price for admission. It had been so wildly popular the museum had extended it by four weeks and promised to bring it back with new paintings.

The silent auction, too, had netted incredible results, with many of the artists receiving thousands of dollars for their work.

He carried the painting inside and returned a moment later. She scooted over, making enough room for him to join her. He wrapped his arms around her and pulled her close.

"Feeling better?"

"Much." She let out a sigh. "It would be nice if Mary's daughter had a baby next year."

"It would."

"It would be close in age to ours."

"Yes..." His voice trailed off as his head whipped around. "What?"

She grabbed one of his hands and guided it to her stomach. His fingers spread across her shirt, his eyes wide, his face full of wonder and disbelief.

"We're...you're pregnant?"

"Yes." She laughed, giddy at the thought that she was carrying their child. "I'm guessing a little over two months, although I don't know for sure—"

He cut her off with a kiss that made her heart sing.

"Rosalind." He leaned back, cupped her face in his hands. "We're going to be parents?"

"We're going to be parents."

He laughed then, deep and joyful.

"It's going to be wonderful."
"But occasionally hard," she added.
"Yes." He kissed her again. "But we'll do it together."
"Together." She smiled. "Forever."

* * * * *

COMING SOON!

We really hope you enjoyed reading this book.
If you're looking for more romance
be sure to head to the shops when
new books are available on

Thursday 15th
August

MILLS & BOON

MILLS & BOON ®

Coming next month

GREEK PREGNANCY CLAUSE
Maya Blake

'You have thirty seconds. Then I walk out,' Ares warned in a soft, dangerous murmur.

Odessa believed him. After all, hadn't he done that once, this man who was a world removed from the younger version she'd known. Or was he?

Hadn't he possessed this overwhelming presence even back then, only caged it better?

Now the full force of it bore down on her, Odessa was at once wary of and drawn to it, like a hapless moth dancing towards a destroying flame.

She watched, mesmerized despite herself as his folded arms slowly dropped, his large, masculine hands drawing attention to his lean hips, the dangerously evocative image he made simply by...*being*.

At what felt like the last second, she took a deep breath and took the boldest leap. 'Before my father's memorial is over, Vincenzo Bartorelli will announce our engagement.' Acid flooded her mouth at the very thought. 'I would rather jump naked into Mount Etna than marry him. So, I'd...I'd like you to say that I'm marrying you instead. And in return...' *Dio*, was she really doing this? 'And in return I'll give you whatever you want.'

Continue reading
GREEK PREGNANCY CLAUSE
Maya Blake

Available next month
millsandboon.co.uk

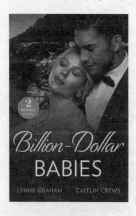
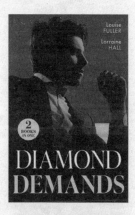
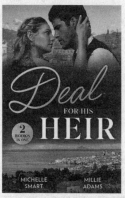

LET'S TALK

Romance

For exclusive extracts, competitions and special offers, find us online:

- **f** MillsandBoon
- **X** @MillsandBoon
- **◎** @MillsandBoonUK
- **♪** @MillsandBoonUK

Get in touch on 01413 063 232

For all the latest titles coming soon, visit
millsandboon.co.uk/nextmonth

Afterglow Books is a trend-led, trope-filled list of books with diverse, authentic and relatable characters, a wide array of voices and representations, plus real world trials and tribulations. Featuring all the tropes you could possibly want (think small-town settings, fake relationships, grumpy vs sunshine, enemies to lovers) and all with a generous dose of spice in every story.

♪ @millsandboonuk
📷 @millsandboonuk
afterglowbooks.co.uk

#AfterglowBooks

For all the latest book news, exclusive content and giveaways scan the QR code below to sign up to the Afterglow newsletter:

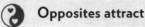
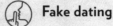
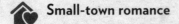
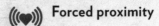
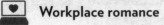